The Scandalous Life of Ruby Devereaux

The Scandalous Life of Ruby Devereaux

M. J. Robotham

An Aria Book

First published in the UK in 2024 by Head of Zeus Ltd,
part of Bloomsbury Publishing Plc

9 7 5 3 1 2 4 6 8

A catalogue record for this book is available from the British Library.

ISBN (HB): 9781035901104
ISBN (XTPB): 9781035901111
ISBN (E): 9781035901098

Cover design: Meg Shepherd

Printed and bound in Great Britain by
CPI Group (UK) Ltd, Croydon CR0 4YY

Head of Zeus Ltd
First Floor East
5–8 Hardwick Street
London EC1R 4RG

WWW.HEADOFZEUS.COM

To my boys: Harry Jack and Finn Jude,
without whom I could never have written this book.

'Every secret of a writer's soul, every experience of his life, every quality of his mind is written large in his works.'

Virginia Woolf

One

With a sense of expectation and a tinge of dread, Marina Keeve opens up her email inbox and sips at the palliative flat white by her side. *Thank God the office manager upgraded the coffee machine*, she thinks, *and not before time*. A bitter cappuccino with inordinate amounts of froth just doesn't cut it when faced with the demands of the British publishing world.

As feared, there's the one email she hoped might have been cast into cyberspace, marked with a star, as is his habit; Marcus Trent not only thinks himself important, he tells you so. Although she's alone in her office at Grantham & Harris, Marina looks around her before opening the document tentatively, with a sideswipe of her finger rather than a determined clunk of the key. Experience dictates that with a hornet's nest it's wise to tap it gently and stand back for the onslaught.

Marina

Lovely to see you at last week's launch, and I hope you are well.

Like hell he does.

I wonder, is there any progress on the topic we spoke about briefly? As you can appreciate, the market is terribly tight at present and I'm getting pressure from the board on contracts that are so far unfulfilled. I'm keen to secure a manuscript from Ruby asap, before events overtake us...

Say it, Marcus – before she kicks the bucket. Because that's what you mean.

It might be the flat white, or the affrontery that she feels on behalf of her oldest client, but Marina reaches for the phone instantly, punching the redial button with irritation. Uncharacteristically, because for those who know her, Marina Keeve is not a particularly forthright woman; she negotiates the publishing arena (gladiatorial often being the correct analogy) with a quiet charm, and – though her modesty means she would never advertise this – she's well thought of by her clients and publishers alike. People tend to like Marina. Today, though, Marcus may not warm to her. She will not be pushed around, not on the subject of Ruby M Devereaux, easily her trickiest client, but oddly her most favoured, too. Though she might never admit that to anyone, least of all Ruby.

'*Mon courage*,' she mutters. Big girl knickers are in situ.

'Marcus,' she trills as he comes on the line, the wheeze of his cigar breath oozing through the receiver.

'Marina,' he says flatly.

Battle lines are drawn, clearly.

'I've just opened your email. Regarding Ruby.'

'Ah, yes. Dear Ruby. Any update on a work in progress?'

'Not as yet.' Marina draws in a breath – nerve and a good deal of resolve tucked into her knickers. 'Marcus, perhaps I don't need to remind you, since you were present, that our *dear* Ruby recently celebrated her ninetieth birthday. Her eyesight isn't good, and she doesn't get out much. To all intents and purposes, she's retired.'

'Has she communicated as much to you?'

'Well, you know Ruby, she would never admit her writing days are over. Not even to herself, I suspect.'

'She rather appeared to be all there,' Marcus says. 'Am I wrong on that score?'

Hard-hearted bastard.

'No, Marcus, she is very much "all there", as you put it. But is Phoenix Publishing really so keen to drag out another manuscript from her? You have plenty of other bestselling authors under your roof, several from this agency I might add.'

This time the cigar fumes are pushed with force down the line, weapons drawn. He intends to smoke her out. 'Lawyers, Marina. Sadly. A contract is a contract, they say, and you know these bastards, they won't be stonewalled. Not even by me. The fact is, she owes us a book.'

Lawyers, she thinks. *Is he seriously quoting lawyers at me?*

'Liar,' Marina mutters under her breath.

'Sorry?'

'Ah, nothing. I did have lunch with Ruby last week,' she adds, 'and I honestly think she's done, Marcus. I mean, she is still writing – short pieces, the odd article about the old days, but...'

'So, a memoir then?' he punts with enthusiasm. With grotesque clarity, Marina pictures him leaning forward with a squeak of the leather under his copious behind, suddenly animated. 'I think the board would be more than happy with that. She's had a somewhat colourful life. I'm sure it would sell very well. Sex sells very well right now.'

This time Marina does sigh. Audibly and with the intent that he must register her frustration through the fug of his cigar. 'Believe me, Marcus, I've tried that tack, many times, about a memoir. She won't be drawn on it. Insists it wouldn't be of interest to her, or her readers.'

The firm refusal from Marina's client was actually intoned with far more verve and colour, but that's Ruby M Devereaux for you – never one word where ten will embroider the point nicely.

'I think, Marina,' – and here Marcus pauses, drawing his voice down an octave, from faux friendly to a Mafia-style low growl – 'that we will have to insist. Or it's out of my hands and the money-men will come looking for their pennies. In court if they have to.'

Bastard. Marina swallows, bitter spit instead of silky flat white. He's let the lions loose in the arena. 'I understand, Marcus. I'll talk to her again, and we'll speak soon.'

'Excellent. I look forward to it.'

No one beyond her office door will hear the frustration Marina takes out on her own desk, because she does it with relative decorum, her hand thudding down on the manuscripts and piles of admin just once, her anguish well controlled behind gritted teeth. *How dare he? Fucking dinosaur!* Marcus Trent started life as an editor back in the 1970s and still resides there, as far as she can tell.

Publishing is, inevitably, competitive and always has been, but in Marina's twenty plus years as an agent, a new breed of editors has gradually pushed out the cigar-toting, hard-nosed old guard. The new swathe are resolute and hungry, but younger and seemingly kinder (and dare she say it, but it's thanks largely to many women who are book-lovers rather than money-rakers). The market still dictates, and there's no fluffy sentimentality in the world of fiction. But there is compassion, too, and a certain loyalty towards Ruby and her legacy among the writing fraternity. Though not from Marcus, it seems, even if his career has been bolstered nicely by Ruby's previous offerings to Phoenix, the last five reaching the bestseller lists.

Bastard. Marina generally loves a good ferret through *Roget's Thesaurus*, but in this case, there's no better description.

She drains the last of her coffee and picks up the receiver. No time like the present, she reasons, driven by anger, fuelled by the dinosaur's blatant disregard, but also by a resignation that this dilemma will not go away. The sooner she sorts it the better, though that's not what people say when facing up to a firing squad. She can't tell if the slight tremble is down to trepidation or caffeine.

The phone rings more than ten times; Ruby's daily help must not have arrived yet, and Marina pictures cautious steps shuffling on the stripped floors of the Highgate mews house towards the phone table in the hallway. Who still has a phone table, complete with a clunky cream handset and a dial-up body? Ruby does, of course, and it's no retro arrangement, either – the real thing, circa 1980. Over the endless ringing, she can imagine Ruby's irritation spiralling.

'All right, I'm coming. Hold your horses. Who the hell is ringing me anyway?'

Except Ruby will know it's Marina. Because it's always Marina – no one else rings her on the age-old machine.

'Hello?'

'Hello, Ruby, it's Marina. Are you busy?'

'Yes.'

'Oh. I wonder, though, could you spare me some time this afternoon? There are a few things we need to discuss.'

'Hmm.'

'Important things, Ruby. I wouldn't ask otherwise.'

'I suppose so then. But, Marina, I haven't got any cake.'

'I can bring some if you like.'

'Well, if you're that keen, the village shop has some nice cream éclairs.'

'Fine. I'll stop by on my way over. Does two thirty suit you?'

'Yes, that will be all right.'

'See you later, then.'

Marina sits, trawling through the remaining emails, then scrolling the manuscript she left off yesterday, one of over twenty in her inbox, from new and young, eager, fresh-faced writers.

It's Ruby who hovers, though, slipping into her vision at the edge of the screen. She wishes she didn't like the old girl so much, but the fact is that she does, despite the complaints and gruff ripostes. Even with Ruby's standing in the publishing world, other agents wonder why she bothers so much. And yet, Marina has a sneaking suspicion Ruby likes her, too. No one else is asked to fetch and share cream éclairs.

And the fact is, Ruby is fascinating. One of the old school, though not in the heinous manner of Marcus. In the times when they do talk, and if Ruby is primed a little with good Scotch, the stories are enchanting, her memory sharp as a pin for detail; colourful is a dull understatement for the life so far reported in the press. More so, the tales never publicly revealed.

And now Marina just has to persuade Ruby to tell her story. Warts and all.

Christ. She marches towards the door and pokes her head into the outer office. 'Jenny, my darling, any chance of another flat white? Make it good and strong please.'

Two

'The fact is, Ruby, they do have the upper hand in law,' Marina says, hoping the cream oozing from the very expensive deli éclair will imbue some courage on her part, plus have a mollifying effect on Ruby.

'You mean they have us by the balls.' The cream lodges on Ruby's top lip, before she licks it off like a child eight decades younger, under which sits – mercifully for Marina – a wry smile.

Mission accomplished. Ruby is in one of her better moods. 'Yes, precisely. So, what do you think?' Marina ventures. 'I mean, it can be something from your bottom drawer, a manuscript we can breathe fresh life into.'

Ruby's gimlet eyes stray from her plate to Marina and stay there. From years of practice, Ruby knows exactly what effect this has on people. 'They are in my bottom drawer, Marina, for a reason. Because they are sub-standard. Shit, in plain English.'

'Well, er…'

'What does that old toad Marcus want?' Ruby demands. The bird-like eyes bore like a diamond cutter. 'Come on, Marina, spit it out. What did he say? I know it will be brash and forthright, just like him. Tell me the worst.'

Marina swallows cream for comfort. 'He wants sex,' she says.

Ruby's raspy roar bounces off the parlour walls lined with books, and whips around the room like lightning. Ruby is genuinely amused. Marina is genuinely relieved.

Ruby chews. 'All right, Marina. Let's give it to him, shall we? If nothing else, I would pay money to see Marcus Trent squirm in his Savile Row pants. In fact, I would write a book for it.' She takes another bite of choux. 'I *will* write a book for it.'

'Really?' Again, unusually for an agent and lover of diction, Marina is lost for words. The power of patisserie.

Ruby reaches with her gnarly hand to wipe away chocolate. 'I'll do it. But with a few conditions.'

'Of course, of course,' Marina agrees. To almost anything. 'Fire away.'

Three

Much to Ruby's indignation, the demands under which she is to write this book are a necessity rather than a choice. Just lately, she feels every one of her ninety years, along with her aching joints and distorted, knotty fingers, the once-loyal tools of her trade. Even with the lighter touch of today's modern laptops, the typing of a whole manuscript is well beyond her reach these days. By contrast, Ruby's brain remains on a different physical plane, continually awash with ideas. Fired by that enduring image of Marcus sweating away in his underwear, she accepts Marina's strategy.

So, the tentative knocking at her door is expected, and the boy – he looks very much a boy in her eyes – is ushered into the kitchen of her mews house and the surroundings of well-to-do Highgate. He looks nervous because he is. 'I'm Jude. Jude Dempsey,' he says.

Ruby's head whips around. If she looks surprised, it's because she is. 'Well, Jude, perhaps you'd better put the kettle on,' she says, lowering herself into the armchair facing the small, neat garden. 'My knees are playing up today and I need to sit.'

'Is this all part of the interview?' he pitches uneasily.

'No, it's making me a cup of tea.' Reluctantly, she checks her tone, bordering on tetchy. Marina has cautioned that it's vital not to scare this one away, the third in a line of not many applicants. Ruby has pondered several times over how her agent will have phrased the job advert: *Grumpy old writer seeks Boy Friday for typing, IT skills and secretarial duties. Cooking essential.* Something like that. Ruby has specified male only, but of course in this day and age, you can't say it outright.

Instead, Marina has assured Ruby the candidates will be vetted accordingly. 'Ruby, I'll just send you the ones with…'

'Stamina?' Ruby had filled in, helpfully.

'The requisite skills,' her agent qualified. Of course, what she really meant was 'guts'.

In this case and on this day, Jude passes the tea test: hot and strong with a dash of milk. Crucially, he joins Ruby at the table with his own mug, and she likes that, always suspicious of those who don't indulge in a hot beverage, because how can you chat without liquid to make it flow amid a curl of steam? He loves to cook, too, and although Ruby's appetite is small, she adores titbits of a cosmopolitan nature. 'I do a mean phad Thai,' he says keenly.

'How old are you, Jude?' Ruby asks, remembering to show her teeth in a half smile so it's less like a grilling.

'Twenty-one. Well, next month.'

'You don't want to be a writer, do you?' Devoid of patience and time, Ruby has no truck with would-be novelists who picture her as some sort of mentor.

'No,' Jude says, in a way which invites belief. 'I'm just scouting around until I decide what to do.'

So, Jude stays, proving his skill first in the kitchen in whipping up a very acceptable lunch, and then at the screen when they move to the office, just a day later. Secretly, Ruby quite likes her new laptop, though she does lament the feel of heavy keys under once nimble fingers, a frenetic motor to keep her running and the words spewing. So, the specialist 'typewriter' keyboard newly acquired by Marina emulates the familiar tickety-tack, even if it falls short of a thundering machine. Another compromise in what Ruby frequently terms 'this bastard ageing process', and which means it's Jude's slim and lithe fingers now playing to her tune.

'Are you ready for this?' Ruby asks. If truth be told, she's not entirely prepared for what may come. And yet the thought of getting one over on Marcus Trent is too good a motivation to pass up.

Jude nods. He's more than a little trepidatious, but hides it well. He flexes his fingers; in time, Ruby will come to know it as an entirely natural gesture, but in that moment it feels truly theatrical. 'Let's go, Miss Devereaux.'

INTRODUCTION

As I've said many a time, I'm not entirely sure of the value of a writer's autobiography, especially when written by one in their extreme dotage. Being habitual storytellers, we fiction writers are notoriously unreliable – we make things up. It's in our blood. In any other guise, it might be called professional deceit. Or lying.

I've pleaded as much to my agent, Marina, who has for years fended off entreaties from publishers for me to wax lyrical about my life. 'It's all in my books,' I've told her each time the subject arises. But, of course, that's an enduring excuse – for laziness, apathy and disinterest. Authors have these indolent feelings in tidal waves, interspersed with spurts of furious activity. Occasionally, it may be touched by genius, though I always think it's up to the readers to make that judgement. Critics may offer their opinions, but with advanced age and twenty or so books in my personal library, I have the luxury of not needing to heed a critic's 'wise' words any longer. It's a rare benefit of being ninety.

So, this autobiography lark. Perhaps, finally, I am beginning to touch base with my own mortality, scraping my scalp on the ceiling of life. Having not expected to live beyond the next decade for many years, I would find miraculously that I did. Again and again. Now, the odds of surviving into the next... well, a betting man wouldn't put his hand in his pocket, and I wouldn't blame him. So I have ruminated, cogitated and somewhat conceded. To a point.

The 'I was born into a shoe box in front of the scullery fire...' type of narrative doesn't interest me, not least because I wasn't. Born, yes, but not into stultifying poverty. My childhood was possibly even worse: dull and uninspired, only shaping the real me by instilling a desperate urge to flee. The points of infantile interest in the early life of Ruby M Devereaux could be etched on a matchbox and still leave room for the price. It is not my parents, my early life or even a dedicated schoolteacher that has moulded me into the woman you might imagine. On deep reflection, a surprising entity that has shaped my life is the opposite sex; I cannot, in all honesty, ignore the allure of men and masculinity – their attentions and sometimes an infuriating bloody-mindedness – in driving the years along. The mystery of men, too. For centuries, women have – quite rightly – kicked against the idea of men sculpting the female form into their desired ideal. The fact is, I have never felt chiselled, or at the mercy of an intensely masculine system. Were I younger and less curmudgeonly, I would certainly be out there, banner-waving with the feminist cause of today. And don't mistake me – the universal balance of power back then *was* uneven. But perhaps I was lucky (or short-sighted). In the moment, I saw it as largely weighted in my favour. I grasped at it and enjoyed it. Those men involved might dispute my version of events, but since all but two of my 'chapters' are dead, they probably won't – another advantage of being ancient and still conscious.

The two still living, well, they can decide to agree or disagree with my depiction, but much like me, at least one of them is probably too old and tired to fight out the details. Breathing is simply a bonus these days.

So, this is for Marina, who will no longer have to petition me annually for the so-say lurid details of my life. I have capitulated. I will tell. Though Lord knows who wants to read the ramblings of a grumpy old woman about to die. It may be feast or famine, but it is you, reader – always my eternal employer – who will decide.

Welcome to my life in twelve men. Enjoy. Because I very much did.

MAN ONE: Michael

London, 1947

He was, first and foremost, my cousin. A second cousin to be precise, but of the family. Before war broke out, I saw Michael only at family gatherings, at Easter and Christmas – he was the son of my father's cousin, and as such probably as bored as I was in the yawning chasm of suburban life on the outskirts of London – all neat semis, postcard gardens and 'nice' couples who moved in across the way and borrowed cups of sugar or the garden shears. Our fathers weren't terribly close, but similar in that they were both extremely dull. Despite being the eldest child in his family, Michael was always labelled the 'naughty' one, and my being an only child, I felt justified in following suit. He was two years older than I, but we seemed to gel as children, always knowing when to sneak off. They had a large garden at the back of their 1930s bay-windowed monstrosity in some godforsaken West London borough, and we would sprint down to the bottom, where it backed onto a small wood, and unburden our pockets of whatever we'd filched from the kitchen, scoffing ourselves silly with our bare ankles in the brook. Once, our feet breeched the icy water at Christmas time, and I can still remember how cold my big toe became, convinced I'd lose it to frostbite. Even then I had a tendency for the dramatic.

When the war came it was like being taken to the funfair every single day. Four children of the family fold, Michael and I included, were whisked off to his grandmother's house in Somerset, along with our mothers, who were so busy herding the two younger ones and coping with Granny's ills and complaints that we were left to run wild. Never again have I experienced such total and utter freedom; lying in the apple orchard under the dappled leaves, bellies pregnant and gassy with eating too many windfalls, Michael and I talked of what we would do 'when'. When we could and would escape, not only the place but the shackles of our parents' dull and lifeless existence.

'I might join the foreign legion,' Michael mused. 'You get to travel a lot.'

'I'd say you get to walk a lot in the sand, and probably to die as well,' I said casually. My mother told me almost daily that I was precocious as well as dramatic.

'All right, maybe not that,' he conceded. 'I could be a writer and sit in a Panama hat on the balcony of a very good hotel in Casablanca, drinking brandy and writing bestsellers. That seems like a good job.'

'That's not a *job*, Mikey,' I huffed. He thought my calling him 'Mikey' suited his wayward persona, like some sort of street urchin. 'Being a writer is a vocation, a passion. You can't just pluck it out of the air. Or present yourself for an interview.' *And besides, that's my passion – you can't have it,* I wanted to say, though I didn't, for fear even Mikey might ridicule me. Without exception, no one knew of my pile of notebooks hidden under the bed, packed with diaries, thoughts, miniscule stories. I think nowadays they might be termed 'flash fiction', but then it was just a stream of thoughts, a telegram wired into my soul. I knew full well it was nonsense, but it was *my* nonsense.

'What about painting?' I suggested. 'Painters can do whatever they like, and no one can tell if they are terrible, talented or simply mad.'

I thought then of poor Van Gogh and regretted that Mikey might become an artist after all. I always liked his ears.

'You can only do whatever you like if you're already successful and people daren't ask what your work is about,' Mikey came back. 'Since I can't draw a stick man, I might not be very good at it.'

'Then you can be avant-garde and penniless in a garret,' I offered enthusiastically. 'I could bring you nourishing soup to cure you of the consumption that nearly kills you every winter, but from which you rally to produce some of your best work, sold for thousands of pounds posthumously.'

We laughed so much that Mikey belched repeatedly from apple over-indulgence and I was almost sick on the grass.

'You know, we weren't that far off the mark,' I said lazily, handing him our last cigarette that we were sharing, him fortunately not dying of consumption at that very moment.

He took it gently from my fingers and drew long and hard on it, blowing a succession of smoke rings towards the ceiling. 'It might not be your classic garret but I do have a damp patch up there,' he said. 'And I am fairly immoral, and produce dreadful art which won't be recognised for its genius until I am cold in my grave.'

It wasn't true, of course. Michael was among the most promising in his art-school year, and he knew it, but he still harboured a fair amount of humility at that point. He turned his naked body towards mine and ran a finger over my bare breast, as if he coveted it both sexually and as the focus of his next life drawing. He was studying its form, the way the anatomy pulped out like a ripe peach, as much as it stirred his loins.

We had already made love, so we made some more and, since it was only mid-afternoon, we dressed and went out into the autumn chill of the evening to meet Michael's friends. He was no longer Mikey, he'd already insisted. In the pub, I was treated as if I was very grown up, despite being all of seventeen.

And before you get the wrong idea and think that Michael seduced me with his bohemian charm, he didn't. Think the other way around.

Halfway through the war, Mikey had been plucked from our country idyll and hauled, kicking and screaming, to a non-descript boarding school on the south coast, one that I heard his mother say 'might knock him into shape, or so his father thinks'. It didn't, of course. He burned down the outhouse attached to the cricket pavilion, and as recompense he was forced to spend the summer painting theatre backdrops for the school dramatics society. Voila! His artistry was born.

Post-war, post-Granny and back in the Gulag of suburbia, with a cabin fever so acute *I* was considering the foreign legion at that point, I got a brief note from Michael inviting me to meet him 'up town' after his interview at the Royal Academy to study art. *I think I've effected the perfect escape, so now let's plan yours,* the note read. I hadn't seen him in two years – our fathers had had a falling out – but we'd been exchanging letters of fond nostalgia since the Somerset war days.

He met me at the bus stop, and I looked straight past him, almost. Michael had changed – into a man. Nineteen then, his blond unruly curls were shorn close to his head, though still desperate to entwine, giving him a cap of hair like a Greek god (I'd indulged far too much in classics at my very nice *gels'* school). He had a newly chiselled jaw-line, shoulders that were square and defined, as if he had played some rugby at that school of his, but his white smile was unchanged. Naughty.

'Hey, Rubes, long time no see.' He grinned and stood back as if to peruse me, head to toe, drinking in the difference. He gave me a hug, and all at once it was exactly the same – and very, very different. I'd loved him since the Somerset days, but oh, what was this?

I was so entranced by his transformation that I perhaps didn't realise how much I had morphed too. Twelve to sixteen is a leap for females, not least in the breast area, and mine were coming on nicely, thank you very much. I was tall and strong, but lean and perhaps fawn-like, my dark hair cut in a neat bob that was neither schoolgirl nor woman. Having not read *Lolita* at that point, I was entirely innocent of quite how coquettish I must have appeared.

'Well, you have changed,' was his final assessment. There was no leer, no suggestion, no boyish tee-hee-hee from Michael. But to my utter surprise, there was an unmistakeable tweaking in a region I later recognised as my own loins, strong enough to spark a cough. What in God's name was that?

We jumped on several London buses and sat in the smoky upstairs, the buses snaking their way past bombsites and the reconstruction of our glorious capital. Since I hadn't seen much of central London before the war, I couldn't take part in the grief of a grand old lady losing her shine. In parts, it looked like a moonscape, in others, a capital we could still be proud of. It was a Phoenix rising out of the ashes, albeit with an arthritic knee. And it was thrilling.

We'd swapped the greenery of Somerset for grey concrete, but it felt like being back together, going wherever we wanted. Michael introduced me to his new-found adoration of art, at the Tate, the National, and several of those little-known galleries, often called 'Institutes' whose unassuming entrances hide spectacular early sketches by the giants of the art world, Picasso and Matisse among them. We rounded off the day at the Lyons Corner House on the Strand, with tea and too many cakes.

'We should do this again, Rubes,' he said, pushing a wayward raisin into his mouth. 'It's been fun.'

'Are you sure you really want to hang around with your younger cousin?' I was two years his junior, but not entirely naïve. I knew good-looking men of nineteen did not frequent Lyons on a daily basis.

'Of course!' he said, a little affronted. Then aimed his very blue eyes at me. 'You saved me, Rubes – in Somerset. You taught me how to dream.'

'I saved you from the foreign legion, that's all,' I countered. 'And I was equally saved from skull-crushing boredom. We're quits.'

'Even-stevens.'

So, I did go again – and again, lying unashamedly to my mother that I was travelling up town with a friend to visit her great-aunt in Hampstead, and no, the old lady didn't have a telephone, but she was very strict and we weren't allowed to go far from the village. *I promise, Mother.* But I would have lied a lot more to be there; time with Michael became my hope, and my solace.

The first time I stayed over it was down to my drunkenness – wanting to be like the boys and consequently consuming one pint of mild too many. I have no idea how I got into Michael's bed, but I was only half-dressed (or undressed) and he was very much on the floor under a thin blanket when I awoke.

'I got one of the crowd to ring your mother last night,' he said lazily as he boiled the kettle on his tiny two-ring gas hob. 'So, make sure to get your story straight before you go.'

He wandered to the bathroom down the hall, and I checked the sheets under me.

Being a woman untouched, and thanks to the derisory instruction at the *gels'* school, I knew very little about sex, but enough to realise there would be evidence if something had occurred. Besides, I trusted Michael. He was my cousin, for heaven's sake. To that point, I hadn't even revealed to myself – let alone scratched such confessions in my diary – the true thoughts that rippled each time I sat in Michael's company. *A schoolgirl crush,* I told myself, though my heart beat like a military tattoo as he stood there in his underwear that morning, nonchalantly ruffling his hair. *Oh Lord.*

And then, suddenly, he was more than a crush against my naïve little heart. We'd been on a picnic in Hyde Park with several of his art-school friends, men mostly, though there were generally several women in the circle. It was one of those sun-kissed afternoons when you have to pinch yourself that life could really be so carefree, having absolutely nothing to do and nowhere to go.

Michael had been at the Royal Academy for a few short

weeks, but the art school, the life and he – well, they fitted each other like bespoke gloves.

'Are you going to life drawing tomorrow?' his friend, Hugh, asked, sipping at his beer that was almost down to the dregs.

'Cancelled, I think,' Michael replied, lying on his back and blowing smoke to emulate the cotton clouds above. 'The model has cried off, sickness so they told me.'

'Isn't there anyone else?'

'Probably not, too short notice.'

Hugh grunted his disapproval – he was good fun generally, but always struck me as a spoiled boy, used to getting his own way.

'We could always draw each other,' Sally piped up. She was the more sensible of the girl group, and a true talent with charcoal, unlike Helen and Phoebe, whose parents Michael swore had bought their places at the art school.

'Naked?' Helen cried. 'I don't think so.'

'No, silly,' Sally countered. 'We don't *have* to paint nudes.'

'But it helps,' chimed in Hugh. 'No decent anatomy on show without flesh.'

Even Michael half-nodded his agreement then, and my mind wandered to an image of them all clustered around a figure on a plinth, staring at the creases or the pink, fleshy folds, wondering what they really thought about as they sketched. Was it really just shapes, or did any of them have that inner, tremulous tweak I'd so recently discovered, as their eyes strayed up and down the bodies, and along the lines leading to intimate crevices?

'What about you, Ruby? Any plans for tomorrow?' Hugh half-laughed, though there was the edge of a real question in there. 'Step into the breach?'

Michael sat up like a jack-in-a-box. 'No, Hugh, Ruby isn't

interested,' he said pointedly, then turned to me. 'Are you?' His brow below his blond hair was wrinkled, like faint waves on the nearby Serpentine.

'No,' I said, though I'd surprised myself by already having thought about it. Not just them clustered around any figure, but around me. Whether they might bustle about, fiddling with their easels and paints, as if I was any old piece of meat to sketch. Or if Hugh would be thinking something else – my eye often caught his focused on me, and he always sliced it away quickly, looking uncharacteristically sheepish. And the girls, perhaps coveting some part of my lean torso they might never possess (Phoebe especially was on the plump side). What would they be thinking? Michael… well, I tried not to think about him at all. So much so, I was utterly blind to the way he leaped to my defence in a heartbeat. I thought I was so clever, never imagining that I was, in reality, shrouded in a thick fog of my own longing. More than anything, I wanted to be a fly on the wall. *Their* wall.

'I would do it, you know,' I said later, when we were alone – or as alone as you can be on the no. 57 to Hornsey.

'Do what?' Michael said, his eyes drawn beyond the window. He never stopped looking – at people, buildings – drinking in every line or curve.

'The life class. Nude too.'

He turned to me and laughed. 'Your father would skin me alive.'

'My father would never know, unless you told him. Or presented him with your sketch as a Christmas gift, though he's such a neanderthal about art, he might not recognise his own daughter.'

Michael scanned my face then in the way I thought he might survey a whole figure, his eyes picking their way around my features, one by one. I could almost feel him scratching away at their every detail. My eyelids itched.

'No,' he said.

'Are you forbidding me?' It was my turn to laugh.

'No. I don't think you should, that's all.'

'I've always wanted to be a muse,' I sang on, knowing it would be irritating him. Silence between us had been a thing of ours – we tolerated it equally well, sometimes for hours at a stretch. Over the long war, Michael and I discovered a way of just being. Consequently, he hated anyone wittering, his mother especially, words just for the sake of them, 'polluting the innocent air,' he complained.

'There's a difference between a muse and a life model,' he said at last, quietly, but in such a way that I felt very stupid all of a sudden, that the age difference between us was way beyond two years. I was a child to his man. It irked me, and a little ember of dissidence sparked into a flame.

I spent the night in Michael's bed, with him on the floor as usual. We had both drunk a good amount of beer, and there was little of our customary murmurings after he switched off the light.

I was up with the birdsong, and he woke to a note from me. *See you anon. R x.* I often drifted back home on a Monday, to reappear the next Friday for a grown-up weekend.

But I wasn't on the train home. The tutors at the Academy were all too grateful at being presented with an impromptu model, and one with experience too – by then, I had added liar to my résumé of precocious and dramatic. The tutor helpfully furnished me with a robe when I said I'd forgotten my own.

★★★

Hugh's face on arrival was flooded with surprise, then bathed in glee as he set up his easel. The three girls simply registered irritation.

'I didn't think Hugh was serious,' I heard Helen mutter.

Michael said not a word as he arrived, although I alone watched the rage in his eyes flare. To this day, I don't know why I wanted to jab at him, like prodding at an amiable old lion in his sleep, just to hear him roar. I adored Michael, and loved spending time in his company, with his adult friends. Why on earth would I invite his wrath? Inwardly, I couldn't admit I was goading for a reaction.

I thought he might simply walk out as I slipped off my robe, revealing all. He stayed, however, perhaps as a way of proving that he was right, to say: 'you wanted this, now you have to suffer it' – the gawping, the muttering about your femur being too long, or your toes too stubby, or your pose too simple; the backache and the draught which makes your nipples stand to attention (which really is quite painful). It was all of those, plus Hugh's resonant breathing too close to me, rising up and down like the pitch of a radio being tuned. Michael looked at me intently, his face peeking out from behind his easel – but only in the way he would have looked at an apple, or an aspidistra. In his eyes, I was flesh and bones only. Inert.

I felt shame then, manifesting itself in goose bumps for long enough that it might well have affected the texture for those using thickened paint. At the session's end, I reapplied the robe and leaped off the plinth, brushing off Hugh's compliments about my modelling ability. I needed to go home and reinhabit my schoolgirl existence, and not continue to fool myself I was an adult in the making. Worse, I knew I'd lost Michael as a friend. And that was the most painful ignominy. His anger I could just about deal with, but not his obvious disappointment in me, thrust entirely upon myself, on an utterly childish whim. Why was I so bent on self-destruction before I'd even properly created a shadow of myself?

'Rubes… Rubes – wait!' Michael's voice was behind me as I charged towards the main doors of the building.

'I have to go.' I tossed the words behind me as I ran out, creased with humiliation. I couldn't even conjure an apology.

'Wait!' He was insistent, though not angry.

Outside, in the fresh dawn of autumn, he pulled at my arm. I spun around – shame and defiance a hard expression to hide. 'Sorry, Michael,' I managed at last. 'I don't know why I did… Look, I'll see you sometime, eh?'

He put a finger on my chin and tipped it up towards him. Lord, he looked more like a Greek god than ever, something to do with the weak sun behind his thick curls.

'I'm sorry too,' he said. 'I shouldn't have said no, spoken for you. That was wrong. It's everything I hate about my father.'

I smiled weakly. 'It did rather make me kick back. Story of my life.'

'And after all these years, I really should have guessed the effect.' His lashes bent towards the floor. 'It's just I couldn't bear… well, the idea that Hugh of all people should see…'

I pulled up his chin then – even though he was a good half foot taller than me, in the same way a nursery teacher would prepare to tenderly chide a small charge.

'What is it?' I said. A burning curiosity simmered within, accompanied by the military tattoo in full swing. I had absolutely no idea what he was thinking. He would not allow me to scratch at his eyelids.

'Oh, Rubes.'

He didn't even go back to collect his things. We didn't say a word, only got on the Underground and walked silently to his tiny flat. And we went to bed. And if you want to be literal about it, he deflowered me, and I let him. He led me and I followed, willingly. I drew in every inch of him, and with every second, I knew it would not so much change me, as entirely transform the direction of my life. Pivotal and precious. A little bit painful too, if I'm honest, in that delicious rite-of-passage way. It was as if I somehow created a spectre of myself, hovering above. Down there on the sheets, I was beguiled by the moment, my skin on fire at Michael's gentle touch, and yet above, acutely aware too of what my second self was seeing, entirely objective in watching my body writhing with pleasure in his bed.

Did I taste regret, too? A little; you couldn't help it, a woman of that age persuaded at every turn that chastity was like a tightly bound parcel to be permanently carried, only to be opened when it reached the right destination of Wedlock, postcode unknown. Equally, I felt grateful, as I lay there grinning and gasping, so pleased I was with Michael, for him to show me, and spare me the awkward fumble of two novices in a clumsy coupling, or the restrained and forced joy of a marriage night, when too late, bride and groom discover it's not all it's cracked up to be. Looking at the wall of starched affection between my parents, I never imagined you could set a match to it with passion. Perhaps I wanted to prove I could burn it down.

But oh! It was some revelation. I walked into Michael's room that day a sheepish, ungainly seventeen-year-old, and emerged a woman, like a rabbit out of a hat. Ta-dah! Not complete (are we ever?) but with one part of the puzzle glued firmly in place. I checked the sheets too; I was Woman. Later, I saw the sketch Michael had made that day of me at the Academy – languid, flowing lines of a near Aphrodite, pencil marks barely skating over the page, some a mere whisper. It was beatific. Yet he captured a defiance and sorrow in my expression, my face looming large on his page. Because there was no full form – no body, bare breasts or shapely bottom. Only my face, and nothing to mark that I was model or muse. Neither naked nor vulnerable. Only Ruby, the girl-woman.

And so that's how we came to be lying there on our backs, smoking and joking in his bed, week after week, as autumn turned to the winter of 1947. The irony didn't escape us – we'd swapped a Somerset wartime sky for the maturing damp patch on his ceiling and were gorging on each other. Drunk on the proceeds. By that time, I had persuaded my parents that I should take a short course in typing at a secretarial school, choosing one which helpfully boarded 'young ladies' in Bloomsbury. In my mind, it would help me type faster when I reached my newest goal of university. In theirs, it was a nice precursor to finding a husband, possibly a rich enough banker if I played my cards right in London.

Of course, I was rarely in Bloomsbury. I applied myself to frenetic typing, because it suited me, and was generally ahead on my exercises, enough that I could dodge the afternoon sessions to write freely in a selection of libraries (I made a mental list of the warmest ones), and meet Michael most evenings after his classes. My father's allowance was unusually generous and meant we could tour the art galleries, followed by a near decent dinner, before landing back at Michael's, where I became his official muse, him sketching me until his eyes drooped and he crawled between the sheets and we made lazy love. I had to be careful to keep enough shillings back to sweeten the landlady at my boarding house, for her not to report my scant presence and unruffled sheets.

The question of our being cousins, albeit fairly distant, never came up, and certainly didn't register on any guilt scale that I recall. It was unspoken, but certainly shared: this was never forever. Michael and I would not have to face the wrath of the family in declaring our undying love, or the uncomfortable prospect of children emerging from a potentially murky gene pool. Perhaps the most awkward moments were in *not* displaying any kind of affection at a Christmas gathering that year, after our fathers had called a truce on their petty disagreement. We skirted around each other over sherry – and he was so good at it, even keeping a straight face as he asked me how my secretarial course was progressing. I swear I nearly gave it away, needing to summon a coughing fit and retire to the bathroom.

After dinner, he suggested I keep him company while he smoked in the garden and we stole a gentle kiss beyond the shrubbery, sharing the cigarette my parents never imagined I smoked.

'You are far too good at lying,' I told him. 'Remind me never to trust you.'

'You and Michael seemed to be getting on well this evening,' my mother said when everyone had left.

'Yes, it's nice to catch up after all this time.' I concentrated hard on drying the dishes.

'Perhaps you should have dinner in London from time to time,' she said. 'The two of you used to be so close – thick as thieves at Granny's.' Then: 'Hmm, perhaps not. You don't know what those art school friends of his are like.'

'Hmm,' I said.

'Bohemian,' she rattled on. 'You hear about it.'

'Hmm.'

I wasn't a complete work of art, at least I never thought so. After all Michael's tuition, I knew full well that even the *Venus de Milo* was left without arms. Perfection in art is overrated and entirely unattainable, he always maintained. I was sculpted, had had some of my sharp edges chipped and smoothed, but I was still a work in progress – and that was my assessment, not his. He never once judged me.

No one decided we should move on, it simply happened, both of us knowing our time was finite. Much like our never, never future that we never spoke about it, we didn't pinpoint when it would be. Correction: *I* made it happen.

I'd been writing furiously and had landed myself a job at a literary agency in Bloomsbury on the strength of a short story – they weren't offering to tout it, but it demonstrated I had half a brain and could spell. My typing was a bonus. Plus it was my way into the book world and everything associated with the printed page, once I'd persuaded my parents that publishers were well off and that I had cured myself of arrogant male writers in the first weeks.

I hadn't, of course. Only evermore enticed. The confidence

Michael had so carefully nurtured in me crumbled to dust in the presence of a published scribe. The more they strutted into the office and demanded just reverence for their brilliance in print, the more I mooned at them from behind my paltry desk. Since it was piled high with manuscripts, they rarely witnessed the mooning, the wall of paper acting as a physical buffer to my sighs of envy. The truth was, I didn't want to sleep with any one of them, or marry them, or bear their children. I wanted to *be* them. Not, in all honesty, for the prima-donna-strutting, or even the adulation, but for that book in my hand – fanning the pages, smelling each and every leaf. My words. For others to see, to marvel at. I had watched Michael grow into his craft, the excitement in his eyes when he made the right mark on the canvas, the pure satisfaction when guests at the art school praised his work. Better still, when they bought it. Someone, somewhere would look at his creation on their wall, day after day, and drink it in. Something that sprang from his hand, out of the ether. I couldn't draw a stick man, but I could paint with words. And I wanted what he had, that ability to create, excite and make wonder. He might not have known it, and I don't think I ever told him, but Michael was fast becoming my muse.

Despite the likes of Virginia Woolf and her Bloomsbury brigade (plus the heroic Ms Austen before her), Britain nudging into the 1950s meant it was rare for a woman to earn her place on the shelf with words alone. Once there, they easily held their own, but the journey onto that dusty domain was uphill. Guile was a valuable currency. Smiles, flirtation and sickening deceit were in there too. It was all part of the game, and everyone understood it.

Gradually, just gradually, I spent less time admiring Michael's marks, and more scratching down my own, being coughed at by the library assistant as they were closing the doors, actually sleeping between my own sheets as I wrote late into the night under a thick eiderdown that smelled faintly of pee.

It was, inevitably, a thinly veiled story of me. What else would an eighteen-year-old female of my background have to write about? I heard it time and again at the agency: write what you know. I made sure the crushing oppression of suburbia featured too, along with the toxic sphere of well-to-do 'gels', but it was essentially about a girl breaking free into womanhood.

And Michael.

As it turned out, it was I who proved to be the expert in deceit, and not my beloved cousin. On the two or three times a week we managed to meet – when I forced myself away from my typewriter – he always asked me how the novel was progressing, hungry to know of the world inside my head. Against my better judgement – *all* judgement – I lied. I told him it was about a girl who escapes her childhood to run free in the metropolis.

'It's about you then,' he laughed. The gorgeous curls had been left uncut for some time and he was, officially, a modern-day Adonis, backlit by the pub's dim-bulb illumination. Michael was too poor to spend out on a haircut, I was equally too busy to oblige him with the scissors any longer. His hole-pocked jumper and paint-splattered trousers completed the artist-in-a-garret look.

'*No*,' I said, a mixture of offence and defence. 'Well… maybe, a bit.'

'Don't sound so guilty.' He swallowed back the last of his beer and looked straight at me. 'I've painted hundreds of self-portraits – the tutors make us. You have to know yourself before you can even begin to pick apart others. I'm sure it's the same for writers.'

I'd loved Michael for ages, in varying shades of love's true sense, but in that second, I adored him beyond anything in the stratosphere, for naturally assuming I was a writer. For naming me as one. And so, my guilt ripped into me even more when he asked, a cheeky, sly smile to his full lips: 'Am I in it?'

I wasn't to know it then, but in that moment I ended us, with a single act of treachery. A large, inky full stop. 'No,' I said. 'There's no romance.'

He raised one eyebrow.

'Or sex,' I lied a second time. 'I'd have to be a man to get that past a publisher.'

'True,' he said, nodding.

How could he be so understanding, and I so fraudulent?

It was that day at the Academy all over again, when I'd taunted him with my naked bloody-mindedness. I had no idea why I felt compelled to prod at Michael's loyalty with a red-hot poker, because he didn't deserve it. My mother had told me since childhood, in my naughtier moments, that I had 'the devil in me'. There, with Michael, I was aware of the evil squatting deep inside that I was powerless to fight against. Even my intense guilt could not hold back the devil, and the page won. The years since have taught me that – whether you like it or not – writers are slaves to words. It was a lesson I should have heeded, only I didn't appreciate their total dominance back then. Which is probably why I have twelve men (and more) to write about, rather than just one.

Maybe, in that smoke-filled pub, I didn't imagine that my writing would ever appear in print, merely a bottom-drawer novel I would pull out one day in my dotage and laugh at the dreadful prose and cringe at such awkward semi-confessions. But I don't remember anything other than the sheer desire to hold a book in my hand and read: *a novel, by Ruby Devereaux* (the M comes later). I was too naïve to know then that the life lived *in* books is – at best – second best.

As with so much in history, it was pure luck that caused my life to swerve in yet another direction, only nudged by guile. For some months, I'd been casually leaving short stories on my boss's desk, tucked in the pile of submissions he needed to read. They were always conveniently unnamed, my hope that Charles, one of the agents and my immediate superior, would be so enticed by the opening paragraphs that he could not help but keep reading, utterly drawn in by the page and my weaving of prose.

He wasn't. Without querying the lack of a name, each came back from his desk with a short and sweet 'No' in pencil, across the title page. It was generally my job to rub out the pencil marks and type up a standard rejection letter to every other disappointed scribe: *Dear... I was delighted to read your manuscript, but...* which I varied and embellished because I felt so sorry for the recipient, hoping someone would afford me the same kindness in years to come.

Like so many fairy stories, the good news came from a fluke, something you genuinely would struggle to make up.

I'd left a rough draft of the now-completed novel on my desk, intending to begin typing it up in my lunch hour, after which I would trawl through the office copy of the *Writers' & Artists' Yearbook* in the hopes of finding an agent or a publisher to take me on. Charles had sent me on an errand to the post office, by way of the tobacconist, to buy his favoured cigars (dogsbody being a large but unrecognised part of my job). I returned to a pile of office duties, and so was entirely distracted until lunchtime when I settled down to my own typing. I figured it would take me several weeks in fifty-minute bursts to complete and craft individual letters, munching on my sandwich as I typed.

My thick-ish tome was gone. I searched high and low, upending a huge pile of manuscripts in trying to locate the precious bundle, panic rising and heart racing. Worse still, the rubbish had gone out that very morning, and the thought of a whole year's blood, sweat and tears, not to mention frostbitten fingers, languishing in some dust cart, made me feel physically sick. Why hadn't I even made a longhand copy? *Stupid girl.* Where on earth was it?

With a face sporting an expression of near-bereavement, I charged into Charles's office, intending to beg another hour of time to face the stinking bins in the back alleyway. He was stretched back in his chair, as was his wont when reading a manuscript – you always knew it had potential when he propped his feet on the desk and settled himself in for the duration. I stopped mid-plead, partly because he held up one hand in a silent 'don't disturb me now' fashion and partly because there was now no need to search the fetid rubbish. I would have recognised those dog-eared pages anywhere, the faux-ageing of one side where I'd up-ended a full cup of tea and sponged off the excess, leaving the paper edges slightly frilly in places.

Unusually for me, I was struck dumb.

'Shocking state these scripts come in nowadays,' he mumbled, not taking his eyes from the page, 'and the grammar is near appalling. But this one definitely has something.'

Never before had Charles voiced any opinion to me, other than in pencil marks, about any submissions, but for some inexplicable reason he did on that day. He later told me he had no idea it could have come from me, the girl in the outer office, sheepishly admitting that he often had trouble remembering my name.

That all changed once he accepted my atypical submission, negotiated a sale and an offer of an advance (one third of my annual income), and set about putting the grammar right. Michael and I celebrated with dinner at the Café Royal – he in his one-and-only mothballed suit – and then a pint at our local pub, where he looked at me not with wonder, but love and pride.

'I always knew you could do it, Rubes. Never doubted it.'

In my new dress, I radiated pleasure and, inwardly, squirmed at his prospective reading of the debut copies due to be delivered in the next months. The deep betrayal of him. Of us. My parents' inevitable and excruciating embarrassment was a ripple in the ocean by comparison. The intimate scenes that Charles had marked in pencil as *vivid!*, but insisted I did not tone down, or the thinly veiled description of my lover, the blond budding architect. In years to come, I would learn the skill of disguising one's characters, but not then.

'To you – Ruby Devereaux – published author!' He held up his favoured pint of mild and beamed. The words I had longed to hear, turned bittersweet when coming from my Mikey.

I was alone in the office when the first proof copy was delivered, hands trembling as I clawed at the box and snatched at the first copy, turning a full circle to make sure there were no spying eyes and then smelled the pages, all 316 of them. I braille-read the blurb on the back: *exciting new debut* – a comment from an established writer that Charles had managed to solicit in return for the promise of a favour.

Michael was itching to lay his hands on a copy, despite my trying to delay it as long as possible. 'Come on, Rubes, surely I get first dibs? I'm dying to scuttle further into your psyche.'

Be careful what you wish for, I thought, and crawled onto his bed, running my hands up his thigh and into his trousers. We had the best sex; I wondered then if he suspected the finality of it when we both ascended, or whether it was just me, the selfish one among us. I left early for work the next morning, his near-naked body sprawled spider-like on the bed, and a copy of the book next to the kettle.

We met in the pub later the next evening, as planned. I was already contrite, pre-empting his feelings of betrayal and preparing my goodbye speech, not so naïve as to expect a reprieve, a forgiveness borne of his own innate goodness. I reasoned that if Michael had done the same to me, I might never forgive him. So why should he? In one overriding fat slice of selfishness, I had swapped the hard covering of a book cover and the feathering of pages for the taut sinews and soft flesh of his body. Worse still, the true loveliness of Michael. How did I feel? Sickened, and yet still under the influence of a drug called 'ego' – among other things, it renders you stupid as well as cruel.

He had a pint in front of him as I arrived, and a face like thunder. He didn't offer to buy me a drink, and I sat without one. Under the golden curls, his eyes were bead-black and watery, and I wondered if he was going to cry. He swallowed, growling through his mean line of a mouth. 'You said it wasn't about me. Or us. Or romance.'

'You forgot the sex,' I said. It was a senseless and glib reply, and his lips all but disappeared in rage.

'How could you, Rubes?' His bottom lip pushed out to quiver. 'That was us. Private. Our love. Haven't we always loved each other, in every way? Since we were kids.'

Ironically, I had no words, much less excuses. As much as he loved his art and lived entirely for being a painter, how could I explain to Michael that it was all about the book in hand? The giving over to strangers who would pore over the pages, a portion who might be affected enough to talk about it, discuss it, buy it. Be moved by it. At the end of the day, it was pure self-interest, tightly bound in a craft that I found exhilarating and addictive and... how could I say it was like the best sex I'd ever had, when I'd only had that with Michael, the object of my soul and heart? The one who had partially shaped me into the writer I was.

I felt like Joan of Arc, up there on the pyre, only I was lighting the matches myself.

I left the pub without explanation, tears streaming. I sobbed for an age into my pee-pong eiderdown, and then I sat down at the typewriter and put in a fresh sheet. *Chapter one,* I typed. I was a writer and so would have to live and die for my art, I decided there and then (the dramatics not having left me at that point). The dying I haven't quite managed yet, but by God, did I do the living.

I saw Michael only twice after that; much like our unspoken non-future, the abrupt end of our relationship was not uttered, with no acrimonious break-up in the pub to sadistic glee from the other drinkers, merely a series of sad, resigned looks that spelled out 'goodbye' through a veil of tobacco smoke.

We couldn't avoid an agonising meeting that Christmas, given that all family events at that point were apt to inflict pain, though seeing Michael made the occasion almost unbearable. His stone wall of silence was far worse than any civility. That, and his slinking away to the bottom of the garden as I went outside for a cigarette, so that I could see his lone puffs rise above the shrubbery while I blew smoke rings, sitting on the patio, entirely alone. It was nothing less than I deserved.

I glimpsed him a year later at a book launch – my own sales were good, though not enough for me to give up the day job. Charles had promoted me to dogsbody in publicity four days a week, allowing me more time to perfect the dreaded follow-up to a well-received first novel, which had sold amply to a select readership of largely older, and very probably married, men. Only years later was it taken to heart by a newly emancipated breed of women, who took it upon themselves to adopt my innocence as bravery in playing men in their own world. Lolita turned Boudicca.

This particular launch was in the upstairs room of a private club, and Michael was in the distance, a champagne glass to his lips, though I recognised his mass of curls hovering above the black, oiled caps of other men. He was still beautiful, still god-like, and I had a heart-stop second followed by a pinch, that I knew to be jealousy, at him laughing with a good-looking woman. He turned his head casually so that I must have fallen into his line of vision – I had on a striking red dress, and he couldn't have failed to note its vibrancy. His eyes lay on me for a whole second. He tilted his head perhaps a millimetre, maybe even less, and sliced his gaze away, causing a thud in my heart like the fall of a guillotine. There was not a semblance of emotion in his look – not regret or hate, or love or forgiveness. Nothing. He, a man who could fashion emotion from one hair of a brush on a bright, white canvas, would afford me nothing.

I only heard of him after that, and not through the family, who largely disowned him in time. After a good deal of success as one of the bright young hopefuls of the British art world, he moved to Mexico to paint in '55, his greatly acclaimed works fed via his agent, refusing all press coverage without exception. I saw only one picture of him before he became a near hermit, and it looked very much like he was wearing that Panama hat, poised alongside his easel. I liked to imagine that he married a Mexican woman, painting in the shade of a sun-kissed garden, with scores of children called Jose and Miguel running around his ankles.

Seems not, though it *was* a Miguel who stole his heart and became an enduring love to Michael's dying day at the tender age of sixty-four. I still wonder if it was our connection which convinced him of his true orientation, and that our affection (I sincerely believe it was love) proved a one-off, not to be repeated with any other woman. I'm sure of such devotion because of the frequent trips I made in the years following, to a small gallery in Kensington that had wisely invested in several of his paintings before he became a bankable and collectable darling. I went to stare at only one of his four works on display, dated 1950, the same year as my book debut, and our break-up. It's of me – he sketched me time and again in the damp-patch flat, lying in bed and reading the Sunday papers, drinking endless tea. It's stylised and stark, not the soft brush strokes of his earlier student works, and although not a true likeness, it is me. I recognise myself. And I look nice. My face isn't contorted, my soul doesn't push out from the canvas as mean and dispirited. His paintbrush then wasn't a conduit for his disappointment, or my betrayal. In fact, my expression is one of indifference. Which is my only criticism, since I was never apathetic or cool, I promise you. Naïve, foolish and misguided, maybe, as well as hopelessly chained to my ego. But never indifferent.

He was my cousin, and my lover, my teacher and my muse. Together, we joined our own, respective foreign legions, and we broke free.

But he was, first and foremost, Michael.

MAN TWO: Jerome

New York, 1953

Eventually, I broke out properly, the sort of escape Michael would have been proud of. Sadly, it wasn't as a celebrated author that I crossed the Atlantic in June of 1953, but as one of Charles's lackeys. He'd been muttering for some time about 'getting into the American market', and somehow pulled one of the many strings to his viola and found me a posting at an expanding and very chic New York publisher, whereupon I would work by day and help forge links for him by night at various book parties and launches, thereby sniffing out the market. My reward?

'The life, my sweet,' he boomed behind his mushrooming cloud of cigar smoke. 'What better opportunity to soak up the metropolis as a writer. Push it out through your pen, or your typewriter, or whatever you use.' He was hinting heavily, since my second offering to the literary world hadn't gone down a storm, merely sunk into the silted, oceanic depths of the follow-up. It was a tale of love and loss in wartime Somerset; I was still on the write-what-you-know track, though the romance was my imaginings between adults rather than schoolchildren. It seemed, however, that the war wasn't far enough in the past at that point, and global catastrophe hadn't yet moved into the genre called 'nostalgia', a time when those who suffer it can cheerfully forget the grim reality of daily struggles. Personally, I thought I'd grown as a writer. My main character was less like a mirror image of myself and there were fewer grammatical wrongs to be righted, but when it came to the cash till and space on the shelves, it was a dismal failure, falling way short of Charles's expectations. I own only one copy of *Apple Days* and I think it's still out of print as I write.

My boss, however, remained philosophical. 'Everyone's second is a disaster, my sweet,' he said cheerfully. 'It's a mark that you'll be great one day.' Though not great enough that he promised to commission a third without exception. 'Let's see what the Big Apple does to your output, eh?'

It was an opportunity not to be sniffed at. As I sailed towards Lady Liberty aboard the *Queen Mary* (my mother having persuaded my father to upgrade my cabin from mere steerage), I was a woman on the brink of an adventure, but by no means looking for a man to engineer it. In a generous offering of his contacts, Charles had secured a room in Manhattan, in the apartment of 'a friend of a friend at my club'. But it was a good address 'uptown', as New Yorkers say. Even without a viewing, it was a good deal better than I could afford on my paltry wage.

How to describe New York in the eyes of a 23-year-old who'd barely been further north than Watford or west than to Land's End? Big, loud, brash, hoots and toots, and yellow cabs flying – the clichés came thick and fast into my head. Weary from peppered sleep the entire journey (nausea from the swell of sea and too many cocktails), I was truly overwhelmed. A porter at the dockside took pity on my eyes the size of frying pans and hailed me a cab, loading in my copious luggage. I'd reasoned my wages would leave no spare cash to buy new clothes and so had packed everything I owned. To this day, I think I forgot to tip the poor man.

It was there, on arriving at West 86th Street, in the top floor apartment of an elegant brownstone, that my pupils dilated a tad more. And I met Mushens for the first time.

Octavia Katerina Makarenkov was the youngest daughter of some form of Russian nobility back in the day when it was suitable to admit as much. She no longer had a recognised title, but more importantly for her, the money was intact. Oodles of it. From first glance, she clearly didn't need my trifling contribution, but since she rarely carried any cash – charging everything to 'my account' – the envelope of dollars I left on the hall side table each week was her 'running about' fund, i.e. tips. My hard-earned rent went into the hands of bellboys and concierges, and sometimes beggars on the street. Mushens, I came to learn, was as rich as Croesus but also quite generous, as a good deal of the wealthy are sometimes not.

'Happy to meet you, Octav—'

'Just call me Mushens,' she said in her Slavic lilt, extending her long thin fingers. For a minute, I thought I needed to kiss them, but she was expecting a shake only. 'Everyone does.'

No other explanation was offered – there it was, and she remained Mushens forever after.

'The apartment isn't huge,' she said, leading me from room to room to room, me trailing like a puppy and gawping at the high ceilings and expensive furnishings, 'but Papa has me on a very tight leash.' This, it turned out, meant she had approximately ten times my weekly income, and no job, bar keeping various commercial services in business; a princess in everything but name. And like a lot of pseudo-royalty, Mushens knew a lot of people, kissed a good many cheeks, fluttered her hands at hundreds over the heads of others at parties, but at the end of the day, sitting there in her insanely large apartment, she was alone. There were acquaintances and suitors, but I came to see in time that she had very few friends to confide in, laugh and be silly with. And so we came to be such.

My first week was intended to be an orientation to the city, and as much as I had packed my flat walking pumps to pound New York's famous avenues, Mushens had other ideas. The New York I saw in those first days was largely through the window of a cab or her father's chauffeur-driven convertible Buick, a gleaming bright red chariot that she loved to ride from uptown to downtown and back again, just parading, or looking, occasionally ordering the long-suffering driver, Teddy, to park up outside a particular boutique, where the poor man risked a ticket every time.

So, by the time I started at Kabler & Bonnet as an editorial assistant, I had a job title but very little street savvy to get around. My duties involved a lot of to-ing and fro-ing on foot, which I actually loved, delivering manuscripts to the nearby printers, and fetching the lunchtime sandwiches from the deli, which was a smorgasbord of choice compared to the regulation cheese and pickle of post-war London. Somehow, being a dogsbody in New York was way more glamorous, hopping across the long, wide avenues, seams of yellow wagons parping just for the sake of it, and once or twice at me as I learned the etiquette of crossing a New York street the hard way. You do it quickly and without fear.

My immediate boss, Mariel, was an alumni dogsbody only just promoted to assistant editor, and so immediately felt she had become top canine in the female office hierarchy. This caused her to consider me as the lowest of all life forms, having had a memory lobotomy about her own origins. Rumour had it, from my fellow dogsbody, Sarah, that Mariel was actually a Mabel, but had given herself a new name and plenty of airs on arrival in the big city. So began a daily contest between Sarah and I, in seeing who could trip up Mariel over her true identity; every so often one of us would sing out 'Mabel' from down the hallway and the other would watch for her reaction. Sarah once thought she saw an eyelid twitch noticeably, but really we needed a good look at her passport to settle the argument.

Mariel's boss, though, was a darling. Harvey Kabler was a man of books, and someone who I considered a candidate for a surrogate father almost the minute I met him. Broad in the waist and with a similarly wide smile, he was generous with his time, despite being in great demand. He was a German Jew and an escapee from the Nazi's anti-Semite scourge, fortunately before war broke out. It was only later that I learned the efforts and the money he gave in helping fellow refugees to flee to America, before and after the war. He never spoke of it, but it did account for the odd, truly terrible manuscripts that would arrive on our desks from time to time, ones that Harvey would uncharacteristically pass for publication. They usually sold to no acclaim but earned enough sales to put the author on their feet and into the American yonder for a new life.

It was Harvey and not Mushens who introduced me to Jerome. Part of my job, not forgetting my secondary role for Charles, was to be a professional mingler, sounding out the potential for a New York branch of my agency back in London. Since Harvey's wife was chronically ill and a virtual recluse as far as I could tell, he often needed someone to accompany him to book launches and publishing parties. He appeared to take an immediate shine to me, much to Mariel's irritation; he once explained it as our both being 'fish out of water – fellow aliens in the big pond, Ruby D'.

Escorting my boss's boss was like being wined and dined by a sugar daddy, but with absolutely no funny business. Harvey was simply delightful company, and munificent in introducing me as 'my associate'.

'Perhaps we need to find you a nice date on one of these occasions,' he said as we sipped pre-party cocktails at the Russian Tea Rooms on West 57th. 'As much as I adore your company, Ruby, it's only right to let New York enjoy you too.'

I didn't like to tell him I'd had my fill of men by then, despite being only twenty-three (who was I kidding?). My love life after Michael had not been a barren desert as such, but neither was it a garden in bloom. There had been one or two men, short but sweet affairs that had never captured my imagination and were a long way from securing my heart. One, however, had been particularly persistent after I cooled off and stopped responding to his messages. The prospect of setting an ocean between us had been rather timely.

Harvey and I downed our Manhattans and moved a block or so north to a reception at the New York Plaza hotel, with its chintzy lobby and stream of A-list celebrities tripping through its doors. I could have simply sat for hours just staring at the entrance, second-guessing myself every so often, but there was work to do. Mushens was already present, surrounded by a gaggle of be-suited men, and I blew her a kiss – she looked to be in her element. Years later, I would have sworn someone present that night used her as the model for Marilyn Monroe in *Some*

Like it Hot, the love and attention so clearly the oxygen she survived on. In turn, she oozed the vapour of their attentions.

On these occasions, Harvey often melted away as we entered the party milieu, happy for me to come and tag onto him again if I was feeling adrift and needing anchoring.

'Drink? I don't see one in your hand,' a voice said as I scanned the party swathe. 'If you're not careful you'll be accosted by a waiter and thrown out for not imbibing enough alcohol.' The man smiled as he said it and pushed a glass of fizz into my hand.

The bubbles popping into my nose and landing on my taste-buds happened to belong to very good champagne. 'Thank you. I will be very careful of breaking the rules.'

With sharp features and a jaw-line that could expertly slice a hefty sirloin, he looked like a young Robert Wagner, and I told him so. In turn, he flattered me that I resembled a cross between Audrey Hepburn and Liz Taylor, probably down to the dress I'd borrowed from Mushens, and which came from the same boutique that Miss Hepburn frequented – or so we were told. Equally and duly complimented, he and I retired to a table at the side.

'Jerome Hemmings.' He offered a solid, all-American hand, to go with his New England accent.

'And yet I'd say that's a very British name.'

'My mother is a lover of all things British,' he explained. 'And it's Jeremy really, but the Hemmings is my agent's idea. He says it sounds more refined than Bronstein. Jewish actors are ten a penny, but British…'

'In Britain, they're ten a penny too,' I countered.

His smile widened. 'Aha, but in New York, it's as well to be distinguished. Or at least appear to be.'

I couldn't dispute it – my accent had opened doors, both metaphorically and literally. Every doorman I encountered appeared charmed the moment I uttered a syllable, and I was often introduced as 'the writer-publisher from England'. Somehow, and thankfully, 'British office dogsbody' was never used.

'So, what sort of acting does your British-sounding name bring for you, Jerome Hemmings?'

He lowered his eyes. 'This and that, bit parts mostly. Until now.' He smiled like the cat that had lapped up all of the cream, and he may have rolled his tongue momentarily around those full lips of his.

'Oh yes?'

'Well, keep it to yourself, but I auditioned yesterday for a new medical TV show that's going on air this autumn.'

'And?' I was aware at this point the conversation was dominated by Jerome, but I was biding my time. We Brits famously don't give too much away. And anyway, who was I going to tell? Mushens didn't know one end of a television soap opera from the other.

'Put it this way, tonight is something of a celebration,' he said, holding up his glass. 'I got the producer's call just before I came out.'

I cocked my head, a movement he later said made his heart flip ten beats. 'And you're celebrating at a book party?' I queried. 'I mean I'm happy to drink champagne with you, but seems like you should be out there', – I gestured to beyond the doors of the Plaza –'with your thespian chums.'

'Say that again.'

'What?'

'Thespian chums.'

'Why?'

'Because you are adorably British when you say it.'

'No.'

'Why not?'

'Because I don't do Audrey Hepburn or Liz Taylor to order. I'm Ruby Devereaux, and this is what you get.'

And apparently, the vital organ in his chest tumbled ten times more. Or that's what he later told me.

How could we not celebrate the newly christened and recently promoted Doctor Tom Bradshaw, Emergency MD at the fictional Angel of Mercy hospital? Even I had to admit that Jerome was born to sport a white coat and be the saviour of small children and the love icon of assorted nurses everywhere. He looked every inch the part, and might never have needed a scalpel with that jaw. How well he could act was, at that point, to be ascertained. But perhaps it didn't matter if the stethoscope looked good enough slung around his neck.

'So, what's the script like? Is it good?' I ventured.

'Excuse me?'

'The script – you've seen it surely? Do you like it?'

He stared at me as if that type of naïveté was not so much endearing, as just plain naïve. What did he care about the quality of the words when he would be the one on set – on screen – wearing the white coat? His name heading the cast list?

I got his drift, though not *the* drift. For me, it was still about the words. I just managed to put it to one side for a time.

Harvey, being Jerome's uncle and godfather (and the reason he wasn't out on the town with fellow thesps) helped in the revelry with more champagne. We were tipsy by the end of the evening, very possibly drunk, but I didn't accept Jerome's invitation to see his new apartment, rented impulsively on the prospect of his Big Breakthrough. I decided on playing to the stereotype of an aloof Englishwoman, which seemed only to excite his curiosity even more, and he requested – very gallantly – to 'see you again, Miss Ruby Devereaux'.

My attempt at aloofness turned to illness in the next week, and so postponed the first of our dates. Thanks to a spectacular summer cold, I spent a whole week holed up in Mushens's very nice apartment. My princess of a flatmate, who had been mollycoddled her entire life, had no concept of care and the human condition when it came to others, and was – to put it frankly – utterly clueless, except when she ordered medicinal chicken soup from Bloomingdales. I'm not sure if the accompanying cream-laden pastries made me feel much better, but they tasted sublime. Did I miss my mother at that point, to bring me tea and feed me sympathy? I'd like to say I did, but no. Perhaps it was because I had officially become a Grown-Up, but in hindsight, it was simply that I didn't miss anything about England at that point. The Big Apple was far too enticing.

The early dates with Jerome were like a forerunner of the yet-to-be-released *My Fair Lady* film, as if he'd got hold of a script and was practising his Rex Harrison to my Audrey H cum Eliza Doolittle, even before it reached the screens (though he'd never have managed it with his awful attempt at a British accent). The all-American boy set about giving me the complete New York experience. We went to baseball games, ate ice cream on Coney Island; we pretended to understand art at the Met and ice-skated in Central Park as the temperatures plummeted… or more like, he skated and I fell over, as befits a Brit who'd never ventured onto ridiculously thin pieces of metal underfoot. To some extent, I played up to my Eliza role, but largely because it amused me. And I liked Jerome – as with so many women of the age, and despite my innate need to kick back, I had also been conditioned to please. In turn, he was good company, subtly self-deprecating, and he made me laugh. And a string of dates on the arm of a small-screen celebrity was nice, I don't mind admitting.

Life slowly became a series of bubbles, some of which hovered nearer to the earth than others, but none that ever registered as reality on any scale I had ever known. There was a point once, in the bath as I readied myself for a party given by one of the many producers floating about, that I remember physically pinching my own arm and laughing when the whole scenario didn't vanish in a puff of wet soap. Discerning readers will know that, in novels, all bubbles are bound to burst. Fated. Meant. Needed. It's a plot thing. It has to happen for the wronged character to pick themselves up and triumph over the tragedy. But do they always, in real life?

The press, at this point, only served to put a sheen on said bubbles. *Medics of Mercy* had hit the tiny black-and-white screens of New York City and state, and was an immediate hit. Doctor Tom Bradshaw, with his glowing smile and faultless bedside manner, officially became a Television Heartthrob. It wasn't at the superstar point where we couldn't go anywhere, but there were often one or two photographers hovering outside restaurants, ready to blind us with their flashbulbs and make me feel slightly important. Jerome played his part to perfection, pushing his hand out – 'hey guys, lovely to see you, but we're having a private dinner, me and my girl' – and delighted to see how it whetted their appetite for more.

My girl? Perhaps if it hadn't been such a casual Americanism, or we'd been in private, I might have challenged Jerome. As it was, I just smiled, and hoped they snapped my best side.

Once, when I emerged from Macy's department store on 34th Street, a reporter trailed me, asking questions about being Jerome's 'lady friend' and what did I think about sharing him with a whole army of women, the implication being this TV armchair militia was metaphorically bent on removing his white coat, and plenty more. I think it was the first time in my life when I uttered the words: 'No comment'. Sadly, not the last.

And Jerome? He lapped it up. If any actor ever tells you they do it for their art and don't care about fame and fortune, you are entitled to call them a liar. Especially those who audition for a daytime soap in the leading man role. Off set, he was the consummate celebrity. His acting ability on screen… well, that was another matter. It's true to say that inwardly I cringed at the flash of his expensively sculpted white smile, when the camera hovered on his face to capture the twinkle he activated at will. The spoken parts seemed distinctly wooden, not helped by a script that was genuinely appalling. 'Nurse, please fetch his family – he may not have much time', featured frequently, with accompanying grave look, along with 'It's fifty-fifty if he'll walk again'. By the miracle of Doctor Tom's Jesus-like hands, the poor acting stooge in the bed always did get up and disappear off set, into the sunset. Along with his TV career.

'Where do the scriptwriters come from?' I asked him one night, lying in bed and sipping tea. The one very British thing that my Eliza persona did introduce was a decent cup of tea, brewed the British way from the parcels that my mother sent across the Atlantic as 'survival'. I was never sure if Jerome enjoyed the ritual (perhaps he did have some acting ability, after all), but he tolerated it. And since it was often drunk after making love, he managed to brave the ceremony.

He stopped mid-sip. 'Why are you always so interested in the script?' he pitched, with a splinter of annoyance.

'I am a writer, Jerome,' I said, though since I'd not written a word in months, I wondered if I had the right to say so. And he hadn't read my debut offering, despite my signed copy sitting on his bedside table for weeks. I regularly checked the spine for use and not a single crease. Never kid yourself – all writers are essentially vain; as actors crave to be watched, we hanker to be read. 'It just strikes me that the dialogue could be, well… a little more original,' I murmured.

'Christ, Ruby, what do you want?' He rose up, buck naked, and headed to the table and his pack of cigarettes, when he knew I hated him sparking up after sex. An angry plume of smoke swirled above his head. 'If you want to go out with Gregory Peck, be my guest.' He spun around. 'It's a living. Do you have any idea how many out-of-work actors exist in this country?'

I said nothing, though I might have looked a little contrite.

'Hundreds, thousands – in New York alone, I'd guess.' He puffed on. 'And I am not one of them – thankfully. And look what this so-called "crappy" script has brought me.' He swept an arm around his ostentatious apartment. 'This. And I like it. I *like* being recognised. I *like* having photographers snapping me outside restaurants, and money in my pocket. It makes my mother proud.'

He stubbed out his cigarette and swept into the bathroom, as if the very act meant he had triumphed in the argument. And was it a real fight, or just a storm in an English teacup? And had I been put in my place as a literary snob? I couldn't decide, though I felt slightly wounded. Crumpled.

At that point, I thought we had run our course. It had been fun, but it was never the affair of the century, not even close. Jerome made love like he was playing American college football; head down and rummaging in the scrum until the ball was won, taking large breaths of triumph. Or is that rugby? It wasn't delicate, either way. Neither was it terrible, and what with the tea and pillow talk after – always my favourite part – it was tolerable. Until the talk turned sour.

I pocketed my small pack of tea as I dressed and left that day, him still seething and effecting hurt in the shower. My tiny slice of semi-celebrity was over. I was slightly sad, though reconciled. I liked Jerome. We'd had a fine time, and now it was over. Back to the reality bubble, if you could call living with Mushens anything like reality.

But I was wrong, and really should have spotted the signs. The newly grown-up me should have had a deeper insight into the human condition, as writers are generally meant to. Perhaps, like Jerome, I was guilty of believing my own press (the small amount generated by my debut). But in the end, I got it wrong.

What I underestimated was Jerome's ego and how he would feel shunned, that in his new-found celebrity, it would never happen to the likes of handsome Doctor Tom. As I walked out, clutching my Simpson's finest blend leaves, I was no longer just a girl he'd once dated. Instantly, I became a challenge. Of course, he could have had many a woman at that point, in or out of the white coat. Except that he couldn't let it – or me – go; Jerome's shiny new celebrity crown was scratched and scarred.

I was flattered for a time by his renewed attentions, the

sending of too many flowers, the finest chocolates and tickets to the best shows at Carnegie Hall. Mushens raised her carefully sculpted eyebrows as another parcel arrived on our doorstep, and said, 'Darling? Really?' As a woman of few words, it was the wrinkling of her perfect nose that said it all. She disapproved, and I should have listened to the assessment of a pro. But I said yes initially because I didn't want to hurt Jerome's feelings all over again. And he was courteous and funny and attentive. What harm could it do?

And then the courteous and funny fell away and all I got was attention that I no longer craved, or even liked. 'I thought you might have worn the red dress,' he said waspishly, as he picked me up in his limousine from Mushens's place one evening. 'It makes you look alluring.'

The fact that I was actually wearing something of my own, and not plucked from my flatmate's wardrobe, was the first shard of hurt to land squarely on me. The second sting was that I had scraped a little of my meagre wage each week and pooled it for this one purple number that Mushens and her fashionista friend, Harry, announced was 'fabulously made to drape across you, Ruby D'.

'Oh, well, maybe next time.' I tried to laugh off his obvious slight, but his gaze was serious. No Doctor Tom twinkle.

'Why don't you go back up and change?' he suggested. Firmly.

I prickled inside the few spare millimetres of space the dress afforded me. 'We'll be late if I do,' I tinkled. He looked at his watch and saw I was right. The evening was nice enough – a drinks party hosted by another television network that had taken up *Medics of Mercy*. Throughout, his palm was placed firmly in the small of my back and he kept it there, piloting me around the room at will. His will. The only time I felt able to squirm away was in needing the bathroom, though I felt he might stand vigil outside if he could have done so without attracting undue attention.

Refreshed, I bumped into Harvey outside and felt myself drawn to him like a limpet, dodging Jerome, who bobbed his head like a baby bird in my direction above the clusters of guests.

'Are you quite okay, my love?' he said. Harvey was ever intuitive, and should have been an honorary female, as well as my father.

'If I'm brutally honest, I feel as if I'm under ownership,' I said wearily. Jerome was his nephew but Harvey had already proven his loyalty went far beyond blood.

'Jerome?'

'Any reason why you would guess that, Harvey?'

'Hmm, I realised some time ago my nephew has a few loyalty issues,' he said, looking over at the crowd. 'I hate to be one of those amateur psychologists, but I think it has a lot to do with his mother, my sister Dora. It pains me to say it, but she was a terrible mother to the poor boy, and it's left him with something of a complex over rejection.'

'But I don't think I rejected him,' I protested. 'We had a minor disagreement, and I felt we'd run out of steam, that's all. Time to move on. I thought he'd be relieved.'

'And that, to dear Jerome, is called rejection.'

'Oh. So, what do you suggest I do?'

'Me?' Harvey was all of a sudden affecting surprise. 'I may be a reluctant psychologist, my darling girl, but I am definitely no agony aunt.'

And with that, he caught the eye of someone he knew, or half-knew, and waltzed into the throng with his glass, at which point baby bird Jerome craned his neck high enough to spy me, making a beeline. The palm slotted back into place.

'Come and meet the producer for the Tri-State region,' Jerome said with his acting smile. 'He says they may be talking of a spin-off series for Doctor Tom.'

I was clearly much less of an actor because even feigning a headache didn't earn me an early reprieve. It was gone midnight before we climbed into his limousine, by which point I genuinely did have a throbbing head, plus feet that were on fire. Funds hadn't extended to buying shoes that were my own size.

Out of my hearing, Jerome had obviously instructed his driver to go directly to his place. As we drew up at the entrance, my heart sank. A bullish session in bed satisfying Jerome's self-esteem was the last thing I desired.

'I've got a busy day tomorrow, Jerome,' I lied. 'I'd really rather go home if you don't mind.'

His face went through a myriad of emotions in just three seconds, one of which was irritation, though he settled on a mawkish Peter Pan/lost boy look. 'Stay with me tonight? Please, Ruby D.' He placed a hand on my knee and began crawling upwards. 'We'll just sleep, I promise. I simply want your lovely self next to me.'

I was largely immune to his thespian overtures, having seen him switch them on and off like a lightbulb on the few occasions I had visited the *Medics of Mercy* set. In the bedroom, I was used to his changeable nature, though generally I held enough allure to sway the mood one way or the other. That night I was simply too weary to object or bicker.

Predictably, we didn't just sleep – the alcohol and an evening of flattery had nourished Jerome's ego, but not enough. He wanted more caressing, except the alcohol only fuelled his harrying, rough attempts at wooing. To the point where they became intimidation. The heroic Doctor and his kindly bedside manner was swiftly replaced by the Mr Hyde hiding beneath the humour I had seen for months. Jerome's true frustration and his need for love erupted that night into an ugly, frenetic lust for punishment and control. Hostile and cruel. And violent.

Did I object? Cry out? We were seven floors up in his well-insulated apartment where the well-to-do residents were cushioned and rarely disturbed. I certainly squirmed, did my best to wriggle out from under his overpowering form, made deadweight by his level of drunkenness, though the strength in his arms and fingers appeared to multiply as he thrashed out his desires.

I decided the only way to survive such an onslaught was to match him and play the actress. Painting on the mask of a coquette, I poured him a tumbler of whisky large enough to fell a thoroughbred and pretended to drink the same. Adding to the substantial amount he'd already consumed, his powerful engine finally began to falter; one by one his limbs succumbed to the deadening effects, and I was able to extricate myself from his grip. Finally, a total, alcoholic paralysis, and he fell deeply unconscious.

I slipped out shoeless and hailed a cab. Tiptoeing past Mushens's room and into the bathroom, the mirror and bulb above highlighted the purple imprint of his grip on my shoulder, a bloody swollen lip and the bruise painting rainbows over my right eye. Those on my lower legs I would be able to conceal, though the shame pulsed fast and bright throughout my entire body.

I know now what women of today's age would do. They would rightly march into the nearest police station and tell all. Jerome would be an abuser, arrested, possibly jailed, but certainly labelled, if not punished. But this was 1953. If it did exist, the language was in its infancy. Plus, it didn't – in all honesty – cross my mind to complain publicly. I had been seen at a party drinking alcohol, photographed on his arm for several months, and he was a darling of the small screen. Who would they believe? And hadn't I seen the signs coming? Surely, I had goaded him, denied him something he had come to expect in the bedroom. Wasn't it a perfectly normal, full-blooded male reaction? That's what the papers would say. Other men. Maybe women too. It was that time.

Me? I felt affronted, abused, sore and stupid. As well as hating every bone in Jerome's pathetic being, mostly I blamed myself. As women are wont to do. I had seen the signs of his subtle and petty attempts at control. Imprudently, I had thought it was well within my talents to handle them. Silly, silly girl.

Feeling foolish, I crawled into my bed and sobbed myself to sleep, knowing full well I had probably signed my own exit visa out of New York. I knew Jerome's dogged nature, and how – with supreme irony – he would be the one feeling injured by my inevitable rejection of him. Whatever his reaction or pathetic excuses, I was resolved. He'd had his pound of flesh and he could have no more. Even if it meant my leaving.

I took the weekend to heal, forced to admit my folly to an unsurprised Mushens, though her evident anger and concern were a comfort. She could be sometimes shallow, but always fiercely loyal – it came out of being persecuted royal blood, she said. Cancelling all engagements, she ordered in food from Bloomingdales and we spent the weekend watching television, resolutely switching channels when Doctor Tom came on screen. Thankfully, there was no immediate word from Jerome, but I knew he would be waiting in the wings, licking his shame like his own emotional wound, before the floral showering began, along with lavish gifts and the pitiful apologies.

By Monday morning, the swelling on my eye had abated, morphed to a fetching shade of mustard and my lip could just be covered with lipstick, though I looked like an old dame who'd applied the bright red colouring with fuzzy vision and a large glass of gin.

None of this fooled Harvey. 'Christ alive, Ruby!' he bellowed as I slunk behind my desk. 'What in the hell happened to you?'

He took me into his office, where his kindness was my entire undoing and I blubbed all over his coffee table and an expensive first edition. Harvey hugged me gently, ordered me a strong cup of English tea, and disappeared next door, where I heard his low, furious rumblings into the phone. I pictured Jerome's shamed face on the other end of the mouthpiece. Was he penitent or merely perplexed? His square jaw clenched with frustration?

'He will not bother you again. Ever,' Harvey announced resolutely when he returned. 'And if he does, I want to know about it. Because if he tries, goddammit, I will throw him in jail myself.' I'd never seen anyone whose anger was the colour of a pomegranate before.

'You mean I don't have to leave?'

'No, my darling Ruby D, you do not. Though I think you might benefit from a vacation.'

Being Harvey, he knew of someone whose house on Martha's Vineyard happened to be free, and who would be delighted to have a guest to employ the otherwise idle housekeeper. He packed me off with a driver and a fatherly kiss, and I arrived in Cape Cod puckered and deflated but wholly appreciative. What Harvey gave me was priceless – space, time and a safe haven, with the added bonus of a stretch of water separating me from New York. In my mind, I firmly cast him as an honorary woman then, as well as being a surrogate father.

Three weeks later, I left the fabulous Cape with my bruise-free skin lightly tanned by the Atlantic winds. Without being overly dramatic, I felt like a chrysalis emerging into a new world, dressed in my refashioned, hardened shell. I had healed and deliberated. More importantly, I had purged. On paper. The germ of what was to become my first bestselling novel – *The Women We Are* – sat in my suitcase, and was developed over the next months as I shunned New York society and feverishly typed into the early hours, leaving Mushens ever more baffled. 'This writing you do, is it really better than cocktails or sex?' she drawled.

My nails were bitten to the quick as I waited for Harvey to read my first tentative draft. I hadn't planned on showing him, thinking that perhaps I'd offer it up to another US publisher when I'd ironed out the wrinkles – a bookman whose nephew *didn't* feature as the villain of the piece, albeit anonymously. Admittedly, I was still writing about things that mirrored my life, but since this was real living, I felt it passed as new.

In a supreme irony, and perhaps a slice of déjà vu, Harvey found it on my desk while scouring for a phone number. When he called me into his office two days later, I imagined it was to let me down gently, that yes, I might have been published twice before, but really, this latest effort had 'no legs'; I had lost my verve with the pen, such was the nadir of my self-confidence. My future might lay in editing, he would say, publishing admin or publicity perhaps. I knew he would put it kindly, but the message would be same. I had already peaked as a writer, and my efforts tantamount to a molehill at best.

But, dear reader, I signed with him. His eyes were watery and his ruddy big cheeks wet with tears as he told me it was among the most profound of stories he'd read in years. I made him promise it wasn't just one of the favours he often afforded poor waifs and strays to set them on their way. He laughed heartily and told me no, and would a two-book deal convince me? Then I did go back out into New York society, with my beloved Mushens, and we became very, very drunk. Just me and her and lots of Martinis. No men. At that point, not required.

The Women We Are was published six months later in the US and back home, to critics' acclaim and very good sales, allowing me the freedom to leave Harvey's cocoon and spread my wings across the States for the next six months. I dedicated the book to abused women everywhere, and to Mushens – not that she was assaulted, though I always felt her shell was in some ways as delicate as mine had been. And she sometimes seemed at the mercy of men and their adoration, despite being funny and beautiful and a hundred times smarter than men gave her credit for.

Harvey never once mentioned his nephew again, at least never in my company. I saw Jerome's picture in the papers – not beaming his white, wide smile amid the gossip columns, where he liked to read about himself over coffee in the mornings. Instead, this was buried in the news section, a tiny snapshot of him looking dishevelled and small as he emerged from a police station. The actor previously known for the role of Doctor Tom had been arrested and charged with assault on a man outside a New York nightclub who had apparently propositioned his girlfriend, the same woman who later accused Mr Hemmings of assault and battery on 'more than one occasion'. He was sentenced to six months jail-time for the nightclub assault, but found innocent of what later came to be known as 'domestic abuse' against the woman. Go figure, as New Yorkers are apt to say. It was 1953.

For myself, I left New York a full year and half after I arrived, with a tearful farewell to the lovely Harvey, and plenty more shed in saying goodbye to Mushens, though we did later spend a riotous week in the Florida Keys, drinking the place dry. She remained my good penfriend until her death in 1964 in a light bi-plane accident at an air show, minutes after she was seen waving down regally at the crowd from the tiny cockpit – fittingly dramatic for the princess she was, and how she would have wanted to go. I knew from our late-night confessionals that she dreaded the onset of wrinkles more than anything.

I suppose I was one of Harvey's protégés in a way. I took off into the wild west yonder, though I was no charity case; both he and I made a pretty penny out of my book, and Charles back in London too. I re-emerged as a writer, with something extra. I had my armour in place and I'd grown a better casing. No man in my life would do to me what Jerome had done, what I had in some way enabled him to do. There, see – still taking the blame. The difference being, I would never do so again. Not this version of me. No sir.

I walked out of Harvey's office, with one more backward glance.

'Cheerio, Mabel,' I trilled to Mariel, top dogsbody in situ, her face a picture of discontent.

And do you know what? She snapped up her head in swift response, and I smiled broadly at the triumph.

Four

'Lunch?' Jude suggests, when he detects that Ruby is flagging a little. After not much more than a week together, he reads her stubborn nature well, and knows she will rarely call 'time' on the writing, despite her frustration at trying to prise out the words when she's tired. A culinary titbit, however, might persuade her. 'I can run up a soup or some fried rice.'

Her crinkly eyes sparkle. 'Rice, with a little bit of spice,' she says.

'Coming right up.'

The phone trills in the hallway as Jude is passing the age-old machine and he picks up the receiver.

'If that's Marina checking up on me, tell her to bugger off,' Ruby calls out. 'It will be done when it's done.'

He doesn't need to, because Marina hears the sentiment perfectly well down the line. 'Oh, like that, is it?' she ventures.

'It's fine, really,' Jude replies.

'It is? Are you sure?' She can't help pushing surprise and shock into the receiver. A frantic week of launches and events has kept Marina from dropping by the Highgate house, plus a slight sense of dread, if she's entirely honest, in predicting an apologetic call from Jude announcing he 'just can't do it anymore'. Or worse still, the same from Ruby, and the subsequent fallout from Marcus. But so far, nothing. 'So, is she writing?'

'Yes,' he says. If he's honest, Jude wonders why Ruby's agent sounds so astonished. Together, he and Ruby manage more than a thousand words a day, in between frequent breaks for brief naps and food, and Ruby's longer snooze in the afternoon. But then, she *is* ninety. His own gran had seemed foggy and moribund at eighty-five. 'The word count says well over ten thousand so far.'

'And?' This fight for words in Marina is becoming a habit when the subject is Ruby.

'Erm, it's… surprising,' Jude offers. 'I mean, I don't know much about memoirs.'

'Can you send what she has so far?' Marina entreats. Unprofessional, perhaps, but the prospect of another disdainful inquisition from Marcus is not welcome. She wants some ammunition, to be able to tell him it's up to standard.

'What are you talking about?' Ruby's hectoring tone echoes down the hallway. 'If she's asking to see it, tell her no. Not yet. Not a word until I say.'

Marina puffs out a sigh. 'Well, there's my answer,' she mutters into the receiver, swallowing some of her stand-by flat white. 'She's a bit scary, isn't she?'

'A bit,' Jude concedes. 'Listen, I'd better go. Lunch to make.'

'All right. But ring me if you need support, moral or otherwise,' Marina says, and rings off.

Jude pokes his head into the office before making his way to the kitchen. Ruby is propped in the lumpy easy chair, eyes closed. She looks serene, though nothing like his soft and squishy grandmother. He tiptoes out.

'A bit of spice, but not too many onions,' she calls down the hallway.

MAN THREE: Enzo

Venice, Summer 1961

I might have easily passed her by without a second glance, except for those stunning legs. She was on the prow of a vessel, one of those small taxi motorboats with a polished wooden front, her glorious long limbs scissoring upwards for a photographer, he massaging her ego and her actions with his silken Italian. 'Bella, bella,' he exuded. Snap, snap, snap. But for the fact that my entire life scenario at that point felt like a film set, I might not have guessed it was the fabulous Sophia Loren, right there in front of me. But it was. In plain sight, her curvaceous figure enhancing the Venetian splendour around us all, the collected gondoliers almost choking on their early morning espresso as they looked on goggle-eyed at a perfect example of Italy's home-grown beauty.

And I walked on, as if it was the most natural thing in the world to come across a renowned film star on your stroll to work. By a process of fault and fortune, I had very much landed on my feet.

It was Harvey who had come to my rescue yet again, in my

endless wanderlust and pursuit of inspiration. By then I had trawled the length of America's west coast, spending a good deal of time in San Francisco and Los Angeles, generally partying and fooling myself that I was harvesting material for another book, when in fact I was simply living the life of Riley, Ruby-style. Quite, quite selfishly. The men were flighty and often insincere, especially the shoals of would-be actors, of which I'd had my fill by then. Their affection was ephemeral to say the least. I indulged occasionally but only at a level I tagged as 'skin-deep' relationships. I had fun roaring up and down the Pacific Highway in shiny sports cars, hair bound to my head by a stylish scarf, but my boundaries were tight and uncompromising. Inevitably, the men lost interest when my shell proved tougher than the lobsters we would crack at expensive ocean-side restaurants.

At intervals, I would retreat to a house either on the coast or in the Hollywood Hills, alternately renting cheaply or house-sitting for those I'd met at various parties, and who had more money than sense in giving over their homes to a virtual stranger. With me, they didn't need to have concerns over their houses being used as social venues, because it was solitude I craved. Then, the butterfly came in to land, and I wrote. I couldn't claim to have writer's block as such, quite the opposite. The prose came fast and furious, but they were bad words and I knew it – the order in which they presented felt clumsy and immature, letters falling over themselves to impress but spilling drunkenly into a heap on the page. The floor was strewn with screwed-up balls of frustration, a completely stereotypical scene of the tortured writer at work, which of course could never happen nowadays with technology and the like. I was both a failing artist and an environmental disaster.

The charred remnants of a near completed book called *Party*

Girl might, even today, be fluttering in the firepit of one of those houses, though it's no loss to the world, I promise you. Everything I thought or wrote was somehow *surplus*. I remain even now a great believer in fiction as fantasy, the nosing into other worlds out of reach to the reader, and I've never intended my novels to be 'worthy', filled with angst-ridden characters. But neither do I admire fluff, sentences that melt like candyfloss and fail to linger in the reader's brain for at least a second. I couldn't grab onto anything that interested me for even a paragraph. And heaven knows, if you're bored as the writer, the reader has no hope.

And then I met Hanna. She arrived one morning to clean the large hilltop chalet I was squatting within, sweaty and out of breath from the hefty climb, despite her lean frame. Starved of company and conversation, I began to look forward to Hanna's twice weekly visits, and I would whizz down the hill in my rented, ridiculously large sedan to pick her up. I made coffee as she dusted and polished, giving us time to sit on the balcony and talk, about her life mainly – her Slovakian parents, the pitiful wage her job brought in, the husband who drank and occasionally thumped her across the face 'though he doesn't know what he's doing', she excused him. You couldn't make it up.

Effectively, I stole Hanna and made her my fictionalised book, a narrative that didn't feel surplus to requirements on the shelves. I had gone from 'write what you know' to 'who you know'.

I can predict what you're thinking – though I was never so mercenary, even then. I did it with Hanna's full permission, so that with her portion of the advance *Valley Girl* brought in, she left the drunken bum of a spouse and travelled off into the yonder, much like I had done. It's termed 'pay it forward'. I created a moderately good seller, and she got a new life. Quid pro quo. I received a postcard not long after, from Seattle, saying she'd landed an office job and a new man, 'one that doesn't beat the crap out of me', and she even liked the constant rain and the winter snow. Fair's fair, I say.

Hanna and *Valley Girl* seemed to put a line under California and the US, and I no longer felt curious enough to stay. But where to go? The Sixties were not yet swinging and London was a few years from being the Beatle-fuelled epicentre of the globe. Enter Harvey and his little book of contacts. 'And, my darling Ruby D, if Venice doesn't pull a book out of you, then you are no writer,' he effused. I stopped off briefly in New York to give him a large (and unbeknown at the time, a last) hug, and down some very good cocktails. And then I was yonder-bound again.

Venice astounded me, far more than I had anticipated. You would have to be blind, deaf and dumb for it not to have that gawp factor on arrival – some type of modern-day *real* Atlantis hovering in the Adriatic, its beauty and solidity rising up in the world's most permanent and fantastical film set.

Harvey, the wonderful man, had secured me a job as a press liaison officer for a small film studio which rented out equipment and set dressings for visiting crews. They needed an English speaker, and well, I might have exaggerated my command of Italian just a little. With royalties from a total of four books, I could have just scraped by in a top-floor garret and ballooned on pasta alone, feeding my inspiration as I gazed over the lagoon. But Venice is for living, and I wanted to linger in bars and eavesdrop on the Italian I was desperately trying to master, to visit the Accademia, to sample squid-ink pasta cooked the right way. Oh, and the gelato! All of which cost money, and so earning a regular wage was necessary.

The work was hardly taxing and I could do it with my eyes closed, turning around press releases and furiously consulting my Italian dictionary cum bible. I liked being on set most of all and, I learned quickly, you can go a long way in Italy with good gesticulation. I was told many a time that my eyebrows were particularly expressive.

It sounds a tad more glamorous on paper; Miss Loren did not come our way, having a crew rich enough to ship in their own equipment, but we had a steady stream of low-budget Italian films in production, travelogues and some English crews with B-list actors counting their lucky stars at working on location in the glittering jewel of Venice. It beat a draughty studio on a West London set any day.

Enzo was not an actor. As stated, I was over those. The Italian variety were possibly more egocentric than the New York clique, swooping onto our little sets with enough hair oil to cause a slick in the sparkling *laguna*. I kept a low profile and my mouth shut much of the time in their presence. The on-screen women were a breed apart, however – hard-working, jobbing actors largely scathing of their male counterparts, quite as beautiful as Miss Loren but paid considerably less.

'Breath like a bison' and 'greasy goat-herder', they would grumble about their male leads when we retired to a bar in the back streets of the Cannaregio district. To the innocent eye, they were goddesses – hair piled high and eyes made Bambi-like with layers of kohl and mascara, men of all creeds hopelessly enticed by their image as they strutted elegantly in a pack across Venice.

But they smoked like chimneys, had mouths like sewer holes and possessed something my grandmother coined 'gumption'. I loved them.

Enzo was the cousin of Livia, a pocket-sized actress who lived principally in Milan and was endlessly cast as the archetypal friend or the sister of the lead, despite the fact that her acting was often far more accomplished. She must have appeared in hundreds of Italian films, though her philosophy triumphed over any bitterness. 'Ruby, it's a far better living than rolling onto your back in the bedroom, or rolling pasta in the kitchen,' she quipped innocently between drags of her cigarette. Like I said, gumption.

So, Enzo. He came to the set whenever Livia was there, first to visit her, and then later to work on an ad hoc basis as a carpenter when we needed extra help with set construction. He was a boatbuilder by trade, in the family business, and he looked every inch the part. Picture an extra from *Ben-Hur*. In the heat of an Italian summer, shirts were often discarded by the set-builders as they chipped and sawed. I could well have gasped when Enzo pulled off his shirt that first time – I recall even now a small noise escaping my lips. His back was a textbook of human anatomy, chest taut and angular, and his face a rare concoction of beautiful and friendly. Michelangelo would have wet his leather breeches on coming across this subject for his pencil.

But underneath his striking beauty, I discovered Enzo was shy. True, our first conversation amounted to me trying to elicit a certain style of woodworking from his skills, using my less than perfect Italian and resorting to pad and pencil, where he and I discovered swiftly that I was no Michelangelo. His flawless brow crinkled in confusion, and I could have laid him in a gondola there and then and had my wicked way with him. But he was far too nice, too gentle, though I was struggling to gauge the line between innocence and aloof at that point.

It was Livia who saved the day, smoothing over my linguistic cracks and suggesting that we should all retire to the nearest trattoria and eat pasta. Who was I to reject such an offer to sample the best of Italian life?

I noted that Livia placed me side by side with Enzo, and my heart swelled at her opinion of me, my being trustworthy enough not to scare off her beloved cousin.

There's a surprising amount you can learn about someone by their command of eating spaghetti. I was somewhat excused my fumbling for being British, but Enzo's treatment of his squid ink was masterful, rolling it around his fork nonchalantly, with a not a drop to soil the shirt he had mercifully reapplied.

'And so, you are a writer of books?' he quizzed, mopping his plate with bread and skill, before admitting he didn't read much, and when he did it was rarely anything other than home-grown literature. 'How can you make up the stories in your head?' He gestured theatrically to his own brain. 'I am in awe, Signorina Ruby.'

'In the same way you can sculpt a tree into a functioning boat, or anything that we ask you to, Enzo. It's just manipulating words instead of wood.' Though Lord knows what I actually said in attempting the complex translation of 'manipulate'. It might have been why he looked perplexed. Mercifully, he also smiled, a full white-toothed expression. I was intoxicated. Thirty-one and falling headlong like a lovesick teenager.

The awe, then, became my preserve. Unlike a lot of Italian men I'd met to that point, who rated their own appearance over substance, Enzo was solid, in mind as well as that magnificent body. He wasn't overly educated, but he listened quietly in the background. I watched him on set, focused on his tools and glancing occasionally at the actions of his fellow Italian men prancing like peacocks, the subtle disdain in his expression at the way they talked down to women. The men sensed it in him, picking him out, either jealous or lustful of his superior looks – depending on which way they leaned sexually – and the result was a subtle but constant jibing whenever Enzo was on set, mutterings about his manhood or his lack of intellect. But like the sweat which poured as he hammered away, Enzo let it fall like water off a duck's back.

Only once did he react, and with vigour. Paulo Fabrizi was a particularly queen-ish lead actor with delusions of grandeur and the certainty – in his own mind – of a calling towards Hollywood. He'd also been sniffing around me since day one of the shoot, and I'd politely declined to view the comforts of his hotel room at least twice. I'd walked across the set to ask Enzo if he could move some pieces of equipment before the next scene, and we were exchanging a few words, when Paulo's voice rose a tone too far above a whisper. His comments were lost in translation for me, but Enzo's reaction was instant and fiery. He leaped forward and had a very shocked Paulo up against the wall in seconds. Judging by the apologetic, strangulated sounds coming forth, there was no doubting Enzo's strength or manhood then. A great deal of hooting and cawing echoed from the other male leads, though not one of them attempted to challenge Enzo. In the opposite corner, the women cheered and egged him on to finish the job like trainers at the edge of a boxer's ring. In the absence of the director, I moved in and gently persuaded Enzo to return Paulo's feet to the ground, and that it was fine. I was fine. No harm done.

'He shouldn't say those things – about any woman. And

especially not about you, Ruby,' he said in his own defence. His face looked pained and hurt. I smelled the pungent musk of masculinity radiating off his body, and watched his face acknowledge my appreciation.

A heady cocktail. And you already know how much I love a good cocktail.

Well, what's a girl to do? I was hopelessly in love, in the middle of my own story, on a film set in the fairy-tale mecca of romance. And my knight had just donned his shining armour, on my behalf. My well-aired but slightly battered heart never stood a chance.

Once we'd wrapped for the day, I plucked up the courage to stroll over to Enzo, and with cheeks ablaze, asked if I could buy him a drink to say thanks for his gallantry. Casually, he seemed to brush it off as 'no problem', and for a second I thought my courage was to no avail. Deflated, I felt I'd never muster a sufficient quantity of it again, but in the next breath he said yes, that would be nice, he'd like that. And for once, he didn't look towards Livia to join us.

We were filming on Giudecca Island, and he led me by the hand from the waterfront facing Venice proper, to the opposite side of the land mass, where it faced directly into the Adriatic and the shimmering *laguna*. I mean, how hopelessly romantic can you get? We sat sipping wine as the water lapped and the sun burned its golden rays on the sparkling water, and I thought I had died and gone to Ruby heaven.

I learned a lot about Italian life on that seemingly endless evening, despite his very limited English and my fledgling (though rapidly improving) Italian. My eyebrows came into their own. He was twenty-seven and still lived at home, as was the case then with many young and unmarried men, given that

Venetian Mamas did not permit the cutting of their apron strings until there was a sufficient substitute to feed their sons properly, i.e. a wife who passed muster in the kitchen.

Enzo was unlike any man I had ever met: satisfied. He had no desire to roam, other than to show me the delights of the slightly more far-flung islands of Torcello and Pellestrina, but his entire world centred in the lagoon. He was a true Venetian, prepared to live his entire life within its watery boundaries, happily.

'Why would I go anywhere else, Ruby?' he said with genuine curiosity. 'I have my family, the most beautiful place on Earth on my doorstep, the best food and true friends.' He stopped and laughed. 'I leave it to the likes of you, you writers, to help me dip into the rest.' Only then did he admit to reading my first and third novels; I'd conveniently forgotten to mention the second, given how poor it was. I was honoured and then quickly nervous.

'What did you think?' I asked tentatively.

A pause, narrowing of those gorgeous eyes. 'You're like Venice, Ruby,' he said at last.

What could that mean? Solid, intricate… dare I think beautiful?

'Shifting,' he qualified. Though he did follow it with a smile.

At least he didn't say sinking.

I'll admit, it took me some time to appreciate Enzo's manifesto on life, me who hadn't set foot in England for years, much less visited the mausoleum of the family home. The words 'family' and 'home' still didn't gel as a concept in my world. But the warmth I witnessed between him and Livia began, slowly, to alter my thinking. We saw each other regularly after work, a sort of drifting into dating, rather than anything formal. And the kiss, the cement of something more, did not come for a while.

I won't dwell on it, suffice to say it was spectacular, and Enzo's manhood did not disappoint. That was merely the *antipasti*, I might say if I were being clichéd or crude (and you know how I can be at times), and several dates later we retired to my miniscule garret and made glorious and satisfying love with the setting sun streaming through the tiny window, and the sound of the downstairs harridan giving her husband what for. Kitchen-sink drama in all its perfection.

In the following weeks, we squeezed every nook and cranny of Venice into our own montage of romance. In Enzo's small motorboat, we sped across the lagoon, me in huge sunglasses and a scarf, pretending to be an amalgam of Misses Loren and Lollobrigida, and him at the helm, as if he'd actually been born on the water. He led me by the hand towards hidden gardens and tiny private islands; we climbed endless towers, kissing with the wind in our hair and the deafening sound of bells alongside. I knew I was smitten when one evening I turned down an invitation – gilded and priceless in Venetian circles – for a reception at the waterfront palazzo of Peggy Guggenheim, the city's adopted New York socialite. Parties at Peggy's were legendary even then, awash with actors, artists and literati, the invitations coveted like the gold dust they were. Enzo would have hated it, and so he and I spent the evening tucked in a beachy cove on the Lido, sharing his mother's freshly made arancini and a cheap but still superior bottle of wine. I will employ literary privilege here and say the stars sparkled for me in a very different way. And no, I did not regret never being asked again to a Guggenheim soiree.

It all sounds too good to be true, and I would forgive anyone for suspecting it as a rich but fictional figment of my imagination. It read like the book I couldn't write. But I have proof – we made our own picture postcard, Enzo and I, which I sent to Harvey as testament, and to say thanks for the life he had steered me towards again. Given Enzo was a boatbuilder by trade, of course he could glide a gondola as well as steer a motorboat. He teased me with the image until I gave in to its charms, guiding me effortlessly under the Rialto in a polished black craft, while I grinned idiotically at the cliché and loved it at the same time. He didn't sing, mercifully, but offered a lilting running commentary of every building and its history, evidence of the intense love for his city. The captured photograph of us, taken by a friend stationed on the bridge, I still have among my prized possessions. I look so happy, so content. And grounded, despite floating on a canal, squat in the middle of the Adriatic. It was around that time I penned a postcard to Mushens, still a firefly on the New York socialite scene. *Dearest M – Wallowing in La Dolce Vita. Come and see for yourself*, even though I knew she was unlikely to forsake her beloved Saks on Fifth Avenue.

I know what you're thinking. Given my life thus far, I should have been wary of perfection in all its forms. It did not bode well. I could have easily fallen from my state of nirvana into the depths of the lagoon, with a resounding splash. Expectation and happiness do that to you.

I defied it though. Or life did, for those timeless few months. The only sticking point in our otherwise dreamlike existence was time. The summer was receding and with it my contract at the film company. I'd earned enough to stay on for a month or two, but beyond that, my royalties wouldn't keep me in Venice for long. Waving goodbye to Enzo and this life was unthinkable, and so another job seemed a better prospect – I could do some translating perhaps, or hotel work. In one moment of clarity, as he lay sleeping beside me amid Venice's unique morning wake-up call, his bronze chest rising and falling like the idling engine of a great steamer, I realised I would scrub floors to stay. Lord knows, I might even do some writing.

Enzo seemed to be of the same mind. He never indulged in wasteful chit-chat, so when Enzo spoke it wasn't to impart some great philosophical deliberation, but something worth hearing; his brain matched the brawn of his woodworking skills, where every word had a function.

'I'd like you to meet my family,' he said one day, and he might as well have recited Shakespeare's most romantic sonnet for how that sentence made my heart flip.

We did it gently. His sister, Stella, first. She was taller than Livia, and I guessed height ran in his side of the family. She was dark and slim and elegant, possessed of that innate style that Italian women have injected in the womb, and Venetians especially. She was also different from Enzo, in that she was cultivating her own slice of wanderlust, and so we got on like a house on fire as she quizzed me about London, New York and the States. Stella worked in hospitality and her English was good, and although she hadn't gone further than Milan at that point, her looks, charm and her need would take her far, of that I was sure. I had stage one approval. Enzo's father was a huge force in his life, having been the teacher of his trade, pottering around the boatsheds and refusing to embrace retirement. He was a chiselled man under a shrinking, leathery coating of skin, with sparkling eyes and a roguish smile. In the boatyard, he held court, but at home Mama was queen. And everyone knew it. Crucially, I had to gain Mama's favour.

***

Rosario Pucelli stood like a sentinel at the door of their house in the Cannaregio, pretty much filling the space, if not north to south, then east to west. I barely stopped myself doing an overt double take in sizing up Enzo's hefty frame and wondering how on earth he emerged from her – a square peg in a round hole, only in reverse.

Since arriving in Italy, I had been perplexed at the transformation of the female form there. The majority of young women possessed bodies to die for – curvaceous and lean, the hourglass figure personified in shop assistants and waitresses, models and actresses like Livia. Then the Mamas – short and square, their squat forms seemingly knitted from the vats of spaghetti they presided over, wiry grey hair held under black hats and scuttling like beetles around the market stalls in early morning, haggling and gaggling over fish and pomodori. I felt sure I was feeding my own stereotype, but nowhere could I find the in-between women – the rounding out of the hourglass, padding of hips and the losing of height, a gradual greying of hair. It was as if Venetian women had their very own missing link. The Livias and the Stellas simply became the Mamas overnight. Where did they pupate in between? And that well-worn, etched-in scowl… there's a tale for another day.

Mama Pucelli, however, greeted me in the way I expected – with manners, hospitality, a healthy dose of scepticism and protection for her darling boy. And a lot of food. Italian women throw down the gauntlet with their table, daring you to match, and in the first place, to eat.

'Have no breakfast,' Enzo had warned me, and it proved to be good advice when I glimpsed a table heaving with lasagne and chicken, octopus and possibly the deepest dish of tiramisu I had ever laid eyes on. Mama's battle lines were drawn.

Papa Pucelli was a darling throughout the grilling. Stella, too. Both shielded and guided me from the force field that was Enzo's beloved mother. And Enzo just sat there, next to me, though his attentions were firmly centred on Rosario as the host. He was charming and deferent, courteous and complimentary. I began to think he'd done this many a time – taken women home for Mama's eye – until Stella pushed her mouth towards my ear as we dried the mountain of pots and pans.

'She must like you,' she whispered. 'There's not many who are allowed within sight of her dishcloth.'

'So, has Enzo brought many girls home?'

She looked at me in surprise. 'Oh no, Ruby – you're the first.'

I emerged, pot-bellied and swilling in cream from too much tiramisu, Mama Pucelli waving us off from the doorway, Papa left snoozing in the armchair. Enzo walked me home, silent against the lapping of the water on the canal-side. Inside, I burned for some sign, his badge of approval. Had I passed Mama's test in his eyes?

'Your family is lovely,' I said at last, when I couldn't bear even the formerly glorious soundtrack of the lagoon tapping its tune on the brickwork. 'They're very welcoming.'

'She likes you,' Enzo said, squeezing my hand.

'Really? Did she say?' I was hungry – perhaps too eager – for praise.

He turned and afforded me his best smile. 'She didn't need to. You were offered a second portion of dessert. Believe me, Ruby. She likes you.'

* * *

I lay awake in bed that night, Enzo having left me at the doorstep; it was expected for him to go home and join in the family appraisal. He didn't say it, but it meant picking over the day's events. And me. Did I want to be scrutinised? Preferably not, but it was the family way.

Lying in bed, I rolled my own feelings back and forth inside my head. I liked them, Enzo's parents, despite Mama's guarded manner, born out of culture, and her maternal self-preservation. They worked as a unit, with their love, squabbles and irritations apparent. But it was real and unapologetic. No one on this Earth was good enough for Mama's baby boy, that was abundantly clear. But *someone* might come close. Could that someone be me?

I did detect a warmth under her slightly gruff, matriarchal air, as if she was wearing her armour and that it would be softened or shed for the right person. Papa was simply twinkly and easy to be with, and I felt he would scoop another daughter under his wing with ease.

My fantasies went into overdrive. I could picture myself in the kitchen, side by side with Mama, making pasta and gossiping in Italian at breakneck speed, being let into the closely guarded secrets of her kitchen, Enzo eating *my* lasagne with the near look of ecstasy he afforded his mother's.

I went further, further than I'd ever been before. Behind my eyelids was a clear image of Enzo and I on the steps of their local church, me in a puffball of white, him in a suit, his muscles tight against good, tailored fabric, Mama Pucelli weeping into her handkerchief, proud at being the mother of the groom. Me as the bride.

I could do it, I felt. It had only been months, but Enzo had taught me, with few words and a good deal of silence, with his quiet fortitude, that simply *being* was fine. It was happiness. I didn't need to gallivant around the globe to find my place. It was here, on my doorstep, on the edge of the lagoon. I could be still. I could stop roaming. With him, I could be content.

I would do it, I convinced myself. I would say yes, if he pulled out the crucial question and a ring, as we sauntered under another stunning Venetian sunset. I would get a job, learn to keep house… hmm, perhaps some of the time. I would be a Venice-based writer (there were worse things to be), and I would have his babies, likely fairly swiftly, given my age. I would have a normal life.

I went to sleep, for the first time in my existence, with the certainty of a future. And quite chuffed with myself that it was mine, largely of my own making.

Work kept us busy and apart for several days, so when I woke to a rapping on the door one morning, I imagined it to be Enzo with offers of breakfast. And yet the knock was chaotic, the voice behind it urgent.

'It's Enzo,' is all Stella said. But it was all that she needed to say, alongside her ashen features and tear-stained cheeks.

He lay resplendent in white sheets against his olive skin, chest bare and muscles prominent, his hair still damp. God-like. But nothing other than dead.

Mercifully, his eyes were closed, or I couldn't have looked, not when I might have seen so little in them. No life, no humour. No Enzo.

He'd been called out by a neighbour, someone's child missing the night before. Infants born to Venice are raised to be wary of the water's edge, but as in the rest of the world, they disappear on occasions, sometimes innocently. Still, the rallying cry goes out and the search parties are sent forth into the lagoon, their lights strafing the water's underbelly. It's just something they all do, and I knew Enzo would have gone willingly.

The child had been found, fit and well, duly hugged and chastised and taken home. Only Enzo didn't return. The large purple welt on his perfect brow pointed towards a freak swell caused by a vaporetto or a larger craft, perhaps tossing him into the water. As a native Venetian, he was a strong swimmer, but another boat in the dark, the heft and speed of a propeller… it would have been enough. We might never know, but as I held on to Stella and Livia – a trio of women in grief – we convinced each other that he might not have suffered. It hardly seemed a consolation to me, but it stood as an odd comfort to the family that the lagoon took him.

'It's where he would have wanted to be,' Mama sobbed. Papa's twinkle had sunk to where his son was discovered, and he looked a broken man.

I stayed long enough for the funeral. I shouldn't have expected anything less than the ostentatious affair it was – a flotilla of crafts in all shapes and sizes bobbing stern to prow on the Grand Canal, a good few that Enzo might have had a hand in making, all paying their respects. His body lay swathed in the grandest of gondolas, festooned in flowers, Mama and Papa solid in black behind, Stella too. And me. I felt that, alongside the second offering of tiramisu, I had already been accepted as Enzo's life choice. Papa later told me, out of Mama's earshot, that Enzo had been readying the question, had already chosen a ring.

'I'm so glad it could have been you,' Papa said, with the tiniest of twinkles rising, and then falling back and dying with the light.

As befits a nearly Italian wife, I cried. The emotion was real but also acceptable, because Venetians know how to live, and also to grieve. And then I could no longer hold myself or my sorrow. Venice and its shine turned a matt grey, every water's edge a potential grave, every splash a reminder. While Mama found comfort in the lagoon as Enzo's life and birth, I saw only his death. I tried so hard, remembering the conversations we'd had.

'If I died tomorrow, I would think of my life as happy,' he said once, looking intently onto the water. Then, I'd passed it off with some flippant comment about not dying young, not yet, since we had too much lovemaking to do. But I knew he was happy, had been, and it should have been some comfort to me. Except it wasn't. *We* should have had a life, he and I. Babies and old age and me morphing into a Mama.

It meant I could no longer tolerate the labile, undulating nature of Venice and its foundations. The very thing I had loved most about it initially – my life floating on a pure whim – became a shaky, unsteady quagmire which threatened to pull me down and drown me forever.

And so I did what I always resorted to in times of strife. I fled, away from a former utopia. I left Venice as the once sparkling jewel, with many a backward glance this time, and a mountain of regret.

I also did something different, heading not into Harvey's comforting arms, or swallowed by the protection of an anonymous, noisy metropolis.

Incredibly, I went home.

MAN FOUR: George

London, 1961

Given my track record on travel, and with a tendency to meander towards my eventual destination, I didn't go directly to my family's suburban seat. With an age-old antipathy towards my parents' house, I wasn't in a rush to burst through the door and reveal what an unmitigated disaster my life had been thus far. I planned purposely to avoid flying out of Venice, not to peer over the aircraft wing as it banked across the lagoon and thereby glimpse from above any one of the tiny islands that Enzo and I had motored to and made love upon. It was simply too painful. My last view of that beautiful jewel was Livia waving me off from the platform at Venezia Santa Lucia, her diminutive form soon receding into the distance as the engine chugged forth and my eyes blurred with true regret.

The train stopped in Paris, which seemed a good enough place as any to drown my sorrows, since the bars and alcohol were in abundance and, more crucially, open day and night. I attacked the task with gusto, in an endless carousel of drunkenness and near misses with opportunistic men that makes me cringe for my own safety even now. After Jerome, I really should have known better. Except I was so blindsided with grief and permanently infused with alcohol that knowing anything (bar the French for 'another drink please') was beyond me. Least of all what a fool I was making of myself.

I woke up after a week, miraculously in a hotel room that seemed to belong to me, in that my clothes were hung in the wardrobe, and I came to. Abruptly. I stank. I was bloated yet thin; I had bruises in unexplained places. I felt old and shrewish, dried up, despite being sodden with alcohol. And I was coated in shame.

Readers will be aware that I was already well acquainted with its brazen characteristics – that leaden, nauseating, pit of fire in the stomach sensation when you know for sure that none of the problems rapping at your door, or the spiralling stack of guilt, is anything other than Your Own Fault. You are in the well of despair entirely due to your own actions. Most of them unwise. Safe to say that shame and I had a bit of a thing going.

Paris was one of those times, an epiphany among the sweat-stained sheets (who's soiling, sadly, wasn't even down to glorious sex). I was not responsible for Enzo's demise, that I knew. But my reaction to it was cowardly and childish. And I needed to damn well grow up. By properly going home.

I cleaned up and spent a day actually appreciating the beautiful sights of Paris, drinking soda water and coffee. From a boulevard café, I drafted a cable to my parents, the few words of which took me far longer to compose than any real novelist has the right to claim. How to make it sound as if I would be visiting for the joy of seeing my long-lost mother and father, and yet hinting I might stay awhile (subtext: I have nowhere else to go)? In ten words or less.

Their return cable was more gracious than I had any right to expect: *Be lovely to see you. Ring on arrival.* I only wondered if their words matched mine for untruths. But then I guessed that was a parent's job – the giving of unconditional love, or something disguised as love. Affection had never been plentiful in the Devereaux dwelling, but they did qualify in being parents, and so perhaps their goodwill was in some way automatic?

I arrived in the late autumn of 1961, a storm lashing against the windows of the taxi and obscuring the full view of Corston Avenue in all its suburban drudgery, beating back the spindles of rose bushes so carefully tended by an army of neighbours. Mother greeted me at the door, smiling, and yet in that instant I knew I had not experienced my entire quota of death or demise; life had some more in store. In the world I recalled before my getaway, my mother had been functional and caring, in that I was cared for. I'd had clothes, an education, there were 'things' and a roof over my head. She cooked, or mostly burned things, the oven being set at furnace level regardless of the recipe. But warmth wasn't Mother's forte, and even if I scratched into the far corners of my memory, I couldn't remember a time when she cuddled me, or comforted, the scent of her apron in my nostrils, or any of those nostalgic maternal aromas you're supposed to list wistfully in a memoir. The smell of her hair I do recall: the chemical equivalent of a tobacco factory with a sickly flowery perfume smell, given that hairspray had a way to go in those days, and Sheila Devereaux probably has her very own hole in the ozone layer to prove it. Her locks were crispy to the touch. But it did mean she was always well-turned-out, eternally 'presentable', as she termed it.

On the doorstep in the rain, there was no evidence of hairspray, and she was simply grey. And thin, with eyes that had retreated back into her head like a glass marble falling down a well. Still, she was smiling.

'Ruby!' she cried, making some effort to hug me, an awkward tangle of upper limbs that we attempted for a few seconds and then gave up, her shushing me indoors like an inept shepherd. I was more surprised to see my father in the living room, in the flesh. Throughout my entire childhood, he was never *in*, always at some business function or another, and not the sort of father who would creep in to kiss his kin on his late return. It was little wonder I shared my bed with a plethora of fluffy animals to take the place of parental contact.

I was so shocked at his presence that I stared rudely for a good many seconds, he getting up from his armchair in front of the television (another first – seeing my father in front of a screen) and inching towards me.

'Ruby, my love,' he said, pushing an arm around me, followed by another. He was warm. And soft. It felt like he meant it. I'd never known the like. It was a day of revelations all right.

More were to come. We had burnt offerings from the kitchen that, to be fair, were equally my fault as I joined my mother in the kitchen and we spent time catching up on the family, Michael's sexual proclivities included.

'I feel so sorry for his parents,' she said, with lips so puckered I thought she'd inhaled the lemon in her G&T. 'You do hear of it – men like *that*.'

Over dinner, I gave them a whistle-stop tour of my travels and adventures, pushing up the highlights of my writing and neatly nipping and tucking at the embarrassment and shame.

'It's just like that TV show on television, isn't it, Dad? What's it called?' said my mother.

'*This Is Your Life*,' Dad replied.

Dad? Had I ever in my life called him that? It didn't feel familiar on my tongue, except that he didn't visibly recoil at my mother's address. I thought for a minute she might have swapped him for a different model, only he looked the same, if a little older, flesh a little looser around his jowls. But the genial bit and the jokes were entirely alien.

Mother (she was never anything other than 'Mother') retired to bed early, and Dad visibly sunk into his chair with something like relief, pulling out a pipe and lighting it with a great deal of ritual. I'd been home only a few hours, as the guest from another planet, but my curiosity would not be quelled. I had to know what sort of world I was invading.

'How is Mother then?' I ventured.

'Your mother? Well, you can see...' His upbeat tone tailed off like the dying squeal of a Catherine Wheel on bonfire night. He turned away from the flickering black-and-white screen, and faced me like he had never before in his life. As an adult. 'You can see, Ruby.'

'How ill is she?' Since I was a child, she'd sounded like a woman who swallowed several Hoover bags for breakfast – the consequence of a thirty-a-day habit – but now it had backed up beyond her voice box, as if her whole body make-up was merely dust glued together with tea or gin.

'Very. Maybe a month. Or two, if we're lucky.'

'Cancer?'

He nodded. 'Lungs. And other things. Luckily, not her brain. Yet.'

'And you didn't think to tell me?' The words were out of my mouth before I had a chance to check my audacity, my complete inattention, my years of gallivanting without a care in the world. Or a care for them.

He looked at me again with nothing like accusation, and everything of resignation and regret. 'We just thought...'

My contrition multiplied. He didn't need to rail at me, or berate me for gross neglect as a dutiful daughter, although in fairness he never did do that when I was a child, because he was never there. Right then, I owned my guilt very nicely, thank you very much, swallowing it bitterly and letting it burn from the inside out, as it should. I deserved to feel wretched. He could have made me feel two inches high in one sentence. But he didn't.

'But it's lovely to have you here now,' was what he said. 'Cup of tea, Rubes?'

My father at the kettle! How much more make-believe could I take in one day?

She lasted six weeks. The last two were hard, the walls heavy under the pending shroud of death, when Mother was bed-bound, and any rattle in the house seemed as if it might be her last, husky laboured breath. But the four weeks previous were actually... fun. Yes, truly – I had a good time with my parents. It's proof positive that some things can never come too late in life.

We played the board games never attempted in childhood, my father taking immense pleasure in beating us both at Monopoly, to cries of 'it's not fair – you were a bank manager!' My mother, though, proved herself a dab hand at gin rummy, sitting there with her cigarette in one hand and her Gordon's and tonic in the other. 'What's it going to do?' my father reasoned. 'Kill her? Too late for that, Rubes.' Clouded in smoke, Mother looked like a poker pro and played her hand with the same guile. My abiding thanks even now goes to Mother Nature, or God, or whatever deity holds power over our fate, that her lungs gave out before the scourge could reach her brain and so suck back what little joy she had in life then. She never lost her sarcasm or her wit at the table, though it had become a little dulled, or perhaps she had morphed into someone softer, I couldn't quite tell. She let me win more than once.

We made our peace, too, as mother and daughter. The creeping cancer meant she needed help day-to-day with her 'personal musts', as she called them. Although the new version of my father probably would have done this willingly, it fell to me as the female in the house to step in. Far be it from me to paint myself as any Florence Nightingale, I was nonetheless happy to do it. Yes, it assuaged a smidgen of my guilt load, but more than that, I found I wanted to.

We talked as I washed her wasted back in the bath, tables turned as I felt for the first time in my life the bare skin clinging to her rack of ribs, and the concertina of bone as her chest heaved with a lengthy coughing fit, my hands almost bracing her entire body together.

'Just a little tickle,' she'd say with a wry smile, emerging to draw breath again, eyes red and rimmed. 'Nothing serious.'

'I know I was never the easiest of mothers,' she murmured one day, as I tucked her in bed and dished out her grade-A morphine.

'Pardon?' As the weeks progressed, she'd become more ponderous, dipping into her memories. Lucid, though nostalgic.

'I know I wasn't very affectionate towards you,' she went on, grabbing at my wrist with real urgency. 'And I'm sorry. But I did – *do* – love you in my own way, Ruby. I really do.'

It came out then, what she'd been through, the long and painful memory noose that had knotted around her poor strangled heart for so long – a childhood of her own, barren in everything but cruelty between wealthy, warring parents, and then sent to a boarding school the likes of which would have turned Dickens's beard to grey. There was little contact, no affection, and absolutely no love. She married the first man to show any interest, affording her an escape. Lord knows how my father had chipped away at her chilliness to create a family. Maybe his frequent absences were his escape from the challenges of living with an ice queen.

'I didn't know what to do with you the first time I held you,' she admitted, her bottom lip quivering like a baby. 'I thought I should kiss you. I wanted to, I felt something hot and hard in my chest, and that smell – your hair was so sweet and soft, your lips so red. That's how we named you – 'Ruby Red Lips' your father called you at first sight. But I didn't know if it was right to shower you. Whether it would ruin you. No one ever told me.'

I'd never heard such words from my mother, that she was capable of articulating emotion. Or that she possessed any. 'It's all right, Mother,' I told her. It hadn't been, back then. I'd felt the void acutely as a child, watched my friends and cousins receive their warmth and the way it moulded them, knocked off the sharp corners in the brittle pain of growing up. But my mother didn't need to know that now. What good would it do? I was me because of where I came from, and there was something to be said for it, despite my catalogue of failures. I wouldn't have run to Michael without that need, or run anywhere after that.

We played gin rummy just hours before she died, me holding up her cards and offering her sips of gin through a straw. The doctor visited as I allowed her to beat me (I'd become worryingly adept at reading hands in just six weeks), and his look towards me and the Gordon's bottle on the sideboard served to chasten.

'What's it going to do, kill her?' I whispered as I let him out. It might well have done, only hours later, but it was the best thing, her drifting off in a G&T haze. It's the end many would wish for.

Dad was with her on the last breath, as I soaked away the stench of imminent demise in the bath. He knocked tentatively on the door, and I knew instantly.

'No rush,' he said calmly through the wood. He didn't elaborate on the death rattle, but I knew her last breath would have been like a chorus of Hoovers needing repair.

We made a cup of tea and sat drinking it around her bed, and it was actually nice. The room was warm, and the odour of death had departed, exited stage left when no longer needed. Dad closed the last pack of her favourite Benson & Hedges on the side, though she hadn't been able to smoke for the last week. He put them in a drawer, where I knew they would stay until disintegrating into dust. Much like the rest of us, really.

Had I been in the literary mood, the funeral was a cornucopia of material, perfect for a wry exposé about simmering envy among the middling classes, ways to prune your roses and snitch on your neighbours to the council authorities. A previous version of myself would have leaped on it and disappeared into the nearest privy with notebook and pencil, scribbling every detail.

But I was no longer that person. I played the grieving daughter to perfection, feeling it was about time I truly acted as a member of the Devereaux family and that I owed it to my mother's memory to give the neighbours something good to talk about. And I was genuinely sad, and sorry she was gone. Contrite, too, for only being there in her last six weeks, and enjoying her company for a tiny snapshot of our lives.

I was mournful too for my dad, pulling his bank manager handshake out of retirement and effecting the 'grip-n-grin' pose until the sausage rolls were down to the pastry flakes and the sherry bottle had finally run dry.

By the end of the day, he resembled a shadow of the man.

'Tea or whisky?' I held up a china cup and a glass tumbler.

'Alcohol, Rubes,' he said, 'and in abundance.'

Two thirds down the bottle, I asked him how it was – truly – living with her all those years. He didn't flash anger at my disrespect, or tell me to mind my tongue, only drew in a long breath and considered.

'Lonely,' he said. 'You know, she wouldn't even undress in front of me on our wedding night, or any other night,' he went on, the alcohol loosening his hold on intimacy. 'That school she went to – they told her it was illicit and dirty to set eyes on her own body. We could never have any lengthy mirrors in the house. She was so ashamed, and yet, Rubes, the few times I did glimpse it, she had such a beautiful body, so elegant.'

'And the years… being married didn't change that?' I prodded gently.

He shook his head wearily. 'It was so ingrained. I think she'd never even seen her own mother in a bathing costume. Her father was a complete brute, so outwardly cruel to his own wife that it was painful to watch. Your mother witnessed that, and

I think she retreated into a very hard shell. I tapped away for so long, and then I suppose I just gave up.' His guilty sigh was covered by a generous slug of whisky.

I was perplexed. In all my dealings with men to that point I had never considered going anywhere near the aisle without sure and certain love to go alongside the lust that inevitably preceded it. As with Enzo, I would have needed to desire and covet and be utterly devoted before surrendering myself to a lifetime with just one man, both in my life and my bed. So how on earth did they get married?

'That's just what you did in those days, Ruby,' he said. 'It was the Twenties, everything was flighty and shallow. We'd not long been out of the war, and people were desperate to put down roots, that perhaps by doing so it might not happen again. And don't forget, your mother had years to perfect that shell,' – I thought of her sculpted helmet of hair as he said it and smiled inside – 'and any man who was nice to her meant an escape. I asked her to marry me and she said yes. And after that, you simply roll along with it.'

He sat up, refilled his glass, and mine. 'But she could be fun, sometimes, in the right mood. We loved each other in our own way, a bit like two old cushions on the sofa, some kind of comfort in familiarity.'

I thought of Enzo again, having managed not to for at least one full day. I recalled the passion flowing between us, the love that multiplied and the way we had peeled back almost every layer of each other in those few, short months. I saw then why my father had been the parent he was – largely absent – partly because that's what fathers did then, but also the pain of being in the house for any length of time, the famine of affection he must have felt.

'Did you ever think about leaving?' I probed.

Another sigh. 'Once or twice,' he said, his eyes suddenly watery. 'I can't deny, Ruby, that I sometimes looked elsewhere for company. I'm not proud of it, but that's how it was.' He looked directly at me, expecting me to remonstrate as a woman might, and when I didn't, he ploughed on with his confession. 'I think your mother knew, and in all honesty, she seemed relieved, that it was taken care of, and she wouldn't be called upon. Hence, I suppose, you as an only child. We never spoke about it. It made our life workable, to be a husband and wife on the surface. The only thing I could give her in marriage was status and safety, and I felt she deserved that, after all she'd been through.'

He looked at me, rheumy-eyed with whisky and fatigue, and I got the first genuine smile of that desolate, endless day. 'But you know, Ruby, the best outcome has been you, was always your spirit. How different you were, how alive you turned out to be. You don't know how proud I felt when I read your first book,' – he hesitated with a half-laugh – 'though I did keep my copy hidden from your mother at the time.' Then pensive again. 'I felt that at least we hadn't infected you with our shame, or our melancholy.'

Blow me down, but someone really had come and replaced my father with a replicant while I was off living my high and lowly life.

I kissed him on the forehead, as I'd become used to doing in those six weeks, and said goodnight, and he seemed even softer, more putty-like than I'd ever know him, as if some sinews within had given up the ghost. I lay awake in my old room, its four walls virtually unchanged from childhood – aside from more suburban debris piled in the wardrobe – and allowed myself to think. I hadn't known my parents as I was growing up, partly because I thought them so dull and lifeless that they weren't worth the effort. Now, I felt for certain I hadn't known them at all. Not because of their outward tedium, but because they had strived to keep their sadness hidden from everyone. So that, along with my shame, I now had tenure of a good deal of guilt. The sadness? I resolved that would be temporary; in her last days, my mother had insisted that life would go on.

'Promise me,' she'd croaked, 'that you will go again and be alive, Ruby. And that you'll make him too.'

What else can you do but grant a dying woman her wish?

But my father wasn't finished there. He had surprises in him yet. A whole bloody Pandora's Box of wonders.

A week after the funeral, we sat in the living room one evening turning out containers of ephemera only women such as my mother could collect: old make-up, brushes and combs, half-filled cans of hairspray.

'How on earth can one person use so much?' Dad said, incredulous. Clearly, he had never come that close to her impenetrable helmet of locks in recent years. I grabbed at the photo albums underneath and relished staring at their wedding photo, my mother smiling in her fashionable 1920s drop-waisted dress, and my father stiff and proud in his suit. Then, one I hadn't seen before, one of us all together, with me as a baby. The camera can lie – we looked a content, happy threesome, with my father's hands resting proudly on each of us. He gave a slight moue as I held it out to him, and moved on. Tucked in the back sleeve of the album, its sepia tones just poking out, was a faded photograph of a man in uniform, officer class. Unless a true doppelganger existed, it was undoubtedly my father. On the back, however, scribbled in faded pencil, the words: *Captain Henry Clarkson, 1944*.

'Dad, who's this? It looks like you.'

In one fleeting expression, he rolled out a film-reel of surprise: shock, fear, guilt, shame, and the unmistakeable 'shit! I've got some explaining to do'. As a writer, and ergo, one of life's observers, I read that one expertly.

'Oh.'

'Who's Henry Clarkson? Don't tell me you've got a twin I don't know about.'

'It's a tad more complicated than that,' he murmured. 'Fancy a Scotch?' His look said he needed one, and I probably would too.

I sat and sipped, open-mouthed a great deal of the time – me, the ever-changing firefly of the new world, was duly shocked. My father *had* been a bank manager, it seemed, but only before and after the war. During the conflict, in the time I was cavorting around apple orchards in deepest Somerset and tasting freedom, he was anything but lacklustre, very much minus his staid suit and briefcase.

'Why did you even keep this?' I held up the photograph.

'I don't honestly know,' he sighed. 'It seems like a different universe. When I look at it – at him – I feel it wasn't even me. Maybe I needed reminding.'

'And yet it is you?' There was an undercurrent of interrogation in my tone that he couldn't easily ignore.

'Have you ever heard of something called the London Cage?' he said at last.

I hadn't, and his grave look told me that was probably a good thing.

'I can tell you now, I suppose,' he breathed, after a lengthy pause. 'They can't do much to me now, can they?'

'What do you mean, Dad? Why did you need to be someone else?' Even my mind, bent as it was towards fiction, was struggling to contend with the truth he might reveal. I'd read a good amount of wartime espionage, but to think my father might be a character in one was frankly ludicrous. Implausible. Though entirely possible, it seemed.

The 'Cage' was apparently set behind a fence but in among some very nice houses in Kensington. George Devereaux would toddle off there each morning in his three-piece suit, changing into his officer's uniform and the persona of Henry Clarkson.

'Why the secrecy?'

'Uh well, what we did there was classified. Some might say unacceptable.' He rolled the words out slowly. 'It had to be that our identities couldn't be traced. No repercussions.'

'Was it legal?' My eyes were like saucers, focused on the man who'd never had so much as a parking ticket.

'Hmm, legal tends to have a shaky definition in war. Immoral, possibly. It depends on your outlook.'

They – he – interrogated prisoners of war, Germans principally, using a whole manner of methods. He alluded, though gave me no details, to torture, to being responsible for harming others. To crimes against humans, if not humanity as a whole. His face spoke volumes on Bad Things being done behind high walls with no windows and even less accountability.

'I'm not proud of it, Ruby,' he murmured, twizzling his glass awkwardly against the lamplight. 'There were times when I baulked at the lengths they wanted us to go to, when I felt physically sick. *Was* sick.'

'Did you ever refuse?'

He puffed out his cheeks. 'You couldn't. Or you simply didn't. It was war and we were under orders. It was our job to think about the bigger picture.' He gave me a look that signalled only those in conflict could understand such a defence, though it was nonetheless wrapped in layers of remorse.

'Well, do you think it achieved anything? Saved lives, or helped others?' I asked.

He sought courage from his whisky and swallowed. 'Sadly, yes. I think those methods, as inhumane and indefensible as they were, did bear some fruit. We wrung out information' – his eyes shot to me at his unfortunate choice of words – 'that possibly did shorten the war.'

I was aghast, bubbling with questions, staring in wonder at my newly pudgy and soft parent who had been under a new light for weeks. And now this. The dull, grey ghost of my father had been swept away in the space of five minutes, to be replaced with what? I felt like I was in my own, drug-induced version of Dickens's *Christmas Carol*. His image flashed as red as the devil in seconds, and then bled out to a tainted hue. Could the man in front of me really have done such things, those morally questionable acts I'd read about in the war memoirs of others? I was all of nine or ten when the war started, fifteen at its end. I'd been sheltered and cocooned in the countryside, while my father didn't just tot up figures in his municipal bank, as we all imagined, but did his bit to shore up the security of our country. And my future. Did I have any right to be appalled at his actions?

'Do you think you would ever have told me, if I hadn't found this?' I held up the handsome officer snap.

'In all honesty, no.'

'Did Mother know?'

He shook his head, bit his lip. 'I was sworn to secrecy – the old Official Act, you know.'

'But how can you… how can you leave something like that behind?' For a brief moment, I was flooded by the shame after Michael, the cold sweep of excruciating self-disgust that caught me unawares for months after my first book was published. The almost sickening success. It was in no way equal, a mere flicker in comparison to the gravity of my father's dilemma, but it had nevertheless tattooed something on me, in me, that I would never be rid of. 'How can you have kept it inside?' I hoped my tone was curious rather than accusatory.

He laughed then, at his own distorted talent. 'Maybe your mother did teach me something useful over the years, how to bury the emotion. I went back to my life and almost pretended it never happened, like so many did. It didn't seem important – my hurt, I mean.'

'And now? What do you think when you look at that photograph?' I pressed. 'Who do you see?'

'Like I said, another man.'

I stared for an age at that photograph, long after my father hauled himself from the armchair wearily and made his way to bed.

'Don't judge me too harshly, eh Rubes?' he said as he kissed me lightly on the head, a slight crack to his voice.

That image of Henry Clarkson posing as my father proved endlessly alluring – the smart, pressed uniform against what looked to be a garden wall, a trellis of ivy behind, his pose a little awkward for someone who looked to be 'high up' in the great scheme of things. Maybe he wasn't telling me the whole story, still shamed by the past. I knew and understood all about that.

The box that had thrown up the album of photographs lay discarded on the floor. It was against my better judgement to pry, but I had trodden that road already. And I was a writer – it was my function to be endlessly curious, intrusive and downright nosy. That was my excuse to keep looking.

In a large, sealed envelope, there were more: faded snapshots of Henry Clarkson as my father, or vice versa, against a variety of backdrops and in civilian clothes, even one where he was dressed as a sailor. It was almost a comical tableau of a man in fancy dress. Yet, clearly, he had been to Norway, and somewhere that resembled either Austria or Germany, judging by the stereotypical scene behind, plucked from the pages of *Heidi.* Notes pencilled on the back only said *1943*, or *Bergen*, but never the whole picture. There was a faded menu from a Parisian restaurant and a ticket for a museum in Brussels, letters scribbled in faint script which I scoured under the lamplight, eyes narrowed to make out anything clear. Codes? Ciphers? My mind raced. My father, seemingly trooping off to his dull desk in a bank, had in fact been a nomad. And was it a stretch to picture him as a spy… or merely my romantic desire?

I wondered if, in truth, my mother had seen these. They weren't secreted in a drawer or under a floorboard, but in among our family memories. All that time we'd been living a good life at my grandmother's, had she suspected or known her husband was abroad for weeks or months, risking his life? I wracked my rose-tinted memories for missed clues. She'd never given any indication, or was it that I had been too wrapped up in my pre-pubescent infatuation with Michael to notice her at all?

Confused and uneasy, I spent another night with images of George Devereaux flickering behind my eyelids. It was odd, because never before had I scrutinised my father so closely, or even thought of him very often. He'd always just been there – or not, as the case so often was. He provided financially for a nice house and a comfortable life, but beyond that, my brief vision was of him palling it up at the local golf club, rustling up bank business. But as had been proven several times, I'd been spectacularly wrong about men before.

More unsettling, more worrying were the workings of my mind after my father's revelations; I had begun to plan, to scheme and, inside my head, to write. *Write what you know, or at least what someone else knows.* My writer-self on a mission was something even I had learned to be wary of.

The numbing grief over Enzo, and then my mother's death, had frozen all words inside me after landing back in England. When a phrase or sentence did struggle to form, it was often blown away like powdery snow in a wintry gust. Nothing planted itself, and there was no motivation inside me to force it. I wasn't overly worried as I'd survived minor bouts of writer's block before, royalties from my small back catalogue keeping me afloat. Cynically, I knew something would turn up, and I just had to wait.

But no longer. Me as the proverbial cuckoo, the parasite to pray on other souls' stories, had hit the jackpot, and in my childhood home of all places.

Staring at my bedroom walls into the early hours, I surveyed, chastised and censured the willingness to exploit my own father; it was *bad,* and I knew it. But there was something else, a feeling I'd touched on when I first met Hanna, the abused and put-upon cleaner from the Hollywood Hills. Like hers, this tale needed telling. Yes, I would benefit, but so would the teller, and the reader, I hoped. I'd be loath even now to paint myself as some sort of selfless campaigner. I wasn't. I was only ever a chancer, but sometimes one with a good story. And in the midst, there was an emotion I had not experienced before in relation to my father: pride. He was no longer boring, an absence in my childhood and a ghost of my puberty. His grainy, black-and-white transience suddenly became colourful, and interesting. I was proud to be George Devereaux's daughter, because of who he was – brave, daring, flawed and modest. And I wanted to show it.

All I had to do was to persuade him to tell me everything.

Perhaps he felt freed too, from my mother and the cloying manner of their life, because it was easier than I anticipated. I approached him only the next morning, too impatient to delay, though allowing for our respective whisky hangovers.

'You want to tell my story, of the war?' he said over breakfast, unshaven and jowly and looking like the dad I craved at last. He might have rejected the idea outright, not least because I'd burned his bacon – *in my mother's memory*, I justified to myself.

'Not just the war. Everything,' I enthused. 'How it came about, why they chose you, the double life, the pretence.'

'But why?' He was genuinely perplexed.

'Because it's fascinating, Dad! Because I'm captivated, and we – everyone – should know what people had to do, rightly or wrongly, on both sides. Because it's human.'

I don't think I'd ever peddled an idea with more enthusiasm, not even to a publisher. But his gentle modesty came round. He was mystified at my fervour, if a little bit pleased.

* * *

We spent that winter holed up at Corston Avenue, filling the coal scuttle and banking up the fire, the teapot on a permanent top-up, him talking and me scribbling. Every evening, I typed up my notes and forged on with the narrative, while he cooked and took great delight in it, producing delicious food that was never once mildly charred, let alone burned to a cinder.

'I never could tell your mother that I learned to cook in the forces,' he said, with lamentable regret.

'But I know now, Dad,' I assured him. 'And to be honest, I'm not sure Mother had any taste-buds left with all that tobacco inside her.'

'True.' He laughed, a full and hearty rumble, the first I'd heard since… well, since forever.

The result of his purging and my typing was both tangible and emotional. It was published in the autumn of 1962, a solid hardback 'novel' of four hundred pages, detailing the life of banker Anthony Townley and his army alter ego officer Richard Penlea. The 'ole Official Secrets Act' put paid to a straight memoir, but it was my father's story, his name on the front, alongside mine as joint authors. My fictional skills were almost redundant in that every near miss, each foreign mission across borders and narrow escape from capture, occurred in real life – to him, my boring bank manager of a father. He didn't embellish (I know, because I had to wheedle out the vivid details at times as he shrunk with embarrassment), and I didn't need to embroider. It was all there, a writer's gift. Dealing with his time at the London Cage was a little trickier; there were often tears of recrimination in his telling, things he'd buried deep inside, and my prodding at a dormant wasps' nest was clearly painful for him. Cathartic, too. He looked brighter, somehow less bowed after those sessions.

The reviews of *Escaping the Cage* were more than positive, though I didn't actually care for once. I almost popped with pride at the sight of it on his mantelpiece – our work. A true collaboration. With my dad.

'Look at that,' he said, his chest all puffed. 'Your old man, in print. Like daughter, like father. Who'd have thought it?'

And I, Ruby M Devereaux, nudged a fat tear into his crumpled, unironed shirt. I felt as if I'd died and gone to heaven, if I ever believed in that sort of thing.

I left, of course, because that's what I always did. George no longer had need of me, for either my company or support, and certainly not as a shoulder to cry on. He'd already joined a social club in the town, one of those thought to be slightly 'common' by my mother, and soon became firm friends with a widow of a similar age. Apparently, his celebrity as a local writer afforded him a good amount of attention. He and Sandra were 'an item' fairly quickly and married two years later; their postcards from endless holidays abroad always gave the impression they were having a fine old time spending her late husband's pension and Dad's earnings from the book. Whenever I saw him after that, he was at pains to point out that married life was 'just dandy', and I thought it not odd that he should want to tell me, but how much he deserved it.

And, as had become my modus operandi, I departed having learned a lengthy and oft painful lesson. Poignant too, in this case: never judge a book by its bloody cover.

Five

It was bound to come eventually. Marina Keeve looks at the name on her mobile as it trills and releases a heart-sink sigh. Marcus bloody Trent. She's been caught unawares too, peering into her coffee cup and noticing just dregs. She'll need a vat to get over this one. 'Marcus! How nice to hear from you.' Lie One.

'Marina, my love, I hope you're well?'

'Fine, fine.' Lie Two, especially when it's this old toad on the phone. She pictures a single fold of flesh bulging over his starched shirt collar, rippling with a faint tremor as he speaks.

'Excellent. I thought it was about time that I checked in on Ruby's progress,' Marcus puffs.

This time, Marina is prepared, since she has no other clients currently writing for Phoenix; the minute she saw his name flash up, the subject was bound to be Ruby. 'Well, it's good – she's definitely working.' Non-committal at best. 'We've set her up with a young chap who's typing for her, given her age and the arthritis.'

'And it's the memoir, as we discussed?' Marcus pries. For all his polished façade, he can interpret bluster talk when he hears it, those carefully honed 'Nuggets of Shit' sprayed profusely in the publishing world. Christ knows, he invented most of them.

'Yes, Marcus, it's the memoir.' He's running with irritation, clearly. Marina is sometimes cautious with her writers' content, but now she's being purposefully obstructive.

'So, have you seen anything yet?' he probes again. 'Is it… up to standard?'

Bastard. 'Yes, it *is* up to Ruby's usual standard, as you say.' Lie Three, the big one. Marina swallows air and wishes to God it was caffeine, or a decent margarita. 'You won't be disappointed, I promise you. Ruby will deliver.'

'And any hints as to the content?' he fishes. 'These men of hers, I mean.'

Through the receiver, Marina almost hears him squirm, can certainly picture him shifting his copious behind and fiddling with the ubiquitous cigar. A point to Ruby already.

'No one I know for sure,' Marina says. A decent pause. 'Not so far, anyway.' Surely that's a point for her, too?

'Well, good. Good. Just checking in, as I said,' he rattles. 'These bloody print schedules are getting tighter and tighter, and it's crucial we meet the deadlines these days. You know how it is.' Even Marcus, with all his bountiful bravado, knows he's backtracking and he'll loathe himself for the weakness. 'Anyway, I know you're busy, Marina, so I'll let you go. Keep me informed, won't you?'

'Yes, of course, Marcus.' Lie Four. She's more likely to give up her flat whites than seek out that misogynistic troll, either in person or by phone. Only the week before, she'd danced around at a book launch, avoiding his company or his gaze, seeking cover behind a large Yucca at one stage.

'Oh Ruby, Ruby, Ruby,' Marina mutters, as she puts down the phone. 'You will come up trumps, won't you?'

MAN FIVE: Benedict

London, 1962–3

He was, first and foremost, married. That alone might have been an enticement into his bed, since the longer the years rolled on, the less I saw myself as marriage material. Enzo was still too fresh and raw.

There was one other factor in that winter of 1962, crawling into 1963, which threw the charming Benedict and I together – it was bloody cold. Freezing, bone-chilling, and not an understatement to say conditions were Siberian. The weather people told us nightly it was the worst British winter on record, in Europe too, with temperatures frequently down to minus twenty centigrade. The Thames froze, the sea at Herne Bay afforded a mile-long 'pier' of ice stretching out from the Kent coast, waterfalls came to a standstill, and birds caught in the bitter air currents plummeted earthwards, like missiles from the sky. It was *that* cold.

Better then to be tucked up in bed, eking every thermal of warmth from another human body, than to be alone and shivering from lack of heat and having to chance moving out of bed to feed my cantankerous gas fire with coins. Benedict's London place was bigger, more luxurious and, above all, warmer than my own tiny, inadequately insulated flat in Camden.

His family – the obligatory wife and two small children – lived somewhere in deepest Sussex, and he 'lodged' in London all week with a job somewhere at the Ministry of Transport. The snow began falling on Boxing Day, at which point he left the cosy bosom of his family seat and hot-footed back to London before the points on the railway froze. And promptly got stuck. With me.

Determined not to be hemmed in by Mother Nature's cruel Christmas present, I had trudged the entire length of Camden High Street the day after Boxing Day and hitched a lift on a snow plough, the only piece of transport still moving. Being yuletide, and with a renewed 'Blitz atmosphere' dawning across the country, the crew happily ferried me into central London, and to a small bar where I proceeded to get a little warm and very drunk. Looking back, I don't recall it being one of my spectacular benders from the past. I was on a fairly straight path by then, writing again, but it was Christmas; I was cold, and smarting from a recent telegram from Mushens in New York. No yuletide greetings, as per her usual missive, but news of Harvey's untimely death in the days leading up to Christmas. A sudden heart attack, she said, 'though partying until the last', and it was that which prompted a sudden urge to toast his magnificent humanity. Despite the elements, Harvey's loss and the surrounding memories aroused a yearning for company and whisky.

'How are you getting home?' was his chat-up line, though it was a fair question, given the conditions outside. By ten p.m., he and I were the last stragglers in the bar. I hadn't given much thought to the return journey, but with buses largely stranded, I imagined getting wet and cold, using my alcohol-infused veins as a form of central heating. I'd get home eventually.

I smiled, possibly the wonky, inebriated attempt of the entirely pissed, and held out a hand. What I could see of his face was attractive: solid like a rugby player, blond hair neatly cut, smile straight (unlike mine). I thought he looked more European than British, German perhaps, although that might have been my skewed vision in that moment. His voice, though, was all Establishment.

'Listen, you'll freeze to death if you walk far in this. My flat is just around the corner,' he offered.

My radar being what it was then – honed to rise above the alcoholic haze – my eyebrows rose an inch at least.

He held up two hands in mock surrender. 'Gentleman's rules,' he assured me. 'You get the fire and the sofa.'

Given that the drifts outside had risen an inch in previous hours, and my best boots were already leaking, I had little choice. I took a punt. We set off, leaving deep foot wells in the snow and leaning on each other for warmth and balance in the deserted streets.

Two floors up in his Edwardian mansion flat, he stoked the fire, served me with hot cocoa and was true to his word – the perfect gentleman.

'Sleep tight,' he said, disappearing into the bedroom.

I woke to the combined smell and spit of eggs and bacon from the kitchen, and the BBC's dour predictions for the day's weather.

'Morning,' he said brightly. 'Shall we renew the introductions?'

Benedict Aloysius Dalybridge was his grandiose name, fourth son of a minor earl and, as such, entitled to no funds from an estate that had 'already gone down the pan'. A private school education was his only inheritance, leading inevitably to Oxbridge and a government job in Transport. Only, to my eyes, he didn't look that run of the mill; there was something *more* about his air.

'So, what is it you do at the ministry?' I said, noting almost no traffic moving outside of the window, and that perhaps he should be in the office helping to heave the country out of this icy standstill.

'Emergency planning,' he said, with no hint of apology.

'Oh.'

'Only we didn't plan for this type of emergency.'

I laughed and he smirked while serving up breakfast, and I think that's when I must have suspected, a doubt somewhere deep down inside. Though I couldn't quite put my finger on it. Accordingly, I went along for the ride, as they say. I told him what I did, and he seemed marginally impressed, reacting with more vigour than most. Those who issue a deprecating 'ooh', denoting a modicum of curiosity and disinterest all in one. Or that you are not Virginia Woolf, whom they might actually have heard of. He said he'd read *Escaping the Cage* and thought it 'good'.

'Are you writing something now?' he asked.

'I am, as it happens – something quite new for me. A love story.'

'And why is that so new?' he said, gesturing that I had a smear of tomato ketchup on my chin. *Maybe he imagines I'm mutating into a trashy airport author,* I thought, *selling sex to bored wives and businessmen in hotel rooms.*

'For once, it's not about me,' I said, and left him hanging.

Replete with bacon and eggs, I left, entirely untouched by Benedict and his chivalrous virtues. He didn't ask for my number, and I didn't offer it, spying the cosy family photograph on the hall table. I ventured forth into the arctic tundra of London, bought myself some better boots, and decamped to the nearest library on my list of Officially Warm Places, where I could spend the day writing and not shivering in my flat or shouting at the inadequate, sputtering gas fire. Relinquishing my typewriter for freehand was a small price to pay for having blood flowing in my feet at the day's end.

The afternoon was already dark as I emerged, flush from two thousand words in my notebook – spurred on by fond memories of Harvey – a quarter of which might survive an editor's merciless pen. A good day. Outside, it was bitter beyond belief, and yet still I didn't head for home. I needed a bath, but was short on shilling change for the meter, and my fridge boasted little to tempt me. I settled on heading for Soho and a good Italian coffee, followed by supper in the busiest bistro I could find, the prospect of collective body heat being more of a recommendation than gastronomy.

He caught up with me two streets away, another clue that I probably did register somewhere, but that was quickly dissipated by the icy bite of the wind. He would have been hard pressed to spot me randomly on the street, as my distinctive black bob was swathed in a large scarf in the style of 'lesser-spotted fishwife' and my features pinched against the oncoming sleet.

'Hello again,' he said, quite loudly over the muffle of snow and wool coverings. I had to peer beyond his thick, expensive overcoat and the Russian-style hat which sat like a black, silken cat on his head.

'Oh, hello.' I stifled a laugh at the Kremlin look. 'Where did you come from?'

'I had a meeting nearby,' he said. It was an obvious lie, but I thought then his pursuing me was because he saw something he liked, and nothing else. I was too flattered by half and, given my past, perhaps not as judicious as I ought to have been. In the moment, however, I was freezing, and my teeth began an involuntary chattering. Any niceties took too long and risked eyelashes freezing over, so he steered me into a convenient hotel and its bar, where we drank warm brandy, ate some food – though I don't remember what – and went back to his flat. In my defence, it was always going to be cosier than mine, and this girl's watchword had always been survival.

'Did you do any emergency planning today?' I asked, several days later. We'd thrown off almost all the blankets after some fairly athletic sex and lay side by side exuding that post-coital warmth that I had been struggling to recall, due in part to the inclement weather conditions, but also my own barren love life.

'Almost impossible,' he said. 'Everything's frozen solid, and so if you get the tracks working, the trains don't. The buses are mostly pre-war – either the diesel freezes in the tank or they cause more accidents by skidding all over the place.' He sighed. 'We need to learn from the Swedes and the Norwegians. The damned irony is that we were planning a work delegation to Oslo next month to do just that.'

'Bad timing,' I said, tracing my finger over his taut chest, and thinking selfishly that it wasn't. He had the body of a man who'd grown up either on a horse or in a stable mucking out. I thought it was the former, but he assured me it was actually both.

'No money for stable hands,' he said. 'Dirty great pile of a house, too, and no one to clean it.'

I turned to look at him, needing to see and analyse the reaction in his profile. 'Were you waiting for me that day, outside the library?' I asked, more with flirtation than accusation.

His nostril tweaked less than a millimetre, and I swear I heard a cog in his brain nudge. He was deciding on whether to lie. Or not. 'Yes.'

'Why?'

'Is it a crime to like someone, and be lonely?' he said.

'No.' If it had been, I was already hopelessly condemned.

He turned, pulling the blanket back over his shoulder. 'Are you glad I did?'

'Yes, as it happens.' He didn't, however, offer up how he found me, or why. And I needed time to ruminate over those details in private.

He slipped from the covers, poked at the fire in the living room, and began clanking about the kitchen. 'Fish for dinner?' he called out.

I couldn't believe my luck: warm and catered for, and in good company. My love life appeared to be heading for a thaw. 'Yes please. And where did you learn to cook?'

'Necessity,' he called back down the hallway. 'No ruddy cook in the house after the age of ten. My mother can't boil a kettle, let alone an egg.'

It was perhaps another clue to this man's mystery, but one which melted away in the warmth under the eiderdown. Normally far more astute, I had been entirely beguiled by a blazing hearth and a good meal. But then it was *bloody* cold.

★★★

Arctic Britain spanned ten weeks, from first flake to the beginnings of a thaw in mid-March '63. The country climbed slowly out of its frozen paralysis; the sea moved again, pond surfaces thinned and became dangerous, the trains ran (though nothing to do with Benedict, I suspected) and people emerged from their hibernation like blinking dormice in a fable, as if sampling a brave new world. I saw that it was neither fresh nor courageous; the nation had simply been petrified in a block of ice and continued to crank forward on its axis pretty much as before. Plus, there was a tidal wave of filthy black slush to contemplate.

But Benedict's fostering in those cold climes had paid off. The result? I became drawn into the shady world of espionage. Or near enough.

Benedict was no man at the ministry; I figured that fairly quickly, principally because the hours he kept bore no resemblance to civic duty, top position or not. He rolled out of bed at all hours, disappeared for a total of two weekends, where he swore blind he was braving the cruel climate to visit his wife and children in Sussex. I'd let myself into the flat to find a note saying as much, adding that I was welcome to stay and write in comfort before the fire: *keep the bed warm!* he'd scrawled as a cheeky afterthought. When the phone rang later that evening I didn't pick it up, not being my own place. But when it rang again… and again, an endless echo on the hall table, I knew instinctively it was his wife. If she ever rang when I was in the flat, Benedict always picked up and moved into the bedroom or living room, shielding me from his domestic orbit. Back in rural Sussex, she would be nurturing her own suspicions, surely.

His demeanour on return, not to mention a case of unwashed clothes, said he'd been elsewhere. Plus the packet of French cigarettes I found in his coat pocket, bearing the price tag in francs. And he didn't even smoke.

I wasn't worried about the trip, or that he didn't invite me (a Gallic frozen romance did not inspire), or even that he might have had another woman. It was the lying, and thinking I was stupid enough to swallow it. That he would contemplate taking Ruby Devereaux for a ride.

We were sitting in front of the fire eating crumpets one evening, the bones of London taking their time to warm through, when I broached the subject head-on.

'So where *did* you go last weekend?' I said, drawing my focus from the melting butter under my knife to his face. And I kept it there. Unperturbed.

I watched the cogs move again, turning faster this time. The right moment for deception? He was picking petals off a daisy: *Lie to her… lie to her not.*

'What I say depends on whether you want a part of it,' he said at last, biting into his crumpet firmly. He chewed and swallowed while never moving his eyes from mine.

I felt something inside me flip, a thing I hadn't felt for an age. Perhaps since Venice. A thrill.

'Of what?' I came back.

'The life.' And in the way he said it, that life was a million light years from directing policy on bus timetables.

He didn't wait for me to answer, only posed another, more crucial question: 'Ruby, do you feel a duty to your country?'

In fairness, he hadn't known me long enough to ascertain that my number one priority was – and always had been – me. My only claim to my country was in being British born and bred.

And yet I was stirred, and moreover, ready for something new. Some *sport.*

'Yes, I suppose, though I'm not a card-carrying member of the Establishment.' In truth, I wasn't so much lying as fictionalising – that enduring curse of a scribe again. I'd never wasted one second of my life on patriotism, aside from persuading my father that we no longer had to adhere to it in writing his wartime experiences.

'I know that – I read your last book, remember?' Benedict shot back. Chewed more crumpet. 'What I mean is, do you feel enough loyalty to work for your country's security? To risk for it?'

I was a big fan of Fleming's work (if not his lowly view of women), having read everything from *Casino Royale* onwards, but I hoped to God Benedict didn't see me as Miss Moneypenny. I would be a true accomplice to Bond or nothing.

'But more than that, to have some fun,' he added. A convincing wife was required for a trip abroad, he said calmly. To look and play the part. At that point, I wasn't a politico, but I knew the Cold War between the US and the Soviets was particularly chilly, with Britain playing a large part. The defection of double agents Guy Burgess and Donald Mclean in the 1950s had done nothing to quell the government's jitteriness, plus the suspicion – yet to be proven – over their Cambridge University comrade Kim Philby, the divide between East and West amplified by the ugly edifice of the Berlin Wall. Any part to be played by yours truly would surely be steeped in this murky mire. And yet, all I recall was a swell of curiosity.

'Not some Transport delegation, I hope?' I asked.

He laughed. 'Ruby, I know fuck all about transport,' he said in his plum public-school tone.

'It shows,' I told him. 'I hope you're a better spy than a fake civil servant.'

'Luckily for you, I am.'

He never said outright who he worked for. It was always 'they' and, unsurprisingly, there was no contract, nothing in writing, and I never got to meet 'M' or 'C' or anyone with a letter for a name. So, no comeback. And zero accountability, of course.

'When did you begin to recruit me?' I asked, as we lay in bed recovering from post-crumpet sex (a lesser-known aphrodisiac, I grant you).

He sighed, as if I was an over enthusiastic newbie, and that he would satisfy me just this once, but after that, no more questions. 'Outside the library,' he said.

'Why? You knew almost nothing about me.'

'When I saw you in that bar the night before, I knew you'd traipsed through the snow when no one else had, out of your comfort zone. And I could tell, even from that first conversation, you were searching for something.'

I didn't like to burst his bubble; that I'd hitched a ride on a snow plough because I was freezing at home and my cupboards were bare. Not least, too, the hot coal of grief that had fuelled an urgent need for alcohol. Perhaps though, I wasn't giving Benedict enough credit. I *was* bored and searching, albeit subconsciously. I had been immersed in my book, though not absorbed enough to prevent me from casting about, scouting rather than scavenging for excitement. At the same time, I felt a concern that his recruitment of the realm's spies seemed to be based on little more than gut instinct and a carnal attraction. But let's face it, despite that first night on the sofa, it was never going to be 'gentleman's rules' forever.

* * *

We boarded a flight for Amsterdam in early March, disappointment on my part that we weren't headed into the belly of the red beast in Moscow, or even East Berlin, though Benedict said we (as in I) had to start small. I did have a nice fake passport clutched in my palm. Eleanor Stafford, fine and upstanding. Posh. Dull. A wife. All the things I felt sure I'd never be.

It made me giggle inside, but on the surface – and even though I say it myself – I played a blinder.

Benedict already had the accent of a man with money, and I was a fair mimic; I'd practised my 'dahhling' in front of the mirror many times. Neatly folded in my suitcase were outfits I only dreamed of buying myself, couture confidently paid for with the sheaf of five-pound notes Benedict casually handed over.

'Is this government money?' I'd asked as he pulled it from his wallet.

'If you mean, did Prime Minister Macmillan himself sanction it, then no,' Benedict drawled into his whisky. 'But I suppose it does come by way of the Treasury. Down a few rabbit holes.'

He was so nonchalant, the consummate spy. And I was his accomplice.

Strap in, Ruby Devereaux.

I liked Amsterdam instantly; the pace of the city marked out by water, though not defined by it like Venice, and thereby not enough to resurrect the painful reminders. Besides, it was still too cold to afford any real comparisons with that life with Enzo. Despite the temperature, chic women pedalled around on bicycles clad in expensive wool, stopped at cafés and blew smoke into the air from cigarettes and their own gossipy breath, while children skated on the few canals still frozen. It seemed anything but sinister to me.

The world we entered, as Mr and Mrs Stafford, was altogether less bohemian, starting with a hotel dinner that same night with a dry executive and his wife. I was bored to tears by the conversation forced upon me, in trading culinary talk with the wife, but it was – as Benedict later pointed out under the awning of our four-poster bed – good training. Lord knows I'd become practised at fabrication over the years, but this alternate, domestic world I'd had to create on the hoof was on another level.

'Did I pass?' I ventured.

'Gold star,' he said, a little patronising. But perhaps I had asked for it.

'Benedict, what are we doing exactly? So far it seems to be just wining and dining.'

'It's what I like to call the "wadding" of the operation,' he explained. 'We have only three days to convince those around us of our lovely but fictional back story, and we need to be seen. Convince them we are merely mixing business with pleasure.'

'Them?'

'Those that are following us. The Soviets. The Americans. Inevitably.' Benedict reached over to pick up the phone and ordered a second bottle of champagne. 'Spying is a very incestuous game, Ruby – they watch us, we watch them. They try to blackmail us, and so on. You get the picture.'

When he put it like that, the whole set-up seemed little more than a childish pastime. 'Do you like it?' I said. 'I mean, do you actually enjoy it?'

Benedict looked at me as if I had just arrived from an alien land, splaying out his palms at the opulent surroundings. 'Of course.'

'And the danger? Don't spies get bumped off, killed?' They did in the world I had read about.

'Sometimes, but not as much as Mr Fleming would have us believe,' he said. 'Besides, it wouldn't have the same edge without that. You only think about getting away, not getting "bumped off". Otherwise, you couldn't do it.'

'But it's still a reality,' I pushed. I was thinking more about his wife and children than possibly he was – the image of a widowed woman and fatherless children being given the fake news by a real man from the ministry that he'd gone under a big red bus in a freak accident.

'Hmm, yes. But it is just boys playing games,' he said. And I genuinely felt he believed it. That he would go home to the Sussex Downs, retire eventually and write his memoirs under a pseudonym. Though maybe not in such minute detail as was playing out in our bed in that moment.

After the champagne, we slept. I woke in the night and felt for his hand, confused when I followed his arm under the pillow and found his fingers firmly wrapped around the butt of a tiny pistol. So this was the life.

'What comes next?' I said at breakfast – the happy couple in the dining room, dressed to perfection as tourists.

'Now, the stitching,' he said between bites of Gouda. 'Or the stitch-up.'

It necessitated being 'seen' a lot in the early part of that day: at the Anne Frank House, lunch at ornate Café Americain, admiring Van Gogh originals (a thrill for me after my art education with Michael way back when), a short boat trip, and then the resplendent Rijksmuseum to gawp at the Vermeers.

Being so absorbed, I'd almost forgotten about the job in hand, that somewhere in a darkened fifth-floor attic apartment, a grainy black-and-white image of my sipping coffee might be revealing itself on a 10″ by 8″ photograph, to be scrutinised by someone from the CIA or the KGB. I was far too engrossed in the exquisite light and dark of the Dutch masters.

Until Benedict reminded me of the purpose.

'Here, can you put this in your handbag?' he whispered, handing me a small envelope as I sat on a backless bench in the middle of the capacious museum gallery. There was no time to ask, or challenge or to say no, as he floated off to admire another masterpiece in the hush of the room. Instantly, the realisation hit me; that when he'd given me money for a new wardrobe back in London, he had not dictated any style of clothing but only to 'bring a decent-size handbag.'

His question hovered like a sulphurous fog: who was being stitched up now? Was it me, the disposable stooge?

I knew in that exact second I wasn't cut out for a lengthy career in espionage. The fizz of excitement turned to fear, the previous thrill became a sludge of dread, my overworked imagination pictured a man ghosting by with a knife that would slice the handbag from my grasp and exact a swift second move into my ribs, and he would be gone by the time they found me slumped and dying, the blood only oozing into my expensive Dior coat. Like I said, I'd read all the Bond books.

Of course, it wasn't at all like that, but it didn't prevent the terror paralysing me. Benedict, hands casually in his pockets, turned his head no more than an inch and looked at me. Just for a brief second. His pinprick pupils signalled: *stay there.*

And I did. A woman, similarly dressed, sat down beside me. She smiled. She didn't look like a Soviet; immersed in my own literary head I had perhaps expected Fleming's toadish Rosa Klebb, complete with razor-sharp blades in her toecaps. This one was young and pretty, with pale skin and a back-combed sculpting of hair. Lipstick I liked the colour of and might, in any other circumstances, have asked where she bought it.

'I don't suppose you have a mint sweet, do you?' she said in English, with an amalgam of accents.

'No,' I went to say, but stopped myself. It was a code, surely. I looked towards Benedict, whose nod barely registered a millimetre's depth. 'Yes,' I said, opening my bag, whereupon she faked accepting a mint while deftly sliding the envelope out and into the sleeve of her coat, all in one heartbeat. There was not a single tremor in her finger.

'Come on, darling, time to leave,' Benedict said breezily. 'We've a dinner to get to.'

And then, the hit, the adrenalin as I strode away, arm in arm with my husband. Champagne didn't hold a candle to that moment, Martini or tequila shots, and perhaps even substances, had I ever indulged. Even the feel of my first book under my fingers came second best.

I *saw* Benedict then: spying is a drug.

'Is that it?' I snapped in the safety of our room, once Benedict had combed it for 'devices'.

'Yes,' he said calmly. 'What did you expect?'

'Not for you to drop me in it, without warning,' I said with sharp retort. As with the true nature of adrenalin, I had come crashing down, leaving me angry, upset and close to tears – something I did not resort to often. The feeling inside was grinding and nauseating, of being out of my depth. Foolish.

'And if I had? Told you the plan?' he said. 'Would you have felt any happier about it? Surprise keeps us on our toes, Ruby.'

He said it like it was the first rule of spy school, though I didn't believe him for a moment. And yet he was right, in my case. I would have baulked with warning, frozen and fluffed the assignment. Benedict had used me, but I had come willingly, been ready to immerse myself in the glitz and glamour and something to tell my wide-eyed grandchildren: 'What? You were a *spy*, Granny!'

Caught out, again, by my own fiction.

'Actually, I thought you handled it well,' Benedict said. 'Very well.'

And with those words, he led me to believe in my own narrative, bathe in his praise: the dread versus that soaring high. When it came to self-reflection, I was – as ever – a hopelessly slow learner.

I gave myself one last chance to prove that the terror and anxiety were merely first-night nerves, that it would not define me as a liability. I never saw myself as a career agent, but Benedict was right, the life was enticing. And I had something to prove now, plus it was pure gold for research: that old mantra of *write what you know*. I'd written on wartime espionage, why not the Cold War?

Benedict was like Father Christmas doling out parcels when he handed me the next set of plane tickets only a month later. 'Not quite the eye of the storm,' he said, 'but the next best thing.'

West Berlin, he explained, and then East, into the growling belly of the beast. What better place to prove myself?

'Isn't there the matter of a dirty great wall between the two?'

'You forget we are ghosts, Ruby. Government ghosts, and as such we can move through mere bricks and mortar.'

We flew into Berlin Tempelhof under the glare of April sunshine after a shower of rain. I remember staring at the sharp deco lines of the vast airport terminal as we taxied to a halt, sun glancing off the beige sandstone, and thinking that while the Nazis were unquestioningly a bunch of murderous bastards, they had known a thing or two about architecture.

In those days, it was as if every traveller promised to be some sort of celebrity as we descended the steps onto the shiny tarmac, where a few photographers waited for their chance to spy Brigitte Bardot or Audrey Hepburn in Berlin's cosmopolitan citadel. Fortunately, I did look quite the part, having been given carte blanche (a 'brief' in espionage terms) to look very 'it', which meant effectively going wild in Mary Quant's Bazaar on the King's Road with the government's purse, thank you very much. The huge, floppy brim of my white felt hat barely made it through the aircraft doors, and the pop of several flashbulbs startled me behind my white sunglasses the size of dinner plates.

Benedict's instincts were sharp, rapidly pulling down the brim and shuffling me off, rather brusquely. 'There's being seen and then there's exposed, darling,' he muttered as he pushed me into a cab.

We were booked into the Hilton, a large black-and-white chequerboard of a building designed to put West Berlin on the must-have tourist map for the well-to-do, and with an interior plucked straight from the pages of *Vogue*. But it had substance too; the Martinis, as I recall, were especially good.

Our cover, Benedict had told me, was him posing as a small-time director searching for locations in which to place his newest film about the Berlin of 1946, well before the messy politics of the big concrete divide. Where better than East Berlin, with its still crumbling streets of pocked buildings, seeming in places as if the war had barely ended?

'The communist government are desperate for revenue, and as long as the script doesn't touch on the Cold War, they'll be inclined to say yes,' Benedict said with confidence. In reality, there was no script to approve, and this was pitched to the East Germans as a primary scouting mission. Our true purpose touched very much on the frosty relationship between the Soviet-backed East German nation and the British Government. Defection, pure and simple. Someone fairly senior in the East German hierarchy wanted a leg-up over that infamous wall, and we were there to scoop him up.

'All very straightforward,' Benedict assured me. 'Nothing really covert.'

Even now, I'm at a loss as to my own artlessness. I put it down to my growing trust in Benedict, fuelled by the fact that I felt myself to be a little bit in love with him, or the spy in him. Common sense would have shaken me by the shoulders, told me to stand back and look squarely at the situation: he had picked me up in a bar and recruited me to a shady organisation with M in its title, staffed by people with no names. But I was too busy tripping down Berlin's glittering Kurfürstendamm, blinded by neon lights and my own idiocy, to give credence to anything like common sense.

We spent a day being obvious tourists, visiting the Tiergarten and the zoo, cocktails at the Hotel Am Zoo, and gazing at the ugly canker of the wall which had risen up and sliced a city in half less than two years before. Looking at the rough breezeblock, I had to stop myself from laughing. Not that it was so aesthetically hideous (although it most certainly was), but a sort of nervous laughter at the very idea of severing an entire metropolis and its people. Whole families, I knew, had been fractured overnight – the sinister barbed wire rolled out in the dark, early hours of one Sunday morning in August '61, followed swiftly by the concrete and cement. I remembered waking up to the BBC news the next morning and thinking it was a joke; if you'd missed your tram home the night before or had one too many and stayed over at a friend's on Berlin's east side, the entire trajectory of your life changed in an instant. In the blink of an eye. It was that mad – and that serious.

To build a wall seemed audacious at best, but western governments were incensed at the Soviets sticking two stiff fingers up to frivolous, nasty capitalism. The Cold War got evermore glacial, with the Berlin Wall as its concrete manifestation.

It wasn't simply a symbol. The wall was damned difficult to pass through, under or over – thanks to the guards, the bricks and barb, the watchtowers and the dogs, all designed to stop the 'jumpers' stone dead. And people did die – men, women and children, old but mostly young – pushing through this ugly but solid edifice towards a little enclave of freedom in West Berlin.

But as up-and-coming film director Spencer Travis (a name which struck me as far too contrived) and his actress girlfriend Amanda Golden (who dreamed up these people?), we simply walked through the notorious Checkpoint Charlie with our foreign passports. We were met on the East side by our guide cum minder, Gunter, who was to drive us around various locations, sites where Soviet-style reconstruction had not touched the old city yet, and where Spencer Travis would potentially set his film. I was there as an adornment and a distraction for Gunter. Moneypenny to Benedict's Bond. Again. I was advised to giggle a lot. I would have words with 'Spencer' later, I decided.

Gunter was nice enough, in his twenties, dressed in a badly cut suit, and grateful for the western cigarettes that Benedict offered him, casually suggesting he keep the packet. 'Die hard communist or not, they all appreciate a good smoke,' he'd told me over breakfast at the hotel. 'It's the currency.'

He failed to apprise me of the fact that Gunter was 'one of us' – a paid-up member of the capitalist classes. Or at least, the money he received for his betrayal bought more food for his East German family than loyalty to any cause. I didn't know that Gunter would drive us to an abandoned factory, where we would secrete the defector in the boot of our large Mercedes and make a switch to a second car before trundling through Checkpoint Charlie. All in a day's work.

I did gather, fairly quickly, that we had a tail, courtesy of the infamous Stasi, the gold standard of secret police – another of the 'tit-for-tat' elements to regular spying that Benedict casually alluded to. Except no one would ever describe the Stasi as being casual. The black Mercedes following us three cars behind was like an ominous raven pecking at our backside.

Gunter was on it, though, and with a deft slice through a line of comical Trabant cars he ditched the tail, and we circled around Berlin, alighted at various points and duly played at scouting, watching for the Raven's reappearance. Taking pictures, we had been told, was not permitted, and Benedict had briefed me to notice anything I could, schooled me into a simple memory game of slotting one image into a box in my brain and moving on to the next detail.

After two hours, Gunter steered us towards an abandoned factory that, in truth, would have made a perfect backdrop for war-torn Berlin. It was vacuous and eerie, the debris crunching under my kitten heels. Out of the relative gloom (and straight out of a spy movie of later years) stepped a plump, sweaty man in a brown suit, whose look of gratitude was matched only by his apparent terror. He could have been an accountant or a nuclear physicist, but on that day he was simply a defector. And a very frightened one at that.

He said little, apart from mumbling his name to Benedict, and some sort of password. Gunter arrived back from checking the perimeter and pronounced it clear, at which the plump man willingly rolled himself into the boot with a squeak of the suspension, and I noted that the back tyres depressed at least an inch.

Two streets from the checkpoint back into West Berlin, we drove into a large garage and the door closed behind us, plunging us all into near darkness inside the car. Adrenalin was nullified by fear and the bile rose in me then: confined spaces, the potential for a dangerous double bluff, Gunter turning around with a slim, silenced gun in his hand. Dim girlfriend or not, I wouldn't be spared, despite the friendly banter we had traded through the day. I definitely did not visualise a career in spying then. Sweat was seeping into my black-and-white shift dress and I could smell my own terror.

We'd drawn up alongside another, almost identical, car with the boot already open. Benedict signalled we get out – I took comfort from his expression, absorbed in the task rather than panicked. Defector man rolled himself out of one car, with no words but several grunts and groans, and into the other, though I noted this time the tyres had more resilience. We said a hasty farewell to Gunter and got in the second car. I chanced a large breath, in case it would be my last.

As we rolled up to the checkpoint, Benedict calmly put a hand on my knee to quell the uncontrollable shaking moving through my body, as the East German guards circled us to measure the height of the tyres, always on the hunt for evidence of escapees.

'Spencer' turned and beamed at me, the perfect expression of a successful man in love with his chic girlfriend. Like a ventriloquist, he sidled out reassurance: 'Reinforced axle.'

As romantic discourse, it wasn't *Gone with the Wind,* but enough to stop me pissing my lacy pants with fear. We were waved through the checkpoint and hit West Berlin at speed – I felt even Benedict relax a little beside me. Depositing defector man in a residential area to the north, we headed back to the Hilton.

After a bath, we made frantic, furious love, undoubtedly a huge release for both of us, though for different reasons: he as a 'downer' to the buzz he so loved, me as a way of reassuring myself (and thanking every deity I could muster) that I was still alive. It was also my swansong, convinced I would not be doing this again. As we lay in the afterglow, ordering room service, the film noir played out a little longer. Benedict didn't ask and I didn't tell, but with his consummate reading of me, I think he knew it was the end of my spying days. And us too.

I woke to find the bed empty, and for a minute I briefly panicked that he'd upped and left on sensing the finale, and I deflated at being a mere pawn. A commodity. But the note on the pillow said differently: *Meet me in the bar. Dying for a margarita.*

I dressed with a bounteous sense of relief. One for the road.

The bar was only half full, but with a rich tapestry of chatter against a gentle tinkle of jazz, and I scanned for Benedict's familiar, solid presence. But he was nowhere. I told myself he'd gone to the bathroom and ordered two margaritas. Minutes later, he emerged from the direction of the gents and I promptly raised a hand and a smile, then dropped both rapidly on seeing his face. It was that millimetre again, the fall of his lashes, and a faint ripple to the line of his mouth which, unwittingly, I'd begun to read as Something Not Right. The two men either side of him confirmed my suspicions, suited in black, determined, trying too hard to look friendly. I could see only one side of him, but the kink of Benedict's body told me the flip side had a gun barrel pressed firmly into his flesh. Or at least the threat of it.

And his eyes – in one blink they wrote chapters of regret and sorrow and foolishness and dread. I'd never witnessed those elements in Benedict before, but each was so firmly embedded in my own being that recognition came easily.

The trio swept out through the doors of the Hilton bar in trendy West Berlin. After ten seconds, I leaped up and followed, witnessing from the balcony his bending into the back of a car at the entrance. Mercedes. Black. The Raven.

I never saw Benedict Aloysius Dalybridge again. And, to my knowledge, nor has anyone else.

Defected, the British side later claimed. Their explanation tended towards him as a double agent orchestrating a clever bluff: Benedict's help in the escape of an East German proved a convincing cover for his own betrayal as a Soviet man on the inside.

I learned as much when a thin, weasel of a man from the Establishment called on me at home a week later, volunteering neither a greeting nor a name. 'A shame really – he was one of our best,' he lamented, though badly. 'Still, I daresay he'll be treated like some sort of hero in Moscow. They'll give him a decent apartment, vodka for life and a medal from the Motherland.'

Even if he'd been a better liar, I still wouldn't have swallowed it. Two reasons: for all his philandering and zeal for the chase, Benedict loved his family. His murmurings in the hallway over the phone to his wife told me that. On that score, I had no illusions. Secondly, that ruddy hat he so proudly sported – emulating the iconic image of a Soviet premier like Nikita Khrushchev, by wearing a sleeping cat on your head on the streets of London, is not double-bluffing. In Benedict's world, it was mockery of epic proportions. Spy or not, I did know that about him. He was true to the British cause.

The suited weasel thrust a piece of paper in front of me and urged me, with very little attempt at hiding the threat, to sign the Official Secrets Act. I did, though it was a signature markedly different to my own, and one that could never be traced back to me. Lesson number two, as I recall, from the Benedict Dalybridge School of Spying.

Signing of the document was a moot point, since I'd already been to see his wife in deepest Sussex and revealed all to her. The Weasel & Co. had pre-empted my visit, feeding her a triple lie of Benedict's disappearance, of his double life and the defection, and no doubt oozing false sympathy over his cruel abandonment of her and the children. Had there been a body, I'm certain they would have happily used the man-from-the-ministry-under-a-bus story.

Following their spurious visit, I put her right – that Benedict was no double agent – while coming clean about us too. She was remarkably forgiving about that side of it, and it was no surprise to her, clearly. She was grateful for the truth. I told her about his face, and that last look.

'Benedict could be a shit at times, but I *know* he wouldn't leave us forever,' she said between gulps of brandy and gazing at her children playing innocently alongside. 'Not willingly.'

I was certain of it too. And we both knew he was dead. Or as good as. Neither of us lingered over an unspoken image of him in a Stasi prison, his body or mind being bent out of all proportion. He was gone, that was the point.

Fleming was right, and Le Carré after him. It is a dangerous game, and spies do die, between the high life and the champagne.

And that's why I bid a concerted farewell to the shady world of espionage, and returned to the only talent I possessed: writing what you know.

MAN SIX: Ludo

England, 1968

The Sixties, mercifully, became warmer, and in more ways than one. Britain, and London especially, felt like the world's central pivot, and as a young, free and single woman it was an experience to behold: music, money, drugs and the unending summer of love made it a perpetual carousel of bright colours and candy floss. Or so I'm told.

I was free and single, but not-so-young, causing the psychedelic colours to bleach a little, though there's nothing to say you can't have a second crack at youth. Let's just say I had a damn good try.

I was in my mid-thirties as the swinging section of the Sixties took hold. Had I been born a decade later it would have been 'my time' undoubtedly – the pace, the fervour, the kaleidoscope of creativity oozing from every scene. Each time you blinked, it was like the shutter on a camera capturing an image that could have been placed in a million glossy magazines, art to emerge from nothing, music bleeding from anyone who ever picked up a guitar.

I'd stayed in London for a year or so after writing the spy novel; my working title had been 'Ice Spy', though my publishers merely laughed at that, and it came out eventually as *The Freeze*. It was well received, though a few reviewers saw fit to point out I was no Le Carré (I'd never pretended to be). That said, *The Freeze* was the first of my books to break out of the 'women's' section of the shelves, and in those days that was like finding gold for any female writer. Mushens finally deigned to cross the Atlantic the year before, on the way to Germany and that ill-fated air show, having fallen head over heels in love with an acrobatic pilot, of all people. And although we were ignorant of her days being severely numbered, we partied like they were, and she pronounced London to be 'swinging higher than New York, darling'. As she left to rendezvous with her flying ace of a lover, I wondered then if I'd lost her to love, and I suppose I had, in a way. My world was always slightly less twinkly after Mushens left it.

Sometime in 1966, there was a brief sojourn in Paris, trying to dig out material for a new novel. London was a circus, but the French capital – with its chic streets and political edginess – would be different enough to inspire, I told myself. Viewing it as a pilgrimage of sorts, I pounded the ornate flagstones, sat in cafés and went to endless showings of French noir films, where I understood neither the language nor the sentiment. Disappointingly, brilliance did not ooze from the so-say City of Light, or stimuli rise up from its pavement pores.

Worse still, Paris only reminded me of two things: my tendency to drink too much, and how poor my attempts at French were. Combined, my diction became frankly diabolical when drunk. Much like the well-timed epiphany several years previously, I woke up one morning and wondered why on earth I was there, since it was possible to get good Italian coffee back in Soho and passable croissants too. Why stay?

I was British, and as such, something to be admired. We had it all: the World Cup, home-grown musicians that were the envy of the world, and we hadn't – as yet – assassinated anyone important on British soil. Clearly, London was the place to be, to scour and absorb. Paris was so passé.

The London suburbs, however, were not a hot bed of 'now', being static in their rose-pruning pastimes. Besides, my father was enjoying a blissful marital state with a new wife and wouldn't have welcomed a lodger, daughter or not. I'd given up my Camden flat, rendering myself temporarily homeless, so I coupled with some old contacts and tail-ended on their generosity, before picking up some magazine work and renting myself a tiny bedsit in Kilburn, near enough to the centre of the world. And with my talent for cadging and slipping between the cracks of conformity, I dived into swinging London.

Approaching forty didn't seem to register at the time, and I shamelessly played down my age, lucky enough that I had never smoked regularly, and so not inherited my mother's roadmap of life upon my face. I had no right to expect it, but good fortune had smiled on my body too, leaving it toned enough to maintain the façade; I could still carry a Quant minidress, though perhaps not too skimpy on the arms. On a good day, hair and make-up carefully arranged, I might pass as mid to late twenties (apparently not considered ancient). In a dark, smoky club where most of the patrons were either drunk or stoned, possibly the early twenties. And they were very often both.

It was among that scene that I met Ludo. He was only mildly high at the time: 'on the next-door planet', he later said, as opposed to 'somewhere in another galaxy'. I'd talked my way into a party in Soho as the friend of the girl on the reception desk, who I knew vaguely as Tina. It was optimum conditions for camouflage, dark and consistently opaque with illicit fumes, against mandarin, psychedelic lighting that settled on everyone's face for no more than a second. Perfect cover.

He joined me at the bar, ordered a strange concoction of alcohol, also a shade of orange, and pushed it towards me. 'I'm a record producer,' he shouted in my ear over the strains of the Yardbirds.

Oh yeah, and I'm Mary Quant's muse. Being the queen of charades myself, I thought he could easily be a window cleaner in good clothes and a Sergeant Pepper moustache. No one could match me at that game, but maybe I should have had more faith.

'Come and meet someone,' he said, pulling me by the hand to a couple huddled to the side, a man talking intently to a woman with long black hair splayed like a tepee about her shoulders.

'This is John,' he said, and John tipped up his chin as if he couldn't give a shit but acknowledged me all the same, perhaps as a favour. I already knew John. Of John. Lennon. That John. Conversing with Yoko. In the opposite corner, Ringo was dancing amid a cluster of groupies. It was that type of party.

Ludo smiled and shrugged as he turned away. 'They're good guys, if you can keep up with their bloody genius.'

Ludo Lindvist may have had the aura of the working-class made good, but he was smack bang in the middle of that 'scene' – for real. He knew everyone, and they knew him. He had his own groups to produce, boy bands mostly, with moderate chart success and a stab at the big American market. But for a music man, he was oddly philosophical too.

'There's no point aiming for anything like the Beatles – they come along only once in a blue moon, and we all missed the boat. It's a mug's game if you try and chase that, so you have to content yourself with the next best thing. If you're lucky.' He had a nice life, he said, but knew it all might go up in a puff of smoke one day. 'Live it while you can, isn't that right, Ruby?'

I nodded. I thought I'd met my soulmate a second time around.

We ended up that night at his apparently 'small' flat in Highgate, roughly eight times the size of mine and possibly furnished by Terence Conran. I felt lost in his vast expanse of a bed, and we decamped to the long Afghan rug opposite the mock fireplace, swapping champagne in favour of tea, toast and giggles. I found him funny and genuine, and he didn't seem to mind when the morning came and the cruel glare showed up the real me. Or he simply didn't show it. He was twenty-nine, he told me in passing, but stopped short of asking my age. I think it was a form of working-class chivalry.

The bookshelves surrounding us were full and the volumes well-thumbed, seemingly by Ludo, and after careful consideration I revealed what felt like my past life as a writer – a good three years since my last submission and no stock in my word bank. He crunched the numbers silently, calculating I had not been a child prodigy with a debut novel at age ten. Even then, he didn't seem to care, or run like the wind. I didn't mind that he made love like an innocent. In fact, I rather liked it. He was neither Enzo nor Benedict between the sheets and I didn't want him to be.

The summer of '67 went by in a haze. In part, the consequence of a steady supply of weed, though nothing stronger on my part. I was old-school and alcohol had always been my crutch. Truth being, I was scared stiff of powder or pills, of any colour, having seen too many reeling with excesses, washed out and wizened in the cold light of day. That purple vapour of loveliness seemed a façade, and I knew all about those. Ludo indulged at times, though I never witnessed any excess. He was serious about his music, and he got up for work each day, frequently infuriated by his fledglings who were living life to the fullest on studio time.

'You can be a genius and a dick,' he sometimes railed, 'but you can't just be a dick. Half of these kids look the part but they don't know one end of a guitar from the other.'

I liked Ludo's lifestyle, his contacts, his party invites and the people he hung around with; Marianne Faithful and I struck up something of a bond, largely glued by alcohol, but we shared a few wild nights as a raucous twosome. But what I liked – loved – more than anything, was Ludo's candid take on the dream; the haze was just that, he told me, lying on our fluffy rug with tea in hand.

'It will pop, the walls of our flimsy kingdom will fall away, and we will move on, Ruby. Maybe together, maybe not. But John has it right – it's all just "Lucy in the Sky with Diamonds".'

'So, go on then, what's your real name?' I ventured, judging he was in the mood for truth and all its warts. 'It sure as hell isn't Ludo.'

'And why wouldn't it be?'

'Because you talk like David Bailey, and you clearly didn't go to public school.'

'Fair point. It's Leonard. Clutterbuck.' He drew on his cigarette. 'Does that make me less hip? Or attractive?'

'No, but I like Ludo better. Lindvist definitely. You don't seem like a Leonard to me, and certainly not a Clutterbuck. The real question is, were you a window cleaner?'

'A builder – a brickie actually,' he said plainly, at which point I awarded myself an internal cheer of triumph. 'I can run you up a nice garden wall while I'm spinning a top ten disc. See what a bloody farce it is?'

He looked at me then. So hard. He scrutinised my encroaching lines, the weather of my life, as if thumbing my history like the books on his shelves. I held his stare but I wondered what on earth he was looking for. If he could see into my truth. And whether he would like me still.

'So, are you a Ruby for real?' he said at last.

'One hundred per cent genuine,' I said without hesitation.

I wasn't lying. But who the hell was I kidding?

We floated into 1968. Compared to '67, it was like the morning after the night before. With his well-honed man-on-the-street philosophy, Ludo wasn't wrong. In hindsight, people imagine the fantasy of the Sixties ended in the last year of the decade, as the Fab Four became a warring clan and set fire to their own castle. But it started much earlier for the rest of us, those still in that circle. John, Paul, George and Ringo took themselves off to meditate in India in early '68, and left the party nursing the bottom of the bottle and feeling distinctly bilious. And weary. The Vietnam War chugged on, played out in horrifying reality thousands of miles away, muted in our consciousness and on the front pages. Nearer to home, the promise of a political bloom in Czechoslovakia's Prague Spring was never allowed to flower by the Soviets. Martin Luther King was lost to hatred, and Robert Kennedy followed his brother into the family mausoleum. Where was all the love then?

'We need to get away,' Ludo announced in late June. 'I'm sick of London and its fakery. Do you want to come, Rubes?'

Untethered and largely unemployed, save for a few journal commissions, of course I said yes. When had I ever not followed my heart, or the very moment?

Into deepest Gloucestershire we went. Landsmere Manor, at my first glance, was something that dreams and Regency novels are made of, the sort of house that wealthy gentlemen inherit and their wives maintain with a legion of servants, all climbing ivy and stone porticos, to which horse-drawn carriages – or in our case, a polka-dot Mini – could sweep between with a spit of the gravel. The wealthy gentleman owner in this case had lost his fortune on a joint venture of slow racehorses plus a decent drug addiction. He was, by necessity, renting it out to a friend of Ludo's called Marlin (did anyone have real names back then?), a music impresario who was also doing his best to inhale his bank account up his nostrils. Luckily, Marlin seemed to have three girlfriends to steer him along the straight and narrow, who industriously kept him 'busy' and away from the limitless brown and white powder as much as they could, or dared.

Since the manor had fourteen bedrooms in total, three large living rooms, a huge kitchen and a swimming pool, there were people coming and going through what felt like an infinite summer, some of whom Marlin seemed not to know at all.

'Are they *all* his friends?' I mused to Ludo, as we whiled away another day on the poolside. The sun was high in a seamless blue sky, our lemonade already tepid and the bees sluggish in their pursuits.

'Hmm, maybe he met them once or twice, said to them in passing to come down, and they jumped at a spot of freeloading.'

'Is that what we're doing? Freeloading?'

'Possibly,' Ludo said unashamedly. 'I mean, we're buying some of the food and booze, but Marlin foots the bill for everything else.' He meant the poor housekeeper who came in daily and fought with the kitchen overload, and the gardener who weeded out cigarette butts from the flowerbeds, very tentatively since the day he chanced upon a couple practising free love at the back of the summerhouse. And the drugs, of course, brought from London each weekend by a man alternately known as Billy or Jimmy. He was the same man, as far as I could tell, who shaved his moustache every other week. Once, I peered closely to see if it was fake; he narrowed his eyes and, I swear, growled at me under his piquant breath.

'Do we feel bad about that? Taking advantage of Marlin?' I pressed on.

Ludo turned lazily onto his back. 'No,' he said. 'He has far too much money, and besides, I lent him his first thousand to set up his business. He's never paid me back, so I think we're even.'

July sizzled on, the housekeeper left in a huff, taking the gardener with her, and yet Ludo seemed in no hurry to depart. The flighty hangers-on turned up less and less, and really, it sort of morphed towards commune life. Marlin's babysitters, Juno, Livvy and April – who I thought of either as a young version of the Three Fates, or the Destiny Angels from *Captain Scarlet* – turned their attention to the garden, and I took up a post in the kitchen, surprising myself at what I could turn out, and that the ceremonial burning of all food had not been genetically inherited from my mother. Surprised also that I enjoyed it, having a purpose, to feed and nourish. At some point, we were joined by a young couple who arrived in a clapped-out Transit van and never left. Willow and Gareth had no money, were not musicians but offered up far more transferable skills, having lived on a commune in the Outer Hebrides. They soon knocked us into shape and, amazingly, we became largely self-sufficient.

Ludo, for his part, kept us amused with music, like some sort of minstrel plucking strings for his dinner. Aside from the odd joint, which in the Sixties was tantamount to breathing, I wasn't 'on' drugs, though it did feel like it at times, as if the world was blowing heavily scented smoke into the foliage and no one would be fazed if the Queen of Hearts or the Yellow Submarine sallied forth and joined the party.

Ludo and I didn't talk of the future, beyond what the evening's dinner might consist of. We had long, meandering conversations about life in endless, lazy hours, but anything that felt like reality was restricted to the hypothetical, and floated away on a cloud into the distance, until the next one came along, a little like London buses.

I was content. 'Happy' was a different dimension; the bliss I'd known with Enzo was another hypothetical and so never considered. But I still liked Ludo, laughed at his unique take on life. Beyond next year, who knew whether we would survive? In that moment, we were good together.

And then two things happened, in unison, to make our happy little land cloud over, and our sun retreat. Ludo joined Marlin in his passion for recreational powders, and me… well, I got with child.

Ludo plunged first into his new world, egged on by Marlin.

'It was just one night,' Ludo insisted the day after, working off the night before by lying poolside. 'It was his birthday – how could I refuse?'

'Every day is Marlin's birthday, it seems,' I grumbled, hating myself for sounding like an old harridan. Or a wife. Still, opiates and the like were a big step up in my book – or down, in Ludo's case.

'Chill out, Ruby – I can handle it. What's for dinner? I'm starving.'

Marlin found something else to celebrate several days later, and then the day after that. Each time, Ludo dropped unconscious into our bed in the early hours like a sack of potatoes, or didn't come to bed at all. More and more, he looked like he'd constructed the Great Wall of China as a solo effort, brick by brick, a sallow, lime dust coating to his skin, ribs pushing out of his chest. Of course, I prodded gently at what suddenly felt like a 'habit', and he sniped back in denial. As addicts do.

I knew the dream was over, but I thought – in my lifelong vanity or stupidity – that I could save Ludo. He wasn't the love of my life, or even a fixture in my vague vision of a future, yet I liked him. Underneath the veneer of substances, he was one of the good ones. But Ludo's increased sneering, in between bouts of oblivion, meant he had a new idol to worship. Eventually, I made some phone calls and fixed up a few tentative commissions for literary magazines. At the very least I could do some temping back in London until the next Bright Idea came crashing into my life. I would leave the Gloucestershire Shangri-La and put it down to experience. In that, I'd had plenty of practice.

Pre-occupied as I was, I hadn't noticed the subtle changes in myself. It fell to April, as one of the Destiny Angels, to point these out. Turns out her real name was Betty and her mother was a midwife.

'Your breasts are getting a little bigger, if you don't mind me saying,' she said casually over the kitchen table as we kneaded the day's bread.

Having never been very well endowed, I wasn't displeased, although I had noticed it went in line with a slight thickening around my waist. 'Too much good food and not enough exercise,' I brushed it off. 'I need to lie around less.'

'Oh okay, it's only that…'

'Yes?'

'I mean have you had your… Are you regular?'

She had the nose, clearly. I don't know if it's a thing passed down from midwives to their daughters, but April pretty much *smelled* something awry.

'Well, no, not very regular, and just being here, Ludo maybe, it's sent me off kilter, I suppose.'

She looked at me from under her blonde fringe and said nothing. But her expression alone set me thinking: no, I hadn't bled for… how long…? Three months. The mere thought sent me scurrying to the local doctor.

There was no purple haze dense enough, and no joint sufficiently strong, to match the flotation as I walked out of the surgery several days later. The result of peeing in a pot was shock, delight, fear, horror and amazement.

A child. In me. Fuck. How did that happen? Yes, I knew *how*, but why? In my mind, I'd said farewell to that particular life, principally after Enzo. I'd reconciled myself, quite easily as it happens. I could barely ground my own life, so how would I manage with a small human in tow?

Had I taken precautions? Not really. Since it had never happened, I thought it never would. My eggs just weren't for courting, clearly. Occasionally, my bed partners would use their own clumsy, outmoded form of insurance and I went along with it. Ludo did at first, and then became more casual and then downright lax. After the drugs, he could barely manage the entire act. And yes, in the limited time when he wasn't pursuing Lucy in the Sky I did want him, lust for him, his touch and his company as the Ludo I once knew. I loved the old parts of him.

The doctor thought I was three to four months gone. There was no legal alternative, and though I'd never been a slave to rules, it didn't actually cross my mind to seek out that choice. Mother Earth I was not, but if this tenacious being had moved heaven and earth to burrow inside of me, it deserved a chance. He or she.

I was having a baby. Jesus. I'd have to live with it. Forever, or as good as. The only semi-permanent thing in my life thus far had been my typewriter and a rent book, and both of those were disposable.

April came through, as did my other Destiny Angels, in caring for me, feeding and releasing me from the heavier work in the garden. They'd long since abandoned Marlin to his new best friend, the insidious opiate, and we women – along with the Outer Hebridean Gareth – ran the place as best we could. By some bizarre coincidence, April's midwife mother lived only ten miles away and visited her daughter, by way of reassuring me too. She paddled my small bump and pronounced it 'perfect', gave me a rough date based on a good deal of guesswork around the conception and talked to me about homebirth.

I'd never been afraid of much in my life, but to this day, hospitals terrify me, since having my tonsils unceremoniously removed at the age of eight. The ogre of a consultant had poked what felt like a baton of hot nails down my throat just a day after surgery. I hid under the bed and never went back again. Nice, comfy cottage hospital or not, I would not be stepping foot inside any National Health facility to be prodded by doctor or instrument.

Besides, we had Willow. She was Gareth's other half (he'd shrugged off his given name of Jupiter, since he looked every inch a 'Gareth'), and a high priestess of birth: pigs, sheep, dogs, cats and, thankfully, humans too. Chanting aside, she knew what she was doing. And if there was enough time, April's mother – midwife Ivy – would make it too. That was the plan, as much as we had one. As to the bit afterwards, the life with a baby, that was still Lucy in the Sky.

So, to Ludo. It was at least a week before the haze cleared enough for me to reveal my news and subsequent plight. He took it remarkably well, though I think his brain was on the way to being permanently addled; he tended to look at me as if we were both underwater and our conversation a series of bubbles to be pricked at and read like a cartoon.

His response to the news was slow and considered. 'So... so you'll have it?' he asked.

If women of today are appalled by his fairly heartless reaction, the reference to a living being inside me as 'it', then be assured it was a fairly common question for the time. He was no worse than any other man faced with a child he hadn't planned and a tethered life ahead of him. For all of our pretence in casting off the shackles of a restrained society and preaching a subtle form of anarchy and free love, illegitimate children were still branded as bastards. Commune or not, our child would push forth into the world as one.

Ludo, love him, made reparations with his next sentence. 'Do you want us to get married?'

'No, thanks,' I said plainly, though I hoped it didn't sound cruel. In my own mind, I was already living on a raft in a sea of sharks, unsettled to put it mildly, but it was the one destiny I felt certain of. A marriage certificate might satisfy the world, but it would not offer succour to my child. At worst, I would be the one swaddled and suffocated. I had no intention of casting Ludo aside at that point, but neither did I have visions of us cradling our baby and growing old by the fireside.

Winter was approaching, and we drew inwards to the house, living off the jars of pickled fruit and vegetables and whatever credit Marlin was still good for in the local village shop. He hardly ever made an appearance then, holed up in his stinking room, either unconscious or throwing shoes at the Destinies if they dared to offer him nourishing food or – worse still – suggest he take a bath. Gradually, Marlin became like Mrs Rochester in the attic of *Jane Eyre*, us shrugging off the intermittent banging from inside his room as if it was just the old house 'settling'. Quite where he got his drugs from at that point was a mystery, though not so much when I spotted Jimmy or Billy skulking around the grounds and hopping back over a fence in the twilight.

The baby, as far as we could work out, would be due in late February, and for a time Ludo and I played at being prospective parents. He cleaned up largely, confining himself properly for three days at the top of the house with only food, water and a vomit bowl. Cold turkey was noisy and painful but effective, and I loved him for doing it – for us. He emerged positive and seemed to be looking forward to the baby. Once or twice, we did lie by a glowing fire, he circling his hands over my bare belly and humming 'Hey Jude' into my burgeoning skin.

'Best fucking song ever written,' he said with a note of sorrow, as if all music should have ceased from then on, that there was no point anymore; all songsters should put down their pens and hang up their guitars, the endgame having been reached. We stopped short of talking about any kind of long-term future, even as a threesome, though we both knew Landsmere Manor would not go on forever. Marlin would either succumb to his excesses, or the bailiffs would arrive, but that's as far as our joint foresight stretched.

Meanwhile, I had begun to nest, way before those pregnancy books say new mothers ought to be sorting and sewing baby clothes, and busying themselves with the layette. Lucky for me, Destiny Juno was a dab hand with a needle and thread. I feathered my own nest with words; ideas and sentences that sprung from me like a wayward firecracker on Guy Fawkes, almost the instant I became aware of the person rolling somersaults within. Nothing would be suppressed, so that I retreated to a bedroom at one end of the vast upstairs corridor, hot water bottle and flask in tow, and typed through the night at times, the baby pounding away in a rhythm to my key-tapping, before it was lulled to sleep as exhaustion flooded and my typing slowed. April would find me in the morning, snoring gently with the imprint of the keys on my cheek, and I thought back to the last time that had happened, in the days when I killed off my virginal relationship with Michael with pure ambition. So many words and plenty of sacrifice under the bridge since then. This, though, was different. This was for my baby. Me and him. Me and her.

Me, Ludo and him/her?

Pregnancy galvanised me. Far from feeling like an over-packed suitcase with more knickers to squeeze in, I wore my bump as if it was already a living, breathing person fastened to me with a fleshy sheath, like pictures of African women, or real hippies on the American trail swaddling their babies close. It helped that kaftans and ponchos were in vogue, my beloved Quants becoming a tad tight all too quickly, though as Ludo so sensitively put it, my figure was still lean. 'You're just Ruby who swallowed a football,' he laughed.

I palmed, patted and stroked at my increasingly taut belly, my heart flipping as a limb kicked out, delight overriding the genuine discomfort. I revelled in it, and for the second time in my life, I'd found something that equalled – no, *surpassed* – the birth of a book. This was something I'd created, with a 'little help from my friends' as Ludo would often croon at me. This, though, would never sit on a shelf accruing reviews or dust. He or she would go on to create more in this world, maybe even a book of their own. How proud would that make me? With or without the pharmaceuticals, it blew my mind. Nothing else required, Mr Lennon.

Having ditched the serious drugs, Ludo took himself to London to breathe some life into his neglected career.

'We'll need more than my flat,' he reasoned. 'My mum had my youngest brother when I was fourteen, and my God, Rubes, they take up some space.'

In the meantime, I settled into a routine. I was up with the lark, cooking, potting and nesting until midday, followed by a brief nap (Willow's orders) and then a five-hour stint at my typewriter, sometimes with my machine piled high on books so I could stand when the squidling went truly wild. *Definitely a writer in the making,* I thought.

What were these words about? A woman, of course, with

child, unexpectedly. A fish out of water. The story of my thinly veiled life. Again. Transported somewhere else in the world, but the location barely mattered, because my world on the page then was limited to a baby-sized egg of flesh, and the smaller dimensions of my brain, which on occasion turned to maternal mush.

There was no question we needed the money, but I honestly didn't care if it sold or not. It was about committing this experience to memory in the form of words and chapters, a love letter to him or her.

I had truly intended to write the book's end before the arrival, or so I told myself. It was all there in my head, though secretly I felt too afraid of that time to lay it down on paper. Like every mere mortal, I harboured silly superstitions. I couldn't commit in ink until the real truth was known. But I knew how it played out, the way it would come right in my own perfect, literary world. I could wait.

The bump had other ideas. April, the secret sleuth of a midwife, detected it first.

'You all right, Ruby?' she said after dinner one evening. 'You look very uncomfortable.'

I stopped washing the soup pot and thought. Yes, I was, and had been for hours. But so much of the past week had been achy, with the baby rolling its displeasure at times, that a hand rubbing at my aching torso had become automatic. I could no longer distinguish between pain and the pleasure of my baby's movements.

'I've got two weeks to go yet,' I said dismissively, at which April rolled her eyes in a sage-like way, no doubt recalling the nights when her mother had been called out to a woman labouring at thirty-eight weeks. As I was then.

'I'll get Willow,' she said.

Willow's wild, long-haired look was all Madame-Giselle-with-her-crystal-ball, but even she couldn't be certain just by palming my bump for signs. 'It might be days or weeks, although you are tightening when I touch.' She tapped a finger on my egg shell to prove it. The baby booted its displeasure.

Should I call Ludo? He'd agreed he wanted to be with me, right by my side, though I suspected he was more influenced by Willow's earthy expectation rather than his real desire. In her commune world, men were engrossed in the entire journey, all hours and days of it. In Ludo's experience, his father had been down the pub with a pint of ale at all seven of his siblings' births. Despite his obvious intellect, and the hype of peace, love and equality, Ludo was still an East End brickie at heart.

Snow was thick on the ground and the driveway to Landsmere under a three-foot blanket, but I chose not to call him then. Gareth said he would get on clearing the path, just in case. My night was fitful, tossing and turning to get comfortable, and included a firm conversation with my beloved child at three a.m. to either 'get on with it, or calm down'. We both gave up the fight around four and agreed a ceasefire of sleep.

My internal alarm call went at precisely 8.21, when I unceremoniously wet myself. Or we did. There was a belter of a kick from inside, followed only half a second later by a rush of wet fluid and the egg deflated enough for me to scrabble upwards into the hallway, a bundled-up sheet between my legs. 'April! WILLOW!'

Even with the weather, and his Mini skidding like a go-kart on the iced-up roads, Ludo arrived in plenty of time. Both April's mother and Willow had warned me first babies take time, and so it was. The day was long and tiring, with Willow's forced route-marching around the grounds and snatches of sleep, pains and blowing, being force-fed soup and retching it up ten minutes later. Willow sat on the sidelines, nodding and knitting, joined at one point by April's mother, who popped in 'unofficially' and pulled out her knitting too. No doubt worlds apart on the midwifery spectrum, they nonetheless concurred everything was 'going fine'. Oddly, I remember a very involved conversation between them over the benefits of seed stitch and casting on, after which Ivy left.

I wasn't so sure about 'fine'. It hurt. One minute, a fiery demon had invaded my insides to burn for all of eternity, and the next, nothing. With intervals at first, then closer and closer, then the measured breathing, panic breathing, the huffing. April and sometimes Ludo on hand to rub at my back that was surely tethered to a torturer's rack, to my bellows of 'Harder... DO IT HARDER!'

Willow stoked the fire, spooned me honey tea, occasionally put a cool hand on my blazing belly. She never broke a sweat. She floated like a tiny, orbiting planet around my scorching sun, occasionally settling to lightly click at her needles.

Somewhere in those meandering hours, Ludo clutched at my hand, trying to think of the best thing to say, which amounted to 'I love you, Ruby D', but all I could see were his demonic dilated pupils and smell his pungent, weedy breath.

Willow finished a row and put down her needles when it was time. She broke her orbit and came near as I groaned and moaned, and then out of the blue emerged a moo. Deep, concerted. The word 'bovine' tottered around my crazy writer's brain.

'Willow, I neeeed to… eeeuurggh… PUUSH!'

'And so you are,' she said calmly.

I wasn't party to the sight at the other end, but I felt every millimetre, every sinew of stretch, every nudge into true life. And I loved and hated it in equal measure. I felt stoned, acutely sober, like a million dollars and a beggar scratching for succour, all in ninety seconds of one push, but which lasted so much more in my mind. At her end, Willow hummed and ummed her satisfaction, with April pushing back my sweat-soaked hair from my forehead, telling me I was a superwoman. I wanted to kiss her and hit her, but I was too bloody busy to do either. Ludo loitered somewhere in the hinterland, looking pained.

At some point I looked up and saw midwife Ivy sidle into the room again and sit quietly, calmly taking out her knitting. She dipped her head towards me in a tiny, cursory nod and smiled. *Well, she's not worried,* I thought. That, and the cocoon of love and care I currently kneeled within, gave me the impetus to get on with the job.

That last effort, the second when I hovered in the antechamber of motherhood, was the hardest. I heard life, a squeak, and Willow told me in her hushed, hippy tones that the baby's head was born, but to rest and gather my energy, wait for it to brew, that it would only be one more. I was suddenly terrified, of it happening for real. Too late in retrospect to have thought such things, but my mother's dying confession came back to haunt me in full surround sound, word for word: how she hadn't known how to love me, dared not trust her instinct. Couldn't give herself. Would I be like that? Some old crone of a mother with wizened emotions, a working woman with no time for her child. It was all possible, but was it inevitable?

No time to analyse; my body brewed all right, a cacophonous, volatile and vocal surge coming at me from inside and forging my child into the world, oblivious to my – frankly very late – objections. The sensation as he slid from me is unequalled to this day: elation, relief, strength, might and potent power shot through me like lightning as his first bleat hit the hot, still air.

'He is gorgeous, isn't he?' I murmured to Ludo as we both lay near naked in front of the fire, our birthday-suit boy sprawled across my chest, one tiny hand pumping at my breast, having had his milky fill. The question was rhetorical. Of course he was beautiful.

'Hey, Jude,' Ludo said, stroking at the dark kiss-curl at his tiny crown. He hummed the first few bars of McCartney's tune.

'Really? Jude, you think?'

'Best song in the world. Best son in the world. That's my choice, but it's up to you, Rubes. You did the hard work.'

'Jude is lovely. It's strong. And he'll have a song, too. The best.'

'Welcome, Jude Devereaux,' Ludo said. 'A superstar's name if I ever heard one.'

'Not double-barrelled then – not your name as well?'

'I would not burden the poor little mite with Clutterbuck.' Ludo laughed. 'Alongside Devereaux, he'd spend more time spelling and writing his name than living. One name is enough.'

'Then, that's it. Jude Enzo Devereaux.'

He never questioned Enzo. I never told him.

I needn't have worried. I loved my 'little bean' instantly and without restraint. Much like the familial cooking gene, I seemed to have dodged the sad, absent maternity of my mother.

In those first few weeks, I also wondered what the hell I had done when I pulled him to me at three a.m. and plugged his tiny lips around my sore nipples, begging him silently to sleep. But come the morning, the sight of his tiny, pixie-like face – the spitting image of Ludo's photograph as a baby – manufactured so much love it spilled like the contents of my overripe, oversized breasts. I was a leaking, weeping, exhausted hormonal mess. And I was in love. Ecstatic.

The women of the house nurtured me as I cultivated Jude – squeaking like a little piglet as he shivered with excitement at the smell of my milk, mooing with satisfaction when it flowed into him. I let go the one night of indulgence when Ludo briefly reacquainted himself with Marlin, who'd been totally unaware there was even a baby expected in the house, let alone born.

'Just dusting the baby's head in celebration,' Ludo said in excuse. 'It's a one-off, Rubes. I've got more to think about now – I'm a family man.'

He was true to his word, taking a real delight in our son as he played the minstrel again and stroked at the strings of his guitar while Jude drifted to sleep. Propped up against his cot was the card that Paul had sent – one Mr McCartney – congratulating Ludo on the baby and the name, a doodle of a thumbs up next to his scrawl of *Hey Jude*.

Watching father and son, I began to itch a little at the perfection of my life, that age-old dread of Something Bad loitering around the corner ready to pounce. I was just too damn tired to scratch at it.

Thanks largely to Willow's post-partum potions, I had just enough energy to haul my typewriter into bed and complete the last chapter of 'Jude's book', as I called it then. Unlike so many of my offerings of the past, it signed off on a high note; to write anything less would have been a betrayal to my own body, my baby, to Willow and April, and the whole of motherhood. Womanhood, even. Life can get right, I decided.

I tapped it out with Jude snoozing beside me, he never wincing or startling as the keys clattered with the zeal pushing through my fingertips. A writer's son, for sure. A future scribe? Or would he follow his father into music, pick up a guitar at an early age and change the world? Even then, I had a picture in my mind of him as a young man, taking his mother to lunch and my being fit to burst with pride.

I was on the phone to my publisher one morning when the dread bore its own fruit. Softly spoken Willow had never raised a tone in my presence, but her bellow that morning coursed down the ornate stairway of that huge house and shook the whole of Landsmere, the howl of a woman possessed. I ran towards it like I'd never run before, finding her in my bedroom, her curtain of hair bent over the crib, sobbing.

His little hands were already cold, his cheeks too when I stroked – in the four hours since I'd fed my precious boy and placed him gingerly back in his bed. In the early hours, I'd been so worried about Ludo's constant tossing and turning on our mattress that I chose to place Jude out of harm's way, for his safety. The supreme irony of life, the Something Bad around the corner.

Why? Why had I not had that instinct, at five in the morning, to change the path of fate, to kick Ludo out of bed instead and into one of the other numerous, empty bedrooms. Why?

Because I was so drunk with the want of sleep that I satisfied my own need too quickly, unthinking.

He looked perfect laying there, the ruby-red lips of his mother fixed in a determined pout. Still my boy. Still Jude. But so still, and no longer my entire future. At six weeks old, he became a remnant of my already chequered, tainted and colourful past. The dark part, but also the light – in time, I forced myself to believe that.

Cot death, the coroner said. Undetectable and unavoidable in an otherwise, healthy, bonny baby. But it didn't stop the guilt, in me, or any other parent, I dare say. It came in waves, and then a flood of biblical proportions. I went through every scenario, wept and tortured my way through his last days and weeks. Ludo was there – and not. He had his own pain, applying his own blame, obliterating the hurt in private, indulging not with Marlin, but in Marlin's tried and trusted methods.

I left Landsmere soon after the funeral, just days before the bailiffs arrived and Marlin was stretchered out to the nearest psychiatric hospital. Ludo and I spent my last night there together, forcing ourselves through hours of tearful and agonising reminiscence, knowing it would be the last time our boy's mother and father would recall his tiny, momentous life. We owed him that. It was eviscerating and painful, but it signalled a determined end to our own connection. Ludo drifted and dabbled, moved to London, and then to the States; the last I heard of him in the early Seventies, he was a small-scale property developer in the vast mid-west of America, creating wholesome homes for post-commune couples. Ever the East End brickie.

The finished book hit the shelves eight months later, simply titled *Mother*. To this day, it stands as my best seller, and the only one where I have the reviews clipped and saved somewhere in a dusty box, the lines that state it was a novel 'written from the heart' and 'a testament to the undying love of parent'.

I never did write the epilogue. Jude's death wasn't an addition; it was real and it hurt like hell, but it did not sweep away those months of joy at feeling him alive inside me, and the six weeks of a dream when another human relied wholeheartedly on me – the flighty Ruby D – for solace and a source of life.

To this day, he is not an epilogue. I was a mother. Without a child to cling on to my hand, for sure, but no one could take that from me, ever. Nor my pride in reaching such heights.

Even now, at my extreme age, I am a mother. Ludo is a father. Together, we made the best boy there ever was. Would have been, I'm certain. I was a parent and I had – officially – grown up.

What could the world offer me then?

Six

'Jude.'

'Hmm?'

'Jude?

'Yes?'

'Are you all right?' Ruby shuffles over to where he reclines on the study's window seat, his favourite spot to lie, knees pulled up, in their breaks between the chunks of narrative she is dictating at astonishing speed. 'You seem a little off today, that's all.'

'Do I?' He jerks up his lanky body and swings his legs to the floor, neatly disproving the point. 'I'm fine, Ruby. Absolutely fine.' He's not. He is, in fact, nursing a hangover of epic proportions after a Big Night, celebrating not much else other than being young and able. Because he can. After weeks with Ruby, Jude is beginning to appreciate what youth offers and old age brings. Her life, as dictated on the screen, has caused him to raise eyebrows on more than one occasion, in surprise, shock and admiration. But looking at her now – the once fickle butterfly in her world – needing help with the stairs, and her tendency at times to drop off if she hesitates for too long in her diction… if a firecracker like Ruby evolves to this, what hope for the rest of them? Hence his abandonment the night before. The one before that, too. And the banging headache he is now trying to keep at bay, and hide from the shrewd senses of Ruby.

After several minutes, she pigeon steps her way down to the kitchen, needing tea. Normally, Jude sorts the food and drink during his time at the house, nine until five most days, but Ruby sees clearly that he's working off some excess. Her eyes might be milky, skin furrowed and her limbs achy, but her nose functions well enough to smell the drink on him. *It's what they do, isn't it?* she thinks. It's certainly what she did at his age. In spades. Even so, he does seem a little 'off', not his chatty, enquiring norm. But then she's wrung out, too, after that last chapter. Purged and lighter in one sense. She hasn't allowed herself to think of her Jude in such detail for an age, and it's a joy to recall the better bits, the life rather than the result. Still, Ruby feels a sadness settling like sediment around her, following her down the hallway, hovering like a bitter smell, not unwelcome, but not exactly pleasant. Maybe the Jude of now feels it, too. And then Ruby is sad if she's made him so, because she doesn't want to drive him away – might never admit it to him, and certainly not to Marina, but she's become very fond of him, this Jude, a man young enough to be her grandson.

The sadness, she calculates, must be part of the process. What else can she do but tell it like it is, warts and all? If there were no warts, there would – in her life – be no substance either.

'Juuuude?' she calls up the hallway. 'Cup of tea?'

MAN SEVEN: Victor

Saigon, April 1970

I'd had enough of death. Too much. It had claimed more than its fair share of me, what with Enzo, my mother, Harvey, Mushens, the likelihood of Benedict and the bud of Jude. What do you do when the grim reaper is bent on stalking your every move? You stick two fingers up to its ugly, deformed morality and go hunting its tail, yearning to come face to face. *Come get me, if you dare.* And where better, as the decade of love rolled over, than the nucleus of death?

The stupid option would be to dive head first into the bear pit. So I went to Vietnam.

By the time I flew into Saigon, I was a month beyond my fortieth birthday, and I felt it. On some days I looked it, too; Max Factor is a marvel but even it has to hold its hands up in defeat where ingrained grief wins out. My saving grace was that a correspondent's uniform was pretty much the same as any jobbing soldier, and my hips had been eaten away by grief, too. I could cut the bagged-out khaki quite well, if no one looked too hard at my eyes, the crow's feet alongside and the dead space behind. Subsequently, I learned the vacant stare was an asset in blending in, but that was a discovery for later.

As the plane circled above the sprawling boulevards of Saigon and the thick dense green of the countryside beyond – the bits of it that hadn't yet been bombed or torched – I was pumped. I defy anyone to resist the pull of that place. Stepping off the plane at Tan Son Nhat Airport, a wall of heat and humidity slammed into my skin in the same second that I heard the iconic anthem to the Vietnam conflict: the frenetic swipe of rotor blades as a Huey helicopter rose upwards, pushing out a belting beat of the Doors's 'Roadhouse Blues', draftees leaning from its open doors and sucking in any wisp of breeze. Even the sign daubed on the helicopter nose – Welcome to Hell – did little to dampen the anticipation in my stomach.

And it was a hell of sorts, wrapped in the faded glory of a once feted country. As a British subject, I'd never been a fan of colonialism or its intent, but there are few who would doubt the beauty that French architects had brought to Saigon, with sweeping, wide boulevards, its solid, ornate hotels and impressive opera house. It must have been a jewel worthy of its title, the 'Pearl of the Far East', before a host of nations tried to burn out its soul. After decades of struggles with the French, and now the full force of a US occupation since '65, Saigon was in ruins, its people dislodged and deposed in their city and beyond. Of the bullet-holes that pocked almost every stone or concrete building, it was a guess as to which conflict the scars had come from.

And yet it was a heaven of sorts. I'd gone there not so much to forget, but to suspend my overarching grief over Jude. I needed to be busy. And we seemed well matched; the air had been seeping painfully out the Vietnam balloon in recent years, ever since the bloody massacre of My Lai and the '68 Tet Offensive left Americans back home doubting the wisdom of their nation's commitment. The larger battles had been fought and the communist Vietcong – the 'VC' – were holding firm, hunkered in their subterranean bunkers and tunnels, an elusive, invisible enemy. The hammer blow for any US hope had been delivered by the illustrious newsman Walter Cronkite. After a fact-finding mission in '67, he'd declared, direct to camera and the nation, that 'we are mired in stalemate... the only rational way out is to negotiate'.

Americans might have chosen to believe their trusted anchorman, but in 1970 President Richard Nixon held the sway and the power. He wanted to win in Vietnam. Badly.

To the world at large, Vietnam was still newsworthy and, from my eye-view, far enough away from my own reality to prove attractive. Unabashed in using my publishing contacts back home, I'd secured a loose contract with a couple of British-based magazines to root out 'anything different'. Anything, they said. The war had been grinding on for so long that little coming out of the Saigon press pack was fresh anymore. How could it be? Over six long years of American involvement, they had photographed the lines of body bags, the burning of Vietnamese villages, covered the politics, the corruption and life in the field. Reporters had lived like soldiers, and died like them too – over a hundred press in total by the bitter end. This was no cosy assignment sipping cocktails as the blazing sun set over Asia. Well, not all the time. But the West still wanted to know what their tax dollars and their boys were doing thousands of miles from home. It was my job to find a new angle on that dollar spend and translate it to the British public.

I'd always considered myself a wordsmith rather than a

reporter, but other novelists had gone before me in Vietnam, notably one of my heroes, Martha Gellhorn. While I could never claim to be so accomplished as the fearless Miss G, I felt confident of combining the long and the short form of writing. And as was my track record to date, the bones of a book might well emerge too.

Hence my arrival in Saigon, with a rucksack, typewriter, a wad of introduction letters and that characteristic chutzpah. Some called it audacity, or pure effrontery.

Turns out, you needed it all, as a woman especially. Gellhorn hadn't been the first; there were other women who blazed a trail through the jungle, both in words and pictures. I'd followed the photo essays of the diminutive but fearless Catherine Leroy in *Paris Match*, who did for Vietnam what Lee Miller had achieved in *Vogue* during the Second World War. The words, too, of Frances FitzGerald in reporting the Vietnamese stance from the front line. But being good wasn't the same as being accepted. Women were still considered aliens on the battlefield, even if the military forces couldn't stop them; the strangest of anomalies meant all journalists had a free pass to observe said conflict. Because it was just that, apparently. The US had never officially declared war on Vietnam, merely involved itself in the battle of the West versus communism, good against purported evil. Turns out death and destruction surrounds both, but the wording was vital. They were merely 'containing communism'. On the ground it meant that, with press accreditation, any hack could jump on a military helicopter and observe war in the making. Sorry… the conflict.

It took me a week to finally hold that precious pass in my hand. In the meantime, I orientated myself by visiting every one of the war-torn but more comfortable hotels patronised by the press pack that hugged the focus of Lam Son Square: the Continental, the Rex, the Majestic, and the doyenne through the war years, the Caravelle. There, in the Caravelle's rooftop bar, the pack assembled each day at five for briefings from a US spokesman – dubbed the 'Five O'clock Follies' by those who always treated the official line with a healthy scepticism. More reliable was the view nine floors up, the best vantage point over Saigon and where to catch a rare breeze from the meandering river, in humidity that could cause a snake to sweat. It was also the place to share a drink with the likes of veteran Peter Arnett, or the *Sunday Times*'s Jon Swain, battle-hardened and slightly cynical, but still there all the same. They were polite and welcoming – to a point. It was all about proving yourself out there, as a woman especially, and then again in print. Me? I felt like a schoolkid coming into the classroom halfway through the term. Once again, I was in awe.

The Caravelle was effectively a work hub, but my favourite place to sit and suck in Saigon was the ground floor of the Continental Palace, an archetypal French Colonial build on a busy corner near to the opera house, all faded glamour and threadbare velvet. In the terrace bar nicknamed the Shelf, all life whizzed by as you sipped at a Coca-Cola or a Tiger beer: decrepit buses, Mini Moke jeeps and battered Fiat 500s, along with swarms of bicycles, scooters and mopeds, the workhorses of the city's trade, laden with people, produce, babies, and a good deal of live chickens. With artillery firing in the distance, it was plain to see that nothing stopped the cogs of Saigon turning. And since the revered Graham Greene had famously lived at the Continental while he wrote *The Quiet American*, how could I fail to be inspired? Way before I'd netted a single penny for my dispatches, I paid my money and took a room there.

★★★

I was at the Shelf, pretending to work on my wish list of assignments, when Victor first caught my eye. Or his reading matter did – a tattered paperback of Dickens's *Hard Times* in his hand, the irony of which made me laugh under my breath. Absorbed as he was, it was loud enough for him to look up.

'Sorry,' I said. 'Just struck me as funny.'

He surveyed the book's cover, as if it was anything but a subject of mirth.

'The title,' I qualified. 'Not much of a respite, in all of this.' I gestured to swarming Saigon beyond the bar, and the maelstrom beyond that.

'Oh, but it is,' he replied. He was serious in the few seconds before a smile began to work its way across his face.

And that was that. We shared a beer, and conversation that was not steeped in offensives or battles, or political directions. Instead, we talked words and books, both old and new. He asked me what I did 'before this', and I told him, and then he – as an avid reader – was in awe of me. At that point in my own dungeon of self-worth, it felt good (and because, of course, writers never get tired of that).

Mercifully, Victor was not a journalist, a photographer or cameraman. Dressed in civvies, it was his build and demeanour that screamed military, thick black hair shaved into the sides GI-style that turned to curls up top. He was taking time out from the field, on a weekend R and R – Rest and Recreation to those not yet entrenched in the language of 'Nam. Unlike his unit colleagues, he preferred the relative calm of the Shelf to the bar-brothels in downtown Saigon, where underage girls made pathetic money from cosying up to soldiers far, far from home. Victor preferred the love of a good book.

I'm sure we gelled initially as misfits. Despite my age, and as much as I imagined sliding effortlessly into that world, I was back to being a rookie. He was no newbie, but as a half-Italian, African American, Victor knew all about being on the sidelines. Being a quiet intellectual no doubt marked him out too, despite looking as if he'd been chipped out of some ancient rock in the Vietnamese jungle. History was etched visibly across skin darkened under the sun, one deep scar under his left jaw and several shrapnel nicks across his face, a sharp contrast to his white, smooth shirt and spotless casual trousers.

It was Dickens, though, who allowed those first introductions. 'He takes me out of here,' he said. 'To another world.'

'Better?' I wondered. Victorian drudgery against modern-day atrocity – which was worse?

'Different.'

We moved on to noodles, the best I'd ever tasted, in some dank, steaming alleyway, then blue-tinted cocktails. We retired eventually to my hotel, sated but otherwise hungry, his own room being situated in the deep, dank alleyway (I was ready and willing for the full Vietnam experience, but I'd leave the crawlies until I was out in the field).

If you are shocked by the speed of our intimacy, I offer no excuses, only that this was 1970, a good portion of the occupied forces were stoned, we were grown-ups, and this was war, however much the US liked to split hairs. You lived in and for the moment. He never admitted to being married, and I didn't ask, since being in Vietnam *was* tantamount to being single, in that we were all alone in this highly populated city. Besides, everybody was sleeping with everybody, bed-hopping like bugs, to coin a blunt analogy.

For him, our coupling was clearly a release. The ferocity of his passion told me that, even though he was gentle and considerate in his lovemaking. Battlefields, I guessed, made men hungry for affection, and the raw act was a physical need after weeks on patrol. And until that point, I hadn't realised how much I needed it too. Anything tactile had been absent since Ludo and I parted after Landsmere, and by then our touch was parched of anything like tenderness, only a grim grasp on the tether that had been Jude.

The heat contributed to the cauldron of my hotel room. With Victor's taut, worked flesh on top of me, I felt his military life under my fingers and between his shoulder blades. It read like braille: grooves meandering like the rivers he'd waded across waist-deep in war soup, plus an entire map of conflict chiselled into is back.

He was battle-weary, and I was tired of life. We were the perfect match.

Quietly doomed.

'So, you volunteered?' I asked when we lay back, a film of sweat draping like gossamer over our naked bodies. Outside, Saigon hooted and tooted in its usual frenzy.

'Better that than be drafted,' he said in an accent that was pure downtown Chicago. 'A grunt is a grunt out here – the VC don't give a damn who they shoot – but a draftee is different in your unit.'

He was on his second tour, he told me, and a corpsman. I rifled through my scant knowledge base of army hierarchy: one of those to scoop up the injured and dying before they are medevacked out, sometimes amid a hail of bullets and mortars.

And when the battle was done, the dead needed to be gathered up.

'It's my job to cut back on the number of body bags we use,' he said, targeting the ceiling fan with his smoke, and then laughing cruelly at himself. 'You could say I'm a saviour on all fronts.'

I wondered why and how a corpsman could accrue so many battle scars, but it didn't seem like the time to ask.

We parted late the next day with a loose promise to form a book club of two; he was keen to move on to Jane Austen, he said, but felt like he would need a translator to navigate the Regency marriage market. I didn't like to tell him it was the same the world over, including the meat market only a few streets away, where beautiful, svelte Vietnamese women sold themselves for dollars and a western utopia that didn't exist.

'So long, Ruby D.' He waved as he headed back to his unit, and what was inevitably another trip into the valley of death. I collected my notebook and pen, and headed out there too.

Decades on, the adrenalin of that time is easy to recall, yet almost impossible to describe, despite a life lived with words.

'You okay?' the airman shouted as the rotors began turning, making our steady climb to a frenzied thwack-thwack above us.

I nodded, because it seemed to be the thing to do. I wouldn't admit that I was terrified, had never been in a helicopter before, or that I'd already left my breakfast in the toilet before take-off. I was press, hitching a ride into *their* war, and rule number one: don't be a burden. Don't be a dick, either. Or sick.

And yet when we left the ground, my stomach stayed with me, and I was addicted from that moment on, as if I became a miniscule passenger on the wings of a bobbing dragonfly, rising high and catching the thermals of thick, warm air over a garden of Eden. Enchanting. Then, when there were four or five Huey's alongside in tandem, the radio spitting with air-speak and rotors beating the particles like drums, we were part of an armada ready to grab at victory, adrenalin stoking at the fire inside. No wonder they craved drugs to calm down.

The men sitting alongside were bored and battle-weary, hungover and half-asleep, though I suspect the pilots – those cool and collected 'chopper jockeys' – were playing it up a little for what they knew was my first trip out. My heart raced in double time as 'Born to be Wild' hoofed out of the speakers and we swooped over a South Vietnam of two halves: the swathes of lush green foliage and back-to-back paddy fields, against pockets of scorched earth, burnt and largely abandoned villages. Under us, the Vietnamese hung onto their hats as we flew over, the conical circles of *non la* headwear dotted across the landscapes, wind from the rotors churning up the soil from which they were desperately sucking a living. It was beautiful and wrong in the same blink of an eye.

We landed on what was then a 'search and destroy' mission. The big battles of the mid to late 1960s – the bloodbaths of Ia Drang and Khe Sanh later made into blockbusting films – had already been fought and won, and the conflict was spiralling down. Everyone on the ground knew it, the people back home sensed it. Only the politicians were loath to admit failure, since saving lives didn't equate to saving face.

The gung-ho volunteers had either been killed or done their tours, and the unit consisted mainly of skinny, badly attired draftees, whose sole interest was in surviving long enough to have a second stab at life. They would introduce themselves to me with a name and a number – the time in days left before their chopper out to civilisation. 'Billy West, 58.' 'Tony Gonzalez, 72.' 'Jimmy Malloy, 88.' As one reporter coined it at the Caravelle, and later in his own dispatch: 'No one wants to die for a dying cause anymore'.

If you skated over their language of 'gooks', 'spooks' and the liberal use of 'fuck', they were just boys hankering to go home and eat all-American pie around Mom's kitchen table.

For three days, in a combination of high sun, insane humidity and rain like stair rods, we toured on foot through a 'no fire zone', where Vietnamese villagers had been driven out and any remaining movement was assumed to be VC, and therefore a target. The enemy were a ghostly but invisible presence, and the army's solution was to burn first and ask questions later. The unit routinely stopped, scanned through their binoculars, radioed in a grid reference for artillery fire and then watched as the bombers soared over, laying waste to the beautiful countryside in front of us. In my mind, anything left alive after that blitzkrieg deserved to escape.

Boredom rather than death dominated these patrols, though death's shadow hung low like a heavy cloud. We walked, looked, destroyed, then camped to eat bad combat rations and smoke.

'I never thought I'd hanker so much for a shit scrub town in Hicksville USA where nothing ever happens,' Jimmy muttered between puffs of his Lucky Strike.

The real paranoia was in booby traps left by the VC, near-invisible lines triggering a grenade which guaranteed a body bag or life in a wheelchair.

'Fucking bad karma if you find one of those,' Billy declared, eyes glued to the ground.

It was a sniper, however, that brought me back alongside the spectre of death, ironically pushed to the back of my mind since arriving, by the muddle and the enigma of this crazy, beautiful country. We'd strayed beyond the no fire zone and come across a 'ville', a tiny circle of huts with squawking hogs and squeaking children, adults that pulled their infants close as the uniforms loped towards them, rifles slung lazily over shoulders to signal no threat. Still, the fear in Vietnamese eyes was palpable. Through an interpreter, the unit commander grilled the village elder – as usual the answer was 'no VC'. Perhaps the commander was too bored or tired to press further, but there was no violence that day, no burning of huts or displacing people from their homes. That had all gone before. We radioed our position, Tony shared out his chocolate ration among the children and we turned to leave.

But there was VC. Perhaps a loner, perhaps one of several lurking in those infamous tunnels and rat-runs – only one whose rifle poked its nose from the bushes, releasing a bullet that sliced through Tony's metal helmet and put him on the ground. Instantly. Life extinguished in a heartbeat. Glassy-eyed, he lay there, without so much as a final tremor. Gone. Someone's son, once a child, a helpless newborn that was dressed and bathed and kissed. Open-mouthed, I thought of how many times it had happened before – a whole lived existence cut down in less than a second – and all when I'd been soaking in the warm, western waters of the Sixties revolution, an entire half decade in ignorance. I barely kept on my feet, bending double in the bushes and losing my rations. Almost my mind, too. 'Jude. Baby boy Jude,' whipped around my head, the clamour deafening over the roar of bombers called in for an immediate strike to 'burn the sonofabitches'.

Someone's son. Her son. My son. Why?

'Poor bastard,' Danny said, closing Tony's eyes. 'He just got engaged by letter.' They tucked a full pack of smokes inside his pocket, scrawled '72' on his body bag as a kind of memorial and carried him tenderly to the evac chopper.

I never again wore a metal helmet on patrol. No point, clearly.

Well, you came here to hunt death. If your number is up, it will damn well find you.

'Wise up,' Tony would have said.

The resulting article was titled 'The Numbers Game', on the men and their boredom, their frustration and the stalemate between nations that still might get them killed: digits that marked the number of days until discharge, cigarettes in their pack, the grid reference on which they might take their last breath. Every number a crucial one. I wrote it at speed on the journey back, the flap of rotors fresh in my ears and my pen a scrawl as the chopper banked and turned. Never had the words spilled so freely.

Back among the tree-lined boulevards surrounding Tu Do Street, I typed and filed my copy, took the longest shower of my entire life and drank four straight whiskies in the space of an hour slumped in one of the ancient wicker chairs of the Continental bar, my warm tears melting the ice. When I looked up through my haze, Victor was standing there. Saviour.

He thumbed away the salty streaks on my cheek. 'Welcome back, Ruby.'

'It all seems so pointless,' I whined in my room, sweat-stained and expunged of frustration again, my need being greater this time. It might not have been the stupidest thing I'd said in my life, but it ranked as close. And as understatements go, it was a humdinger.

Victor laughed throatily, enough that his body bucked under the sheet, and he reached for another cigarette. 'Put that in your newspapers,' he said, though I sensed it was a statement rather than his scorn.

'And if you're going to ask why,' Victor went on, 'either to me or in print, then don't bother. Vietnam is like a thousand finely spun cobwebs layered over each other – delicate, complex and strong as a damn ox. You can't untangle it. Those who try end up in the madhouse or the bottom of the bottle. It just is.'

'So why do you stay?' It was the next obvious question. I was there through desperation and naïveté, but Victor had a choice, could have headed home after his first tour. More to the point, why was someone so obviously intelligent – one of life's natural philosophers – still there, if it was all so bloody clear-cut?

He drew in smoke again. 'Reparations, Ruby. Reparations.' He pulled back the sheet. 'Come on, I'm starving, let's get some food. I know a place to get *the* best chicken rice and steamed rolls.'

'Is it by any chance in an alleyway that's a hundred degrees, cooked up right next to a sewer pipe?'

'You're a marvel and a psychic, Ruby D. How did you guess?'

The next month flew by – on Hueys and Chinooks, B-52s and troop-carriers. The US Army proved the best travel agent; you could book a seat to a base up north or a skirmish down south at the drop of a hat, since they needed us to remind the world that communism was still being contained, albeit slowly and at great expense. The bad publicity – those hacks rooting out the corruption and the US indiscriminate bombing of neighbouring Laos – didn't seem to bother them much. 'The US Army is *not* in Laos,' they stated, straight-backed and po-faced at the Five O'clock Follies. It was a war of attrition as much as anything else. Sorry, still a conflict.

In words, I kept to my own brief, which was the people – the grunts, the Vietnamese who serviced them, the women who coveted all things western, the babies who were born blond but with unmistakably Asian features. The men who left those newborns back in 'Nam, to fly home to their wives and 2.4 equally blond children. That was the Vietnam I sought out.

Satisfied? No. I rarely saw or spoke to any Vietnamese who weren't sweeping, serving, cooking for or sleeping with western foreigners, aside from the hats scurrying under a helicopter's violent descent onto their plundered soil.

'Are you telling me, Ruby, that you want to see the *real* Vietnam?' Victor couldn't keep the sarcasm out of his drawl. It was what every newbie reporter who strolled into the Caravelle stated, until they saw the reality, and fell into apathy, and their real need became an ice-cold beer after three days in the field. Victor, though, was not party to that particular cynicism – I kept him out of the press swamp and very much to myself.

I sat up, naked and affronted. 'Don't mock me, Victor! We can't all have our own private stand-off with death. Nor do we crave the insight quite as much. I can't solve or even explain fuckin' Vietnam, but I would like to justify my presence here by telling it like it is. Perhaps just once. Make some readers give a shit over their cornflakes.'

Even I was shocked by my reasoning, which came shooting from the heart, brittle as it was. Must have been the heat softening those charred insides of mine.

Victor sat up too, surprise across his normally controlled features. 'Okay, I hear you. So be it.'

We left on a transport chopper, one of those laden with supplies to aid the US 'pacification' programme, bent on rewarding those Vietnamese who shunned the Vietcong and pledged to be good anti-communists. Sitting close to the doorway and drinking in the warm gusts, we followed the winding route of the Mekong south into the lush, fertile green of the river delta, with its patchwork paddies and water buffalo plodding lazily in the heat. Only the large pocks of scorched earth told us the war had been here, B-52s dropping their noxious napalm to flush out VC. To my eye, it said nothing about containment and everything about excess.

Where we landed had no sign, or name, yet Victor was at home instantly. He shook hands with the pilot and arranged a pick-up for the next day. 'Come on,' he beckoned. 'Meet some friends of mine.'

We walked through dense foliage for a good half hour, and I pined for the thick khaki fatigues that Victor had suggested we leave behind, my thin western clothes proving no match for hungry flies and an unforgiving jungle. It gave way eventually to a clearing, which revealed itself as a village, twenty or so huts and one-storey wooden buildings in a loose ring, the ubiquitous hogs in their pens or rooting in the scrub. Victor was an instant magnet, children hanging like limpets to his muscled legs, squealing gleefully as he opened his rucksack and dished out cheap plastic toy-tat and army-issue chocolate. The adults were similarly pleased; I watched them gather with true delight on their faces, something I'd not witnessed in Vietnam before when East met West. There was no evidence of suspicion or false diplomacy born out of fear or an inequity of power. He really was their friend.

Around the edge of the group, I noted a woman hovering. Quiet, unsmiling, though no displeasure on her serene face. Lean and beautiful, too, with sleek black hair pulled into a braid. She simply waited.

Victor's bag depleted, he stood up and caught sight of her. The children dispersed with their spoils, and after handshakes with the elders (I was introduced as 'my good friend, Ruby'), the woman walked forward, head slightly bowed. He extended a big, dark hand, and her tiny, pale palm was swallowed into his. They said nothing when she looked up under her blunt cut fringe, but everything. For a minute, I thought Victor had brought me to the middle of the jungle to meet his woman, more so when a small child sidled up and clutched at her leg, an ugly plastic doll in the other hand. Mother and daughter. *His* daughter? I looked at her browned skin for signs of him, but saw only a tiny, sweet girl bronzed by the sun.

Is this what he meant by reparation? And why would he bring me here, if not to prove a very large point?

'Ruby, I'd like you to meet Linh,' he said.

We'd had laughs, Victor and I – our union wasn't all intensity and angst – but I had never seen anything like the look he wore then. He adopted her serenity instantly.

'Linh is a friend,' he added.

My having just been presented as such, what on earth was I supposed to make of that?

'Pleased to meet you,' she said in perfect English. I shook her delicate hand. She smiled and led us to a small hut with a bed made up on the floor, palm mats and a small veranda. 'You'll stay here.' There wasn't a trace of jealousy in her tone.

She left us with tea, at which point Victor must have sensed an explanation was necessary. 'I worked with her husband,' he said, and swallowed the choke back down. 'Best man I knew.'

'Worked?'

With his huge, muscly arm, Victor placed his cup delicately on the floor. 'Worked and fought. My first tour. Tam Duong was an interpreter assigned to our unit, from the South Vietnamese Army.'

'But I don't understand. Why would a corpsman need an interpreter?' It seemed crude to point out that the dead and dying don't have a lot to say.

'I was a sergeant then, in a front-line corps. A few big battles.' His staccato sentences were born out of pain, I assumed, rather than pushing the drama. 'I took Tam with me to check out a forward position, where the scouts thought they could see a tunnel entrance. Sure to be VC.' His voice trailed off into a difficult memory.

'They saw him straightaway, held him for, oh, a good three or four minutes before they cut his throat in front of me.' Victor's big hand hovered across his neck before wiping away the tears on his cheeks. 'I looked into Tam's eyes in his last minutes on Earth, and I knew he was thinking of Linh. I saw what he was asking of me.'

Through the rush walls, the persistent hum of the bush beat into a brief silence.

'Let me tell you, Ruby, I've seen and felt a lot of men die under me. But when it's someone you know, whose hand you have shaken, whose smile you can recall again and again. Who shares his dreams of fatherhood with you…' He broke off and shook his head, as if to stir the grief. 'Well, it feels like hours when you watch their last, painful breath.' Victor swiped again at his sodden face. 'He didn't even get to see the baby. Kim was born just two months later.'

'And so?' It was all I could say as the emotion welled inside of me, the touch of Jude's tiny, soft fingers in mine all over again. The loss. That great big fat fucking hole, black as night.

'So now I look after them. I volunteered back into this hellhole to make sure they were all right. And if those bastards out there' – he flung an arm out to the world beyond – 'complain that feeding money to the problem is no solution, then they should come and see how many widows have been created. In the thousands. Linh is clever and educated, she speaks English, and yet she can't make enough money to support her child. Not unless she sells herself in downtown Saigon. So she came home to the delta, to her family.'

The anger pulsed off him, and I felt the heat of it as I touched his shoulder. 'So, how do you square that?' I asked.

Why couldn't I keep my big mouth shut? These were the times when I hated being me, the one to always question, to pry, never to let it go. It was the writer, and latterly the journalist, in me. Fucking nosy. But I had to know: how could a serving soldier in the US Army, complicit in the search and destroy, the stark annihilation, feel like this?

Victor was too smart to miss my insinuation, but there was no anger in his reply. 'Tam's death was my last day in combat,' he said. 'I was in the hospital for a while,' – he gestured at the scoring on his back, and then pointed a finger to injuries deep within his head – 'getting my shit together. I transferred to medics after that. Like I said, Ruby, it's reparation. Tiny, miniscule, but it's what I can do.'

'And when this tour is over? What will you do then?'

He sighed, turned and kissed my cheek. 'Honestly? I really

don't know. Got any need for an assistant, you being a hot-shot reporter and celebrated author?'

Victor had lied to me. *The* best noodles in Vietnam were not in a stinking Saigon alleyway, but from a pot over a simple pit fire, laughing and sharing in pidgin English and Vietnamese with good people who hailed from neither north nor south, only a country seeking control of its own destiny. I'd had good and bad times in Vietnam, in a relatively short space of time, and this rated as the best. I felt less on edge than walking some of London's dodgier thoroughfares.

'That, Ruby, is the real Vietnam,' Victor said, drowsy as we lay side by side on our floor mattress that night. Beyond the thin walls, the cacophony of Saigon had been replaced with a soundtrack of an industrious jungle. 'Put that in your paper.'

'I will,' I told him. 'I bloody well will.' But he was already asleep.

We woke in tandem to a sound from outside, seconds before Linh's tiny feet padded across the rush floor and she bent to Victor's ear.

'Come with me – quickly.' Her whisper was clipped and fearful. 'They're here.'

'Where?' I heard Victor say. No prizes for guessing who.

'The elder's house. But they suspect we have visitors. I don't know how. Just come with me.' She was devoid of all serenity, and the tension fired in Victor wasn't to be underestimated either.

Me? I was shitting bricks. All that blasé talk about stalking death turns to dust when it comes close enough to sniff at your fear, like a lion's hot breath on the other side of a flimsy curtain. Linh led us behind the hut and into the pitch-black of the rice store, told us to stay put until she could come back to move us again. That's when it became noisy outside, the entire village woken by a raid that was designed to scare the villagers into submission, as well as gather food supplies for the mobile VC units. Shouts and threats echoed, a single gunshot causing the babies to wail and the women to plead. The VC were famous for their stealth and their silent incursions into enemy territory, taking entire US units by surprise. But not where they felt entirely confident of control. Not then.

My Vietnamese was limited to pleasantries, but Victor was silently translating the threats echoing around the huts. 'I have to go out there,' he said into the darkness between us.

'What? Are you insane? No!' Exasperation mingled with pure terror, emerging as a strangled whisper.

I saw only his blazing eyes, wholly determined. 'They are going to kill women and children unless we show ourselves. That's what they're saying. I can't have that, Ruby. I just can't.'

'They will kill us. You know that, don't you?'

'I'll go. Just me. It'll buy you time enough to get away.'

'Away where? It's a fucking wilderness in the pitch-black, Victor. I won't last ten minutes.'

Think. It's what you pretend to be good at – survival.

'Listen, I have a camera in the hut,' I said in desperation. 'If we can get it, we might just persuade them we're both press. They could still kill us, but right now that is our only chance. Worth a shot?'

This particular bunch of VC didn't like the press, that much was obvious. A sharp blade against my neck proved that; Victor opposite me, a machete up against the scars already scored into his flesh. It pressed dangerously close to his carotid artery, the one I watched throbbing, prominent against the firelight of their torches. His face portrayed just the right amount of terror for a shit-scared photographer, but behind the gaze that I'd stared at in bed, inches from mine, I read a strange calm. One that I recognised, too, because I had at one time owned it myself: a welcome for death. The release. He would only care what happened to Linh and Kim, and the villagers. Me too, I liked to think.

They wanted blood and they took it. Principally mine. The nick to my neck, just under my left ear hurt like hell, and I wanted to howl out loud like a child. It took every ounce of me to stymie that pain, but I took my lead from Linh's tranquil expression: *Be in control, take the hurt, because that's what VC do. It's what they admire.*

It's true that a previous incarnation of me may have secretly relished the small wound as a souvenir, proof for a war yarn to impress while propping up the bar at a writers' convention. This older (perhaps wiser) version absolutely did not. I realised in that stinging second I did not want to die. This irresponsible pursuit of death was merely a coward's way to escape the pain of Jude. I should live, if only to remember my precious boy. And I did not want my end to be in a jungle, at the hands of a stinking, sweaty bunch of men whose own bravery was in threatening women and children.

I felt blood trickle down my neck and snake downwards, but since I wasn't losing consciousness within seconds, I had to gather it was a warning, rather than fatal; a red poppy flowering on the breast of my white shirt. Blooming for a time, until it stopped. Thank fuck for our body's natural ability to survive.

The villagers were silent around us, submissive in the light of flaming torches, because they knew that was our best chance of survival. Let the VC rant and scream, let them thieve the precious rice and food, taste a small amount of blood, just enough to slake their desire for dominance.

They guessed right. In time, the rangy, twitchy leader of the VC raid was calmed by the attention and the food in their taut bellies. Like a storm, the tirade blew itself out.

Then Linh, rather than the village elder, began to speak. Calmly and persuasively, as if she were a lawyer in the highest court room. I couldn't interpret her words, but in the way she moved, bowed her head at the right time to his supremacy – as animals do in the wild – he came round. She pointed at the camera slung across Victor's neck and my notebook. Why not tell your side of the story? she coaxed him, appealing to his vanity. The Americans get all the coverage, don't they? Why not tell them why you desire a unified Vietnam? Why Ho Chi Minh was a great leader?

He considered, the propaganda gears revolving. Finally, he nodded and my near-to-bursting lungs functioned again.

Which is how we got to sit around the fire, the knife and the machete hovering at the corner of my vision, but no longer skimming our flesh. I conjured questions designed to draw out the ideology and flatter their intentions, though my hand and the resulting notes were so shaky I knew I'd have trouble deciphering later. If we ever got to later.

Victor danced around the group like a bona fide 'tog', the shutter of my camera clicking with enthusiasm. He didn't let on there were only three shots left on the film, the rest being a performance worthy of an Oscar.

And that is how I came to interview the Vietcong while being held a sort of captive, snatched from the claws of death to land on my feet yet again. And a scoop, too.

One in the eye for the grim reaper.

The VC skipped into the night soon after, and we, at first light, relieved to hear those rotors swipe into the still delta air and lift us back into Saigon's crazy arena, only slightly less demented than the scene we'd left behind.

I departed Vietnam a couple of months later, swamped by fresh commissions after my 'hostage' piece syndicated worldwide across magazines and newspapers. I was true to my word, telling their side and ours, and it was run alongside one of Victor's snaps of me amid the VC, taking tea with the enemy. He did a pretty good job, with no evidence of a shaky hand on the shutter.

But my Vietnam was over, flooded as I was with a real need to crawl back to my own universe. Thanks to Victor, I had seen the reality – not for long, but long enough.

His parting gift was to see me off at the airport and press a small keepsake into my hand, his dog-eared, well-thumbed copy of *Hard Times*.

'Victor, I will never forgive you if you quote some worthy words of Dickens at me,' I said.

'I won't then.' He threw me the same winning look I'd seen in the Continental bar all those months before. 'But, as the great Mr Dylan says, the times are always a-changin'. Let's hope so, Ruby D. Take care of yourself.'

Bloody poet as well as a philosopher.

No book, either fact or fiction, emerged from Vietnam. How could it? There was no gain in a country ravaged by decades of conflict, or a people dominated by hardware whose only purpose was to kill and maim. Certainly, I had been enlightened, but by sorrow instead of hope. By a single man rather than the enormity of the US machine.

The Vietnam I left in late 1970 was still five calendar years and eons away from the peace or tranquillity I'd witnessed in so many of its citizens. In the past, I'd been no stranger to assimilating and using a situation, a love or a man, and binding it into the pages of fiction for my own advantage. Royalties, too. But in Vietnam, where nothing was right, it steered way beyond my moral radar.

Victor was worthy of words. Except he would have told me in no uncertain language to write about something else more important, and he would have been right. In the end, it was so gargantuan, so much of a moral haze that I couldn't have strung a coherent sentence of a novel. At the same time, the universe didn't possess enough paper to explain away the complexities of Vietnam. By the power of its many pharmaceuticals, or by base reality, it was mind-blowing.

I'd survived, and that was enough. As did Victor, I later learned. Sometime in '73 a friend of mine returned from Thailand, having stayed in a small bed and breakfast outside Bangkok while writing his book. It was run by an ex-US soldier and his Vietnamese wife, with two 'beautiful' children running about – Kim and Tammy, he recalled. Genuinely, I smiled to myself: Victor's reparation with a capital R. But his love, too. That much was obvious the moment he took Linh's tiny hand in his, in a dusty village in the Mekong Delta. I'd been guilty of vanity on many an occasion, but I was never blind.

So, I left it at survival. I was changed, for the better, I hoped. It was no mere chapter, but – if you're one for that book analogy – there was no other option but to close it for good. Or die. And my time there taught me I wasn't ready for the end, however much I'd welcomed its solace on arrival. Amid a devastating theatre of death, one person was saved.

Back then, I flew out of the maelstrom under the flapping 'wings' of a Chinook; those chopper jockeys went for unabashed irony and switched up the volume on the Doors's 'The End', thundering out above the twin roar of the rotors.

'This is the end, beautiful friend,' chanted the once stunning Jim Morrison, whose own end, sadly, wasn't too far away, '...the end, my only friend.'

Thanks guys. A perfect full stop.

MAN EIGHT: Johan

England, 1973

Wanderlust is exhausting. Much like age, it catches up with you when you are least expecting it, and in my case, it was after a long night at a London club frequented by writers, where I might well have confidently held court if I hadn't been so wearily drunk. I slunk into my tiny flat in a corner of Camden and woke to a fuzzy vision of four bland walls, only my typewriter a clue that it was actually my room. Even the cheese plant was on loan.

After Vietnam, there had been a brief stay in Rome, followed by an assortment of rooms, bedsits and frankly appalling flats, all short-term, and all of which seemed little more than cheap hotels without the luxury of room service. What I badly needed was a home, one that would make me think twice about going out for food, followed by the inevitable glass of wine. A place where I felt happy to live and work, and invite guests in. Something grown-ups were apt to do. Lord forbid, it was high time I put down some roots.

Tentatively, I paid a visit to my accountant, Leo. Well-heeled, well-fed and feathered in Savile Row cloth like a fattened goose, Leo totted up the figures behind his large, mahogany desk. To my great surprise, he reported I was actually quite solvent, thanks to the royalties still trickling in and a life spending very little on rent.

'But you have nothing in the way of assets,' he declared, in the tone of a schoolmaster to a pupil who is in danger of squandering great talent.

'Assets?' I imagined that I possessed plenty – a functioning brain, limbs that worked, hands that could still type.

'Something for your later life, Ruby. The twilight years. You might want to think about property.'

I had never, ever imagined reaching the sunset of my existence, let alone the twilight. But judging by Leo's fat fingers dripping in gold and his Rolex watch, he knew a thing or two about investment.

Comfortable as I appeared to be, there wasn't money enough to buy a house that I might choose to live in, not least one that didn't warrant a good deal of TLC and a huge builder's fee. I was left to rummage in my little bag of tricks. It wasn't entirely putting aside principles (never owning a great deal in the first place), but it did go against my personal grain to seek employment. However, there was a book out there that needed writing, and the last time I checked, I was still an author. A simple trade, you might imagine. And so began a painful but mercifully brief episode as a ghostwriter.

He was erudite, wordy, talented, intelligent, and a complete pain in the backside. The sixty-something actor with a capital A – one of Britain's premier thespians and the nation's darling – could have written his own autobiography if he hadn't spent half the day swimming in his own ego, and the other half in a vat of port. Enter the paid-up wordsmith. No one told me that five other scribes, all experienced ghosters, had already 'declined' the task. My own agent, Charles's son Robert, assured me I could 'do it standing on my head'. Which is what it almost drove me to, or at least banging said head against a stone wall. Just think of the money, I told myself. And hope to God my name isn't on the cover.

Each morning, I travelled to a large house in Richmond and sat with my tape recorder and notebook in a study overstuffed with shiny accolades, waiting for him to sashay in, statesmanlike, in his smoking jacket. Mornings were a necessity, because by lunchtime, he was gin-pickled before starting on the port. This we did for eight weeks, until I arrived one morning to find him being stretchered out to a private wing at St Mary's, and thence on to a drying out clinic. After which point, he was incommunicado and I just had to get on and fill in the gaps.

Word for word, the fee was quite generous, but I'd accrued several greying hairs and ghosting was henceforth struck off my résumé. I was ever thankful that no one got wind of my writing the 'self-penned memoir' which became a posthumous top-seller (the national treasure having drunk himself to death at the addiction clinic). With unusual foresight, I'd opted for a portion of my fees as percentage of sales, and with the proceeds I bought myself a nice little mews house in Highgate, a city-village of writers, artists and BBC types just north of the capital's beating heart. But London of the early 1970s had lost its spark, beset by the Irish Troubles spilling over onto its streets. It was also dirtier and more drab than I ever remembered it, not helped by the miner's strikes dimming the lights in a very literal sense. Even the chameleon Mr Bowie had retired his colourful alter ego

Ziggy Stardust. And like Ziggy, I decided to bow out. I promptly rented out my new home at a ridiculously exorbitant rent and set off for Cornwall.

St Ives is virtually the most southerly tip of the British Isles without actually falling off the end, and so suited my need to get away from it all, plus it was the scene of a single family memory that felt soft – the setting for that photograph where my father had looked dashing in his miniscule bathers, and we appeared gelled as a family. The rest I must have embroidered, but I was drawn to Cornwall by that warm, familial ideal. With it, I also harboured some dreamlike vision of being able to write like Virginia Woolf, all solitude and long walks on the beach, pulling the next book from its place adjacent to my soul, though I'd no idea if that's what actually happened to dear old V. I would follow in her well-trodden footsteps along the multiple romantic coves of St Ives and hope something – more than merely sand between my toes – stuck.

Securing a room of one's own, as Miss W famously encouraged, was easy in St Ives. Renting an entire fisherman's cottage, all quaint inglenooks and whitewashed brickwork, proved even easier. In the days before en-masse tourism, it remained a small, cobbled fishing village with an added population of creative types, hauling their easels westwards in the wake of the renowned sculptor Barbara Hepworth and her co-op, to capture the light of the dawn, fresh fish and the camaraderie of being an 'artiste' in a fisherman's smock. Wisely, some of the bona fide fishing families had decamped from their dinky, draughty cottages to a nice semi inland and were making a tidy rental profit out of the arty brigade, myself included.

But everyone seemed happy enough with the arrangement. I lugged my portable typewriter out of a recently purchased Mini clubman, lit the fire in my bijou cottage and prepared to live the life. If Miss Woolf could do it, no reason why I shouldn't. Minus poor Virginia's tragic end, I hoped.

I lasted a month in my self-induced purdah. It's true that I drafted the skeleton of a novel in that time, the first where I'd attempted to write beyond myself or those in my sphere. Inspired by the sea and the crashing waves (how could you not?), it was a semi-fantastical tale of modern love, interwoven with a siren-esque theme. And for once, the siren in question wasn't me.

My agent was a little sceptical, in reading between the lines of his dutiful and cheery publishing speak: *Glad to hear you're writing again,* Robert scribbled. *Can't wait to read a chapter.*

Me? I was bloody chuffed with myself. After Vietnam, I had finally mastered sleeping again, not waking with horrifying visions of Tony ('72') lying side by side in my bed, with his glassy-eyed gaze upon me. That lifeless glare, with the seeping of blood into my clean white weave of a pillow. I'd gone as far as writing to his mother in the US, hoping it would discharge me of some kind of self-induced culpability, that I hadn't spoken to the poor boy a minute earlier, or made him stoop to help me hoist up my heavy pack. Anything to have removed his head from the sniper's sightline. That type of misguided guilt.

I wrote to her of Tony's generosity in dishing out his chocolate ration and that he was kind to the Vietnamese, but not of the abject fear in his eyes when we suspected the Vietcong were stalking us, or the marks on his pack scoring down the days until he could hug her tightly again. She didn't need to know that. I couldn't fathom if she would ever be blessed with sleep again, but having discharged my letter, I felt Tony's ghost move on to pastures new.

The novel then. A departure from previous efforts, and as such quite hard work. Words for a writer sometimes flow – on a good day they come thick and fast, too speedy to be captured by the pads of your fingers at full stretch, snagged and grasped at from a mind racing with the pace of a whippet, and so end up as shorthand to be unpicked once the intoxication has worn off. That's a rare day of abundance. More often, the words have to be mined from a subterranean seam, chipped at syllable by syllable, fished from the deepest of oceans (see where I'm going with this?). They get trawled up through a sludge of clichés and muddied by pretentious prose, hollow and showy. Much like those last two sentences. Fight your way through the morass and there may be one or two paragraphs that warrant space on the page. Physically, it's nowhere near a real shift down a dark and dingy mine. Mentally, you're in need of a good scrubbing at the close of it.

Christ knows how Virginia did it without a decent pint at the end of the day.

Johan came to me in the cleansing. Dating from the seventeenth or eighteenth century (or the thirteenth, depending on which plaque you chose to believe), The Sloop Inn was *the* pub in St Ives, facing on to the picturesque harbour and a favourite of those sporting the arty fisherman's smock. Real gentlemen of the sea tended to gravitate towards one half of the pub with their talk of net quality and quotas, while the painters and sculptors huddled in the other, swapping locations and light. No acrimony as far as I could tell, just a natural division of labour, brought together by a love of Cornish ale. In the midst of a busy pub that evening, there remained only one spare seat between the two halves, opposite a lone man nursing his beer. I could detect no allegiance by his looks – no smock, but his shoulder-length greying hair was swept back, with a full, tamed peppered beard: fisherman or fauvist, it was hard to tell. He appeared to be in a deep quandary, staring into the honey glaze of his pint glass.

'Is this seat taken?' I said, with unaccustomed reservation.

'No, I suppose not.'

'Well, do you mind?'

He looked up, perhaps at the irritant in my voice. His irises were grey, too, and he struck me as a man who had grown into his eyes, a matching combination that had been years in the making. Mental note: squirrel that little gem away for the book.

'No,' he said. Unconvincingly. But I sat anyway, in silence for a while, until he drained his ale and stood up.

'I'm going to the bar, can I buy you a drink?' he offered, in an accent I couldn't pin down, neither Cornish nor Home Counties. I only knew that it stirred something in me.

He was Danish, which in 1970s St Ives was about as cosmopolitan as you could get. And blow me down, he was a writer too. As I was sucking inspiration from Miss Woolf, he was on some kind of Hemingway track, with the surrounding sea as his constant muse. And as with Ernest, there was also a good deal of fishing, even if mackerel made a poor substitute for the mighty marlin.

All this he told me with an economy of words, in his softly spoken Scandi tongue.

I promise you faithfully that love was not in my sights. Solitude was my only quest, plus a chance to reflect on life gone by. At forty-three, I was becoming acutely aware of middle age, alongside my remaining years potentially alone, with only brick-and-mortar assets for company. I felt St Ives and my tiny cottage was a rehearsal for the real thing.

But think about it – Johan wouldn't be 'man eight' without numbers one to seven having gone before him, and my life thus far was proof positive of 'things' popping up when they are least expected. Love and its attendant baggage being the most inconvenient and immersive of them all.

I hadn't read any of Johan Sogard's books – they had only been published in Danish at that point – but he'd read two of mine. Despite my not fishing for an opinion, he pronounced them 'interesting'. In the same way you might describe a dose of athlete's foot as 'thought-provoking'. I drained my cleanser of cloudy ale, thanked him (though for what I wasn't sure) and wished him a good evening.

'And is it not the custom to buy me a drink in return?' he said, in perfect command of English – the language and its people, it seemed. His grey eyes were suddenly not so steely.

'Oh, yes, of course. Tomorrow night?'

'Perfect. Do you have a car?'

Not a classic start, I grant you, to any rip-roaring romance we scribes might create, but this was real life. Since when did anyone's day-to-day existence read like fiction?

We drove out to another hostelry, this time near to Land's End, and sat for a time in silence watching the spray arcing over the magnificent rocks in a faultless framing of the sunset. To continue a previous, awkward analogy, I sensed he was mining the scene for words. I'd known men in my time who were streetside philosophers, Ludo and Victor among them, but none whose silence spoke so loudly, whose quiet presence was instantly comfortable to be with. What follows is the type of sentence I might easily write in a book and expect my readers to swallow at face value. But hand on heart, I really did believe from that moment I had known Johan all my life. Truly.

Later, inside the warmth of the pub, we exchanged words, and lives. Mine was heavily edited, of course. No need to frighten off a potential friend, let alone a suitor. His forty-seven years on this planet had been quiet in comparison, certainly much less gadding about than yours truly. And yet his stock of knowledge and self-worth was rich and carefully cultured, as if he'd stuck a conduit in the earth – I pictured it as a giant straw – and simply sucked up all that he required. He knew things. Moreover, he knew about himself, his place in the world, and where he wanted to be as a writer, happy enough to be well respected in his own country. Not a household name, but a constant presence on the shelves as a reliable teller of tales imbued with meaning. I was to learn later that nothing much happened in Johan's novels, but it didn't need to. Reading his carefully orchestrated words was like spooning the best dessert into your mouth and holding it on your tongue until it melted (Enzo and his mother's tiramisu came to mind at that point). He was an artist with a palette of words – what good old Charles would have dismissed as 'one of those bloody literary types'.

Except I couldn't dismiss him. Despite my wannabe Woolf-dom, all solitude and sacrifice to the writer's cause, he reeled me in. Hook, line and sinker, if you can excuse yet another appalling use of cliché. It does seem apt, though.

Hang it – I might as well go the whole hog and employ blatant plagiarism. *Reader, I married him.*

⋆⋆⋆

Not straightaway, of course. That would have been madness in a purely clinical sense. And I was beguiled rather than crazy, entranced by Johan's inner calm. As with Enzo ten years before, I needed to be certain of giving over my future to any man before waltzing up that aisle. Along with all my assets, which Leo continued to remind me almost weekly after I broke the news: 'Sign away *nothing*, Ruby,' he warned. 'Marry the man, if you must, but do not offer up a single signature on your assets.'

But I was – utterly certain. This was it. He was IT. Though, strictly speaking, there was no aisle to waltz up. In the physical sense, I'd known Johan a full three months when we tied the knot at the St Ives registry office, tripping out onto the municipal steps and very pleased with myself at finally laying down a real documented history, our wedding photo to sit on the mantelpiece alongside my fading family image. There was me in a ridiculous purple trouser suit with flares the size of boat sails, and Johan in his trademark leather jacket. I'd cut my hair, and he'd trimmed his beard. My only regret was that my father remained too frail at that stage to make the journey from London – I wanted more than anything for him to see me 'settled'. A friend from The Sloop took a snap and ran it down to the local chemist for processing. In retrospect, we look a sight. But even to this day, I think we look happy.

So, we two – his Ernest to my Virginia – set up the marital home in my own rented cottage, his being smaller and draughtier than mine. We typed in opposite nooks by day, and came together by the fire at night.

We talked, walked in silence, and sat on the rocks overlooking

Porthgwidden Bay, soaking up the spray. 'Let's go mining,' I'd say when our brains had run dry.

For goodness sake, we even got a dog! Our small, terrier-like charge had been a long-term resident in the local dog shelter, with a wayward front leg and blind in one milky eye. As a result, he ran in circles like a crab, which I thought very apt for our location. He looked like Snowy from the Hergé adventures, and was already tagged 'Tintin', so we'd stumbled on a literary connection of sorts.

'He's a bit of a misfit,' the shelter worker said, as Tintin peered with his one good eye from inside the cage, forlorn and unloved. We bonded instantly.

Can you picture it? Me, in living, breathing domestic bliss? Minus the free-range children, but I'd already reconciled myself to that. Too old and enduringly selfish was never a good combination for revisiting motherhood at forty-plus. I knew about Johan's family back in Denmark, his ex-wife and two children, then teenagers. He saw them twice a year and, yes, I suppose, I did wonder how he could relinquish that precious contact, but then who was I to cast judgement? I'd been a physical presence to Jude for all of six weeks. Johan had read *Mother* and we spoke of my boy only once or twice.

'It's all there in the book,' I said, as if I believed it myself.

Our self-imposed seclusion, save for a social pint or two at The Sloop, lasted eight months. Happy months, by and large. In my new-found guise of kitchen goddess, I perfected a handful of recipes that I could lay on the table without shame, and Johan taught me the art of the Danish sandwich (which, let me tell you, is an art, and light years from cheese and pickle). We made lazy love in the afternoons under a sloping ceiling, and once or twice I was sucked back to 1947 and Michael's garret, with a dusting of memory rather than envy. My breasts were looser, for sure – more like a wrinkled peach past its sell-by date – but my resolve and direction were firmer. Johan kissed the tiny scar under my earlobe, but never felt the need to explore its origins. Nestled next to me, I had a husband whose only need was to absorb. I was his lover, and – unbelievably – a wife.

The books, or our 'babies' as we called them, dominated our nightly conversations and the air around us, either sitting like sediment in the winter months of high, coastal winds, or wrapping us in a blanketing balm, dependent on whether the words flowed or turned to cold ash in the grate. It was a love-hate tug-of-war in the way writing a book is meant to be.

For the first time since *Mother*, my own world on the page consumed me. The characters I'd created were, in my own view, more selfless than I could ever be, the women especially, a depth to them that I recognised in others I'd met, but had so shamefully been absent in my personal endeavours of the past. Ursula was strong and fierce, and yet giving, willing to put others before herself, her sister Caroline headstrong but equally selfless, and together they formed a wall around the family, their minds given over to the fantastical swell of the sea as a method of inspiration and survival. They became like the imaginary friends of my childhood. Sometimes, I'd stop typing and wonder how I could write it but not *be* it, and where in the hell it was coming from. Bloody hell, was this how Virginia had felt during her famously prolific spells?

I didn't think for a minute that writing it would fix me (far too many broken parts), but I fancied I might learn from it, use it as a mirror to hold up to myself – it was a line I'd often heard other writers use in interviews, but one that I'd never really understood. Now it became crystal clear. So much of my past work had been about a thinly disguised me, and not what I could imagine myself as. Maybe this was it. Perhaps I'd discovered a way of facing up to my own inadequacies, and producing not just a good seller, but quality work. A book to be proud of. Four years before, I'd been proud of *Mother*, but the subject was so marred with distress, I'd not been able to read a single word of it since.

So prodigiously smug was I about this new work in progress that Robert's request for 'a peek at the new chapters' fell on deaf ears, endlessly rebuffed or ignored.

'Patience,' I teased him over the phone. 'But I promise you won't be disappointed. This is a new take on my writing. One that you've not seen before.'

Only Johan was my bouncing board, only Johan asked the awkward questions of my characters that an editor was bound to pounce upon at a later date. 'What's the message here, Ruby?' he would push me. 'What is Ursula trying to say?' 'Think about the underlying theme.'

In the past, I had always reached that point, usually after a painful push–pull process with Charles or Harvey, and latterly Robert, to produce something worthy of publication. But my technique had always been just to write. I put a sheet into the typewriter and I started, like a greyhound out of the traps. Some days proved to be more of a three-legged race, but I was consistent when the muse saw fit to bless me. There was a certain level of forethought (to call it planning might be excessive), but much like my life, I relied on the words turning up when needed. And I did recognise rubbish when I read it. I produced plenty and condemned a good deal to the fire grate. But I'd never exposed my work to such scrutiny in the process. Johan, by contrast, *interrogated* my motivations.

'It has to have meaning, Ruby, or else what's the point?' His beautiful, ashen eyes narrowed with serious intent. The accent still made me weak at the knees.

Up until that juncture, I thought the whole point had been to entertain, but I only shared that notion with Tintin in private. Johan pitched his argument with such calm surety that he could only be right. What had I been playing at all these years?

While I beavered away in my nook with new-found purpose, I barely noticed when Johan's typewriter became increasingly silent. He took to walking alone in the mornings and the afternoons, to the level that poor old Tintin was exhausted, hiding under my feet when summoned for another hike along the beach.

When asked if there was something wrong, and whether I could help, Johan brushed it off as normal. 'This is how it is with me,' he said. 'I have to work through it. It'll come right, don't you worry. Tell me where yours is going today.'

A month on, his typewriter had been virtually mothballed. His mood has gone from deep to detached, and then one step further into depression. Our exchanges became limited to courtesies, and sometimes not even those. At night we teetered on our respective edges of the bed, afraid to make inroads, let alone love. All too easily, I recognised the signs of our threads beginning to fray, but we were married, for goodness sake. Even in the presence of a municipal registrar, wasn't it supposed to be forever?

'You won't let me in,' I moaned, and then railed like a fishwife. 'How is this a two-way process when I'm not allowed to know what you're thinking?'

I'd never before had to dig so deeply to find someone I thought I knew inside out, only for a mere wisp of him to fall away from my fingers in the rare moments he did speak. A sensible woman would have let him be, but the tantalising nature of it only fuelled my appetite for more. Typical me – always craving what I can't have. With Ludo, and Enzo before him, I'd been content with a long fuse, in the knowledge they would emerge fully, and that the slow burn of a relationship was actually quite fun. But with Johan and I, the fuse had been short and burned bright. Perhaps too vivid. Now I was having to rekindle my own husband, the man who was supposed to be the last in a fairly long line of lovers. It felt like trying to light a fire with wet seaweed.

'Perhaps we need some space, Ruby,' he suggested one evening. 'I'm overdue a visit home.'

'Home?' I screeched unreasonably. 'Isn't this home now?'

Tintin whimpered under the table.

Distance, and the 'space' Johan so craved, came our way several days later. The news of my father's death from a serious stroke cut through our near wordless existence, and he waved me off in the Mini the same afternoon. He didn't offer to accompany me, and I didn't ask. I needed to share my grief with those who would miss George Devereaux and not with a stranger to my father, who was fast becoming one to me. In that, Johan read it right, but he promised to postpone the Danish trip until I returned.

'Someone has to look after our furry boy,' he said.

If I'm being brutally honest, the morose face of Tintin sparked more of my tears as St Ives receded into the distance.

I spent eight days in London without word from Johan, since we had no phone at the cottage, and when I rang The Sloop for any sightings, no one had laid eyes on him. Picturing him sprawled in bed, in a murky pool of dejection, I sent a brief note detailing the date of the funeral and when I'd be back. I signed it *Love Ruby*, but even writing it, I wondered if it was a falsehood. After such a short time, had our seam of love been scraped clean?

George's farewell, as funerals go, was fine: well attended, full of golfing puns and the opposite of what my mother's had been, in that people laughed, and they celebrated the chirpy, satisfied man my father had become in his second stab at happiness. A copy of *Escaping the Cage* perched on the coffin as it sat in the church, the one he'd insisted I sign.

'And he said it must go with him,' his widow Sandra told me. 'He was insistent.'

She and I sat for hours over recent photo albums, cooing at their tanned, happy faces on various cruises and new-style package holidays, swimming and toasting with cocktails, his arm around her waist, in a proud rather than proprietorial fashion. He'd been happy, and she had been good for him.

My dad left this Earth a contented man, causing my own lifetime of losses to be cushioned by his late gain.

Arriving back in St Ives, the sight as I descended the hill into the coves and the tumbledown of whitewashed cottages was beautiful and bittersweet. I yearned to get back to Tintin and my typewriter, but did I relish the sight of Johan, or the ongoing tussle with his unfathomable depths? Which welcome would prove the warmest: man, dog or machine?

I needn't have worried. My desk was as I'd left it at the top of the house, a little dustier but ready and waiting.

Johan was not. Nor was he in The Sloop, or any of the cafés he'd come to frequent through not wanting to be at home. His minimal wardrobe was gone, and his own typewriter – passport too. My stomach lurched in the knowledge that he'd left for Denmark without telling me. And likely for good. Yet my heart cranked painfully at the whereabouts of Tintin. Surely, Johan wouldn't have been so cruel as to flee with our four-legged charge? My *baby*?

I sat in the damp and vacuous cottage, with the full realisation that I was more upset about a dog than a husband; certainty dawned that we had run our course. The seam was barren. A timely, distinct yapping from next door's cottage set me smiling again, and in limped Tintin, spinning his crab-like circles and offering up wet, licky kisses. The best of greetings. Johan hadn't been so heartless as to take what I clearly treasured the most.

Oh, but he took something else instead. He stole what was within me, that I'd dragged out over the months, a part of me shaped and worked so diligently. I hunted high and low for that manuscript and my notes, any scrap of what I'd put down, all ninety thousand words of it. Sure, the general idea was in my head, but once I'd discharged a stream of thoughts onto the page, my brain rescinded any responsibility for it. There were other things to cram into the empty corners, new ideas to chew over. These were the days before word processors and computers, no discs or chips to use as the brain's holding pen. You put it down on the page and hoped a gust of wind didn't blow away a year's work. Or that a thieving, conniving husband might not abscond with your life.

Eventually, I spied the note propped between the tea caddy and the kettle: *Sorry*.

Sorry, my arse.

Three pints down at The Sloop, I weighed up my options. I could go after him, on an adventure reminiscent of the real

Tintin in tracking down my work, seizing it back in a physical fight, with reams of paper floating down like confetti (a good scene to write, potentially). And accuse him of what? 'You have my work, you *fiend*!'

'Your work?' he might say. 'Prove it.'

In all truth, I couldn't. There is no copyright on the ideas rattling around in your head, or the copious notes on random scraps of paper. Which meant the apparently enigmatic Ruby Devereaux had been very foolish in not logging the book's premise with a much shrewder agent. Such was my trust in Johan that no one else knew what was in my head, inked onto three hundred plus pages.

I harboured little hope of seeing it again, except with his name under the title. I wrote to him, of course – letters that were duly returned. My solicitor eventually tracked Johan down via his new publisher, if only to issue the divorce proceedings that he didn't contest. On subsequent evenings, I sat with Tintin at that very pub we'd been to on a first date, watched the waves arcing as they had, and wondered at Johan's motivation.

I had loved him, and I think he loved me, in the small window we had. Clearly, he coveted the idea of being a writer more, and for him it was vital oxygen. I'd always fed off words, or what they brought me, but I did not starve without them. By contrast, Johan had begun to fade away as his talent deserted him. I watched it happen, day by day. His entire identity had been in danger of shrinking to almost nothing. It led me to view the betrayal as an act of survival on his part, rather than any spite or greed towards me. He was desperate to feel like a writer again, and there was a book to save him, within his grasp. Tantalising. Never mind that it was written by someone else, the woman who had pledged her life to him.

I wasn't in any mood to forgive him, but for the first time in a while, I could understand him. Lord knows, I had known desperation over the years and appropriated my fair share (Michael lurching into my vision), skimmed reality and used it to my advantage. I'd even purloined my own father as a subject. None of which I'd done with any intended malice, but as a way of perpetuating who I identified with: Ruby the writer. For years, words had been my only constant. Johan's too. We'd both hurt people along the way and, like me, he'd displayed weakness. Not exactly quid prod quo, but near enough.

In time, I might not hate him as much.

The Virginia dream was over, but I took inspiration once again from the sagacity of Miss W: 'You cannot find peace by avoiding life'. I packed up the house and typewriter, made room for beloved Tintin in the front seat of the Mini, and we motored out of St Ives with a fair amount of regret. And a lesson learned. No more weddings, white or purple or otherwise.

I would miss the soundtrack of the surf, the sand between my toes and the sense of trying to be a writer proper, à la Ms Woolf. As with my life mantra: it was good while it lasted.

Time, though, to rejoin the real world. And Tintin needed to explore London, with his all-seeing single eye and wayward crabby gait. Highgate and homeward-bound we went.

MAN NINE: Alex

London, Spring 1976

Tintin navigated London famously, or the little corner of Highgate that we inhabited quite happily as a twosome. My tenants had decamped to a new and 'more exciting' borough of London, crossing the great Thames divide into Brixton and a much cheaper rent. But my little mews house was perfect, the boy and I walking every morning into the 'village' to buy our copy of the *Guardian*, since it was against the law to live in Highgate and not patronise that paper. We'd peruse the pages in a selection of cafés, and chat to several other writers, all of us perhaps hoping to be remembered in the same vein as other Highgate alumni, notably T. S. Eliot and Samuel Taylor Coleridge. I'd never aspired to poetry, however, feeling myself more aligned with the local cemetery's renowned resident Karl Marx, having a certain sympathy with his political aspirations. And I liked his beard.

At times, we two would go as far afield as Hampstead Heath for our stroll, where Tintin had fun terrorising the puffed and preened handbag-style dogs of old dowagers and ladies who lunched. Once we even fell in step with a python – Monty Python's Michael Palin, no less – embarking on a very involved conversation about books, he never asking what I did, and me never letting on I'd adored him for an age. Tintin didn't try to make whoopee with his leg, and so that was a good day all round.

Despite being in the latter end of my forties, I was a content sort of cheery. I'd begun a loose liaison with a newspaper editor; he offered sex and made me laugh, and I gave him respite from his enduring marriage that was – and I quote – 'as cold as mackerel on a slab'. He proffered insight and gossip, too, always valuable when you're on the hunt for an engaging hook for the next novel. There were no expectations, ties or tantrums between Ed and I, and Tintin liked him. It worked well.

The shadow of Johan had long left me, though I continually described myself as single rather than a 'divorcee', and my decree absolute was propped in my office, directly in my eyeline, as an aide-mémoire never to venture there again. As if I needed reminding.

Better still was the pile of proof copies squeezed next to it, a divorce present to myself, I liked to think. It was called *The Plotter*, a fictionalised account by yours truly, concerning two writers who fall deeply in love, then out again, and the theft of an idea by one from the other. You get the gist, having already read the reality? I wrote the entire novel in a frenetic three months holed up in the house over the winter of 1974, typewriter steaming (to the extent my keys bent on more than one occasion and the ribbon detached itself), emerging blinking into the spring sunlight, expunged of my wrath and his betrayal. It wasn't that heavily disguised, just enough for everyone in publishing to recognise the key players, but without Johan's lawyers being able to sue me for defamation. Better still, it sold. Oodles, compared to Johan Sogard's sea-theme literary effort, which sunk to the bottom of Denmark's shelves, and – the last time I checked – remains out of print. *The Plotter*, by contrast, sat in the Sunday Times Bestsellers List for ten weeks. Revenge is indeed cloyingly sweet.

So, my life was good, and it had settled into some sort of rhythm; God forbid that dreaded age was creeping up on me, but for the first time in decades I did not have itchy feet. My wanderlust had gone on holiday.

Suffice to say, I was pootling along on another project, and holding it very close to my chest, in between enough book parties and soirees to keep me out of trouble, courtesy of my married editor – since his wife lived in the sticks and rarely ventured into London – plus my own circle of London literati. Spring was warming up the earth, and I sat with Ed (the only man here I honour with a pseudonym) in Highgate's pub hub of The Flask, musing over the world as it stood. Fairly humdrum, we concluded. A middle-aged pseudo-socialist had just taken over the reins of Downing Street from another middle-aged would-be-socialist, both of them claiming to be 'of the people' in as much as they didn't speak with a plum in their mouths and hadn't been schooled at Eton. A Swedish group of four dominated the music charts with inoffensive songs that were catchy, but hardly likely to raise the barricades of any revolution. In fact, the only proper revolt occurring was across the Atlantic in Argentina, a long way from Sweden and the UK.

'We need something to hot up,' Ed said into his gin and tonic. 'Or I might be forced back to the sticks once in a while. Save me, Ruby, from a fate worse than the Homes Counties.'

What could I do but oblige? And lo, did it heat up, in every way.

Those of us who lived through the haze of Britain's summer of

1976 mark it even now as a turning point. In hindsight, it should have been when we woke up to the warning signs of climate change, but then it was just hot. Bloody hot. The intensity of a sauna not in your back garden, but in your house, every room a tropical sweatbox. The sort of heat that breaks thermometers and meteorological records daily. Waking up to a scorching sun was very welcome in those first few weeks of the school holidays, a relief to Brits fed up with years of rain-soaked summer months. The heat morphed to lingering, and then tiresome, while we as a nation rapidly became seared, cooked, broiled and spoiled. After several months it progressed to downright dangerous, when the great British lawn came under attack from the inevitable hosepipe ban. But enough of the weather report – suffice to say that as the Siberian winter of '62 had been a bit nippy, the summer of '76 felt a tad warm.

Alex first floated into my orbit in June of that year, just as the barometer began to wobble. With his tie slightly askew and a glass of warm champagne in hand, he loitered uncomfortably on the fringes of a publishing garden party. I stood on the sidelines for a minute or so, amused by his inability to decide between sinking the champagne and heading for the exit, or dutifully sticking it out. Eventually, he sat on a convenient chair, as if grounding himself physically might aid the decision.

'So, why do you have to be here?' I slipped into the seat opposite.

'Oh, me? Um, no it's very good. I mean, a nice party.' His stammering justification didn't match what I assessed to be the 'smooth, silver fox' look. In his fifties, I guessed, a trim salt'n'pepper beard (which was not de rigueur at the time) above a well-cut, neat navy suit. Expensive but not ridiculously so. On looks alone, suave came to mind.

Watch out Devereaux – you know what suave can do.

'Tell me, are you an editor, long-suffering agent, or some poor accounts manager dragged in to boost the numbers when required?' I posed, assuming he was none of those, but I felt like a game of twenty questions. The party was lifeless, and my energy had to go somewhere.

He laughed. 'Mistaken on all counts, I'm afraid, though I'm flattered you think I might be. Sorry to disappoint, but I'm the politician wheeled in, no doubt to entice the 'serious papers' to send a reporter to one of these things.' He sunk the dregs of his glass. 'According to the press office, my media profile needs "bigging up".'

'In among a bunch of inebriated book-types?' I countered. 'I doubt it. Crucial question then – which side of the political fence are you on?'

'The right side,' he said, as if he was suddenly enjoying the game too.

Oh, hadn't I heard that one before? Maybe when super spy Benedict once insisted he was on the side of right, of justice. Look where that got him. Should I leave well alone, or chance it?

I was bored and flighty from the fizz in my glass. Always a dismal combination for good judgement. He didn't look like a Tory, not with that beard, and no evidence of a plum in his cheek. There was actually a hint of the regional in his accent. 'Are you something important then, or one of those politicos that likes to do earnest work from the back benches?'

He laughed a second time. 'Can't I do earnest work from the front benches?'

'Earnest and champagne rarely go together,' I said, as if it was a widely known fact. 'What's your speciality?'

'It's been said that I make a nice omelette.'

I frowned and surveyed again: earnest with a sense of humour. Far too interesting to let slip. 'Work, I mean,' I pushed. 'If you're in government, where do you govern from? Treasury, or the Home Office? The Arts perhaps?'

He blew out his cheeks. 'I'm going to disappoint you again, but it's Agriculture and Fisheries, for my sins. In my defence, I am a mine of information on fishing etiquette.'

The penny dropped for me then. 'Ah, this book.' I gestured at the surrounding launch party 'It's got a sea theme. But isn't it about a mystical ocean creature in the Norwegian waters of the 1600s?' I'd read the blurb in accepting my invite, but not much else.

He smiled with resignation. 'I told you I'd been wheeled in. The Arts ministry contingent are eating canapés and making merry at the Tate this evening. Don't you just love the creative mind of a government press officer?'

'Well, shall we wheel out of here?' I suggested. 'If anyone asks, you can claim to have been kidnapped by some monstrous kraken of the deep.'

'Total fiction,' he said. 'And nothing less than the bloody papers will print anyway.'

We scooted out like a pair of overgrown kids dodging school for the day after assembly, running with glee to a very nice restaurant three streets away.

'I spend all my life eating nibbly bits at receptions and parties,' said Alex. 'I'm dying for a solid meal.'

So we ate very good food, with wine that was chilled, and

the man from the ministry – Alex Kincaid – proved a very good catch of the day.

'You're Scottish?' I queried.

'Way, way back in the family tree, but I wonder if that's why they thought I would be good in Ags & Fish. It helps to know one end of a salmon from the other.'

'And do you?'

'I know which end I like to eat.'

He was fifty-two, had been a Labour MP for ten years in market-town, semi-rural Cheshire, rising to ministry level fairly quickly. And biding his time for what he considered a desirable posting in Transport.

'My dad was a bus driver, and if he can live long enough to see that, he'll be bloody proud of me for directing traffic in a different way.'

'No ambitions for the top job?' I wondered aloud. 'If you made it to Downing Street before fifty-five, you'd be a baby PM.'

He shook his head with conviction. 'I'd hate to lose sight of the ground level. Believe me, my constituents make sure I don't get ideas above my station. I've got an 84-year-old woman who takes me to task every week at my surgery. I'm thinking about adopting her as my gran, just so she'll be nicer to me.'

We talked a little about me – the potted version, as per usual. His wife had read *Mother* and was profoundly affected, apparently.

'Have you got kids?' I asked.

'Two boys, both flown the nest. Nowhere near politics, thankfully.'

The easy mention of his family didn't unseat me. When had it ever? I'd felt oddly comfortable with married men throughout my adult life, and Alex Kincaid wouldn't be sitting opposite if his conjugal home was all roses above the cottage door. I'd never snared an espoused man – every one of them had wandered willingly into my path.

'And your wife?'

His eyes rose above the menu. 'Disinterested.'

'In politics?'

'No. Me. She does the obligatory charity rounds at home, but only comes to London under duress.'

My inbred nosiness compelled me to pry. Why stay, with children old enough not to be injured by divorce?

'I would make the break and start afresh,' he said, 'but she won't. She's intent on keeping up appearances, maintaining a front. And I owe her that, for her sacrifice in the early years. She willingly puts on her blinkers when it comes to my London life. And the Labour press office are not keen on any marital split making the papers.'

'That sounds to me more like the other side of the House,' I said. 'All for Queen, country and family – nothing else matters. Sure you're not a closet Conservative?'

It was the only point of the evening where he looked truly affronted. 'My father is not yet in his grave, but it would send him there if I ever switched to the other side of the political spectrum. Which I wouldn't anyway. So, more wine?'

He got me drunk, and I let him. Aside from the understanding Ed, he was the only man I'd been physically attracted to for months, that pleasurable tweak-in-the-groin thing. I liked it, that he was older, that I might finally be acting my age. But I also liked Alex and his evident humanity, replacing any pretence of machismo.

His London flat was in my old stomping ground of Camden,

and so we further repaired there for a nightcap. I stayed, of course, most of the night spent on the sofa talking, until tiredness drove us to the bedroom, where we slept, and only slept.

But we made up for it in the morning.

Ed understood. He was true to his no strings pledge, and mindful of my history, he simply told me to give him a ring when I felt like some company again. Alex and I rapidly became a 'thing', as much as we met, talked, laughed and made love, and then went our separate ways. I was halfway through a new novel, he had sittings in the House, and then up to his constituency every other weekend to play happy families and be chastised by his elderly voter cum surrogate granny. It suited us both. In typical fashion, I thought several times that he might be too good to be true, in that he seemed to respect the needs of women like me, but in general, too. It was no mystery as to why his wife didn't want to let him go fully.

There was just a tiny fly in the ointment. Naturally, we led quite separate lives, but on one or two occasions, I thought it would be nice to attend a publishing soiree together, if only to share the humour and give Alex a taste of relief. At a press launch or a drinks party, you could find fun even in the stuffiest of events, given that booky types are quite gregarious people. Engagingly odd, too. There was plenty of the peculiar in his Ags & Fish circles, he told me, but I saw my half of the equation as less dry, if you catch my meaning. It was, however, a non-starter in the eyes of the Labour Party press office. Whatever their political leanings, the British public apparently wanted wholesome, family-centred representatives in parliament, no matter the reality. A man from the ministry could not be spotted with a once girl-about-town. Especially one who was single, and with a past life such as mine.

It meant that for a month or so, we remained close but relatively cool to the outside world. We ventured out occasionally, to a selection of discreet and local restaurants, but with no obvious displays of emotion until we reached his place or mine. Reluctantly, I reasoned it was the price to pay for his company and the closeness that, surprisingly, I had come to rely on.

July limped towards August. The sun burned and the days got hotter and seemingly longer, waking up to a blistering white glare at eight a.m., relentless until the sun disappeared, only for the heat to continue in a clammy, toss-and-turn night of fitful sleep. The daylight hours were a desperate quest for shade, or ice, or lollies from the local shop, or a single moment when sweat wasn't forming at the nape of your neck or trickling down that awkward crevice between your breasts. Tintin and I rose with the lark to fit in some sort of walk before he became a panting, huffing casualty, after which point he stationed himself under a large garden shrub for most of the day, rolling in the dank, slightly cooler earth. I roamed with my typewriter like a house nomad, seeking out a rare wisp of wind to drink in, careful to sate my thirst with innocent lemonade rather than anything stronger. I carried a hand fan with me at all times, like some crusty old duchess.

Alex was busy at work, with parliament approaching recess – their long summer break to mere mortals like you and I – but the heat was beginning to pose a problem. If it continued as the weathermen predicted, the country would run dry. This was a time before 'environment' became a separate issue, with a ministry of its own, before the phrase 'global warming' had even reached the public domain. It was simply a bloody hot summer. But the reservoirs and rivers said otherwise, their levels falling rapidly. Alex being in receipt of these facts (not least via his bulging postbag from concerned anglers), he was under pressure to 'do something'.

'A rain dance,' I suggested unhelpfully, after a pathetic show of trying to make love in heat that reminded me of Vietnam's sweat-stained existence, minus the air conditioning or even a ceiling fan.

'Funny, Ruby. Though I think the PM may not reject that idea,' Alex said. 'I do believe I saw him take off his tie the other day. It's never been known. Everyone in the room thought it meant the end of the Earth.'

'I don't mean to insult, Alex, but as an expert on fishing, what are you expected to do?'

'Their reasoning is that fish live in water, ergo I must deal in water, and so that puts me in the prime position for a solution. It'll be an inevitable hosepipe ban…'

'Killing my roses! You evil despot.'

He ignored the ill-placed humour. 'And then maybe rationing. Popular will not be my middle name. Not least with my wife.'

'Seriously? Rationing?' My thoughts went back to wartime and that post-war scrabble for food and clothes. I was too old not to wash anymore, much less stand out in the street at a standpipe with my bucket. 'Oh God, Alex, I'm beginning to think a rain dance is not such bad idea after all.'

There's no doubt the focus upped his profile as a parliamentary member, and those wily enthusiasts in the press office capitalised in every way. Already jaded with the endless stories of sunburn and children cavorting in fountains, the newspapers turned their focus inwards to the grim forecast this unprecedented hot spell might create: the lack of water, a potential famine of ice cream (God forbid!) and mounting cases of the elderly dying from the heat. Alex was wheeled out again, this time to the television studios, where make-up women pecked at his beard with their scissors, and he tried not to sweat under the lights while being grilled about every climate aspect under the sun. He even got fan mail, and not merely from anglers. One reporter tried to label him the 'Fisherman's Friend'. Mercifully, it didn't stick, despite plenty of encouragement from that zealous press office.

At first, I thought it amusing, teasing him in good spirits about his media presence. Then it got boring. Soon, we weren't able to eat at our small selection of discreet restaurants, for fear of being recognised in public, or the prospect of lurking photographers, who really had become bored of chasing 'scorching' Britain.

Having never courted publicity, Alex began to itch with unease at being manipulated by the party machine. There was, however, no going back or ducking under the limelight. The PM was apparently pleased at having something positive to counter the nation's distinct fatigue, where each and every citizen was hot, sleep deprived and tetchy.

'The Home Office is concerned that irritation sparks flames, and flames get fanned by unrest,' Alex said as we lay naked in my bedroom. 'Before you know it you've got a riot. Riots breed fire, and that's not good. Physically, this country is a tinderbox, dry as dust.'

I scoffed, irritably. 'Are you sure that's not your own blasted party using some emotional blackmail on you? Come on, Alex, do you imagine the consequences of your not turning up for a press conference will be anarchy and destruction on our streets?'

He looked hurt then, for a second time. I realised instantly that it was not his vanity I'd dented, but his purpose as an MP.

Moreover, his life purpose, to make some small change. His entire working life had been about making a difference. He was that rare thing – an honest member of parliament.

'No, I don't, Ruby. I don't for a minute think *I* matter. But I think what we *do* matters a lot.'

So, that was me told, and I – awash with a familiar shame – retreated to a silent, sorry position, heaving myself off the bed and into the shower for the fourth time that day, before the man in my bed pulled the plug on my daily water supply. I apologised before he left the next morning, and it wasn't a deal breaker as far as I was concerned. A tiff. I would make it up to him, be more understanding.

But to the journalist skulking outside my door at seven a.m. that August morning, it was a deal maker. A very profitable one.

Said journalist was young, ambitious and hungry – everything I'd been once in my life, which is how I spotted the dangers of his interest, once I'd opened my eyes to the fact. He wasn't after a salacious flash-in-the pan splash on the front page, though his sidekick photographer got the picture all right, one of Alex departing, the image that could easily have been captioned: *Government minister Alex Kincaid leaving the London home of a friend before the heat of the day dawns. While Mr Kincaid is busy as the appointed spokesman for Labour's newly formed drought committee, his wife remains at their constituency home.* Presumably, the same photographer was still lurking when I left to walk Tintin, and from his resulting snapshot, I recognised that morning as one where I looked less than my best.

Neither Alex nor I spotted our pair of stalkers that day, or the day after. But this wily hack had sniffed out a story and he was biding his time. As with all successful journalists (I hesitate to say 'good'), he was prepared to play the long game. Situated along the length and breadth of Fleet Street were the 'cuts' libraries of every national newspaper in the country, the equivalent of today's internet to any reporter searching for a back story or an identity. Vast files of paper and magazine clippings lay on the shelves, cross-referenced under names and events. If you were important enough, you had your own file. I knew this because Ed had once taken me on a late-night tour of his own paper's library situated in the basement, and we'd been caught being indiscreet somewhere between A and G.

Even with an attendant librarian to point you in the right direction, it was a time-consuming and laborious search, but our press hound had determination. Clearly, he smelled some intrigue, too, because he went digging into those archives, and he found me: the times I had been pictured at parties in the company of Ludo, once side by side with a Beatle or two, possibly a small clipping from *The Times Educational Supplement* when my father's book was published, and the most recent article in a Sunday magazine where I crooned about my bestseller and was almost legally imprudent about Johan and his thieving ways.

Something he found piqued the interest of our boy, because he went deeper still, to his contacts within the Establishment. Squirrelled away somewhere in the bowels of Whitehall was that picture of me oh so long ago – 1963 to be precise – descending the steps of a Lufthansa flight into Berlin Tempelhof Airport, under a hat the width of a sombrero and behind enormous white sunglasses. But it was undoubtedly me, taking the hand of a man later identified in the papers as one Benedict Dalybridge, late of Her Majesty's Secret Service and a suspected defector to the insidious Soviet side. So, he had his connection, albeit a fairly tenuous one: a home-grown writer, who had once slept with a man labelled as the enemy, now sharing a bed with a British Member of Parliament. And not just any MP – a government minister, and *the* man of the moment.

Our dogged reporter had cultivated his prize. He had his very own Profumo.

Blissfully unaware, Alex and I continued to enjoy each other, despite the restrictions of his fame and heat combined. Once again, I was under no illusions he would leave the comforts of his marital home and live in blissful bohemia with me. Neither was it my desire, too old by then to share my space or change my irritating ways. Tintin, increasingly deaf in his old age, was the only man who could put up with my moods on a bad day.

Our life suited us both – weekday nights at mine, generally, as his London flat was little more than a bed and sofa. Every other Friday he would head up to Cheshire and return late on Sunday. His wife may have suspected, but since she and I were never likely to cross paths, she ignored the existence of another woman. Everyone was happy. Clammy but content. And as with most of the country, we couldn't imagine a time when these alternately heated and halcyon days would end.

'Do you think they'll toss you on the heap for used MPs when the winter comes?' I asked glibly. 'How competent are you on snow?'

'Very sure-footed, as it happens,' Alex said, 'but as for my knowledge of the fluffy stuff, I am doomed to be thrown aside. And to be honest, Ruby, I'll welcome it. Though there are rumours of a ministerial opening in Transport, so you never know, I could well become an expert in the art of snow ploughing. Destined to be wheeled out again for the cameras.'

'Then I shall place a ban on snow for this coming season, but not until we've had some cooling rain. After that, I want you all to myself. My very own Right Honourable.'

'I don't feel very honourable at times,' he said. Maybe he was thinking of his wife, or the potage of personalities which made up the House, a good many of whom seemed the opposite of respectable.

'Oh, but you are, Mr Kincaid. The most right and proper I've known for a long while.'

'In which case, you can come and vote for me anytime.'

The phone call came early one Saturday evening, on a weekend when Alex hadn't travelled to Cheshire.

'Ruby, it's Ed.'

'Oh, hello stranger.' I disentangled myself from Alex's arms, as if one lover might see through the receiver and catch me with another.

'I just wanted to warn you.' He didn't sound like the Ed I knew and gossiped with. More like Ed the editor of a large national newspaper.

'Warn me? What about?'

'Listen, I'm breaking all sorts of unspoken codes here, but the *Telegraph* are running a piece on their front page tomorrow. They're leaving it as late as possible, but you can expect a phone call from them very soon, to get your comment.'

'Comment? On what?' I stood naked by the bed, while a furnace took hold inside my body. 'Sorry, Ed, but you're not making much sense.'

'You and the spy, Benedict. Dalybridge. Ring any bells?'

Of course it did. A whole blasted belfry full of them.

'But what about him?' I quizzed. 'I mean yes, he worked for intelligence, but on the right side. Our side.'

'And you're sure about that?' Ed's suspicions carried down the receiver.

'Yes!' I said with conviction. 'And the poor man is likely dead because of it. He was swooped on by the Stasi and never seen again. I saw it happen.'

'If it's any consolation, Ruby, I don't think it's much of a story – too far in the past to have any bearing. But I'm biased, I suppose, and I don't want to see you hurt.'

'Thanks, Ed,' I murmured. 'What do you think I should do? I mean, what should *we* do in the face of the press.'

'Well, I think Mr Kincaid should leave straight away and call his press office, and you should stick to "no comment" until you see a solicitor. Make sure you get some supplies in tonight, since the whole of Fleet Street will be camped on your doorstep by tomorrow morning. You'll be a hostage in your own home for a few days at least.'

'Will that include your own reporters, Ed?'

He sighed down the phone. 'It has to Ruby. I'm your friend, but I also run a newspaper. This is the silly season on news, and after the dry summer we've had, it's the spark we all need. At the end of the day, it will sell papers.'

Alex had heard the entire discourse, his ears pricked by the obvious panic in my voice. I put down the receiver, and in the short time we had, I relayed a candid but condensed tale of Benedict and my limited stint as a spy stooge – to call me a bona fide part of the intelligence service would have been fiction – and the ending which, to that day, I trusted to be true. That

Benedict was no Soviet spy and had gone to his fate as a British subject, loyal to the last.

I hoped Alex believed my version of events through the obvious shock and the political incendiary I had just tossed into his naked lap. In all honesty, I wasn't worried for my own future – by my own reckoning, I'd done far worse in the past, and a touch of infamy generally worked wonders for an author's book sales. No doubt, my agent would be delighted. 'You can't *pay* for that kind of coverage in the Sunday's, Ruby,' he'd coo.

On behalf of Alex, whose humility, honesty and decency far outshone my own, I felt sick. He tried to hide his own agitation, while rushing to pull on his trousers.

'I need to phone my father,' he kept muttering. 'I have to let him know before it… or the shock will kill him.'

Wary of prying eyes and a long lens, we pulled the curtains on our goodbye. Possibly very dramatic, but that's how it felt – a carefully scripted tear-jerker of a film, or a scenario I might struggle to write. A final scene before the hero strides out into the wilderness of middle-class England.

'I'm so sorry,' I said. 'It honestly never occurred to me that any of it would come back to haunt me. He was, like you, an honourable man. Who just happened to be a spy.'

'I do believe you, Ruby,' Alex said. 'But they' – he gestured to the prickly, testy world outside – 'will take some convincing. I owe it to my family, and the party, to try.'

I used every facial muscle to raise a smile while I stroked the beard I had come to know and love, every single grey bristle. 'Nice while it lasted, Mr Kincaid.'

'Wonderful while it lasted, Ruby M Devereaux. Thank you for my long hot summer of love. And passion. And fun.'

I can tell you with absolute certainty that when you kiss

with tears flowing, it makes for very slippery lips. The salt, too, renders a bittersweet taste.

Waiting for that phone call, and the inevitable incursion upon my home and privacy, was like expecting a time bomb to go off any minute. Unusually, I found myself cowed, skulking around the house, peering through the drawn curtains and jumping like a jack-in-a-box when the phone finally trilled. I delivered my dutiful 'no comment' down the receiver, left a message for my solicitor (apparently partying at a golf club fundraiser), and opened a bottle of wine. Or two. Tintin must have sensed the sadness in me; despite the intense heat of our bodies, he curled up on my lap and panted away the evening.

Reporters are nosy and noisy individuals, I discovered at eight o'clock the next morning. They hammered on the door for an hour or so, found their way around to the back kitchen window – at which point my elderly neighbour unleashed her substantial wrath upon them – and then sat smoking, eating and drinking on my doorstep.

When I finally set eyes on it later that morning, the *Telegraph* article was largely accurate. I had embarked on a relationship with Benedict, travelled willingly with him to East Berlin and shared his bed. I'd also slept with Alex, albeit a good thirteen years later. Quite what state secrets might have been relevant or lodged in my memory was beyond me, though not the suspicions of the British press or public. The only tenuous link for me was the Ministry of Transport, where one purported to work, and the other desired to. Yet, my Right Honourable friend was right – the country would take some convincing.

After hours of constant ringing, the phone had to come off

the hook. I craved any breath of air that could make it past the curtains permanently pulled shut. Agent Robert visited the next day with more essentials – milk, wine and dog food, and vital news.

'Have you heard the radio broadcast?' he asked, helping himself to the drinks cabinet.

'Sadly, yes.' The PM had issued a statement which admitted nothing, but in the meantime Alex had been suspended from the party and the House 'pending enquiries'. Like Profumo before him, it was a fait accompli that he would have to resign eventually, and the very thought broke my heart. It would break Alex in two.

'Have you caught sight of him on the television?' I asked Robert, since my own set was temporarily on the blink.

He nodded. 'I must say, he looked very pale. And his constituency house is equally besieged, though I detected a brief, self-satisfied expression on his wife's face as she swept past the reporters. Far be it from me to say, but I think she might have been practising for this.'

She would stand by her husband, the wife stated stoically in front of the cameras. Of course she would. It was in the MP's manual, and Alex would very possibly never stray again. I pictured her spousal face trying to mask the triumph through an expression that was *so brave*.

As for me, I lasted another twenty-four hours as a hostage in my own home. Poor Tintin was desperate to stretch his legs and pee on a new patch of grass, and I wasn't far behind in my own need to escape four walls that had rapidly become a prison. I decided to brazen it out; if Mandy Rice-Davies could do it in a British court of law, then so could I, albeit older and much less of a coquette.

Make-up in situ, hair pinned to battle against the heat and perspiration, I threw open the door to the shocked faces of a languid, bored press pack and sallied forth with Tintin. Flashguns fired, reporters scrambled to their feet, pushing notepads and microphones in my face, a battery of questions aimed in my direction: 'Did you discuss state secrets while in bed, Miss Devereaux?' 'Were you a British agent?' 'Have you ever been a member of the Communist Party?'

'No, but I've always liked Karl Marx's beard,' I said tartly and strode away. They gave up following as Tintin got on with his business, and we breathed again for a short time. On our return, I pushed through the crumpled, hopeful group and battened down my hatches again. I realised this would go on until we all got very weary, or there was no more story to tell. Already bored, I decided to be cowed no longer, and picked up the phone.

'Hello, Ed.'

'Ruby! How are you?'

'I'm fine. For now. But I want these arseholes off my doorstep. Would you like an exclusive?'

I would have opted to pen the article myself, but Ed convinced me it would carry more conviction from another source. He sent his best feature writer, one whom I recognised instantly as a carbon copy of me twenty years previously: confident, sassy and assured of her own brilliance. Well-dressed, too, and unwilting, even in that heat. It was quite irritating that she also had the talent to match her own conviction, steering the questions around to her readers' hunger for detail, unflinching in her demands: *Did you sleep with a known spy, Miss Devereaux, and take part in a clandestine operation in Soviet-led Berlin? Did he have a gun in his bed?*

What else could I say but 'yes'? I qualified that Benedict was a patriot and – mindful of his wife and children enduring a second wave of grief – that he loved his family above everything. I was merely a bit part in his existence, I added, though it pained me to say it. It was the only lie I allowed myself.

And no, I did not swap Soviet pillow talk, I told her, either then or thirteen years later. Why would I? It was the men, the sex and the life I craved, not dull politics. Bit by bit, I spoon-fed her the salacious details that were so craved (still diluted from the reality), and satisfied the British thirst for scandal. At the appropriate points, I turned on the tap for an abundant flow.

'Thank you, Miss Devereaux.' She switched off her tape recorder, we sunk two glasses of wine, gossiped about the lack of decent men in Fleet Street (Ed notwithstanding) and she left to write the week's front page exclusive. Oh, for the benefits of youth and chutzpah. Tintin and I snuggled up in bed and tuned out the still attendant press pack with a good drama on BBC radio.

Miss Star Reporter earned her decent crust – I tweaked the piece only slightly. It splashed under Ed's carefully constructed headline and simmered on the inside pages for three days until a fresh wave of indignation over national water shortages became the newest scandal. My doorsteppers peeled away, and once again, Tintin and I took our morning promenade. I also said a silent thank you to the government press office for orchestrating those 'outrageous' pictures of youths stealing precious water barrels, subtly leaked to Fleet Street. By comparison, 'the writer, the spy and the MP' was already yesterday's news. My book sales weren't bad either.

A few months later, in the icy grip of temperatures that had finally plummeted, a hand-delivered note dropped through my letterbox. In Alex's distinctive script, it read like a heartfelt apology, but also a thank you for my 'sacrifice' in exposing my own story. *It steered the focus from me, and spared my family further damage,* he wrote. *You'll be glad to know my father survived the shock. I'm indebted to you for that blessing.*

I'd heard at the time that Alex did 'the decent thing' soon after and resigned from Ags & Fish, but British politics has a notoriously short memory, and his latest news was soon to be released. *My father is delighted with my new position – Transport ministry, with special responsibility for buses.*

Above all, Ruby, I hope you are well and not scarred by knowing me. Take care of yourself and enjoy life. No regrets, only sadness for what might have been. Alex.

Who'd have thought it? A politician with enduring humanity.

I smiled. I'll admit to smudging his words a little with my tears, and then I burned them. Like any good spy would.

Seven

Ruby takes a breath and lays her head back, a sign that Jude has come to recognise over the months, in reaching the day's end. Dry of words. At times, she stops halfway through the telling of a man, and he's sitting there with his fingers hovering, glancing over to find she's suddenly absent. Propped in her usual chair, head slightly tilted, but somewhere else entirely, eyes closed – not asleep, because when Ruby drifts properly, her breathing changes to a subtle whinny that he finds comforting, like growing another gran all over again.

Today, though, it's the end of that chapter. He knows it, quite pleased with himself at sensing her literary ending, that he agrees when the tale is done. Maybe he is learning something after all, in a job that some of his friends tease him about – being a 'carer' to an old biddy. That hurts: he's no carer, nor a lackey. And she is light years from being an old biddy. Old and infirm, yes, but never that. It's well paid, and it has purpose, too. *He* has a purpose, so who are they to mock?

He saves today's words to the bulging document and shuts down the computer, tiptoeing out of the office, just in case Ruby needs to take her 'brain nap' for twenty minutes. In the kitchen, he's careful not to clatter about while preparing the dinner she'll heat up and eat later – a mild curry requested for tonight, complete with samosas that he'll buy from the deli later.

Jude ponders. This won't go on forever – it can't possibly, and for so many reasons. There are a finite number of chapters (and men surely?), and let's face it, a limited number of years to Ruby, though he thinks she's out to prove the world and Mother Nature wrong on that score. It's a shame, because he likes this job more than he ever anticipated. But no one goes on for eternity. Is that why she's ripping through this book at breakneck speed? He likes to think his presence has something to do with it, and not just the relief to her gnarled and pained fingers in not having to type.

Even so, he's certain Ruby M Devereaux will go out of this world kicking, screaming and sticking two of said fingers up at those left behind, and that makes him laugh as he pulls out the mixing bowl. A fresh Victoria sponge for today's afternoon tea. One of her favourites. 'She'll like that,' he says, breaking eggs into a bowl.

MAN TEN: Maxim

Budapest, February 1982

Life tends to offer up surprises from time to time, and of all people, I should have been accustomed to that universal quirk. Equally, having moved without too much rancour beyond my fiftieth year (aside from the inevitable aches and wrinkles), I imagined reaching a point where one gains immunity to certain conditions, like acne or chicken pox. You've done your time and escaped scot-free. It's pure arrogance, of course – aged or not, bombshells and monsters are often lurking around dark corners to scare the hell out of you.

And my behemoth came back to haunt me.

So debilitating is this scourge of my profession, I did actually make a trip to Highgate local library to seek out the word for it – in the same way aphasia describes a loss of verbal words, or alopecia a loss of hair. For goodness sake, even a fear of clowns gets a word ('coulrophobia' should you ever need to know it). And yet writer's block does not. It's just that. A great bastard of a boulder.

There are no -isms or -obias to describe the anguish of facing the expansive white tundra of the page, day in, day out, a complete dearth of anything Remotely Good. Or Remotely

There, in my case. Paralysis of the prose, a desert of dialogue, a scarcity of script; suddenly, I could furnish neat alliteration until the cows came home, but a lengthy readable narrative? No sir-ee.

It was an acute onset. Incurable? I hoped not. At fifty-two, I had little else to offer the world except weaving untruths and calling it a story.

Never before had I endured such a prolonged attack; there had been short, dry spells, and sometimes a stream of complete twaddle pushed its way out, entire chapters at a time, but I generally managed to rein it in, tame or exorcise the demon prose, enough to produce something that was neither Booker nor Pulitzer, but palatable and publishable. Or so my readers told me.

In the years previous, with the sweaty and unfashionable Seventies drawing to a close, my second spy book had finally come to fruition. A good decade and half after Benedict, it was driven less by my experiences as a James Bond stooge, and more by that brief spell as the hunted of the Alex episode, focusing on the notion of information as power, pervasive and all too freely available. Once again, I surprised myself and the bookish fraternity, all too ready to write me off as a butterfly in her choice of subjects. Le Carré would be forever safe on his pedestal, but I was among those 'snapping at his heels', as one kind critic wrote. I thought for the first time that I might have found my niche. On the back of the spy book came a frankly dull 'family drama', that even now I struggle to claim as my own work (later, I felt convinced the Dreaded Block was something of a penance for its mediocrity).

And then it hit, like a bolt from the blue, some fiendish virus that caused my beloved words to be snatched away. Kaput.

Initially, agent Robert was unfazed. 'Happens to the best of you,' he twittered over lunch. 'It's not a catastrophe, darling. Don't force it, and something will come.'

The drudge of a decade turned over to the slick Eighties, and still nothing, whence even Robert become twitchy, and thereby suggestive. 'Perhaps you need a trip,' he said over the phone, the lunches having dwindled with my output. 'Something to inspire.'

Determined not to be beaten or defined by it, as with Johan before me, I took this as sound advice. His suggestion fuelled a dormant itch – that familiar need to escape having washed over me from time to time during my Highgate tenure. For the previous few years, I'd resisted it. In truth, the tickle was also prompted by the loss of my beloved companion, Tintin, succumbing to his age in dog years and upwards to the great kennel in the sky. Aside from my daily café trips reading the *Guardian*, there was very little to keep me in London, or the great British Isles. Even Ed had crossed the pond and was now heading up a New York daily, very much living the life, or so I'd heard.

Robert was right – perhaps a retrospective was in order? Luckily, I was still in possession of both hips, and enough money to avoid roughing it for a few months. I mothballed the house and called a taxi for Heathrow. My tour would take me to New York, if only to entice a fabulous meal in a good restaurant from Ed, and forward to San Francisco to call on some old friends, before Venice and then Paris. Being winter, I should have perhaps craved the sunshine of the Caribbean, or emulated Martha Gellhorn and settled cheaply in Mexico for an entire season. While attractive, neither of those could deliver what I needed: a firm kick up the arse. It's a fact that indolence comes to us all if you don't feed a constant desire for change, myself included. And I had to confess that, since Alex, I had coasted, both personally and professionally.

New York and Venice especially would mean facing past demons, but if the proverbial arse kick doesn't wound, then what is the point? Did I want to revisit those very places that had, in the past, exacted a searing hurt? Yes and no. The enduring pain of those stark lessons maintained a tiny flame within, enough to singe and burn. Equally, each one had had a hand in shaping me, pushing me on to the next adventure. Prior to my limbs finally giving out, I wondered if there remained one or two exploits ahead, before old age snared me with its suffocating grip.

If I'm honest, there was also love, since the men of my travels had undoubtedly moulded me. Women of my own age – those that I knew – became swiftly aware on hitting the big 5-0 that the allure of any mature female was largely down to brains and wit, since few of us are blessed with the gene pool of Sophia Loren. Ms Loren's spectacular measurements aside, the men of our age wanted bed partners twenty years younger, while we were expected to prop up the male race twenty years our senior. 'Prop' being a key word.

Not me. I was sensible of my age and not inclined to men too much younger, but I was still lean and fit enough, without prescribing to the latest, irritating fad for Lycra, no thanks to Jane Fonda and her bouncing band of aerobic acolytes.

So, yes, I was prepared to face the sting of the past in my pursuit of Something Different. At the very worst, it would pitch me head first into another agonising episode, but at least I wouldn't wither.

***

On landing, I found New York still mad and unstoppable, though it no longer held the charm of sailing up and down the vast avenues in a red, shiny Buick. Instead, the soaring skyscrapers haemorrhaged money-men in suits and sharp haircuts, talking millions over exorbitant cocktails. There was no Jerome, but equally no Mushens or Harvey to guide me through this new chrome façade. Ed was attentive but otherwise 'involved', leaving just a tense, needy nation in my sights, one ruled over by a third-rate movie actor.

Was it me, or had the Big Apple lost its lustre?

After San Francisco, I had high hopes for Venice, once I'd overcome my grief over Enzo and the deathly water's edge. What I found was a city still utterly fantastical and beautiful, but no longer frozen in time, and no chance of spying Gina Lollobrigida enticing a camera lens on the water's edge. The fabric of Venetian magic was there in the ancient bricks, but under a sheen of corporate tourism that was both inevitable and sad. I sought out the pint-sized Livia, who – in the interim of twenty years – had grown a family and made a near transition to Mama, squat and square, but with her glorious dark mane and sense of humour intact. We caught up, cried a little over Enzo, and went our separate ways, she back to her Venetian kitchen and me to the train station. It had been neither painful nor cathartic, but it was enough.

Lining up at the ticket office for my train to Paris, I tuned in to a nearby conversation in English, since any writer – stricken by paralysis or not – is inherently nosy.

'Paris is so overdone,' one woman professed. 'So expensive, too. If you want ornate, and somewhere cheap, then Budapest is your best bet. I mean, it's known as "the Paris of the East".'

'But isn't that behind the Iron Curtain?' the other voice replied.

'Well, yes. But it's not grey like East Germany. They know how to live, the Hungarians.'

I left the queue there and then, in search of the nearest consulate to issue me a visa. Chance, fate, serendipity – label it what you will – but I recognised the calling. And that's what took me to Budapest, and ultimately to Maxim.

Snow from the park bench seeped through my thickest coat as I gazed up with continuing admiration at that staunch, stone beard and mused on how Mrs Marx coped with all that hair, probing beyond the great man's flowing locks and the facial bird's nest to reach her darling Karl underneath. Since they had seven children, she must have journeyed on a few occasions. It was, I judged, a granite representation to match that in Highgate cemetery, nudging up alongside his ideological stable-mate, Mr Engels. Say what you like about them, but the communists did a good line in statues.

Just beyond the square, and out of the corner of my eye, stood the bleached brick of the 'White House' – the Communist Party headquarters – often given a wide berth by native Hungarians trying to avoid its sweeping security cameras. Having already been accused of spying and tainted red by my own countrymen, I lingered, quite unperturbed. They'd let me in, after all. I'd filled in the forms, passed muster at the police station and all under the beady eye of communist customs. The man who had been tailing me, more than likely from the Hungarian secret police, gave up after just a week. Perhaps they viewed me as a kindred spirit? It was true that in a little over two weeks, I'd become very much at home in Budapest.

Into this scenario, a distinct bear-like form moved through

the monochrome landscape of Jaszai Mari Square, a shuffling cloud of Gauloises smoke, like the opening credits to a foreign arthouse film.

He paused to move in next to me, lit a fresh cigarette from the first, sat back and followed my gaze upwards. 'Nice beard,' he said in English, heavily accented in French.

I turned and surveyed. The bear was equally hirsute, and perhaps just as portly, salt-and-pepper locks tumbling over his thick scarf. But for the accent, he might have been a living effigy of comrade Marx on the plinth.

'Hmm,' I said. I'd been picked up once before in a snowy scenario, by a man who looked like a Soviet and really was a spy, leaving me cautious to this approach.

He moved his eyes from Karl and shifted his solid body sideways, swathed in a large and worn black leather coat, the Hungarian winter uniform. 'Would you consider posing for me?' he said, eyes crystal blue and alive against the neutral surroundings and his own grey.

What was this? A contrived effort at my own life in flashback? Even Michael hadn't pitched it so bluntly.

'No,' I shot back. Bluntly.

'And why not?'

'Because I don't make a habit of taking my clothes off for strangers.'

The resulting laugh had a throaty Gallic edge to it. 'Oh, but I don't want to paint you nude. People are much more interesting covered up.' He leaned in closer, giving off a certain musk under Gauloises and soap. 'Your face, it's so beguiling. You've lived an interesting life, I can tell.' But he didn't reach out to probe or touch. He just looked – at me, through me, as if I was already a hologram and he could examine any part of me at will.

I shivered and said nothing. Critically, what I didn't say was no.

'Coffee?' he offered. 'I know the best place around here. Good torte too.'

Despite the shortages of life behind the Iron Curtain, I'd learned quickly that Budapest did not want for coffee and cake. In my first days alone I had recognised it as a staple – of life, soul and socialising, so that any shortage could have easily sparked a second revolution. Any man promising the best was to be given a chance.

'I'm thirsty and cold,' I justified, 'so one cup would be fine. And perhaps a slice, too.'

He pushed out that Gallic rasp in response, thick with delight rather than triumph.

Over a grubby Formica table, we drank rich, exquisite coffee and ate creamy Dobos torte, incongruous with a traditional gypsy folk sound pushed out of a tinny transistor and the surrounding Hungarian chatter, loud and urgent.

'So, Ruby Devereaux, what brings you to Budapest?'

'Life, loss, a search.' I scraped the last of my torte, eager not to give too much away. 'And you, a Parisian in the Paris of the East?'

'Frustration and poverty, and the fact that I can't afford a garret in my own home city because of all those moneyed bankers buying up Paris wholesale.' He smiled under the copious beard. 'And, of course, this glorious communist regime, which is prepared to pay me to be an artist.'

'Does it follow you're a socialist?'

'You know us French – Vive la République!'

Up until that point I'd had no friends in Budapest, and Maxim Joubert became one instantly. And then I was among his entire circle of ex-pats and local artists, of which he seemed to be the heart, the pivot of so many gatherings and wine-soaked, late nights dancing to an impromptu Hungarian band, talking politics, philosophy and nonsense into the early hours.

Life was tough for a good many Hungarians, but they were generally regarded as the 'happiest barrack' of the Eastern Bloc, wary of the regime but much less fearful than East Germans, I noted. Despite the snow and cold pinch of winter, there was a vibrancy, in the bars, and the 'Presszok' cafés that held the same communal reverence as fish'n'chip shops back home. Together, Maxim and I soaked in the famous spas dotted around the Buda Hills, sauntered down Andrassy Avenue, the city's equivalent of the Champs-Élysées, and ate food flavoured by omnipresent paprika, served by waiters who were gruff and grudging at best. And the cake! With wide eyes and sated tongue, I soaked up the Baroque, stately cafés of old, where dissidents had once chewed over the country's future under high ceilings and gilt edges. The ideologies had been and gone, leaving these magnificent 'kavehas' as testimony to the country's greatness and devotion to coffee.

What wasn't to love? As with so many Eastern bloc countries, officialdom was a slow train to exasperation, but if – like me – you had time and hard western currency, there was a way to almost enjoy the excessive order over a bedrock of chaos. I *liked* the slow, smelly trolley buses known as the 'Geriatric express', the dreadfully dubbed episodes of *Starsky & Hutch*, and I positively revelled in the infuriating, aged telephone system, which meant I couldn't possibly call Robert and report my lack of progress on any new work. Instead, I rekindled the art of letter writing, plus the excitement of receiving one in return – tangible and crafted with care. It meant I was rapidly in my happy place, still entirely dry of ideas and prose, but as the weeks went on, it seemed to matter less and less. Life was good, busy and cheap.

Just being in Maxim's orbit wholly absorbed me, aware that I was in the presence of an intense, complicated personality, a tortured creative through and through, who would disappear for days into his old, high-ceilinged apartment near to the Chain Bridge and refuse to answer the doorbell. When I called, his long-suffering neighbour underneath confirmed he was alive, at all times of the day and night apparently. Within the week, Maxim always emerged, hair lank and spattered with a rainbow of oils, his pupils pinpricks from lack of sleep and light. His mood I can only describe as a strange, catatonic zeal, as if his mind was worlds away, yet talking ten to the dozen while I ran him a bath, stripped off the clothes stiffened with dried paint, and spooned him food like a baby. After several hours' sleep, in which his hands twitched with an imaginary brush, he was revived and back to the ebullient Maxim we all loved.

The resulting canvasses – always bold, brash and impressionistic – sold for a pitiful price in the impromptu art fairs across the city, mostly to tourists looking for a bargain and hoping they'd stumbled on the East's Picasso of the age. To Maxim, this ranked as success, and it was something I understood, in recalling how I held the first Ruby Devereaux novel in hand and marvelled at people parting with their hard-earned cash to read my words. It was enough for Maxim that walls across the world would be hung with his work, something sprouting like magic from his brush.

Extra money, to fund his expensive Gauloises and brandy habit, he made from painting large and impressive works commissioned by The Party, enormous depictions of comrades with chiselled jaws holdings arms aloft in triumph at the success of communism. Once or twice, he portrayed the heroic Marx and used his own reflection as the model. And because he was a genuine talent, he could do it all. Maxim had no airs of being a master; painting was all, and he lived the life only to fuel his passion.

Unquestionably, he was complex, and perhaps that's why we fell into each other – it was like holding up a mirror to myself, minus his facial hair. When or how we became known as a couple I can't actually recall, since we never actually lived together (his mess wasn't complex – it was chaos, plain and simple), but probably when I moved into the lofty apartment above his in the spring of '82, just as the world's focus shifted to a previously unremarkable set of islands in the South Atlantic, known as the Falklands.

Maxim and I fell into an easy pattern, eating together – he just tolerating my cooking that contained a 'pathetic' amount of garlic, and me enduring his countless attempts at the best poppy seed strudel.

'Shouldn't we just go out for cake?' I'd say, to his dogged assertion that he was French and, as such, 'I can cook anything!' He couldn't – the Hungarian cake shop always triumphed. Our circle of friends quickly referred to us in the plural, and we were invited once or twice to parties at the French and British Embassies, as oddities I liked to think, but certainly as a pair. Aside from his painting purdahs, we spent almost all our time together. After all, what else was I doing, aside from a constant quest for literary inspiration? *Something will come out of this,* I wrote confidently to Robert. *I'm practising at being patient.*

Truth be told, I was too beguiled with Maxim, hot Buda spas and kavehas to worry about The Block. His conversation inspired my thinking, his presence lifted every gathering. We had everything.

Except the sex.

Maxim was true to his word that first day; he painted me, time and again. In my dressing robe, huddled under a blanket on his sofa, once in the bath, my face peeking out from behind the shower curtain pulled across to preserve my dignity. Yet he never touched, or kissed, except in that rapid, flamboyant French way on either cheek. We shared a bed on occasions, where we simply slept, our bodies separated by a thick eiderdown or a thin sheet, depending on the inconstant nature of our building's heating system. Equally, there was no significant other in each of our lives. We were committed. Together.

'*Ma chérie*,' he purred at me constantly, but never to another man or woman in our little cluster.

You'll have deduced by now that I am a tactile creature by nature, and a big fan of sexual liaison. I still liked it. Amid this odd coupling, I asked myself time and again: did I crave it over and above the relationship? Maxim and I spent hours discussing the world at large, setting the universe to rights in lazy, late-night parleys of too much wine and liqueurs. We talked of love as the world's pivot, of sex in art, art as sexual, but never what wasn't between us, as if Maxim thought the act so unnecessary it simply didn't warrant a debate, that sex between us would be a mere distraction. Oddly for me, I fell into his way of thinking.

But I was a woman still. The absence prompted a critical surveillance of my own body in the bath, pondering on how unattractive I might have become to men of Maxim's age – parts that were once taut, now flaccid with age and overuse. Was I sexually attracted to him? Not especially, with his broad, fleshy frame and tendency for shapeless clothes, the unkempt beard. The unwashed episodes of frenzied creativity. Like so many people, though, I couldn't ditch the innate need of being wanted. With Maxim, there had been none of the chase so vital in previous liaisons, the 'will we, won't we' period that fizzles and fuels, raises your heartrate and pinches at the secret space below your umbilicus. We'd skipped that part entirely.

I'd had male friends aplenty over the years, and what I believe younger people now refer to as 'friends with benefits' (we practised it, just didn't name it) but never a platonic love affair, one where the engine of sex doesn't reflect the smooth running, or an intermittent idling and a necessary thrust to keep a relationship well-oiled.

Did I like this sexless coupling? Was it sustainable? Could I live the rest of my life without the glue that had been so vital in every other emotional connection? I didn't know and – what seems even more incredible to me now – I didn't think too much about it, bar the odd bodily perusal in the bath. I was enjoying life far too much, a happy existence behind the Iron Curtain with my very own French (sort of) lover.

Those in our tight-knit group had become accustomed to Maxim's zealous disposition and his mercurial moods, the times when he became so loud in a bar or café that even unabashed Hungarians winced at his fervent nitpicking of the system, eyes everywhere for lurking secret police. Gradually, though, these outbursts became more frequent, his vitriol forming into spiny, verbal arrows aimed at his closest allies. Come the morning, he'd put it down to drink, or frustration, always apologetic after the fact. Like our friends, I tolerated it, because it was Maxim and we all loved him, never imagining that his '*chérie*' might one day become the target.

We two were having a perfectly reasonable discussion one

afternoon in the Central Café, an age-old kavehas boasting a proud history of academics, thinkers and writers sitting among the dark wood, sparring over the future of their country. Given that I'd written nothing aside from a journal in months, the glorious Central served as a reminder that others did put pen to paper from time to time. Perhaps, if I sat there long enough, it would light my dampened fuse. Maxim simply liked the rich gateau, a soothing panacea for his frustration at losing out on a recent Party commission.

Our conversation was interrupted by the face of Zoli at the window, peering in, gesturing he had something urgent to pass on. My face lit up at the sight. Zoli was all of fourteen, around the same age that my Jude would have been, which is possibly why I took him under my wing so keenly. He spoke some English and was eternally resourceful – I gave him a monthly retainer, helped to improve his English, and in return he acted as translator in wading through the maze of government papers, visas and endless red tape. Above all, I liked him, and yes, I might have been guilty of just a little mothering. Until that point, I imagined Maxim liked him too.

'Huh, you're very pleased to see your boyfriend,' he scoffed.

'Pardon?'

'Your fancy man, your *chérie*.' He covered his disdain with a gulp of coffee.

'Maxim! What on earth are you talking about?' My indignation was postponed by Zoli's breathless arrival at the table.

'Miss Ruby, I've got you an appointment at the ministry in half an hour,' he panted. Built like a string bean, Zoli appeared to run everywhere in fitting all his errands around his school studies. 'If we don't make it, then you might not be able to renew your visa.'

'We'd better leave now then.' I reached for my bag, catching Maxim's expression as I did. A look of thunder under the facial froth. I knitted my brows in return, but he only shied away.

'I'll see you later,' I said pointedly.

Later was no better. I'd never seen the supremely confident Maxim jealous or slighted, since people came and went in our circle with fluidity, and he welcomed them all. But something had changed. Pacing in his apartment, he hurled wild accusations at me with abandon, that I was having an affair with Zoli; I had never loved him; I was merely using his circle of friends; I would leave him like everybody else. He raged in self-doubt.

Against every instinct, I bit my tongue. 'Maxim, where is this coming from?' I pleaded instead. 'Zoli's young enough to be my son.'

He circled the room, head down, eyes closed. 'It wouldn't stop you. Any of you. You're all the same.'

'Who, Maxim? Who is "all the same"?' He was making little sense, not helped by a bottle of the black and fiercely bitter Unicum liqueur in his hand, already half empty, giving his lips an eerie, inky taint.

He rounded on me, eyes blazing. '*Women*,' he hissed. '*Witches*.'

Eventually, I wrestled the bottle away and steered him – exhausted by the endless ranting – to bed. What had I just witnessed? Such venom wasn't conjured by alcohol alone, and sitting in his apartment as he slept, the cold ugly shadow of Jerome crept across me. Maxim hadn't touched me physically, swaying wildly and venting his frustration on several canvasses instead. But it's not true, that old adage about sticks and stones: his words stung me. They punched low, my loyalty torn to shreds.

By the next morning, Maxim was groggy and contrite,

hungover too. There was an element of surprise on his face when I confronted him with the bitter accusations he'd fired at me.

'I'm so sorry, *ma chérie*. You know I don't mean it. I drink too much, and it's like the devil's cocktail when I'm burdened with frustration. I love you, Ruby. You do believe that?'

I did, then. Because I wanted to. I needed to.

Maxim was all attention over the next week; he drank very little and even cleaned his apartment, to a degree. More importantly, he didn't bat an eyelid when I announced a short trip south to the city of Baja – with Zoli. For months, my young charge had been keen to introduce me to his grandmother and reveal 'the real Hungary'. We set off in a borrowed, battered Trabant, the power of a hairdryer under the bonnet, waved off by a smiling, munificent Maxim.

Four days later, replete with enough goulash and torte to nourish me for a lifetime, we arrived home. Having driven almost two hundred kilometres without suspension, I staggered up the stairs to my bed, only to be met by one of Maxim's fellow painters, Balint, and several others in the circle. On the landing outside Maxim's apartment, Balint was bent with his eyes to the keyhole.

'Ruby!' he cried with relief. 'We've been trying to get hold of you.'

'What's wrong?'

Of course, I knew. The noise from beyond the door was proof enough, sounds of furniture being turned over, a bellow of anger followed by the whimper of distress. It was the sound of a hungry bear with agonising toothache.

'How long has he been like this?' I asked Balint.

He shrugged. 'We haven't seen him for two days. When I

came to check, he wouldn't open the door. I've been trying to reason for three hours.'

Against the audible anguish, the friends were silent. Knowing looks were exchanged.

'Has this happened before?' I asked.

Balint shuffled his feet. 'About eight months ago,' he sighed. 'We called the doctor, and he seemed fine after that, like it was just an episode.'

It took me almost an hour of pleading and cajoling, promising and stroking at his fragile mood before the latch was reluctantly lifted.

'Oh, Maxim.'

He stood half naked, bloodied from the turmoil of his own destruction, having done battle with easels, palette knives and scalpels. Who knows how much was intentional, or the result of his frenzied misery. We touched then, as I cradled his big, wiry head in my lap, sitting on the floor amid the paint splatters, the debacle and genius of his world.

He sobbed like a baby, nonsense spewing from his swollen lips, into which crept a lucid second or two, and he looked at me – in me, through me – and apologised, again and again. 'I'm so sorry, Ruby, I thought it could be different this time.'

I stroked at his head, and told him everything would be all right. But that was a lie, wasn't it? It's just something that desperate people say. Because I had nothing of truth to tell him.

Zoli had already run for the doctor, and they took him first to the city hospital to patch up his wounds, and then on to what people once called an asylum. In 1980s' Britain, they were long gone, but not in Hungary. Much like their expertise with effigies, communists do stark very well, and here they had surpassed themselves – greying empty walls of a long vacuous corridor led into the room where Maxim's large form perched on a wire-frame bed, slumped. His beard seemed to have grown longer but thinner in the three days it had taken me to gain a visitor's pass. Zoli, as a reluctant but vital interpreter, inched in behind me.

It could have been Bedlam in the true sense of the Victorian horror, but it wasn't, largely down to the caring staff, who gently coaxed their patient, urging him to at least look at us.

'Maxim, how are you?' I asked, stowing my own distress.

His eyes fought to focus through the medication, pupils wavering, and I saw him desperately searching, scratching at his memory in trying to find his own self and the world. And me.

'Ruby,' he slurred. 'Did you have a nice time?'

'Yes, Maxim, I did. But you haven't, have you?'

'No, Ruby. No.' And then he was gone again, head into his chest, somewhere else entirely.

Once I'd heaved up my despair on Zoli's bony shoulder, he came with me to consult the overworked and encumbered psychiatrist. Between Dr Varga's limited English, my pitiful Hungarian and Zoli, we began to understand the man that was – had been – Maxim.

'He first came to us eight months ago,' Dr Varga confirmed. 'A short but very similar episode, and with medication he seemed to improve very quickly. I can only assume he hasn't continued to take it?'

I shrugged. I'd never seen Maxim swallow anything but food and alcohol. And a lot of cake.

'Unfortunately, it's very common,' he went on, with the tone of a man who knows his work will never be done. 'Patients feel better, imagine they are cured and become convinced they no longer need the treatment. Often, they continue quite normally for a while. And then this.' He gestured to the vast, grey mausoleum around him.

'And do you know the cause of Maxim's' – I almost choked on the word madness – 'distress? What's triggered it?'

Dr Varga sighed again. 'We spoke at length during his last stay. Did you know he'd been part of the French resistance during the war?'

I shrugged. Maxim could talk for France, but actually spoke little of himself prior to being an artist. I made a mental calculation – he was eight years older than I, a mere seventeen when the war had started. It was entirely credible.

'From what I gather, he saw a great many things a young man shouldn't,' Dr Varga explained. 'Too much death, and I suspect it's never left him.'

'He doesn't like to touch – intimately,' I found myself revealing, to a man I'd only just met, with a fourteen-year-old boy alongside. Except this was no place for embarrassment or vanity. Understanding Maxim was my priority.

Dr Varga nodded sagely. 'Hmm, he did touch on this.'

'He did?'

'Just once. He spoke of a terrifying incident, where the resistance were caught in an ambush. Apparently, many of his comrades were mown down instantly, and he found himself trapped underneath the bodies, having to play dead until the Nazis were satisfied everyone had been wiped out.'

'And how would that—'

'His lover's face was wedged into his as he lay there,' Dr Varga said, cutting me off. 'Her mouth was open, as if about to kiss him, he told me. Only very dead. After that, he was never able to... physically.'

Any armchair psychiatrist could make the connection, the enduring agony Maxim had hidden for years with his affability: a sixty-year-old man living more than four decades with the nightmare of his teenage years, trying so desperately to love again.

And he did. He loved in his own way. I couldn't have asked for more.

'And so, what are the chances of his recovery?' I asked hesitantly. I'd seen friends before, several writers become slaves to their own spiralling mental anguish. One episode was bad, two and beyond was like being hurled down a greasy stairwell with neither rungs nor rope.

'Only time will tell,' Dr Varga replied, equally hesitant. 'But seeing familiar faces is good for him now. You should keep coming.'

'One more thing, Dr Varga – do you have names of any family we could contact?'

He shook his head. 'Sadly, no. Only that he'd recently updated his details here. And your name, Miss Devereaux, is listed as his next of kin.'

Outside, the spring sun shone brightly as I picked over Maxim's apartment, tidying, righting the chaos of an artist's world he'd so creatively fashioned. On that particular day, what I unearthed revealed itself as a cruel paradox – the blinding light of spring streaming through the window, against the darkness etched into sketchbooks hidden under the bed and tossed into cupboards. Maxim's copious, ferocious markings in charcoal were of gaping holes, into which death and bodies and evil had been flung, the same picture scored heavily into the paper over and over again.

He'd tried to exorcise it all, to satisfy his role as the gregarious raconteur we all adored. And yet the affection he must have craved throughout so much of his life was clearly one touch too far. He so clearly wanted to love, in every way, but simply couldn't.

For weeks, I walked that long corridor every day, to sit with Maxim, often in silence, then to reach for his hand and control my tears when he flinched and pulled away. Then to have his hand finally in mine, and by degrees his head on my chest, stroking at his hair and murmuring to him how we would travel beyond Hungary to the coast for a holiday, or even to Paris, and drink champagne on the Champs-Élysées. 'Where I can finally call you a champagne socialist,' I joked, and thought I detected some tiny response, maybe even a slight spasm of humour.

It was a month before Maxim talked a full sentence, when the powerful drugs were reduced by degrees, and his light switched on again, the fog lifting. I banned him from saying 'sorry' ever again, and he began to talk, at last, of a future without Dr Varga as his keeper and saviour.

And then one day I caught it. In one second. The terror. Abject horror in his eyes of a world beyond the grey walls. If I'd been looking away or fixing him a drink, I might never have seen it. But I did. And it flooded me with a black dread sea in the same way it drowned Maxim in that moment. Fear of the future, stuck in his own head.

I'd like to say I was surprised when Zoli came hammering on the door one impossibly bright Sunday morning just a week later. I should have been horrified and instantly grief-stricken, running to the mausoleum to hold him, but what would have been the point of caressing his big, grey dead head? Instead, I sat stroking his brushes, and feeling a cool wave of utter relief for Maxim. For the escape that he'd chosen for himself.

On my last visit, just the day before, he'd been lucid, smiling as I waved goodbye. 'Bring me some cake next time,' he said. 'I'm yearning for some Dobos torte.'

'Yes, Maxim.'

'And, *chérie*? Not just one slice. The whole damned cake.'

So, it had been his decision. His choice, muddled by despair and depression, but his choice all the same. And how could anyone deny him that?

Too many times in my life I had departed after a funeral, and so it was with Maxim, leaving beautiful Buda two weeks after the 'celebration', where we all drank the medicinal Unicum in honour and ate too much gateau. I bid a sad farewell to friends and beloved Zoli, departing with a large bear-shaped hole in my heart.

Quite unexpectedly, I found myself blessed with a precious souvenir.

Maxim's lasting bequest was in prising open my own floodgates, words soon spilling thick and fast onto the page, cramming almost an entire notebook on the train to Paris. They began as a memoir, and then when I reached his home city, the facts of an extraordinary life that I uncovered, little by little. The aunt who had looked out for Maxim after his parents were taken to the death camps midway through the war, the Parisian art school where he shone, friends who remembered a svelte, shy boy endlessly scribbling and scrawling, the handful of women who recalled him as 'very much a gentleman, perhaps too much'.

It was impossible to ignore, for a writer especially. Besides, it wouldn't let me – pushing, begging, nagging day and night for Maxim's story to be told, for his life and art to be celebrated. To allow his legacy to fizzle into ash would have been a crime.

Something's popped up, I wrote fervently to agent Robert. *Be prepared.*

The French Bear of Budapest emerged on bookshelves the following spring, my first foray into non-fiction, aside from my father's very thinly veiled memoir twenty years previously.

On the cover, his painting of me peeking around the shower curtain in his huge, ancient bathtub. 'Keep still, *chérie*!' I can hear him chiding even now while I flicked bubbles in his direction. 'How is an artistic genius supposed to work like this?'

In the end, there was nothing about Maxim that I *could* make up, though a few sceptics questioned the likelihood of our love affair without the obvious 'benefits'. Given my reputation thus far, who could blame them? It didn't matter – I knew it to be true.

Both then and now, I wanted only to pay proper homage in print to Maxim Joubert's life, his incredible work, and his departure, too. In the press, it provoked a lengthy discussion about the fragility of the mental state in a modern world, and the choices we make over our own lives and deaths.

He would have loved that – people thrashing out the morals and principles in a smoky room over good coffee.

As long as there was plenty of cake.

MAN ELEVEN: Daz

England, 2000

'Eastbourne? Isn't that where people go to die?'

'Well, not quite,' stuttered Marina, 'I mean, I'm not aware of their funeral rate being significantly higher than...'

'Bloody Eastbourne! I mean, no offence to those who live there, but it does have that reputation. Seriously, Marina, am I really *that* old?'

'No, well, but I simply thought...'

Poor Marina. She'd been my agent for all of three months, the others at Grantham & Harris having probably drawn straws for the unenviable task of managing a seventy-year-old scribe likely to produce few words in her remaining years, let alone a bestseller on which to propel one's agenting career. Patently, Marina had drawn the shortest, and then found herself quickly promoted to chief babysitter, after one part of my body decided not to follow the rest into the new millennium.

So there I was, an inmate of the Royal Free Hospital in Hampstead, minus my womb, which vexed me greatly. Like others of my age, I had no further use for my uterine cavity, quietly sitting out its retirement in situ. Even so, I didn't want to lose it. As the anaesthetist put me under in the theatre, I do remember asking if I could keep it – my womb – and the look of horror above her surgical mask.

'Just put it in a jar, one of those pickle things,' I mumbled incoherently before the blackness descended.

Truth was, I couldn't bear to part with the last physical slice of motherhood still within me. Memories of Jude were, by then, a mere imprint; he'd never left me, and never would, but it was increasingly difficult to conjure an image without the dog-eared black-and-white photograph I kept close, static and precious, and unable to be refreshed. I'd never identified my womb with myself as woman, the organ of some great spiritual female status, but it was a maternal badge I felt loath to relinquish.

Unwittingly, though, I'd been nurturing some fibroids over the years and cultivating them far too well, so the A&E doctor had said. It was their turn to revolt, or grumble, or whatever it is that the little round buggers do. Painfully. Hence my sudden stay as a guest of the great British NHS – with no time to dwell on my age-old terror of hospitals – and the need thereafter for 'recuperation'.

'Can't I just employ someone to help me at home?' I pleaded pathetically with Marina, almost tearful and certainly desperate. Anything but Eastbourne.

'Ruby, you've three flights of stairs at home, and well…' She faltered on stating the obvious. My life, personality, work – the very essence of me – meant I had no one to afford me care in the twilight years. Such is the existence of a single and aged woman clinging to independence.

'Anyway, it's not really a nursing home,' she pressed on.

'I should bloody well hope not.'

'More like a hotel for—'

'Old gits?'

'People who need peace and quiet, and a little bit of help. And Eastbourne does have a very good choice of these places. I'll come down and see you, I promise. You might even get some writing done.'

'I suppose I haven't got much choice.'

'Well…'

Like I say, poor Marina. I've apologised many times since for being Extremely Difficult, given it was more than a baptism of fire in her life as an agent. Still, she duly shipped me off to Eastbourne, and what was actually a very nice residential hotel with a glorious sea view and, more importantly, a working lift to my first-floor room. Surveying the clientele, I thought Heavenly Heights was both optimistic and a tad misplaced as a name, but I've always been partial to a good bit of alliteration.

Waiting in my room was a large bunch of flowers, plus a box containing a small flat typewriter called a laptop computer. It was ready and loaded – the accompanying note said – with the necessary files and the phone number of a local man who would take me through its mysteries.

Just in case inspiration comes calling, Marina had scribbled. Fat chance. Didn't she know I was convalescing?

Much to my annoyance, the hotel's owner was very keen to get all her residents 'mingling', and the idea of serving my sentence in peace faded when we were metaphorically wheeled into the residents' lounge for tea and, for those either upright or cognisant enough, a little dance around the room. Mrs Gardner, a woman who paid homage to Margaret Thatcher in every aspect of life, used the word 'spin' and we all tittered politely at her forced irony.

Oh Christ, Marina. What version of Hades have you pitched me into?

'So, what's your crime then?' He eased himself down on the sofa next to me, and I rapidly sensed that a kindred spirit had landed.

'Hysterectomy,' I said with the petulance of my childhood.

'Hip,' he countered. 'Only the one, so there's a blessing. Though I suppose I can look forward to another spell of being decrepit in a few years' time. I take it you don't have a second womb to give you grief?'

We cut the quiet reverence of the room with our laughter, and a veil of instant relief descended. Someone to be naughty with.

'And what did you do before we joined the ranks of Eastbourne's majority population?' he asked.

'Ageing writer. I mean, I am a writer. I've recently added ageing to my CV.'

'Ageing rocker,' he said, and extended a hand. 'Daz.'

'Daz? Like the washing powder?'

It was a measure of his gallantry that he pretended not to have heard such a poor riposte a thousand times before.

'That's me, whiter than white,' he said instead, laughing.

'What's it short for?' I hoped it might be Dexter rather than Derek, something to reflect a man untethered to the ordinary.

'Dazzling,' he beamed.

He wasn't – luminous I mean. 'Weathered' would have been top of my descriptive prose list; less crumpled than Keith Richards, but a way off Cliff Richard – a better-looking Mick Jagger, I judged, with that thin, wiry look of those who'd worked and partied with equal enthusiasm in the music world, not unlike Ludo. A decent covering of greying hair, too. Better still, his eyes sparkled irreverence.

'I'm all for a good cuppa, but what about hobbling out of here for a decent drink?' Daz offered. 'We can prop each other up.'

He had a walking stick – 'my temporary third limb' – but it was a metal type painted with skulls and crossbones that he sported like a roguish dandy.

I held on to his arm, mobile but with that post-surgery tilt. 'What a sight for sore eyes,' I said as we shuffled up the front.

'Give us two weeks and we'll both be in there.' He gestured towards the lapping waves beyond the promenade.

'Is that a challenge?'

'If you like.'

'Then you're on.'

It was almost two weeks before we tiptoed into the very cold surf, a few more attempts before wading waist-deep in the British briny the colour of cold tea. And considerably less time to fall into bed. I say 'fall' with a good deal of licence, since it was more like a considered lowering.

'I'll go first,' Daz suggested, hovering on the edge of his mattress, 'then I can help you in. Just try not to roll on me.'

'And who says romance is dead? Do you think Liz Taylor and Richard Burton ever got to this stage?'

'But we don't want to have to call an ambulance, in flagrante, do we?' he said, a wise man with a metal hip joint.

'True. Mrs Gardner may succumb to heart failure. She'd jump the queue for our ambulance and then where would we be?'

We giggled so much it was a miracle there was time for any lustful pursuit. Somehow, though, between the positioning and the careful avoidance of tender bodily parts, we managed. Experience counts in these matters.

He was gentle and considerate, while I did my best to make up for a lack of balletic grace that had once been my forte in bed. The act was neither frenzied nor aerobic in its execution, merely nice. I hadn't had the pleasure in some time, and this was all pleasure. We both had our own teeth, and so that was a bonus too.

'Do you think it's against house rules, this fraternising?' I murmured as we sat, propped, looking out on the English coastline. My being slightly more agile, I'd opted to lever myself up and make a post-coital cup of tea with the room's miniature kettle, and agreed that it tasted better than any brandy or cigarette we'd had in past lives, nestled in together.

Daz took a sip and sighed. 'I do hope we're breaking some kind of regulation, or else, what's the point?'

More than anything, it was this I'd missed: the pillow talk, the 'post-play' that, in later life, replaces the thrill of the chase. Nobody of our age had the time or the anatomy for a lengthy pursuit.

Satisfied, I looked sideways at Daz, at his sinewed wrinkly chest and hoped I wouldn't scare him away, for a while anyway. Since returning from Budapest, intimate liaisons in my world had been few and far between. When Ed returned from New York, I thought we might pick up where we left off, but he'd been feted by much younger models than myself across the Atlantic, and so I found myself side-lined to being a friend, in the strictest sense of the word. We drank G&Ts at The Flask and gossiped, but his carnal gaze had settled on another generation.

There had been one writer of my own age in the mid-Nineties, both interesting and nice, fairly agile in bed too. After several months, though, his company had begun to grate, and I grew to think of him as selfish, self-centred and too focused on his own work. On painful reflection, the irony was not lost on me – through the years, I'd moulded myself to be alone, and at seventy it was now cast in stone. It was also fine by me. But a bit of sexual relief here and there was never to be turned down lightly.

'Mr Talbot... Mr Talbot... ARE YOU ALL RIGHT IN THERE?' Mrs Gardner's voice pushed through the keyhole, with equal amounts of concern and curiosity.

'I'm fine, never better,' Daz cried, a hand over my mouth to contain the giggling I could barely control. Instantly, I was fifteen again and smoking behind those proverbial bike sheds. 'Shhh,' he hissed.

'Mr Talbot, the physio is here for your treatment,' Mrs Gardner projected through the door. We could almost hear that infamous landlady radar crackling through the lacquer of her hair.

'I'm err... fine, thank you,' Daz stuttered, suppressing his own laughter. Badly. 'I think I've had enough exercise for today. A little bit sore.'

That sent me into another fit of contained hysteria, until Mrs Gardner shuffled away with 'well, rest up, then'. She wasn't convinced. But we were adults, weren't we?

'The doctor told me to keep moving,' he said impishly, after we'd made love again. 'I'm simply following instructions.'

'Then I shall add therapist to my CV.'

What proved even nicer – and so pleasantly surprising – was

that Daz courted me after the event. Properly, with dates and dinners, where we dressed in what passed as our finery, his being the troubadour-meets-pirate cum eighteenth-century beau.

I liked it, including the one gold earring he sported and which his daughters begged him constantly to cast aside, 'in line with my bloody age. I ask you, Ruby – what exactly does acting your age mean? I hope I never find out.'

Daz was of the old school, a working-class boy who'd made good with his guitar. Being two years younger than I, his youth had been in the Fifties, an archetypal Teddy boy ('longest sideburns in South London'), but a career in a small-time rock'n'roll band peaked briefly in the late Fifties, and so his love of music straddled the Sixties too.

'I would have sacrificed a limb to be a teenager when the Beatles came on the scene,' he lamented. 'Fabulous band. But I had a wife and two kids by then.'

Judging by only a handful of Daz's tales of life as a session musician, he'd managed to have a Very Good Time, despite the demands of fatherhood.

'My poor wife was the long-suffering type,' he recalled over fish and chips on the beach. 'And I did test her patience a fair amount. No regrets about the work, but I could have been a better husband and father. Something my daughters are keen to remind me.'

'And your wife?' It was a perhaps a little late to ask, since we had already 'fallen' into bed by then, but oddly, I didn't want to be the cause of any more of her angst. We were all too long in the tooth for that.

'Died. Cancer, three years ago. We had all these plans to travel the world, and then bang! The rug is pulled from under you. So now...'

'Carpe diem, and all that.'

'I still don't know what that means exactly, but yes, that's the gist,' Daz said. 'You live every moment, chase every dream, even when you can only hobble towards it.'

'So, what's the next dream? Skydiving?' I tossed a chip towards a very fat seagull threatening to mug me of my battered cod.

He nudged at my shoulder playfully. 'Immortality,' he laughed. 'You up for that? I want to be on that first rocket to Mars.'

'Not me, Daz. Life lived, plus a good ending.'

'Shame you don't get to write it, Ruby.'

'Who says I don't?'

She might have been a novice of the publishing world at that point, but Marina was more intuitive than I gave her credit for. Or else she'd been reading up on my reputation.

'Ruby, you look very well,' she said on her promised visit from London, the emphasis on 'very well' and her eyes widely suggestive.

'I am, thank you, Marina.'

'So, Eastbourne suits you? Have you made friends?' There was a tiny note of triumph in her voice which I couldn't let slip. I still had a reputation to uphold.

'Marina, Eastbourne is the death end of nowhere. But I have found the people to be nice, and I have a lift to my bedroom.' I wouldn't give her the satisfaction of being right, or of knowing I was having a bloody good time. And I definitely didn't let on that I'd started writing again.

It was Daz who pushed me to it finally. We had levered ourselves into my bed on that particular afternoon, and after the intimacy and post-pillow tea-talk he found the laptop computer discarded on my side table.

'Hey, this is fairly fancy,' he announced with the whistle of an East End barrow boy.

'I wouldn't know,' I came back. 'I've never used it.'

'Then how you can possibly write about me? About us?'

He'd been researching me since out first meeting, he revealed, absorbing one or two of my books, though not *Mother* I was somehow relieved to discover – we were having too good a time to waste any energy on pity or sympathy.

'Come on, Ruby, surely I get a mention in your next work – the handsome and desirable rock'n'roller with a heart?'

'Are you serious?'

'Deadly. And believe me, I don't utter the word "dead" too often.'

After a lifetime of tinkering with guitars and amplifiers, Daz took to my laptop like a duck to water, and so there was no need to ring Marina's nice IT man for my own plunge into the world of technology. He showed me simply and in syllables I could understand. I can't claim an overnight conversion, but once I accepted this gizmo as merely a glorified typewriter (and mastered not zapping great chunks of text with one swipe of my gnarly knuckles), the old gal wasn't too bad. I'd finally evolved from being a lifelong Luddite.

Living in such close proximity, the lack of 'thunk' in my laptop was a revelation. How many times had I heard voices through walls of flats and hotels when the muse took me at two a.m.? 'Give over with that racket!' had been the general, irritated refrain. Or similar, more colourful requests to stop the infernal clattering of my little portable typewriter.

Now, I was happily tiptoeing and finger-skating over the keyboard into the early hours. Where my body was at times weary and unwilling, the mind took up the slack.

I'd never been to Eastbourne before in life or in a book, and I wasn't au fait with internet surf-travel, so it was back to first principles: write what you know, and combine it with my own maxim that had served me so well over the years – 'write where you are'.

For Jeanie and Terry of my text – free-spirited characters looking for love and its perks – read Ruby and Daz. I had played with romance several times before, though largely with a sad mournful narrative of blighted relationships, written from a wealth of painful experience. Inspired by the billowy sea skies and the company, I was in the mood for something light, this time without death, shame or destruction. I did think twice about writing in a style I'd publicly denounced as 'foolish froth' in the past, but perhaps it was time. As Daz pronounced so frequently on a variety of subjects: 'Fuck it, Ruby. We do what we want, when we want.'

And we did just that, much to Mrs Gardner's paranoia about the dangers of 'losing' a guest on her watch: ice creams on the front and hours in the penny arcade, even a slow and tentative tricycle ride along the promenade. Religiously, Daz and I dipped twice weekly in the bubbly brown surf, with him coaxing and cajoling so that finally my shoulders would disappear into the freezing water and I felt bloody cold but very much alive. Such was my fondness for Daz, he even persuaded me to an over-sixties Pilates class at the local community hall. As the only man, he was hailed as some type of visiting celebrity, swarmed over by a gaggle of women, charming each and every one. 'He looks like one of those Rolling Stones,' I heard one of the flock whisper. 'No, not the one with the big lips. But I wouldn't say no. Would you?'

Lying side by side on our yoga mats and stretching our crumbling anatomy, I couldn't be jealous when he shot me *that* look, the one where I knew his only thought was of flopping into bed (we'd progressed from a lowering of bodies to the gay abandonment of the flop), and perfecting our own form of callisthenics.

Sod convalescence, I was having the time of my life.

On our sunny horizon there was but one bump. Churlish to refer to a person as a hurdle, but there was little love lost between Daz's daughter and I from the outset.

'Amanda, I've heard so much about you,' I chimed when she came to visit her father one weekend.

'I've read so much about you, too,' she smiled, the bitterness held back behind her teeth. That was me warned in one noxious breath.

Daz loved his eldest daughter, of that there was no doubt, but he was also a little afraid of her. His youngest, Lucy, was – by his own admission – 'a little more relaxed'. She also lived in Paris, which meant they met rarely, and when they did, it was to have a darned good time. Amanda, by contrast, adopted the role of her father's keeper, principally to steer Dad away from trouble. And women. Maybe it was that thing referred to as female intuition, but I saw in Amanda a desire to subtly punish her father for the sins of his colourful past. For being absent, and perhaps playing away – she sought to remind him of this constantly on behalf of her dead mother, a name mentioned more than once in our brief introduction.

'I know she just wants the best for me,' Daz said after she left (and with an extended sigh of relief). 'She wants me to sell up and live with her after I leave here, and they're promising to have a granny annexe built. She says I could help in the garden. I do love her and the grandkids, but God forbid, Ruby, I'd rather build my own rocket ship to Mars and die on take-off.'

For one brief moment, I let my mind wander to where I might be with Jude if he were alive. Would I be a doting grandmother, he harbouring a duty of care to his mother's ageing body and mind? In truth, I hoped not. I'd rather he took off, maybe not to Mars, but on some crazy adventure. There were few benefits to death, but his end had given us the freedom not to agonise over it.

'I'll come and help you,' I said to Daz.

'Do what? Move in with her?'

'No, build the bloody rocket ship.'

'Rubes, what do you say to a dip in a proper pool?' Daz suggested one morning as we shivered under a towel after our regular dip. August had given way to September, taking with it some of the warmth, Eastbourne's promenade beginning to empty of all but the old and infirm. 'I'm fed up with freezing my bollocks off in the English Channel.'

Never let it be said that Daz was not supremely articulate, in his own special way.

'My nipples are of the same opinion,' I agreed. 'Where do you have in mind?'

On a whim, we took the bus along the coast to Saltdean, in one moment feeling a lot like pensioners on a day out, then tasting the salty sea air of six-year-old Ruby, on one of the few family holidays I remembered. 'Young at heart,' Daz crooned at me in his croaky, old ex-smoker's voice, clutching my fingers with one hand and his bathers in the other. We might have been all of seventeen in that particular moment.

Our destination and his desire was the slightly faded but once spectacular lido nestled behind Saltdean's seafront, the smooth white icing of the fantastically curved art deco build now smudged to a dull grey. Undeniably shabby, it remained beautiful and charming – think Hercule Poirot strutting his stuff in an ivory summer suit and you're where we stood, in the waning light of an English summer.

And facing a padlocked gate.

'Shit!' Daz expressed eloquently. 'We're a bloody day late.'

Closed for the winter, the sign stated bluntly. *Reopening in the spring.* Through the bars of the gate, the cool blue water of the pool rippled under a sinking egg-yellow sun, empty of bodies and so tantalising after our clammy bus ride. Unusually for Daz, he deflated.

'Cup of tea, or something stronger before we head back?' I offered by way of recompense.

But Daz would not be fobbed off with a good brew of either. He wanted his swim and, no longer reliant on his stick, clearly pictured himself as a reborn Superman in achieving it. 'Here, hold this.' He thrust his swim bag at me and began scouting for an opening.

'Daz, what are you doing?' I said, suddenly horrified. Not by his purpose as such, but the potential embarrassment of being caught red-handed trying to break in. For all my mischief over the years, the risks and living life on the edge, I had never actually broken the law (the spying I slotted into a category of 'dubious employment'). Even something as innocent as scrumping had always terrified me, or the consequences of it – grabbed by the scruff of the neck and made to face the music in full view.

'What if someone comes?' I pleaded to Daz. In vain, because he and his NHS hip were already up on a large commercial bin-skip and contemplating the drop on the other side of the wall.

'Here, take my hand,' he beckoned.

As I later wrote in Terry and Jeanie's escapades, it was the twinkle in his eye which made me do it – the smile, too, beaming and infused with so much 'fuck it' mentality that I was powerless to resist. I couldn't. I took his hand, feeling every one of my seventy years as I grunted and panted my way on top of that bin, then a teenager again as we stood aloft and surveyed the prospect before us.

It stands as the best swim I've ever had. The angst of being a trespasser slipped away as we lowered into the cool blue, two bodies circling in the vast expanse of the pool, spliced dramatically by a late afternoon shadow, so that we swam from a darkened chill, to floating and basking under the golden glow. My grumbling, achy innards were instantly weightless and free. The world in that precious half hour existed for us alone.

'This is living, Ruby, isn't it?' Daz beamed, with the look of a man who was having his cake and determined to savour every last morsel.

I hadn't canoodled in water since my teens, when Michael and I smooched our way across Highgate ponds, to disapproving looks from the oldies diligently taking their daily exercise. Now, I was the oldie, but still a way off diligent. If memory serves me right, the canoodling was equally pleasurable.

'This is the best date I've ever had, Mr Whiter-Than-White,' I murmured.

'I'm glad you think so, Miss D. All tailored and planned in advance, of course.'

Had that been true, we might have dried off and repaired to a nice restaurant, emerging warmed and replete before bumbling back along the coast to Eastbourne. As it was, tepid tea and a wilted cheese sandwich – courtesy of the local constabulary – came as a poor second.

Caught. Red-handed and mid-smooch, though I surprised myself by feeling neither horrified nor embarrassed. Mildly amused, as it happened.

The poor young policeman called to escort us off the premises was easily more rattled. 'Afraid I'll have to arrest you both,' he apologised. 'It's the new chief constable, she's very hot on stamping out trespass and vandalism.' He was kind enough not to bring out the cuffs, having watched us scramble with difficulty out of the pool, gauging that a high-octane pursuit was unlikely.

'That's two to add to my CV,' I said to Daz in the back of the patrol car. 'Trespasser and vandal.'

'You know me, Ruby, always aiming to please.' The twinkle in his eye was perhaps dulled by the prospect of having to admit such delinquency to his daughters, Amanda especially.

They put us in the same cell, which I thought was sweet, and we heard the laughter run through the depressing echoey cell block, the inevitable tittering and allusions to pensioner porn. I was oddly glad, though, that the young officer would have a career anecdote to relay into his old age.

'Sorry, Rubes,' Daz said, offering me the last of his tepid tea as we heard the clang of the heavy metal door.

'Oh, don't be. I always meant to see the inside of a police cell – it's excellent for research. And just think of the escapades that Terry and Jeanie will get up to now.'

'And that's why you're the writer you are, Ruby D.'

Mercifully, neither Amanda nor Marina were required to spring us from custody, arriving breathless at the station to post bail, as in TV drama-land. Within hours, Daz and I were released to appear at the magistrates' court, and Constable Stevens drove us home, justifying the distance and expense as part of the force's initiative on 'disability awareness'. Daz helpfully embellished his limp as we walked towards the patrol car.

I may have tarnished my otherwise unblemished legal record, but it was worth every ounce of standing just to witness the look of horror on Mrs Gardner's face when we drew up at Heavenly Heights in a police car, red and blue lights pulsing. Constable Stevens couldn't justify the siren, he said. Instead, he escorted us to the door, with a cheery 'see you in court'. Her stiff lip and reputation wobbled in tandem.

Priceless.

In a perfect comedy-drama script, we might have fallen into bed and made frantic love, tittering over the day's antics. Terry and Jeanie almost certainly would. But that was for the book. In truth, Eastbourne's dynamic duo were exhausted; we passed on the aerobics and settled for a hot cup of tea while I massaged Daz's sore hip and he sang 'Hey Jude', making me smile instead of cry for the first time in decades. Sometimes, real life trumps even fiction.

Of course, it made the papers. When the magistrate struggled to maintain a straight face and uttered a passing, comedic reference to Bonnie and Clyde, it stirred the local press box to wake from their reverie and start scribbling. Then, as it became known Bonnie was a writer of some note and Clyde had played session bass for Led Zeppelin, the wire to Fleet Street began to sizzle – the internet in this case, but you catch my drift. Luckily, any suggestion of 'lewd behaviour' was put to rest when Daz stood up in court and announced, 'Loving someone is never lewd or unsavoury, Your Honour.' By that point, steam was seen rising from press notepads.

Bonnie and Clyde in Lido Lust ran one of the more popular papers, leaving out the crucial fact that both Daz and I were appropriately dressed for a swimming pool, and our desire extended to no more than kissing, or – as one tabloid phrased it – *a good snog.* I will admit to being quietly delighted by three paragraphs in the *Guardian,* under the strapline *Writer claims after-hours research in lido.*

Daz's daughter was anything but pleased, keeping her stony-faced vigil in the public gallery, and then equally sombre once we emerged to a smattering of press on the steps of the court, having escaped with a small fine after the indecency charge was dropped. Dear Daz – I watched him torn between the limelight he so adored back in the day, and the family he loved for a lifetime. Me? I was the perfect and smiling piggy in the middle.

'You know what they say about publicity…' Marina whispered as she steered me towards a large waiting car and chauffeur, the contrived façade of me as a literary dame of some renown. Snap, snap, snap went the tabloid shutters. She was learning fast.

Mrs Gardner didn't ask us to leave Heavenly Heights in so many words, only hinted that Daz and I had attained a 'level of improvement' in our physical health and her facilities were required by others 'in greater need'. I imagine she meant those who wouldn't drag her establishment into disrepute.

He left before I did, hustled away by Amanda, looking daggers at the woman who had apparently enticed her own father into a life of crime. I'm being dramatic, but sadness does that to you.

'Sorry, Ruby,' he said, out of earshot from the dreaded daughter. 'I really might have cooked my goose this time. It's time for the old man to play at being a proper father. I owe it to them.'

I understood. I might have felt the same duty, if only I'd had the opportunity.

In my room, a postcard had been propped on the pillow – a picture of a young and quiffed Elvis Presley, one of his long-time heroes. *Never let this be Heartbreak Hotel,* he wrote in his spidery hand. *See you on the launch pad for a Life on Mars? Love always, Mr Whiter-Than-White.*

'Are you sad to leave?' Marina asked as we watched Eastbourne retreat into the distance.

'A little,' I said honestly. 'Mercifully, it wasn't where I inhaled my last breath. Far from it, I feel quite alive. And there's a lot to be said for a holiday romance.'

'Hmm,' she said, knowingly.

I dedicated the book to *Daz, aka Mr White,* and I didn't mind that every reviewer saw through the fiction of Terry and Jeanie. Light romance wasn't my forte, but I had fun producing it, reminiscing and laughing out loud in writing the scene of a flushed and naked Terry emerging from the lido. And it sold by the bucket load. That's faction for you.

Better still, Daz came to the book's launch, minus the daughter/gaoler. The gold earring was in situ, plus the ever-lasting sparkle. We drank too much champagne and repaired to a very nice hotel in Russell Square, where we brewed tea, properly fell into bed and I experienced the new lease of life in his very stable hip. A second nod of appreciation to the fabulous NHS.

I heard from Daz only once after that, a postcard a decade later – one of those you can get printed on the internet – of a man mid-air in helmet and goggles, suspended against an impossibly blue background between white, puffy clouds. Beaming from ear to ear while falling through space at speed.

RUBY! The NASA lot are a bit slow on the bus to Mars, so this skydiving lark is the next best thing, I promise you. Got the second hip in place (though the recovery wasn't half as much fun). This is my 25th jump – think of you on each and every one. Carpe fucking diem (whatever the hell it means). Love always, Mr White.

I looked again at the image. Yes, there it was behind the goggles – that irreverent twinkle. Definitely Daz.

The twenty-sixth jump was his last, so the obituary later said. Heart attack mid-air. Absolutely the way to go for him. Amid his long list of credits as a musician was being present when the Beatles recorded 'All You Need is Love' in their hippy splendour, surrounded in the Abbey Road studio by a posse of friends, fans and flowers. He never boasted of it, but then he wasn't that type of guy.

Wishing to avoid the death stare of Amanda, I passed on the funeral. I'm fortunate, however, in that I can conjure Daz in an instant, by merely opening a small cabinet door in my living room and laying eyes on my slightly withered but nonetheless present and pink womb, floating in a jar of formalde-whatsit, the chemical soup used for preserving bodily bits for posterity, and batty old women. And if you think that's macabre, then you might not have the measure of me after all.

Each time I see it, I pay homage to my maternal organ and thank my lucky stars that it sent me on a trajectory towards a man who, every single day, looked for the twinkle in the sky.

Eight

The phone rings at least ten times in her ear, enough for Marina's anxiety to rise. She checks her watch: 3.30 p.m., the time when someone – be it the home help or the typist – should still be at Ruby's, though she does know they are often sent on patisserie errands around now. Still, someone other than Ruby usually answers the phone these days, unless of course, there's been an emergency. They might be with her in the ambulance. Marina's catastrophe gauge runs riot in the space of two more rings.

The ringing finally stops. 'Yes?' comes a surly voice.

'Ruby, oh, I was beginning to think you might be out.'

'Where on earth would *I* go?' Ruby challenges.

She's upset, Marina can tell. There are grades to Ruby's gruffness, and this is high on the irascible scale. 'Is everything all right?'

'Yes. I *am* working, Marina.'

Marina pushes a silent sigh into the receiver. This is tougher than her previous call to the CEO of a vast publishing house. She draws on what residual patience she has left. 'Ruby, I'm not ringing about the work. I simply wanted to make sure you're all right.'

'Well, I am.'

The voice has gone down a scale, at least. 'And the new assistant, is he not there?'

'No. He left early,' Ruby says flatly.

'Is there a problem? Do you need me to have a word?'

'No, Marina, I'm perfectly capable of whipping the young lad into shape. I'm not totally decrepit. Not yet anyway.' A pause. 'But yes, I will ring you if there's an issue.'

'All right. I'll pop round next week – with éclairs. Bye.'

'Bye then.' A cough. 'And, Marina?'

'Yes?'

'Thank you for ringing.'

Ruby moves towards the foot of the stairs and frowns at the newly installed stairlift, hesitating before crossing the threshold to her office, always her world of comfort, where hundreds of thousands of words have been spun, and shaped and splurged, depending on the topic or mood. Suddenly, it feels almost alien. Not her space anymore. Not without him.

For three days, the tickety-tack keyboard has been silent. 'I need a break,' she'd told Ralph, the second – or is it third? – of her assistants. 'Take a couple of days off.'

She's not been in the sanctuary of her office since. Now she ventures tentatively towards the desk. Something is brewing; she recognises the feeling, that 'itch', the nagging voice that won't go away. Time and time again, it's happened, sometimes to good effect, with what she considers to be pleasing work. Now, she's not sure. The one certainty is that it needs to come out, and it won't be denied.

It takes her some time to switch the infernal machine on and locate the file, her fingers stiff and ungainly. She tries flexing them like he did, but it brings only pain. Finally, the screen is ready, the icon winking at a hectoring pace: *come on, then, get on with it!*

'No bloody time like the present,' she mutters.

Within view of her beloved, retired typewriter now skulking on the shelf, Ruby emulates the thunk with her awkward, arthritic rhythm on the keyboard, squinting as the words appear, black on white, if not in ink. It's slow and painful, but then so is the telling. Necessary, too.

When has Ruby M Devereaux ever shied away from exposing herself on the page?

MAN TWELVE: Jude

London, 2020

It was a fait accompli. From the first tentative knocking and my opening of the door, I was stopped in my tracks, halted by a memory somersault which took me back six decades – to Michael and his adorable curls. These were darker and the boy on my doorstep was taller. Looks alone might have been enough to engage my interest, and thence my heart, but there was more.

'Miss Devereaux? The agency sent me, for the position. I'm Jude. Jude Dempsey.'

Like I said – the deal was struck. He could have had two heads and spoken a bizarre form of double-Dutch, but I would have invited him in anyway.

Marina must have known – his name and the implications for me. But then, she could hardly demand a deed poll change, or for the applicants to adopt a casual nickname. Especially as the pool of willing contenders was running dry. But help was necessary, with my body running aground and a book to write, to satisfy my contractual obligations. I might even enjoy the process, too.

My mind was already flitting from place to place as to the content of this memoir, like a busy bumblebee in summer, succour from the recall of me in my prime. I'd been writing consistently, my brain awash with ideas, but my physical orbit had become limited in the previous two years and the pieces were short. Add to that my frustrations with the flesh, and an ongoing tussle with that blasted internet, which seemed like a conduit to the outside world if only I could master the damned thing. Instead, I hoarded precious memories as if they were gold dust, desperate they shouldn't lose their sheen or slip through the cracks in my psyche. I'd made Marina promise that if my recollection began to fail then she was to do 'the decent thing' and scoot me over to Switzerland as soon as possible for a dignified end. Without a functioning mind, I was mere dust.

Jude Dempsey sat in silence in my kitchen as we sipped tea. Another tick for him. Radio 4 was a mere flick of the dial when I wanted a dose of wittering voices, and I admired anyone's ability to read and respect silence. Especially a lad of twenty-one.

'What have you been doing so far, since school?'

'University,' he said, 'in Edinburgh. Political science.'

Another tick. The last thing I needed was an English graduate cum wannabe writer hoping to tap me for tips or introductions to publishers. I'd never possessed the patience for teaching, and age had sucked away any remaining tolerance.

'So, no plans for a job in government, or as a lackey to some worthy backbench MP?' I probed.

He shook those impossibly beautiful curls. 'Maybe someday. For now, I'm just scouting around, taking my time to find out what I'd really love to do.'

Tick, tick, tick. I would have hired him on the utterance of Jude, but name aside, Master Dempsey was emerging as a worthy candidate as my conduit to realise the memoir. We chinked our china cups to seal the deal.

Marina's sigh of relief over the phone was pleasing. And cautionary. 'Ruby, do remember he's only employed nine to five, Monday to Friday,' she counselled. 'He's a help, not a carer.'

'And since when do I need a carer, thank you very much!' I flashed. On reflection, who was I kidding?

'Well, try to be patient, eh?' she sighed. 'It will take a while for him to get used to your ways.' Said with the wisdom of someone who was only just getting to grips with me, twenty years on. 'Besides which, Ruby, there's no one left to interview. So, it's Jude or no one.'

He would arrive on the dot of nine, cycling up from his home in Crouch End, at which point I would be up and dressed, with a purpose I hadn't possessed for some time. Every morning, we pottered out to my favourite café, me on Jude's arm. While stubbornly refusing a stick, I needed something or someone to lean on in life, though it was an entirely new and loathsome state. And yet, with Jude, I found myself not minding at all. At his tender age and with his dark looks, he could easily have passed for my grandson. Once or twice, I indulged myself a little, imagining what it would have been like, out to lunch with Jude's own issue. *Hopefully like this,* I mused. *Simply pleasurable.*

Sipping at our requisite two coffees apiece, Jude and I pored over the *Guardian*'s pages, swapping the news and features sections and flagging up anything of note as we scanned. With Britain just recovering from another General Election, we talked politics (being of the same persuasion, luckily) but also of climate change and gender issues. He told me what young people were feeling, hating and loving, and – on invitation – I told him what it was like 'back in the day'.

'People experiment much more these days, Ruby,' he said. 'Man or woman, it doesn't really matter. It's just about loving a person. Actually, not even loving – merely wanting to be close. To share something.'

'And you don't think we did then?' I remarked casually.

His big eyes grew wider. Curious and hungry.

'Women simply didn't flaunt it, that's all.' I swallowed some coffee. 'Of course, the men had to be more careful then, because of the consequences – imprisonment, or worse. Look at poor Alan Turing and what it meant for him. Women were able to hide it more easily, mostly because men in power didn't comprehend women could love any other species but themselves, and therefore didn't imagine it existed. I'm not sure if that was a good thing or not.'

'And?' Jude's coffee was going cold.

'Well, that life was easy to find if you went to the right pubs and clubs.'

His curiosity was aroused, I could tell. 'Did you ever lose your heart… to a woman?'

I smiled, knowingly. 'Men were my thing,' I said. 'Though in hindsight, I might be better off now if I had. I do think women of a certain age are more suited to living together, whatever their orientation. They just rub along better. I might not be in this pickle if that were the case.'

I wanted to retract the last statement there and then, at the flash of hurt in his eyes – the 'pickle' being my need of him, as a helper.

He recovered admirably. 'But we wouldn't have all this, would we?' he said cheerfully. 'Chewing over the world's fat every morning with a good cappuccino.'

'No, you're right,' I agreed. 'We wouldn't.'

Early on, when the conditions seemed right and our conversation sufficiently casual, I tackled him over the name. 'So where does Jude come from?'

He paused, then sort of scoffed. 'Oh, my mum. She's a fan.'

My heart might have stopped temporarily, kick-started by a nuance of Ludo washing over me. 'Of the band?' I pressed.

'Actually, the book. Though I can't fathom what she sees in Thomas Hardy. I remind her frequently that it doesn't do much for my confidence to be named after an obscurity. I'd much rather she'd been inspired by the Beatles.'

'You like it then, the song?' I was conscious of holding my breath, like some sort of lovesick teenager craving a glance or a wave from a hero.

He looked up from under his thick lashes, working his mouth into a smile. 'Of course, who doesn't? It's the best bloody song ever written.'

And I promise you, readers – I did not make it up.

To this day, I don't know why it was so important, but my heart went into freefall again; it was one of those times when I thought the coincidence was too much, that it – and he – were a dream I'd conjured to plug the holes that had once been my real existence. And I was good at that. It was my job, after all, to sell fiction as credible.

'Come on, time to go, Mrs D,' he said, unaware of such musings, humming as we walked… 'Nah-na-na-nana-NAH…'.

I didn't mind it one little bit.

It was on these occasions, and after righting the world over croissants, that we'd walk slowly back home via the delicatessen and greengrocer, where Jude picked up supplies for lunch and dinner. For an hour or so, while he prepared lunch, I did my 'tinkering', a creative word for procrastination and avoidance of the blank page facing me, or the one littered with shambolic prose from previous attempts.

By that point, I could exchange emails and access websites in a fairly limited way, but if I sent myself down a cyber rabbit hole, I would have to call through the open office door. 'Juuude! I'm stuck again.'

'What have you done now?' he'd chastise me playfully, striding up through the hallway and wiping his hands on his chef's apron, the one I ordered especially from Liberty after his first few weeks, and which hung on the kitchen peg for his use alone.

Invariably, he'd fix the glitch with a flick of his finger on the keyboard. 'Stay for a minute, will you?' I'd often say. 'Just in case it happens again.'

The truth was, I liked him in the room. Far from being a distraction, his presence was a comfort, a grounding somehow, and I could begin to concentrate, to let my ideas settle and ferment. I liked to see his curls in my eyeline as I glanced up, his smooth brow creased just a little as he folded into the armchair opposite and picked up a book, rubbing unconsciously at his temple while his pupils crawled over the words.

'Is everything all right now?' he'd say after a while, unfurling his long limbs and levering himself off the chair. 'Only I've something in the oven. A nice cake for later, and I don't want it to burn. It's your favourite.'

'Yes, fine.' But I had rather he stayed, to just be.

After a small lunch of something exquisite and a joint stab at the crossword, Jude would clatter in the kitchen for a bit, tidying up. Then he'd follow me into the study, where we would continue where we'd left off. It was in those hours, against the gentle industry of Highgate beyond the window, that we laid down my life. With him at the keyboard, I could forget the mist in my rheumy eyes and my one cloudy cataract, or the aching in my arthritic fingers; with the speed of his tapping came clarity in thought – I was flying again, defying the limitations of the bastard ageing flesh. I became a runner drunk on endorphins, intoxicated with the freedom that writing brought me all those years ago, when I'd scribbled silly thoughts in the notebooks I stowed under my bed, or sat under my smelly eiderdown, confident of penning the publishing debut of the century.

For those hours with Jude, I shed more than sixty years in my mind, more so when – as the typewriter-like keys cowered under the speed – he would look up from his own focus and smile. So knowingly. Like he knew exactly what I was about. What the process meant for me, and the soaring sensations it produced.

The value of a muse wasn't lost on me, having once been one under Michael's brush and seen how my presence calmed the frisson of creative unease inside him, even when I wasn't the subject of his work. And Maxim, of course. I'd known fellow writers, too, who admitted to a need for a particular presence in their orbit, and then crumpled when the relationship came to a sticky end, putting a full stop on their artistic flow. After the ups and downs of all my involvements, I was mindful of the reliance and the problems it might create. Except, of course, when it was happening in my own house.

Unconsciously at first, I began to live for Monday to Friday, with weekends as bookends to my enjoyment. Those two days felt like a mere existence, the hours stretching like a road without any horizon, and only Badger – my fat and cantankerous black-and-white cat – for company. We growled away the weekend together, tetchy and petulant.

Aside from Jude, I did have a loyal band of friends who would escort me out to weekend showings or launches, arranging transport and offering an arm on which I could lean. But there was scant enjoyment in feeling like a mere observer, tottering on the periphery. Often, age became a convenient excuse in those times, using my frailty as a crutch (oh the irony!). I was tired, I told both them and myself, or 'sorry, I've got my head in a book'. All genuine sentiments – to a degree. What I desired more than anything on those occasions was Jude's company, his arm as a perch as we mingled at a gathering, his whispered opinion of the room in my ear. Deep down, I knew exactly how it looked, and what it was – an old woman of ninety craving the attentions of a grandson she could never have. But would I ever admit such a dependence to myself?

Having made it to this page, you'll be attuned to my reactions when faced with any kind of life hurdle – to divert and sidestep, rather than confront my own failings. With so much practice over the years, I'd become a virtuoso. I simply told myself Jude was a help, who had evolved into a friend. A good and willing friend, regardless of the wage I paid him. I'd been no angel in life, but no devil either, so didn't I merit some small reward in my waning years? Didn't everyone deserve amity as a comfort? Conveniently deluded, I simply ploughed on.

Largely down to Jude's accomplished cooking, I began to invite the world into my home, and to host little soirees in the mews house. There were sometimes up to ten or twelve of us, principally from the book world, plus a smattering of people from television who were near neighbours. Once the food was laid out, it was natural for Jude to join us in the lively debate darting back and forth across the table. Amid the literary talk, I noticed he tended to be quiet and attentive. But with such a mix of minds the conversation inevitably turned to politics, and that's when he came alive, always the most well-informed among us, and by far the youngest.

No one questioned his presence at the table, since Jude was cast as a 'friend'. Whether my guests pictured him as a ridiculously young lover, I couldn't tell. I hoped not, since the image ranked as grotesque in my mind – there had been few points in my life where the opinions of others mattered much in my pursuits, but in this I was loath to injure Jude in any way.

The truth was that I'd grown to love him, implicitly and quite innocently – for his wit, his youth and the way he made me feel in his company. I hadn't told him, of course, adamant that I wouldn't make the mistake of embarrassing the both of us by giving voice to my old lady affections. Perhaps I *had* gleaned something from my back catalogue of fiascos?

For my part, I chose the role of elderly aunt cum grandmother and hoped it came across convincingly. I don't mind admitting that I bathed in the fondness Jude displayed at those evening gatherings, always coming to me first with the food, making sure I was comfortable, and the gentle way in which he mocked my infamous testy nature. When had this woman – old or young – ever shunned such attention, and why would I start now?

One night, Jude asked if he could invite a friend to help with the cooking, and then to join us at dinner. It being a larger than average gathering in the garden, and therefore a good deal of work for one person, it would have been grudging of me to refuse.

'Can he cook as well as you?' I asked.

'I'm bound to say no, aren't I?' He raised his eyebrows over a wry smile.

'That's good, then. No one is allowed to be better.'

First impressions of Billy as I answered the door to him tended towards scruffy. Long and lean like Jude, he strode into the kitchen in jeans and a grubby T-shirt, his lank hair equally untended. A scant greeting aimed at me gave way to a focus that immediately fixed on Jude, eyes wide with… well, it was lust, plain and simple. Age and poor sight had robbed me of plenty, but the radar remained fully functioning. For his part, Jude acted the go-between perfectly, making introductions and using his amiable charm to smooth over what he must have perceived as a frisson of unease between Billy and me. The word 'interloper' nudged its way into my head and wouldn't shift. He was perfectly polite and made all the right noises, but there was something in his manner that grated – an ingrained arrogance that I recognised from men of import and influence, those who simply *knew*, without a doubt, that they were destined for great things – the mildest of sneers perched under their well-bred noses.

I didn't like Billy from the outset, though plainly Jude was of a different opinion. From behind my cup of tea in the corner of the kitchen, I watched them jockey with each other, chattering and laughing as they chopped and prepared the feast, their body language about as subtle as a billboard on Piccadilly Circus. Either they were already an item, or they soon would be.

How did I feel about that?

Bruised, if you must know. Equally, I had no right to feel anything, and I knew it. Jude was not mine, and had he been my grandson by birth, I still would have had no sway over his heart or intentions. That emerald shade of envy, however, does not play by the rules. I found myself jealous of their youth and potential, of the fun they could have together, of Billy and the portion of Jude that he might enjoy. Was allowed to have. 'Stop it, Ruby!' I told myself aloud as I dressed upstairs. *Silly, silly woman.*

Jealousy of this level was a new sensation for me, and I wasn't sure I liked it. Yes, I'd known envy before, mainly towards other writers with a bigger bite of the publishing cherry, but rarely with men. Over the years, if they'd chosen to decline my company, or moved on to pastures new, I simply put it down to experience, confident there were more attendees on the horizon. But this feeling had never burned, as it did when I heard Jude and Billy giggling downstairs, flirting openly over the canapés, and getting flighty with the fizz.

'Is he going to change before dinner?' I asked Jude in a quiet moment alone before the guests arrived. Billy was smoking out on the patio, where Badger was eyeing him up suspiciously. Had my grumpy feline not been so obese, he might have assaulted this newest trespasser, claws and all. In my ungenerous mood, I might not have minded.

'Umm, I have a spare shirt he can borrow,' Jude stammered. I felt his embarrassment glow hot, torn between his loyalty to me and lust for the boy in the garden. How did I not know – with all my years of experience in the arena – that loyalty has no chance against the demands of the flesh?

The guests loved Billy and his assured, public schoolboy demeanour, nurtured to hold court in any scenario that promises to benefit. Encouraged by Jude (and duly hinted at by me), Billy had transformed himself from the great unwashed to someone capable of being noticed, clad in Jude's clean shirt, his hair pulled back into a casual tail. Some necessary deodorant had been utilised. To me, he came across as a minstrel who had no intention of singing for his supper. For the rest, Jude included, he was simply divine.

'What is it you do, Billy?' one of the table asked, entranced by the addition to our group.

'Oh, this and that,' he drawled languidly. 'I'm waiting for the right opportunity, something exciting to come along.'

I'll bet you are, I seethed. Silently. Jude looked on quietly, awash with adoration.

They stayed that night, the both of them. Jude often did after a soiree, in order to clear up the next morning. I paid him extra, of course, but it was his presence in the kitchen that I especially liked, whistling as he put on the coffee pot, and calling up the stairs that breakfast was ready. It felt like an extra treat to have him there on a weekend, with eggs cooked just the way I liked them and time to crawl lazily over the glossy Sunday supplements together.

But that morning, there was no whistling, only Billy as the cuckoo in our nest, plus the same puerile jostling between the two of them that I found instantly irritating.

'So, where do you live, Billy?' I queried over breakfast. Hinting.

'Uh, Hampstead. For now.'

'Still with your parents, then?'

He glared out from under the loose strands of lank hair. 'Not for long, though. I'm moving out soon.' He looked across at Jude as he said it, as if for confirmation.

'Yes, we might share a flat,' Jude said, shooting a look at me.

'Expensive in North London, though?' I pitched. Was Billy about to take Jude away from me? Steal him properly, and for good?

'Oh, just a room in a rented place,' Jude qualified. 'There's one or two near here we could afford.'

'You'll have to give him a raise, Mrs D,' Billy quipped, the sneer under his nose descending towards a smirk settling on his mouth.

'Ruby,' I said plainly. 'It's just Ruby.'

'You'll have to give him a raise. Ruby.'

'Do you like him a lot?' I conjured the courage to ask a day or so later, over coffee and papers.

Jude looked at me squarely. 'You don't. Clearly.'

'Well, I thought he was quite casual, that's all. And a bit brash.'

'Which is it, Ruby? Casual or brash?' He looked annoyed, a new expression I hadn't seen before.

I considered. 'Both actually. There seemed no… *commitment* in anything he said. As if he's waiting for something, like stardom or infamy, to come and land in his lap.'

'Don't beat around the bush, Ruby, will you?'

I shot him a look. Was this our first disagreement? A tiff? Had I stepped over the mark?

Jude blew out his cheeks. He looked tired, and I didn't like to hazard why. 'Billy is actually a very good actor,' he said with a hint of petulance. 'He's taking some classes near here.'

'Paid for by Mummy and Daddy?' *Oh, Ruby, shut the fuck up.* But I couldn't help myself, because I truly believed that Jude deserved more, was worth a hundred of Billy.

He stood up, more than irked. 'Oh, Ruby, you really are…'

'What?' It took everything I had, but I held him with a milky gaze and my best Mona Lisa smile.

He sighed. 'Tiresome, sometimes. As well as opinionated, cantankerous and curmudgeonly. Grouchy, too.'

'Keep going with the thesaurus,' I said. 'If nothing else, I'm an education.'

He didn't, though, pull his arm away or try to toss me onto a pedestrian crossing as we walked home. I took that as an armistice.

We rarely spoke about Billy over the next few weeks, and Jude avoided another potential clash by not meeting him at or near the house. For a brief spell, I thought Jude and I had weathered that squall of a storm, wondering too if their liaison had blown itself out after a short time. With nothing to gain from Jude, I imagined Billy had moved on to a new lover, someone more useful to his personal trajectory.

As with many other episodes in my existence, it was largely wishful thinking. Along with the passing weeks came a shroud over Jude, a greyness in his temper, though he tried to work and smile through it. More than once he arrived late with dark circles under his eyes, needing coffee as a drug, as opposed to our small pleasure, yawning through our morning ritual.

'Am I keeping you up, Jude?'

He shot a contrite look in response to my acidic tone. 'Sorry, Ruby. Not feeling a hundred per cent today.'

'Are you ill?'

'No. I told you, I'm just tired.' He slurped more of his necessary drug.

'Sad?'

'*Ruby*. I'm fine. I need a night's sleep, that's all.'

'With or without Billy?'

He glared at me then, partly with annoyance, but principally because I'd found him out.

It took me until lunch and the crossword to tap beyond his shell. 'Come on, tell me what's wrong,' I badgered. Gently, and as kindly as I could manage – something I'd had to practice. 'You're not yourself.'

'Why do you want to know, Ruby?' he said irritably, clearing the plates. 'You've made it plain you don't like him. Unless it's to gloat and say "I told you so". Just like my mother.'

It was rude of him, but no less than I deserved, and he was hurt, trying to hold back tears as he splashed water and dishes in the sink, until nature's flow won out. He did tell me then, as I made him a cup of tea, necessarily strong and hot, and he sat with reddened eyes over the wisp of steam.

'Billy wants us to be free,' he sniffed.

'What does that mean?' I'd known freedom half a century ago, but the goalposts had shifted to another ballpark entirely. 'Free from what?'

'Convention, he says. For us to be non-exclusive. To be with other people, whenever it suits us. When it suits him.'

'And you don't want that?' It seemed a reasonable question, given what I *didn't* know about young people and relationships right then.

'No, Ruby!' Jude wiped a stray tear from his cheek. 'I don't. It's taken me long enough to find where I'm at, *who* I am, and I want to be with someone, maybe not forever. But I don't want to share them. Or him.'

'So maybe Billy isn't that person?' I ventured, softly and without spite (I really had been practising).

'Maybe.'

He knew a good portion of my history by then, as a woman

of flight, so why would he be listening to a damned word I said? Me, giving advice of the heart. It was beyond farcical. But I so wanted to deflect the hurt, to stop the torque beyond his skinny, vulnerable ribs and dry his painful tears. Anyone with eyes and ears could have seen it plainly: I was bent on saving Jude. Obvious to everyone but me.

Despite Jude's distress and his desire for monogamy at that point, Billy hung around like a bad smell. He didn't want Jude exclusively, but neither would he set him free; there was some inexplicable hold, like a fish-hook firmly snagged. I struggled to understand Jude's dependence on someone who could injure him so coolly and cruelly: why on earth would he stay, hoping to suck up the crumbs from Billy's overstocked table? I'd only ever sensed that profound connection once, with Enzo – the feeling that I could never hope to move on if he was living and breathing in the world without me, in the arms of someone else. My marriage vows to Johan I put down to some temporary madness, an illness I was swiftly cured of.

Jude's moods during that autumn became undulating to say the least, his smile fed by Billy's attentions one day, or starved by callous neglect the next. I tried to ignore the times when I smelled alcohol on his breath, or extra strong mints, or when his curls gave off that sour weedy odour of Ludo and the late Sixties. Why? Because I loved him, and I didn't want him to go away. I couldn't bear it. Not again.

My patience and Billy's disregard combined to make Jude reckless. On several occasions he accompanied me to book launches, where he availed himself of too much free alcohol, and while he was never outwardly embarrassing, his voice became louder, opinions were less of a whisper, and once or twice I needed to remind him: 'That's enough, Jude.' I hated it – being his keeper, clipping those beautiful wings, but I'd both seen and used booze as a prop. He was far too young and bright for it to make him dull and ugly.

One such night at a *Times* reception, Jude was especially 'up'. I watched him from my seat, flitting like a butterfly through the room, fuelled less by fizz than the energy he exuded since we'd left Highgate in the taxi. Either he'd taken something, or Billy had been particularly kind to him, bathing Jude in this new-found confidence. With a lifetime of catastrophe behind me, I couldn't help my own private predictions of a fall, that he would come tumbling from up on high.

Jude, however, was having none of it. 'Hey, there's a new club opened up in the next street,' he said as we waited for our taxi back to Highgate. 'It's supposed to be amazing. Come on, Ruby, how about it?'

'I'm tired, Jude,' I protested. 'And in case you've forgotten, I am ninety.'

He looked disillusioned then – at my lack of adventure. And stupid though it was, I couldn't abide that: to be a disappointment to my boy. 'Just half an hour, then,' I relented. 'You never know, it might be good research.'

'That's my Ruby,' he beamed.

To my great surprise, I didn't hate it, not entirely anyway. The music was far too loud, pulsing endlessly in one unswerving beat, but squatting in my corner booth, I was soon beguiled by the energy of the dancing crowd, Jude lost in the throng. The rhythm was more frantic, but the dynamic I recognised from more than fifty years before, that night when I first met Ludo – the abandon and the permission to let go, to surrender yourself to the music. Then, it was Yardbirds and the Stones, and now, who knows? But on the faces of the crowd, that thirst for freedom was identical. Nothing had really changed.

Jude bounced over, drunk on the beat, his eyes spinning, stoned certainly. 'Isn't it brilliant, Ruby?' he hollered. 'Come on, you need to dance.'

'Jude, no. Shouldn't we go?' I felt a sense of panic, that he was slipping from me and I couldn't hope to hold on.

He shook his sweat-laden curls like a child digging in their heels. 'No, no, not yet. Come on, one dance? I'll hold you tight, I promise. You need to *feeeeel* it.'

God knows we were attracting the stares of other club-goers, this ancient woman and a young boy who had – to all intents and purposes – brought his great-granny to a nightclub. I could have asked any number of people to help me towards a taxi and the safety of my own home. But if you could have seen his face in that moment, his eyes bright with promise as well as chemicals. And so much expectation of me in that look. I hadn't harboured that much belief in my failing body for an age, and here was he – Jude – asking me. Needing me.

You'll understand why I did what I did. Won't you?

Accident and emergency on a Saturday night is no place to be in London, though being of advanced age does shunt you up the queue a little. I imagine that if you expire in A&E with nothing more than a broken ankle, it tends to create a lot of paperwork and prompt an internal inquiry. They asked me lots of questions about my breathing, until I told the poor junior doctor, in no uncertain terms, that my lungs were nowhere near my feet and where he did go to medical school? We were wheeled off to X-ray soon after that.

'Ruby, I'm so sorry, really I am.' In between bouts of silent regret, Jude's apologies played out like a broken record. The shock had caused him to sober up quickly, almost the moment we toppled and fell on the dancefloor in a heap, becoming my Boy Friday instantly, the one who could read my genuine expression of pain, the one who tended to me in the ambulance. Quite rapidly, he and I realised he would soon become my carer, too.

He stayed after we arrived home, almost with the lark. And the night after that. For two weeks, Jude became my live-in nurse, for want of a better phrase. We even joked about it: 'Nurse, can you get me my crutches?'

'You're an extremely impatient patient, Miss Devereaux,' he teased. 'Do you know that?'

I paid him the going rate for live-in care, but I think Jude's attentions were driven by remorse, even after I banned him from saying sorry ever again. 'It's one of those things, Jude. I've never broken so much as a toe before,' – the multiple clefts in my heart somehow didn't count – 'so my time was up. I do think my dancing days are over, though.'

'Oh, Ruby.'

We never mentioned the reason why – the wildness in his mood that night or the drugs fuelling his rashness. Not when he was there in my mews house, day after day, constant and caring. Back to the old Jude.

When I was free of the aching that old broken bones are apt to give you, we continued working, and that's when Jude would run out for food supplies and fresh air, a respite too from his eccentric old charge. Early evening, we would have our single

G&T in front of one of those vapid game shows on television that I'd become curiously fond of, in a fierce competition to score points off each other on general knowledge questions. And then just before bed, sipping my herbal 'sleepy' tea that Jude convinced me was good for slumber and health (insipid dishwater, in my book), he often steered the conversation around to my life.

With Badger on my lap, purring and pumping with his big fat paws at my abdomen, Jude probed in a different way, gently grilling over my exploits and travels through the years. 'You didn't, Ruby, did you? *Really*?'

Given the nature of his questioning, I suspected that he had also been working his way through my fictional back catalogue and wanted ever more detail. He never said as much, though, and I didn't ask. There was never mention of Jude, either – my Jude, that is. He seemed especially curious about the Benedict episode, about Berlin, the Stasi and espionage. Looking down at my big, fat NHS boot on the end of a rangy old leg, it seemed like fiction from another life entirely.

Still, I delighted in it: his interest, and the recollection, scraping my mind for detail we hadn't already laid down in print. It served as a necessary tool, I thought, for keeping the demon dementia at bay.

But for the fat foot, life seemed perfect.

Oh dear.

I hobbled to the door one day into the third week in response to a loud knocking, bent on intercepting an expected delivery – a silly present I'd ordered of a child's nursing kit, an in-joke I hoped would raise a laugh between the two of us.

I flung open the door with delight. 'I thought it wouldn't come so quick... oh.' Billy hovered on the stoop, still the great unwashed. The sneer had diminished slightly, replaced with something approaching wantonness.

'Is Jude there?' He looked at my foot, bound with padding and Velcro, and needed no other clue.

'Ruby, who is it?' Jude's voice drifted up the hallway. 'If it's a parcel, I'll deal with...' Billy and I waited in silence as his footsteps drew closer.

'Oh.' Jude stopped, wiping his hands on the tea towel slung over his shoulder. 'Hello, Billy.' There was shock and anguish in his tone, mixed with anticipation and elation. A soupçon of triumph, too, if I remember rightly. And hope.

All of us endured a brief, three-way stare-off until I shuffled backwards. 'You'd better come in,' I said, in the best welcome I could muster.

I left them to it in the kitchen, retiring to the office and switching on the radio. Part of me wanted to tune into the conversation, but a bigger portion didn't want to hear Billy wheedle his way back into Jude's life, with his lies wrapped in charm. That sneer hadn't disappeared completely.

And wheedle he did. Laughter was soon rippling up the hallway while I tried to wade through emails, the tinkle of their attachment chiming over Classic FM and the clatter of my machine. I heard the door latch click half an hour later, and Jude's tentative steps approaching.

'And?' I barely looked up from the keyboard, pretending to wrestle with a Very Important Message.

'He says it will be different this time,' Jude uttered, almost with apology. 'He wants me, and only me.'

'Absence makes the heart grow fonder. Is that his pitch?'

'Ruby!' He sounded shocked, and hurt.

'*What?*'

His lips pursed, containing disappointment. In me. 'Don't be a cynical old woman.'

'I am an old woman.'

'But you don't have to act like one.' He was already halfway down the corridor, gratified, no doubt, at having had the last word. 'Guess what?' he sang.

'What?'

'Noodles for tea. Vietnamese. My new speciality.'

Over the next month, the love/lust/Billy triangle played out again, with Jude pitched in the middle. Again. I was nowhere to be found, cast out by Billy principally, like some wretched soul on the outskirts of a maze, peering through a dense hedge and yet desperate to be let in on the conundrum. Jude was present less and less as my ankle healed, but metaphorically absent, largely due to the other guests in Billy's orbit – a dusting of drugs and a deluge of alcohol. It was both inevitable and painful to watch, Jude's second slide into this dual dependence, courtesy of Billy, the serial, entitled abuser.

I put up with it for so long. Too long, probably, adding my own layer of sugar coating to his chemical dust, in the times he sobbed, or was sick in my toilet or elsewhere, lying comatose in my office, not working or musing. Or even being. I did it out of love for Jude, but even I had my limits. Our banter had become bitter and was in danger of turning toxic.

'Don't go *on*, Ruby,' he railed at times, body and temper frayed.

Would my Jude have spoken to me like that? From

conversations with my parent-friends: yes, probably he would. But then he was my son, flesh and blood. Reluctantly, painfully, I had to admit the old adage harboured some truth: blood *is* thicker than water.

'Jude, I think you should go today,' I told him at last, my voice the coldest I could manage. 'And not come back. I'll pay you to the end of the month.'

'But, Ruby…' He didn't ask why, because he knew. I hobbled from the room so as not to see his wounded face under the unwashed curls, my wooden stick as a new and inevitable crutch.

He loitered for a second in the office doorway on his way out. 'I'm sorry, Ruby. I really am.'

Oh God, I could have taken it all back there and then, looking at his gorgeous face and the remorse upon it, the whump to my heart. I almost hopped up and put the kettle on for both of us. But the dark circles under his eyes were ingrained, as was his addiction – to Billy and Billy's world.

'Look after yourself, Jude. I mean it.'

'You too, Ruby.'

I didn't watch him through the window, trudging down the street, because I was busy sobbing into my keyboard. It's a revelation that your body shrivels with age, but your tear-ducts remain fully functioning. I cried for Jude, his future and the loss of his beautiful youth. And if I'm honest, for me too.

The realisation hit with the might of a steam train: I hadn't managed to save my boy. Again.

It was a good six months on when Marina rang me at home, one bright spring morning, a nervous strain to her voice. Kazia, my new and capable domestic, was singing away in her native Polish down in the kitchen.

'What's wrong?' I said, cutting off one of Marina's lengthy of preambles.

'Erm, I've just had the heads up from a publisher friend of mine, on the quiet.'

'Why on the quiet?' Senses were already tingling, my own preamble to a recent and concerning ache in my chest, the one that came at all times of the day and night. Uninvited.

'Do you remember that boy who worked for you?'

'You mean Jude?' The ache pushed inwards and grew spikes.

'Yes. Well, he's only gone and written a book.'

I had our respective agents negotiate a face-to-face meeting, being too impatient for some immature spit-spat over emails and in the publishing press. I wanted to gauge him, and have Jude look me in the eye, before I would believe his treachery. I had prepared myself by reading a proof of the book that was soon to hit the shelves. It was in novel form, though didn't put up much of a pretence of being fiction: tales of a young man pitched into the publishing world as a carer for an established writer. Sound familiar? The term is 'thinly veiled memoir'. I know, because I'd fashioned an entire career out of them.

Much as I was loath to admit it at the time, it was well-written. Perhaps my influence had rubbed off a little, except that his style was particular, and innate, a mere sheen of my own evident in his prose. Jude was a born writer. I found myself turning the pages out of curiosity rather than duty, plus a sense of pride if I'm truly honest.

It was all there – the frustrated scribe of eighty-plus, the nightclub debacle, the drugs, each one nicely embellished for literary effect (or were they?). So that as I turned each page, I no longer expected to be surprised.

Silly, silly me. Always the worst at self-reflection.

The man-boy character in Jude's novel had a grandfather, one who he never knew. One who had died before he was even born. One who was evermore branded a Cold War spy and a traitor.

'Hello, Ruby.' His curls were tighter and shorter, and clean. In fact, he looked so unlike the Jude I had last seen leaving my house – smartly dressed, with a healthy pink hue. Yes, he confirmed, Billy was gone – permanently – along with the drugs. There was a new addiction in writing.

'So I did give you something,' I said glibly.

Marina shuffled, and Jude's agent coughed, no doubt keen to move the meeting along without blood being spilled on his nice office furniture. 'So, how shall we play this?' he said nervously.

Jude splayed his hands in deference. 'It's up to Ruby.'

There was only one question really. The one I'd lost sleep over, the one that reignited the ember of unease over Benedict, nestled inside me for almost half a century.

'Why? Why wouldn't you tell me, Jude?'

His sigh was that of a man much older, the baggage leaden on his shoulders. 'I tried, Ruby, I really did. The intentions I came with, well, they got waylaid, and the deeper I got, the more impossible it became, and then…'

Then Billy, and the drugs. Without utterance, we both knew any logic he'd owned had been addled beyond that point.

All along, Jude had known of my relationship with Benedict Dalybridge, his mother's father, and so when he turned up on my doorstep to interview as a potential assistant, it was to… What was he planning?

'I don't know, Ruby, and that's the truth,' he contended. 'I only know that it affected my mother's life profoundly – the lies about her father, not having him to grow up with. She'd kept every cutting in a box, stowed away like shame. I wanted to discover everything I could, for her.'

I cast back to the post-Berlin visit I made to Benedict's wife, and the small children playing alongside as she sniffed back her grief with stoicism. 'But I didn't kill him, Jude,' I said firmly. I'd been a lot of things, but never a killer. 'And I didn't lure him to Berlin, either.'

'But you were one of the last people to see him alive…'

'And to defend him, don't forget that! If you read those cuttings, you'll realise that. I said to the last that he was no traitor, and I still believe it now.'

Jude hung his head. 'I was confused, for a long time. I had intended, not so much to confront you, but to question you…'

'Interrogate?'

'Yes, if you like,' he confessed. 'To get some sense of the man who became my hero because of his absence.'

'So, what happened, Jude? I don't remember any interrogation, or bitterness. Only an interest from you.'

'*You* happened, Ruby.'

Was I pleased that – at ninety – I had beguiled him (his words)? Of course I was. Like tears, vanity doesn't decrease with age. It was recompense that he had applied for the job fully intent on staying only long enough to illicit the truth he needed. But stay he did, because he wanted to, because of what we had.

'I came to love you, Ruby,' he said, eyes down in his lap. 'That's the truth of it.'

Still, I said nothing. If I had, my dowager tears would have drained me to a husk. But when he drew his eyes up again, he knew. Like men before him, he recognised every frailty in me.

'And so, what of this book, then?' I coughed, back to business. 'Did you plan that from the outset?'

A second sigh pushed from within his skinny chest. 'No, Ruby, it wasn't planned, but the result of an odd kind of recipe, I suppose – a chance meeting with one of your old publishing friends, my own bitterness, and circumstance.'

'That circumstance being Billy?' I was certain he would have grabbed at the opportunity, felt entitled to his portion of the 'kill'.

'Yes, I suppose he encouraged me.'

I'll bet he did. Yet I was glad. I wanted there to be a villain of the piece, someone other than Jude.

He said the intention of the content wasn't personal; the more he wrote, the more the story inside burned, like limestone in his belly. 'Suddenly, everything about you and your writing fell into place, Ruby. I had to coax out this dark spirit inside.'

I just happened to be the pivot on which to hang Jude's tale.

'Just one more thing,' I pitched, before we parted. 'The name. Is it real?'

'Yes – and no,' he said. 'It's actually Finn Jude. A total fluke, thanks to my mother. So no, not a lie, not really.' He smiled, in a very Jude way. 'Still the best bloody song every written. And that is the complete truth.'

I wasn't angry, or even disappointed. How could I be? Michael's pained, betrayed face of seventy years before flashed up, crystal clear; Jude had only done what I had, time and again – used the material to hand. And so, this final 'man chapter' of mine is no attempt at revenge, I promise you, but more of a redemption for my own sins. And the fallout from his very successful book, the publicity it generated in the press and publishing circles? Frankly, it was water off a duck's back to someone with a reputation already besmirched. And while Jude wasn't my flesh and blood, he might as well have been then. I simply couldn't hate him. Much to his agent's relief, I merely wished him well. After a lifetime of manipulation of facts and people and emotions, what could I say?

Quid pro quo.

Epilogue

Ruby M Devereaux in my Life

by Marina Keeve

It falls to me to write the epilogue, though I can just picture Ruby's furrowed brow at my inadequate attempts; irritated beyond belief that she has been forced to relinquish control of it. Nothing less than death could have robbed it from her.

She'd started – I found the beginnings in note form, in her spidery script, spread across the chaos of her desk. *So that's it, as much of me as I can give, my soul turned inside out like a paper bag, crumbs and all*, she'd written. The rest of the page is empty.

One sentence. But I have no doubt of its honesty. And really, she has summed it up perfectly, so there's not much more for me to say. Except that I want to.

I want to tell you as readers how much she loved you, for absorbing her words, giving over your hard-earned cash for 'her ramblings' as she liked to paraphrase 'the gorgeous Miss Austen'. But also how she was one of you, how she read voraciously, even when her eyesight was failing over the last years, still purchased books by the dozen, fingered the pages and smelled the ink. I am writing this at her desk, frankly in fear of the shelves groaning under the weight of texts, and had Ruby finally succumbed under an avalanche of books in this very room, she would have been content.

She loved books and words – and men, of course. Their physicality, and predictability, but also the deep need in them for a woman's company and touch, the game that had to be played, and which she admitted was her favourite foreplay. The chase. Ruby liked women, too, but I often suspected she was wary of her own sex, as if in danger of being found out by the intuition that she so admired in the female race. I didn't know her in the younger years, but even beyond her seventies I noted that whenever Ruby entered a new arena, she carefully assessed any of those in her midst, like a lioness protecting her pride *and* vying for the man with the mane.

So, to have finally amassed her tales – those men of influence – is both a coup for me and a jewel for you as readers. I know each element to be true, because of the stories circulating for many years in the publishing world, well before I knew her, but also because of the twenty years I've been privileged to be her agent, and to have sat with her in front of a fire and listened without interruption (or drawing breath, at times) to the facts of her life, recalled with pinpoint precision. They may read like fantasy, but Ruby D lived every second of every minute.

Editing this text, I have learned things too. The one topic on which she wouldn't be drawn was her son, choked still by the nugget of pride and hurt smouldering inside her for decades. Those precious weeks with Jude gave her pain and succour at the same time. Given the fragrant, drug haze of the late Sixties, that episode surrounding the tragedy seems especially hard to believe. And that's from someone who's read the most bizarre of fictional texts in more than two decades as an agent. Even now, I would never have the courage to admit my actions to Ruby, but I tracked down Ludo – aka Leonard – for some corroboration. I trusted her, of course I did, but like she says at the outset of this book, writers are unreliable. Memories sometimes too. Of all the man chapters in this memoir, if I knew Jude to be written with precision, it would be my foundation of fact.

Without prompting, Ludo told me his side from across the Atlantic. Like Ruby's pain over their son, his grief has dulled but remains ever present. It was exactly as she wrote it, he told me, 'Every light, rainbow, ugly line of coke and unending day of summer in that crazy, crazy house. The hard bit, too. She didn't make it up because you couldn't.'

I thanked him and went to replace the receiver. 'I want you to know, I would have stayed with her,' he said on a parting note. 'For as long as forever was then. I've never met anyone like Ruby, and never have since. She was incredible, so much so that I couldn't begin to put it into words. People like her don't come along very often.'

It's true – she was a one-off. Talented, whip-smart, beautiful, quirky, effervescent, but also chaotic, infuriating, angry, incorrigible and increasingly frustrated with 'this bastard ageing process'. If I don't spell out those latter characteristics, I know full well she will come back and haunt me to the end of my days. 'Tell it like it was, Marina,' she said only two days before her final departure. 'Don't let them pretty it up in my obituary. Tell them I was a bitch if you must. Only maybe a nice bitch on occasions.'

What you saw in Ruby was what you got. There are those in book circles who called her a chameleon. But that doesn't do her justice, because chameleons only wear their colours as a covering. Ruby, by contrast, lived hers, in full technicolour. If she hated you, then she truly hated you. And then when she loved you again, it was heartfelt, and you knew it was genuine. I have had the privilege of knowing more affection from her than any of her other myriad emotions. Professionally, I will miss reading her extraordinary words, because she was a much better writer than she gave herself credit for. Along with those hilarious, ranting messages and texts, spoken into a 'blasted mobile machine' she could not fathom. Mostly, though, I cannot imagine my life without that raspy voice coming over the phone line late into the evening.

'I suppose you're very busy,' she would punt, followed by a well-timed pregnant pause.

'Not especially. Would you like me to come over, Ruby?'

'Only if you're passing. Don't let me put you out.'

'It's not a bother. I'll be there soon,' I'd assure her.

'Oh, and Marina?'

'Yes?'

'I'm quite thirsty. A half bottle of whisky will do. A good one, mind.'

I will miss every aspect of Ruby M Devereaux. The world, too, will be a bleaker place without the kaleidoscope of Ruby

D. But we thank you for this last episode, as the navigator of a meandering and wondrous magical mystery tour.

M.K. December 2021

Nine

Marina sighs and reaches for her tissue, already a saturated and mangled mess, much like her heart and the make-up shifting from her face. She reads over her narrative, rewrites and deletes a string of words several times, laughing out loud to her computer screen at the sentence she would dearly love to include. The one referring to a sudden sprouting of perspiration on the face of Marcus Trent when Marina finally handed over the draft manuscript detailing the men and the life, chapter and verse.

But this little nugget, she decides, is best kept between her and Ruby, a delicious secret not for public consumption. She leans back in her chair, stares at the slightly dusty ceiling, the sky and whatever else nestles beyond.

'Oh Ruby, the old man didn't just squirm in his pants. He near on shit himself in that Savile Row underwear.'

Acknowledgements

Those friends and readers who dipped into Ruby during her journey have often posed the same question: where does she come from? The honest truth is, I don't know. For some years, I had a short story rumbling around, of an old actress reviewing her past life, and so *The Life and Times of Kitty Winkhorn* lends itself to Ruby, but is by no means her whole. The character name I have had for some time – I was allowed to ferret in my dad's record box every so often as a child, and the 45-single I selected time and again was Kenny Rogers' *Ruby, Don't Take Your Love to Town*. I loved the song and the name way back then, as I do now. Inevitably, there are elements of me in there, too. I am a huge fan of the Beatles, and 'Hey Jude' is among my all-time favourites. My second son is named Finn Jude (I lost out to family politics on the first name), I recall living through that scorching summer of '76 with sweaty clarity, and back in my previous history as a midwife, I knitted through many a homebirth. As per Ruby, we writers just can't help little bits of us sneaking in.

The biggest influence on Ruby's evolution, however, is another scribe. I read William Boyd's *Sweet Caress* in awe, not only for its writing, but the fact that I believed wholeheartedly the character of Amory Clay had been a living, breathing soul, even to the point of web searching her name, then being disappointed not to find it in the archives. *Wow,* I thought, you really can invent people and their lives. Their pasts, too. *For real.*

So, that's the germ of Ruby. The rest she wrote herself. Much like Jude, I was merely the typist.

Character aside, this tangible book of Ruby's did not emerge out of the ether, and I am indebted to a host of champions. My wonderful agent at DHH Literary Agency, Broo Doherty, was the first to be drip-fed Ruby, chapter by chapter, and from the outset she 'got' her mindset, using her own tenacity to turn my words into print. Huge gratitude to editor Rachel Faulkner-Willcocks, then at Aria, for recognising Ruby's potential. Along with Aria's Bianca Gillam, Laura Palmer, plus the extended team at Head of Zeus, they have allowed her trials and tribulations to flower. Much appreciation goes to copy editor Katrina Harvey, for grappling with my woeful grammar and polishing the text. To anyone who markets, shouts about, stacks on a shelf or chirps in the social media world about Ruby, I thank you.

Friends and fellow scribes have endured a good year and a half of my bleating about Ruby, always with forbearance and words of support: writers Sarah Steele, Mel Golding, LP Fergusson (Loraine, off the page), and the lovely Lorna Cook (Elle Cook), plus all those who sit in a Stroud cafe every other Friday for 'coffee & carp' about a writer's life.

Precious friends – well, you know who you are, and I really couldn't do life without you, let alone this publishing malarkey. You kept me sane when my head was in Rubyville, and still do. Partner Simon – yes, I may at last stop talking about my imaginary friend.

Of course, enduring thanks goes to my No.1 fan – my mum, Stella. Not only for the loan of her maiden name, Devereaux, but for the touting of this text, that she will inevitably do. I say 'cheers' also to a four-legged inspiration in the real-life Tintin, complete with his one good eye and crabby gait. I owe you several bones, mate.

Lastly, to Mr McCartney. It *is* the best bloody song every written.

M J Robotham, April, 2023

About the Author

M J Robotham saw herself as an aspiring author from the age of nine, but was waylaid by journalism, birth, children and life. After twenty years as a midwife and an MA in Creative Writing, she is now a full-time author, writing historical fiction as Mandy Robotham. She lives in Gloucestershire with her partner and muse mutt, Basil.